Tropic of Ruislip

Leslie Thomas was born in South Wales in 1931 and, when his parents died, he and his younger brother were brought up in an orphanage. His first book, *This Time Next Week,* is the autobiography of a happy orphan. At sixteen he became a reporter on a weekly newspaper in Essex and then did his National Service in Malaya during the Communist bandit war. *The Virgin Soldiers* tells of these days ; it was an immediate bestseller and has been made into a film with Lynn Redgrave and Hywel Bennett.

Returning to civilian life, Leslie Thomas joined the staff of the *Evening News,* becoming a top feature writer and travelling a great deal. His second novel, *Orange Wednesday,* was published in 1967. For nine months during 1967 he travelled around ten islands off the coast of Britain, the result of which was a lyrical travelogue, *Some Lovely Islands,* from which the BBC did a television series. He has continued to travel a great deal and has also written several television plays. He is a director of a London publishing house. His hobbies include golf, antiques and Queen's Park Rangers Football Club.

His other books include *Come to the War, His Lordship, Onward Virgin Soldiers, Arthur McCann and All his Women, The Man with the Power,* and, most recently, *Stand Up Virgin Soldiers.*

D0864328

Also by Leslie Thomas in Pan Books

The Virgin Soldiers
Onward Virgin Soldiers
Orange Wednesday
His Lordship
Come to the War
The Love Beach
Arthur McCann and All his Women
The Man with the Power

This Time Next Week
Some Lovely Islands

Leslie Thomas

Tropic of Ruislip

Pan Books London and Sydney

First published 1974 by Eyre Methuen Ltd
This edition published 1976 by Pan Books Ltd
Cavaye Place, London SW10 9PG
2nd printing 1976
© Leslie Thomas 1974
ISBN 0 330 24721 2
Printed and bound in Great Britain by
Hunt Barnard Printing Ltd, Aylesbury, Bucks

To Clarence Paget
... with thanks

Woe unto them that join house to house,
that lay field to field, till there be no place.

Isaiah 5 : 8

1

For a man facing both Monday morning and utter defeat he did not feel too bad. The morning sun, beaming like a cheap salesman, burst from the direction of Breakspear Crematorium (a reminder that Nicholas Breakspear, the only English pope, was of these parts), there was a wide optimism about the sky and the grinning fields, and the girl from Cowacre, the one with the bum like a deftly closed tulip, was walking by on her way to the station.

Andrew's double-glazed kitchen window was higher than all the others at Plummers Park, for his four-bedroomed house (garage and carport, Blo-hole heating, bland picture windows, sun patio, old tree incorporated into the garden wall) was on the prow of Upmeadow. From his sitting-room a variety of sunsets could be witnessed through the seasons, a ritual dipping which, the estate agent had assured him, would be an asset if he ever decided to sell. From the place where he stood this first working morning of a June week he could look, in fact he had no choice but to look, out on to the flat roofs of all the other houses on the estate, scattered in the valley like bamboo rafts on some wide eastern river.

The girl from Cowacre wore a pale shirt, tight across her brassy little breasts, their noses prodding through the material. His coffee-cup immobilized at the tilt, he watched her stride by, her legs long, her face clean and confident as the sun, and waited in anticipation for the promised view of her backside.

Scarcely more than a remnant of blue denim had gone into that skirt, a mere pantile at the front, so tight behind that her buttocks pushed at it like imprisoned faces jostling for a view. They collided beneath the light blue fabric with each neat, blatant step. The road before her extended vacantly to the horizon, to the junction of Upmeadow with Risingfield, and she walked as though she were happy but alone in the world. Behind her in ragged file followed Mr Brewster, Mr Reynolds,

Mr Burville, Mr George Jones and his brother Mr Henry Jones, Mr Shillingford, and poor old Mr Henty trying to keep up.

'I swear they crouch behind their front doors until that kid passes by,' said Audrey. She was standing a yard behind him, on her toes to see what he was seeing.

'Which kid?' he asked, innocence always being his first reflex.

'The one that made you spill your coffee down your shirt,' she said, wiping at the stain. 'If you're going to ruin your clothes with mental sex then it's time I had a new washing-machine. The man says this one is going to blow up at any moment.'

'I'll try and finish my coffee before she goes by in the morning,' said Andrew. There was no heat in their discussion. They knew how they were.

Audrey bit into a piece of toast and considered the men following the girl. 'You're as bad as that sorry lot,' she observed. 'You stand on that same spot every morning waiting for her. Her and her arse. It's a wonder the lino isn't worn into a hole.'

She laughed with off-hand bitterness. 'Dirty lot of sods,' she said. 'Just look at old Shillingford dodging about so that horny Bertie Reynolds doesn't block his view. If she were older, if she had a bit of know-how, she would turn round suddenly. I bet they'd all fall over in fright.'

'If she were older maybe they wouldn't be following her,' argued Andrew.

'They wouldn't know what to do with a girl like that,' she said, sharpness hardening her voice. 'And nor would you. She'd scare the life out of you.'

He nodded solemnly. 'I wouldn't know what to say to her,' he agreed. He did not believe in fighting in the morning – or at any time if he could avoid it. The best thing about defeat was that there was no more war.

Suddenly Audrey laughed. To make a joke was frequently her way out of their disputes. 'Imagine if one fell out,' she said. 'One of her cheeks. Can't you see it bouncing down the road?'

8

'There'd be a scramble,' he agreed, glad of the let-out. 'Like a rugby scrum.'

'Please can I have my ball back?' mimicked Audrey, but not sounding like a young girl.

They both laughed, and he put on his jacket. He said, 'It's going to be hot again. And I'll be in the lousy magistrates court.' His basset hound, Gladstone, a hung and drawn dog, saw that he was going out. Its face sagged even lower. Andrew stooped and examined the perpetually red eyes, shaking his head in mock sadness at the diagnosis.

'That creature stank like a hayrick all day yesterday,' said Audrey. 'I don't mind when it's Sunday and you have to smell him too. But on Mondays he's got me to himself. You'll have to bath him or have him destroyed.'

Andrew looked into the hound's ravaged eyes. 'Action-Dog,' he said to the sagging face. 'You are not wanted. You and I will run away together. The world calls us. We will voyage to the Land Where The Bong Tree Grows.'

'The Pong Tree,' corrected Audrey. 'And the furthest you'll get today is Bushey Magistrates Court, so stop building up my hopes.'

'Nine years,' grumbled Andrew. 'Nine years before the bench. Nine years of Monday and Thursday mornings. Soon I'm going to carve my initials on the press table.'

'It's a wonder you haven't before this.'

'Ah, well, I wasn't sure I was going to stay.'

'Is that why you haven't carved your initials anywhere in this house?' she asked, apparently absently. She had turned away and was brushing her fingers against some flowers on the kitchen table, touching them into a token arrangement. Andrew put out his hand to her shoulder and another on a chair. 'I'd hate to damage the place,' he said. 'Anyway, I think you've got me for ever. Like the *Journal*.'

'Hooray,' she said quietly, still keeping her face from him. 'At least you've made it clear. At last I can plan my life too.' She walked to the tear-off calendar on the kitchen wall and tore off another day which she rolled up deliberately, kissed, and dropped into the waste-bin. 'Goodbye, June the second,' she sighed.

'Stop it,' he said. Sometimes he felt sorrier for her than he did for himself. 'It's a nice day.'

Audrey glanced at him almost coyly, then smiled and went towards him, her step apologetic. She said, 'So it is,' and put her arms limply about him. 'Poor old us,' she said. She was tall; his eyes only had to descend a fraction to meet hers. She had kept a good figure but her face had a sort of tired patience. They embraced and he pressed her crowded chest into his for a spasm of familiar comfort but, as though by tacit agreement, they did not kiss.

They relaxed their arms, and as though that were a signal for the resumption of normality she bit into her toast again. She said: 'Listen, Lizzie wants to go up to the canal again tonight with this youth group they've started. She says they want to do some more work on the barge. Do you think it's safe?'

He was on his way out and he stopped. 'She can swim,' he said simply.

'Christ,' she groaned. 'For a newspaperman you're really dim at times. I didn't think she was going to fall into the canal, you idiot. She's fifteen, if you've had a look lately, and she's up there with two or three boys inside a boat where, by all accounts, they just about have to lie down because there's no room to stand up. Now do you understand?'

Andrew nodded thoughtfully. 'She's all right,' he said. 'Lizzie's not stupid. Ask her if she can work up the mast. Let them have a look at her knicks.'

'You casual sod.'

'Well, what do you want me to say? Perhaps we ought to tell her to keep away from boys and barges.'

'All right, all right,' sighed Audrey. 'I couldn't help thinking they've been spending a hell of a lot of time up there, that's all.'

'Maybe it's a big barge.'

'Perhaps we ought to go and have a look at it. Just to see.'

'All right,' he agreed. 'Let's go up tonight.'

'Do we let her know we're coming? She's out to tea, so I won't be seeing her.'

'We'll play fair,' he said. 'We'll sing as we walk along the tow-path. Give her time to pull her pants up.'

'Shut up. Don't be so bloody nasty.'

He was going out of the door now. 'Nasty, nothing,' he retaliated. 'Just want to give the kid a sporting chance.'

He walked down the front path, his feet among the marigolds which had gone on the rampage. She called after him, on impulse, desperately, as though she had to shout something before he went. 'You!' she called without venom. 'You're mad, you are, Andrew Maiby!' It sounded like a child's taunt.

'So are you!' he returned blithely. 'Mad!' He had the sudden pleasing awareness of the sun on his face. 'We're all mad! All of us!' He spread his arms to take in the multiple boxed houses of the estate. 'Look,' he exclaimed. 'Look where we live!'

*

Each of the thousand flat roofs had a quaint tin chimney projecting from it, the antithesis of the bare and functional boxiness of the rest of the house. It was like a stove-pipe sticking up and was topped by a pert pointed hat, like the chimneys of prospectors' cabins in gold-rush days or the pixie houses in children's books. In cold weather wraiths of smoke wriggled out as the Blo-hole central heating puffed. This fine morning they were smokeless and Andrew could clearly see the farming fields on the other side of the main road running from Harrow to Watford. He enjoyed seeing the busy smoke rising from the little chimneys and lolling in the valley on frosty mornings. It made the place look inhabited.

Plummers Park was thirty miles from Central London, in the latitude of Ruislip, in the country but not of it. The fields seemed almost touchable and yet remote. Wild roses bloomed and blew in seclusion just out of reach; rooks and flashing magpies in elm and rowan were merely distant birds in distant trees; the fox and the rabbit went unseen from the human windows. On Sundays the people had to drive out in their cars to witness a pig. The estate was the strangest crop ever to grow on that old Hertfordshire farming land. When it was built some trees were permitted to remain like unhappy captives spared because they are old. They remained in clusters, sometimes embedded in garden walls as selling points for house-buyers desiring fresh air, twigs, greenness, and autumn acorns for their children. It was rumoured that the builders had a mechanical squirrel which ran up trees to delight, deceive and decide prospective purchasers.

The streets had, with commercial coyness, retained the sometimes embarrassing names of the various pastures and fields that now lay beneath concrete, crazy paving and statutory roses. Cowacre, Upmeadow, Risingfield, Sheep-Dip, The Sluice, and Bucket Way. Some of the new people said they found it embarrassing to give their address as Sows Hole Lane – provided for a policeman it always provoked suspicion – but others liked the rustic sounds.

This was the home of Flat-Roof Man, and Flat-Roof Man had topped the agrarian names with his own fancies. As Andrew walked that morning he passed gates labelled 'Ponderosa', 'Khartoum' and 'High Sierra'. One, called 'Dobermann Lodge', was both a name and a dog warning, while his own uncompromising cube bore the name 'Bennunikin', old Navajo Indian for 'The Wigwam on the Hill'. In these houses lived men who played patience and others who played fast and loose; women who wanted love and others who desired only an automatic dishwasher. Dreams were regularly dreamed, ambitions thwarted, folded away or modestly attained. Love visited and sex sniffed around. Pottery and French classes were popular in winter; people booked their summer holidays as an antidote to the cold terrors of each New Year. Husbands polished cars; wives polished windows or fingernails. On summer and autumn evenings sunset gardeners burned leaves and rubbish, the smoke climbing like a silent plea for deliverance that forever went unanswered.

The estate was divided from a monster council-housing development, built to rehouse families from slum London, by the fortuitous incision of a railway line raised on an embankment like a dyke or a dam.

At the top of his own street, where it met Risingfield, at its junction with Upper Herd, Andrew was able to look down the residential slopes to the frontier-line of the railway and beyond that to the council estate where the terrace houses lay like long grey ships. There were no garages over there but the trees in the streets freely canopied, in season, the lines of cars outside the houses; the churches, the shops and the schools, except the primary schools, were beyond the embankment on the wrong side of the tracks. But the morning sun visited there only after it had spread across the squared, castellated fortress hill of Plummers Park. Those people, whoever they were, in that hinterland, had to wait for it.

The main rush of morning movers, head-down for the station, had eased, the streets had almost emptied. Soon they would be left to tradesmen, occasional housewives and lonely-eyed infants scraping the pavements on tricycles. Andrew had to travel only one stop to the *Journal* office in Watford, so he could take his time. There were some stragglers, though, and some with easier hours, still making the downward journey from the summit of Plummers Park to the station established like some border post in the valley.

Beneath the station burrowed a pedestrian tunnel nervously joining Plummers Park to the council estate. To venture through it was to leave one country for another: on one side fuchsias, and on the other sheets of newspaper drifting in the street winds. The path though the tunnel was their only direct link. Vehicles had to drive south or north and take the roads joining through neutral territory. Trouble was rare between the tenants of one side of the railway and the residents of the other (except for one violent morning in the launderette where some council clothes and some private garments became somehow mixed in a washing-machine). Otherwise the people were not well enough acquainted to fight. They were merely strangers.

From the gate of 'Eagle's Cranny', as Andrew sloped towards the station, emerged Simon Grant whose brand new wife Ena had the breasts at any party within fourteen miles. (At Uxbridge, it was whispered among the men, a better pair had been spied, but this was hearsay.) The indigestible elation with which the young man was filled even at the mundane outset of a working week was emphatic in the way he closed the gate and waved with jaunty triumph at the farewell hand, slender and disembodied, from the bedroom window.

'Great morning, Andrew!' he exclaimed. Then he sighed as though viewing a private memory: 'Fantastic. Just fantastic.'

'It's going to be a hot summer,' nodded Andrew, staring up at the window in the hopeless hope he might see something forbidden.

'No! I don't mean the weather,' chortled the young man. He fell in beside Andrew with a nudging excitement. 'Christ, Andrew, you ought to wake up every morning and see what I see.'

Andrew glanced half behind with assumed innocence. 'Wouldn't have thought the view was all that much this far down the hill,' he observed. 'We've got the whole valley, the farm, the golf course, the crematorium . . .'

'Stop playing games, mate,' beamed Simon wickedly. 'You don't *want* to know what I see in the mornings. I'm talking about what's right in front of my peepers. Soon as I open them. Right under my own private bedclothes. There *they* are . . .'

'Oh, yes, I see. I get you,' said Andrew, hurriedly. 'Yes, that must be a nice sight.'

'Better than the crematorium,' smugged Simon. 'People around here don't know what sex means. They've no idea, Andrew.'

Andrew did not feel at all hurt. Instead he said: 'Oh, I don't know, Simon. Who knows what passions are broiling in the breast of a man washing his Ford Cortina on a Sunday morning?' Then he asked: 'How long have you and Ena been married now?'

'Ten months last Saturday.' Simon almost hugged himself. 'And listen, just listen to this! On our anniversary she's promised to buy a black body-stocking with a hole between the legs. As advertised in the Sunday paper. How about that, then!'

'How *about* that,' agreed Andrew. He was relieved to see another late-leaver opening his rose-cluttered gate twenty yards further down the hill. Normally he might have groaned at meeting Ernest Rollett so early in the day and the week, but he knew that the additional companionship to the station would douse the hot young man who now walked with him.

'Oh God,' breathed Simon. 'Earnest Ernest. I wonder what the week's good cause is? Petitions to the council, the Ratepayers' Ragtime Ball, or the fouling of footways by other dogs than his?'

''Morning, 'morning, 'morning,' Ernest challenged in the way of one briskly disposing of a paltry argument.

'Nice week-end?' Andrew recited the acknowledged Monday greeting.

'Worried,' said Ernest, dropping his tone eighty per cent. 'Damned worried. You've *heard*, of course?'

'I could have done. What was it?'

'I jolly well hope your paper is going to do something about it.'

'Yes, we might. What is it?'

'The waste land.'

'Eliot's poem?' said Andrew deliberately.

Ernest stared at him malignantly. 'I'm talking about the waste land behind my house,' he grated. He nodded fiercely at Simon. 'And yours.'

Simon became abruptly serious. 'What's it about?'

'School for maladjusted kids,' announced Ernest with dread triumph. 'Plans all ready, all drawn up behind our blasted backs. They'll start building in the spring unless we stop them!'

He glowered at the other two. 'You know what that means, don't you? Drugs. Violence. Delinquents. Madness even.'

'You think we've got enough of that now,' suggested Andrew.

'No, I blasted well don't!' hooted Ernest. A ring of sparrows meeting on a square of lawn hummed off in hurt formation. 'You always seem to have some fool answer, Andrew,' he growled. 'This is bloody serious. Unmarried mothers, shoplifters. That sort of type.'

'Sounds like it's going to be a big place,' observed Andrew. 'How come you know about this?'

'I was told. Someone at county level,' said Ernest bumptiously. They were levelling out at the bottom of the hill now. Ernest's voice took on a piteous tone. 'We need play space for our children . . .' he began.

'Didn't know you had any,' said Andrew.

Ernest flushed. 'I'm talking generally,' he said huffily. 'Or I thought they might use it to build a church. Why not? We haven't got a church over this side of the railway. We could do with a nice church.'

'A church?' repeated Simon as though the idea shocked him more than the maladjusted children. 'A church – over here?'

Andrew laughed: 'In this pagan place?'

Ernest argued: 'Perhaps it wouldn't be pagan if we had a church. That vicar from the thing on the council estate seems frightened to come under the tunnel.'

'Don't blame him, mate,' said Andrew. 'This is cannibal country.'

'And here's one of the cannibals,' said Ernest dolefully, looking ahead. 'For God's sake, he's still swinging that invisible golf club.'

'Gorgeous George,' smiled Simon, glad to see him. 'The hole-in-one man.'

'Wish I were, old chap,' laughed George waiting for them to catch up. 'Had the flaming Hole-in-One tie stuck in my wardrobe for two years now, you know. Still not entitled to wear it.'

'Why don't you just wear it and say you've done a hole-in-one?' asked Simon reasonably.

George looked quietly aghast. 'But that's lying,' he said. 'You can't lie – not about a thing like that anyway.' He shook his head as though saddened by a whiff of great evil.

'Didn't see you up there at the week-end,' he said to Andrew.

'Oh, I get cheesed off with the game,' shrugged Andrew. 'It's too difficult.'

George nodded agreeably. He was a man like a pile of sand. He had gingery hair and a moustache exploded like cordite at each end, pale brown eyes and a baggy fawn suit. 'Cheesed off, that's right,' he said. 'Nobody gets more so than yours truly. Unfortunately I just can't leave it alone.'

'Some things get you like that,' agreed Simon, glancing at Andrew as if they had some private secret.

'Have you heard about the waste land?' asked Ernest irritably. 'Or have you spent the entire weekend in a bunker?'

George was pacing beside them now, and the remark set him off on a series of sand iron shots as he walked. 'Waste land? What's that about, Ernie?' he said.

Ernest bridled at being called Ernie. 'Behind the houses,' he said, haughtily pointing over the flat roofs like someone who alone knows an odd and remote region. 'Not on your side of the road, of course. But you'll be affected like the rest of us.'

'What's going to happen?'

'Just a school for maladjusted kids,' sighed Ernest portentously.

'Damn,' exclaimed George. 'I thought that might be just the size for a pitch-and-putt course. Very handy that would be.'

'Then *you'll* have to fight,' pronounced Ernest, swallowing his inclination to wrath. 'We'll *all* have to fight. I intend to call a meeting as soon as possible. And I'm telephoning your editor this morning, Andrew. We must get the paper involved. It's got to stop before it starts.'

They paused while a small and apologetic sports car, the top pulled raggedly back, emerged rear-first from a scarred double gate. The house was one of the oldest on the Plummers Park Estate, all of ten years (when they were cheap), and they did not know the owner's name. His privet hedges were sturdy and cluttered with summer dust. A wan-faced middle-aged man tugged nervously at the wheel of the car as it backed in jerks. His hound eyes rolled towards them, as though in urgent mute warning. At that moment a rainbow of wet salad, potato peelings and carrot tops curved through the air from somewhere behind the privet hedge. Obviously projected by an expert it lobbed over the windscreen of the little car and covered the man in the driving seat. 'Fuck off!' screamed a raw female voice from the hidden house door. 'And don't fucking well come back!'

Andrew, Ernest, George and Simon stood in almost military rank, transfixed alongside the car. The driver, hung with lettuce and festooned with long potato peelings sat as though about to weep. Weakly and apologetically he turned to them, seemingly confident they would understand, and shrugged: 'Monday morning.'

Politely they said nothing as the trembling man backed the trembling car into the road and there stopped it while he miserably picked the vegetable debris from his head and clothes. They walked on, in silence, Andrew, Simon and George not daring to look at each other, and the proper Ernest, feeling it only decent to ignore the drama, returned to his former subject. 'No,' he affirmed loudly and conclusively, 'We've got no place for the maladjusted in Plummers Park.'

*

Audrey Maiby was a quietly sensual woman married to a lazy man. In her teens she had been more promiscuous than either fashion or safety had recognized. She had met Andrew one night on a riverboat shuffle on the Thames, and they watched the growing dawn while sprawled amid the damp dock leaves and dewy dandelions of Temple Island. She and he, hung against each other, drunk with exultation and the unused smell of five o'clock sun, had walked the bank along the length of the Henley Regatta course, she carrying her damp knickers in her hand. Now they lived at Plummers Park like all the others who had merely held hands in the cinema. The wild times had gone. The winds had been thrown to caution. She, who had so perilously enjoyed her love, was securely on the pill.

She watched him leave that airy morning, sixteen years after Temple Island, still worth looking at, his longer hair not looking incongruous as it did on some of the other men, but his stride now eased to something like a shuffle, and no riverboat shuffle either. He spent a lot of his time reading. That far night among the dandelions, as they lay wet against each other, he had told her rhymes and things he had heard and what he had dreamed. He seemed to have read every book in the world, and he knew words, quite short words, of which she had never suspected the existence. 'You,' she had said in her teenage way, massaging her fingers around his uncovered loins. 'You're a poet you are, you know. And I've heard poets are dangerous.'

Now, she thought with a comfort, wry and contrary, he was about as dangerous as one of the pied milking cows she could see mooning in the slanting fields beyond Plummers Park, and at times she had caught him wearing the same expression. And yet he would worry if they had not made love for a week; she had sensed him, in bed, mentally calculating the days and wondering whether he ought to ask. He had once run off with an extraordinary and attractive woman, but he had come back because, she suspected, he missed their furniture, the colour television, his books and his smelly dog.

Gladstone, the brown bolster, the emitter of noises and odours, lay now, already defeated by the growing sun, having watched his master walk towards the station with the smashed expression of one convinced that a beloved one has gone forever.

'You ought to go with him,' she suggested to the basset. Then spitefully: 'You ought to have gone with him last time.' The tubular dog looked up with a red hung eye and ingratiating smile. She closed the front door on him, stood indecisively in the hall, then went into the kitchen to finish her coffee. She stood, as he had stood earlier watching the girl from Cowacre, looking out over the emptied estate. Andrew was always one of the final husbands to leave, and it seemed that the entire valley had been quit by its people because of some plague or disaster and not merely by the daily necessity of employment. It was left flooded with the silence of sunshine, populated by toddlers, routine housewives and, with the exception of the French onion man, unexciting tradesmen.

On this morning, however, there were two early and abnormal interruptions. First Herbie Futter, the taxidermist, left his house later than usual, with a smothering embrace for and from his ash-grey wife on the step. She reflected on the way Jewish people said goodbye as though they never expected to see each other again. She had once asked Herbie to change a five pound note in the Watford supermarket, and he had produced his wallet and proceeded to kiss, both feverishly and fervently, fading pictures of his wife and grown-up children before finally giving her the change. He was a perpetually nodding man, followed, sometimes pursued, by dogs attracted by the smell of the chemicals he used in his trade. Especially in hot weather. He had come to Plummers Park because, he said, he despised the regimentation of the German mentality in his own country. It was not so much the gas chambers, he once complained, but the indignity of lining up for them.

Now he walked quite briskly along the paraded ranks of English houses, free he believed, towards the station and then to his workshop where he was engaged in stuffing a bison, a tiring and exacting task for someone no longer young.

He had only just completed his exit from the wide screen of her kitchen window when from the other edge appeared Hercules, the singing tramp, bent like a tactful enquiry over the laden perambulator which he pushed all day, all week, all year, all life, on some mysterious and never accomplished journey. He was the Flying Dutchman of Plummers Park, restless, unresting, regarded by the new people as something quaint and traditional, to be fed and preserved. He lent atmosphere to the place.

'Hang on a minute, Hercules,' Audrey said to herself, and tugging her dressing-gown round her she went out of the door. She thought she would call him first, but since he travelled at something below a mile an hour she refrained and hurried instead under the carport and to the garage at the rear. Wedged at the side of her white mini was what had been, in its heyday, an elegant baby-carriage. Now it was scratched and dusty and the wheels complained as she moved it. She withdrew it from the garage and then pushed it down the front path.

Hercules was singing in his plodding voice, his head down as if he were tired or ashamed:

When I survey the wondrous Cross
On which the Prince of Glory died
My richest gain I count but loss
And pour contempt on all my pride.

'I say,' she called, 'I wonder if you'd like a new pram.' She did not call him Hercules, because that was just a nickname which people around there had given him. She did not know whether he knew it or would like it.

He stopped walking and singing, bent so low he was scarcely half her height. His face turned upwards. It was like a piece of bruised fruit, but his eyes were black and bright. 'It squeaks,' he pointed out at once. 'I heard it squeaking when you wheeled it.'

'That old thing squeaks too,' Audrey said, nodding at his rusted pram piled with sacks and blankets and with socks hanging over its side like the fenders of a tugboat. They were rumoured to be full of gold sovereigns.

'Right,' agreed Hercules. He swivelled on both heels, a miniature military movement, to view his present pram. She noticed that, apart from a minimal parting from the knees downwards as he walked, his short legs were kept close together all the time. 'It squeaks as well,' he conceded. 'But I'm used to this squeak, ain't I? I don't reckon I could change it for another squeak, not now, missus. Mine's regular. Sends me to kip sometimes when I'm on the road.'

'I wondered why you never got any speed up,' she said, hurt that he viewed her gift with such off-handedness. 'Well, do you want it, or don't you? It's not been used for a few years but it's all right.'

'It squeaks,' he said doggedly. 'Better the squeak you know than the squeak you don't. Let's have a look at it, anyway.'

'I don't want anything for it,' she said hurriedly, in case he thought she was trying to sell it.

'You won't get nuffink neither,' he confirmed, without change of expression. 'I can't see me taking it off your hands. I'm very busy just now.'

He mistook her incredulous expression for disappointment. 'Okay, all right, missus,' he said reassuringly. 'Let's see what it goes like.' He waddled towards her and she pushed the pram a little nervously his way. 'The tyres ain't much good,' he said.

'God, you'd think you were a second-hand car dealer!'

'I was once,' he said, glancing over the bodywork. 'That's why I'm on the road. Too easy-going I was, missus.'

'Look,' she said in exasperation. 'Do you want the damned pram or don't you? If you don't, just say, and I'll get rid of it elsewhere.'

'Where?' he inquired challengingly. 'The dustmen won't take it, and the council will charge you to take it away.' He had shuffled round the rear end by now and she saw with alarm and embarrassment that he was so bent by his years of pushing his low pram that he could not reach the white polished handle of hers. He turned accusingly as though she had perpetrated some cruel joke. 'I can't get my 'ands up that 'igh,' he protested.

'Shit,' she said angrily to herself.

'I can shit, missus. Shitting's nuffink. But I can't reach that 'andle. My old one's a foot lower.'

'All right,' Audrey sighed. 'Let's forget it. I'll take it back.'

'Naw,' he said, with a sudden surging smile of generosity, black teeth projecting over his lips like cigarette stubs. 'Naw, I'll take it off your 'ands. I like the look of you.'

She stared at the innocent wickedness of his face. 'Listen,' he said. 'Don't you worry. I'll tow it behind. I might be able to get rid of it for you.'

'Oh good, all right then,' she said.

She thought he was going to ask her for money, but he merely said: 'I can't stay chatting all day, missus. I'm way behind schedule already. I'll 'ave to go or I'll be in trouble.' Still far from understanding, she nodded seriously and watched him attach the newly acquired pram to his boyscout belt by a piece of cord. Then, one conveyance ahead and another behind he recommenced his eternal journey. For the first time she noticed he had a bunch of wild flowers in a jam jar in the hull of his pram.

She returned gratefully to the house, but for some reason turned at the door and looked out. The bland sunshine seemed wasted on such an empty place. The houses looked like crates waiting on a wharf. On the most distant road, Hedgerows, she could see a post-office van like a ladybird. By her own front path the dew remained like glass on the roses. Birds were sending their summer songs from the oak tree incorporated in their garden wall, which itself was constructed of *old* bricks. That tree and the rough wall put five hundred pounds on the house. The primrose telephone rang in the hall and she went in.

'In the street accosting men,' whispered the accusation. '*I* saw you.'

'Hello, Cynth.' She smiled to herself. 'You and all the neighbours, I bet.'

'Old Hercules might be fun.'

'You haven't seen his teeth.'

'Come to think of it, I don't think I've ever seen his face,' said Cynthia Turvey. 'He's always got it facing the road as he pushes that pram. Do you think he'll take our old pushchair? You do hang on to these things, but I can't see us needing it now.'

'He won't look at it,' said Audrey, as though Hercules were a fine art dealer. 'He was doing me a big favour, believe me.'

'Fancy the poor bugger being all bent up like that,' sighed Cynthia. 'Have you seen Bill Shillingford? He's getting like that. They say he's digging an extra room out of the earth. He can do it because he's got a split level on his side of the hill.'

'Really. I must tell Andrew, though I can't see him ever doing anything like that.'

'You have to actually be on the *side* of the hill,' pointed out Cynthia pedantically. 'Apparently if you go round there he's liable to walk through the lounge stripped to the waist and wheeling a wheelbarrow full of clay.'

Audrey said, 'Come to think about it, I wouldn't mind seeing Andrew hauling a few barrows about. He spends all his time reading, thinking great thoughts or playing football with the kids over the waste ground. He comes back soaked with sweat and boasting he's scored three goals.'

'He'll have more kids to play with soon,' said Cynthia, in the manner of someone who knows something.

'How do you mean?'

'They're going to build a place for retarded children over on the waste land, didn't you hear?'

'No! They wouldn't do that!' She felt the leaden sensation in her stomach that arrived whenever there was a threat of any kind to the security that so bored her. 'Who told you?'

'It's all over Plummers Park,' said Cynthia glibly. 'They're starting work any minute.'

'Oh, Christ, Cynth, that's terrible. It'll knock thousands off these properties. Just our damned luck.' Her fear flamed easily into anger.

'Didn't Andrew know anything about it? I thought *he* would.'

Audrey sighed. 'He's usually the last to hear even though

he's on the paper. Maybe he knew and forgot to mention it. He would. He didn't tell me that Greta Humphries had committed suicide until everybody else for miles around knew. He said it wasn't the sort of thing he thought ought to be bandied about because of her kids.'

'Well, he's very thoughtful, very kind, old Andrew. You know where you are with him. Safe.'

'Old Andrew, indeed,' agreed Audrey. 'He was being nice and thoughtful this morning when that girl, what's her name, Hewkins, from Cowacre came by, with half the men in Plummers Park sniffing after her like randy dogs. You're lucky Geoff goes off early and you don't have to put up with that.'

'He gets his thrills in the office,' said Cynthia confidently, then added a cautious 'I expect'. 'They think nothing of it. It's part of being male. They'd kick up murder, though, wouldn't they, if *we* went around fancying *men* left, right and centre?'

'*Don't* you?'

'Don't I what?'

'Fancy men, Cynth?'

'Yes, I suppose I do, really. I fancied Geoff when he was married. Do you?'

'Naturally I do. Isn't it funny how they think only *they* get the urges. They think we're not the same, we're not allowed to be.'

'I suppose you're right, Audrey.' Cynthia sounded as though she was becoming wary of the conversation. 'Listen,' she continued quickly, 'tonight, if it stays decent, we thought we'd go out and have a drink somewhere in the country. Do you two want to come?'

Audrey waited. 'Well, we'd thought of going out ourselves,' she said cautiously. 'Lizzie is up on the canal renovating that old barge with the other children and she keeps asking us to go up and see what they've done. You've got to show willing, haven't you, when they ask? So we thought we'd wander up there and have a look.'

'Oh, yes. Perhaps we could come with you.'

'No.' It came out more sharply than she had intended. 'Well, you know what kids are. They'll think we've brought the whole neighbourhood up.'

'Oh, all right then.'

'No, but you do understand, don't you? Kids are funny these days. They don't like the idea of grown-ups breathing down their necks. Listen, why don't we meet you and Geoff in that pub up there, the one with the seats in the garden and the old mill-wheel . . . The one with the funny name. Remember we laughed about it?'

'The Jolly Grinder,' said Cynthia, but still coolly. 'All right, I'll ask my Geoff if he wants to go there. He might have somewhere else in mind. You understand that, don't you?'

'Of course I do, Cynthia. Andrew's the same. I always like to ask him. Anyway, maybe we'll see you in the garden.'

'All right. 'Bye, Audrey. Sorry about the home for maladjusted kids.'

'So am I. It's a liberty. 'Bye, 'bye.'

*

Audrey went up to the bathroom. They had knocked the lavatory and the bathroom into one so that it was now a tufty-white carpeted room of a good size. They had found some dignified Delft tiles in an antique shop and put them into the wall to give the area around the lavatory pan more character.

One of the results of making the two rooms into one was that the only place for a full-length mirror was now directly in front of the lavatory and anyone squatting there was faced with their own reflection. She had put a coy flowered curtain on the wall so that visitors could pull it across the mirror if they felt embarrassed by their own presence. She sat naked on the pan and regarded herself seriously in the glass. You could hardly expect to look better every day, not when you were a day older, but the summer tan helped. She smiled at herself and was glad to see that her good teeth showed very white against the deepening brown of her face. Two fatty rolls lay across her stomach, so she folded her arms, formally, as though in a photograph, to hide them.

When she had finished she turned on the bath taps and then felt her breasts for lumps as she did every day, as instructed in the Sunday supplements. None had appeared. The breasts were full but dull, strong but with a touch of sloth about them, like her husband. Andrew enjoyed her breasts. He still told her so, and when he felt like feeling her affectionately that was always where his hands went. Now, when they had overcome the natural laziness of familiarity, they sometimes lay on their sides, face to face, in bed, while he sucked at them, holding her buttocks in his considerate but firm grip.

She now rolled them firmly with her hands, enjoying the minor sensation, and then laughing at her reflection in the mirror. She struck a series of odd poses, like a Balinese temple dancer, legs akimbo, arms and hands projecting like angled wings, head clicking from side to side. She turned and adjusted the cold crystal bath tap. She put the lid of the toilet down and sat on it, the candlewick cover comfortingly soft against her buttocks. She took a bottle of almond oil and began to rub it into the broad tops of her legs, where the week-end sunburn was blushing and sore.

Afterwards she stood in the bath and soaped herself and then lay down in the warm water and let her eyes close. The house seemed very vacant and quiet. She stopped moving and the sudsy water around her settled to stillness. Now through the left-open door she could hear the chronic movements of the clock from their bedroom, the birds outside the window, and miles away the half-sound of a lofty aeroplane. No one was there but her, no one to see or care or listen. It hardly seemed to matter what she did. If she simply drowned herself she wondered if Andrew would keep the truth from Lizzie. Would he be so considerate with a suicide of his own as he had been over Greta Humphries? The solitariness and the frustration gathered within her like indigestion. She felt like having a good swear, but instead she began to sing, like Hercules:

When I survey the Wondrous Cross
On which the Prince of Glory died
My richest gain I count but loss,
And pour contempt on all my pride.

Then she began to cry. It was brief, and she wiped the tears quickly into the bathwater. 'I'm mad,' she thought lucidly. 'I must be potty. I thought I had another ten years or more before I started this sort of thing.'

She climbed from the bath and began to dry herself. 'You ought to snap out of it, my girl,' she told herself loudly. 'You ought to get out and do some charity work.' She would not mind helping with the maladjusted children, she thought, if only they would build their rotten place somewhere else, over the railway line perhaps. Or maybe she ought to go to London more often. It was three months since she had been to London.

She dressed, did her hair and her makeup, and then went down to the kitchen and made another cup of coffee. She turned the radio on and allowed Jimmy Young to twitter three sentences before turning it off again. Then, through the window, she caught sight of the French onion seller.

He was the most beautiful man anyone had ever seen in Plummers Park. Tall, slim, black-haired and dark-faced, with violinist's eyes, everything about him was exciting, sexual, even the onions hanging from his bike. He toured the English streets once a month, he and his wares, leaving tears in many eyes. He wore the *bleu de travail*. He was said to come from Normandy and he had little English. He had never been seen to enter any woman's home. She watched with womanly cunning from the spot a yard inside her window and saw the housewives come to their doors and simper as they purchased his onions. Two were in bikinis and another was in her nightdress. He did not appear to notice. Poor drunken Mrs Burville was already in her garden walking in circles among the flowers, trying to pick a few stems. She was wearing a fat nylon overall and white knee-length socks belonging to her brilliant daughter Sarah. She made little darts at odd roses as if trying to capture a butterfly, but after several indecisive circles picked only one bloom which she gave with the caring smile of the truly inebriated to the French onion man. He accepted it courteously and gave her a single onion in return. Then he turned, crossed the road, and made straight for Audrey's door.

She pretended not to take a glance at herself in the mirror as she went to the door, but she caught herself doing it. She opened the door and he stood there smiling, his dark hair curling down his brown neck and his forehead, and his arms festooned with naked onions. He had left his bike on the road.

'Not today, thank you,' she said firmly.

He looked theatrically concerned. 'A long time,' he said, 'you have not onions.'

'We're not great onion eaters,' said Audrey politely. 'My husband doesn't care for them.'

'And you, madame?'

'No, nor me either.'

He shrugged and his onions shrugged with him. 'It is a pity,' he said. He paused and looked at her with blatant steadiness. Christ, she thought, those eyes are ridiculous. 'Perhaps, my dear, there is something else?'

Audrey felt her blush cover her face and her chest. 'No, I don't think so, thank you. Not today.'

He went and she retreated into the house bubbling like a spring inside. She sat in an armchair and laughed unbelievingly into her hands. Dear Jesus, there was nothing like an onion man to make you feel like a desirable woman.

2

Andrew went directly from the station to the magistrates court, a cool and carbolic place, the high windows letting in the murmurs of a June morning to those who would be brought from the cells to the dock. Clean sunlight slanted tantalizingly from the upper windows, but the lower panes were frosted as though not to aggravate the envy of the prisoners and the others who had to be in that serious position on that fine day.

He collected the charge list from Sergeant Fearnley, the officer's bald, official head bronzed from his garden. He carried it to where Big Brenda, the girl reporter from the opposition paper, squatted at the press table. She was a red, chatty soul, who had once been reprimanded by the chairman of the magistrates for clicking her knitting needles throughout the preliminary hearing of a murder trial.

It was a meagre press table and it was their Monday habit to squeeze together on the bench, their thighs wedged in the confined space between the bulbous table legs. No words were ever said about this comforting tradition. Big Brenda was hung with woollen garments, whatever the season. She knitted most of them herself, often beneath the reporters' table during long and doleful cases. The work finished, she would appear dressed in these sheepish scraps, a bobbled hat, a shaggy scarf, a cardigan growing wooden buttons, toggles, acorns, and, in the meanest part of winter, bright red mittens on her bright red hands.

Andrew placed the charge list on the table between them, and Big Brenda's large fuchsia lips flopped into a smile of genuine greeting. They leaned forward to study it together, nudging hard against the table's legs and each other's, her swollen, woollen bosom resting on the oak top like two bags of damp laundry.

'All the usual,' sighed Andrew, running his eye down the list. 'Drunk, drunk and indecent, drunk and not indecent, drunk and incapable, drunk in charge of a bicycle . . . that could be all right . . . theft from a gas meter, non-payment of arrears . . . parking without lights . . . thrill upon thrill . . . everything but knocking on doors and running away . . . theft from Waitrose Supermarket . . . theft from W. H. Smith's . . . theft from MacFisheries . . . looks like this chap did a round tour . . .'

'Strange for it to be a man,' murmured Brenda. 'They're usually women, shoplifters. And he's seventy-four. Charles White, seventy-four. Morrison Way. That's your direction, isn't it?'

'Other side of the railway,' replied Andrew immediately, and surprised at his own defensiveness. 'On the council estate.'

'Where else?' said Brenda. 'You'd hardly expect anyone from your bit to nick half a pound of hake from the fish-shop.'

'We have other faults,' said Andrew. 'False idols, fornication . . . getting up the Joneses.' She giggled primly and his voice trailed off. The court had been filling, and now the elevated oak-panelled door opened in a mildly dramatic way and, to the bellow of 'Rise, please!' from Sergeant Fearnley, the three magistrates made an entrance of modest majesty.

Andrew's eyes turned idly around the court. It looked like the stage of a bad amateur theatrical company, as though people had been hastily gathered from the street, briefly told their parts, and put into the scene. Some characters were constant, Sergeant Fearnley; his coughing constable; an old boy who always sat in the oaken public gallery, side-on like someone sitting up in their coffin, pouring himself relays of tea from a grim flask; Miss Bishop, the probation officer, an anguished soul screwing up pieces of paper and leaving them on the floor like a castaway's pleas for help. Then there were the witnesses and the relatives of the various accused, sitting resigned, tired, frightened, puzzled or amused, and Mr Henry, the court clerk, his nostrils so close to his large ledger that in the winter dew-drops from his nose seemed to join him like tacky glue to the legal pages. Above him, in the manner of a trio of coachmen above a lone, head-hung horse, were the magistrates: on one flank Mr Walter Brownlow, a baggy seed merchant, and former mayor, who left trails of barley and oats dripping from his pockets and trouser turn-ups wherever he went; on the other Mrs Matilda Prentice, a sexily severe young woman who peered with a sharp but beautiful face from beneath a variable but gay hat at accused men who had never so much as touched one of her kind; at their centre the chairman, Mr John Osmund, a scraggy man who uttered thin comments to himself through-out the hearing of a case and doled out sentences either sadisti-cally severe or idiotically liberal as the mood or the morning took him. Andrew watched them without sensation until he fell to thinking that because of the enclosed gallery on which they sat he had never seen Mrs Prentice's legs. She was the type of woman who still wore stockings and a small suspender belt.

'Number one, sir. John Smart,' Sergeant Fearnley called.

John Smart, sparse and dun, tired, a shred of coloured tie tight around the neck of a grisly army shirt, the very denial of his name, blinked through sore eyes from the dock. He seemed anxious to get the matter done. ''aving a piss, sir,' he announced loudly towards the magistrate.

Mr Osmund leaned pedantically over towards the back of his clerk's head. 'What did he say?' he inquired. Andrew saw how much the magistrate and the accused were physically alike, the meagre heads jutting forward, but one a small, demanding pump, the other a hopeful, hopeless nod.

The clerk rattled his throat, half rose, half turned, and replied: 'He says he was . . . er relieving himself, sir.'

'Oh, for goodness' sake, why can't we start at the beginning, in the proper way?' sighed Mr Osmund.

'Of course, sir,' replied the clerk. He turned from the one sparse man to the other. 'John Smart,' he began . . .

'Just 'aving a piss,' reaffirmed the accused almost smugly.

'*John Smart*,' said Mr Henry doggedly. 'You are charged with being drunk and indecent at Church Lane last night. Do you plead guilty or not guilty?'

'Guilty, sir,' sighed the red-eyed man as though at last they understood. 'Just 'aving a piss.'

He was fined a pound, which he did not have, and so was sentenced to one day in prison, which meant he sat down in court and watched the other drunks and miscreants with the scorning amusement of one whose debt is paid.

The pathetic Monday morning carnival trailed through the official room. To some, thought Andrew, it was probably the best room in which they had ever been. A man with a black eye wept in the dock; two earthy young women, wild as gipsies, sniggered and then fell upon each other with unashamed laughter as a police constable produced two groundsheets, said to be an essential part of their open-air trade; a youth with a broken arm nodded dumbly when it was suggested that he fell down the steps of the cells and was never pushed; a man found at midnight with a glass-cutter adjacent to a neat hole in a shop window protested that it was a tool of his trade, that he was entitled to carry it and had merely been testing its sharpness on the window. It was a poor parade even for that petty area, and the advent of Charles White, aged seventy-four, charged with shoplifting, did little to raise the general tone. Except that with him, sitting in the public seats, watching with studied anxiety, was a girl, small and serious: a round, conventionally pretty, salesgirl face framed with fair hair. She was shadowed below the eyes as though she did not sleep well. When the old man in the dock spoke her lips formed the words with him, as if together they had rehearsed every line.

Mr Henry read the monotonous accumulation of charges. Two tins of cling peaches and a plastic tube of cocktail sticks from Waitrose Supermarket, two paperbacks and three coloured pencils from Smith's, a cod cutlet and a live eel from Mac-Fisheries ...

'Peaches, cocktail sticks, paperbacks, cod and eel,' muttered Brenda as she wrote in her slow shorthand.

'Ivory, and apes and peacocks, sandalwood and cedarwood and sweet white wine,' sighed Andrew quietly.

'Do you plead guilty or not guilty?' inquired Mr Henry lifting his head from his big ledger, as if annoyed at intrusion into some personal and private study.

'Guilty,' the old man almost shouted. Andrew watched the girl's lips say it with him. 'I ... I ... I'm guilty all right.'

'Yes, yes,' said Mr Henry impatiently. 'Evidence, please.'

A young constable was in the pouch of the witness-box, crouching at the neck, holding the Bible above his head as though sheltering from a local shower. He took the oath with religious care and then proceeded to describe the crimes and apprehension of Charles White, aged seventy-four, now standing like a failed suicide, dying of consumption, in front of a firing squad. The old man sported three worn and pathetic medals on his chest, one bravely pulling the lapel of his weary coat forward like a derisive tongue.

'A *live* eel?' said the magistrate. Andrew nodded to himself, grateful that the chairman had brought it up. It was the best part of the story.

'Yes, sir,' replied the constable, carefully referring to his notebook. 'Live. Extant, your honour. This is why the accused was apprehended, sir. A woman complained to me that the accused had dropped the eel on to her baby in the pram. He was trying to make his escape from the fishmongers at the time. The accused, that is, sir.'

'Guilty, guilty,' insisted the dry old voice from the dock, wanting to get it done.

'The supermarket, Smith's, MacFisheries,' recited the chairman. 'Went on the rampage, didn't you?'

He glanced towards the press bench, making sure they were writing 'on the rampage' down. He liked to see his notable phrases in the paper. 'Why did you do this?' he demanded towards the dock.

'Forgot to pay,' said Charles White. He pushed forward one side of his chest so that his medals gave a brief jangle. Mr Osmund ignored the action. Old men were always jangling medals in court.

'You forgot to pay in three shops,' sniffed the chairman. He glanced at the court generally. 'Is there any other evidence?'

'His grand-daughter's here, sir,' said Sergeant Fearnley, touching the girl on the shoulder. 'I think she would like to say something.'

The girl and the grandfather in the dock exchanged quick, trapped looks. 'Take the oath, then,' sighed Mr Osmund. The girl, slight in a red dress, walked nervously to the witness-box and whispered the words on the card before her.

'I swear that the evidence I shall give will be the truth, the whole truth . . . and nothing but the truth . . .' She stumbled along the trite lines and it seemed that she was going to cry. Brenda had gone scarlet with pity. Andrew leaned forward.

'Come on, come on, young woman,' said Mr Henry, with soft severity. He liked young girl witnesses. 'Don't let's have any tears. Lots of people have read that oath.'

'*I* haven't,' said the girl, jerking her head up and staring defiantly at him. 'Not before.'

The clerk seemed unable to find an argument. 'What's your name?' he asked impatiently.

'Bessie White,' she whispered.

'Speak up, girl. Everybody wants to hear you. The magistrates, the press, everybody.'

'The press?' breathed the girl, her face hardening. 'What's the press got to do with it?'

Andrew had often wondered that himself. Now Mr Henry and all three magistrates turned, grinning knowingly at him and Brenda, and they dutifully returned the stupid grins.

'The press are always in court,' said Mr Henry with bland

pride. 'Now let's have your name again.'

'Bessie White,' she repeated, staring across at Andrew as though she could scarcely credit her eyes.

'That's Elizabeth, is it? Bessie?'

'Bessie,' she replied firmly.

'I see. How old are you?'

'Eighteen. Nearly nineteen.'

'And you live at 22 Morrison Way, Attlee Park, with the accused?'

'He's my grandad,' she said hurriedly, and looking around for understanding as though anxious to correct any wrong impression.

'Quite, quite so,' murmured Mr Henry. 'Now, you have heard him plead guilty to this charge . . .'

'Guilty! Guilty!' croaked the old man gladly from the dock.

The girl and Mr Henry both looked at him sternly but in different ways. He dropped his forlorn eyes and began to rub one of his medals with his sleeve. '. . . you have heard him plead guilty,' repeated the clerk.

'Guilty, guilty,' muttered the man.

'Shut up, Grandad!' cried the girl suddenly and fiercely. Her voice, which had been soft, touched with an edge of Cockney, flew like a knife. The old man dropped his ashamed chin on his chest.

'Thank you,' said Mr Henry. 'Now, what have you got to tell us?'

'Just that he didn't mean it,' she said. 'He's just an old fool. He just saw the things and he took them. What does he want with cocktail sticks?'

'We appreciate you coming to espouse him.' It was the sharp young Mrs Prentice leaning over her wooden parapet to look down at the girl. 'What sort of person is he?'

'He's an old man,' shrugged the girl as though it answered everything. 'He's even older than he is, if you see what I mean. He just walks around and does silly things. I don't want his name in the papers.'

Andrew looked up sharply from his notes and saw her hard expression directly at him. He began to scribble aimlessly.

Brenda's thigh nudged him. Mr Brownlow, the corn merchant magistrate, a kind man, took out a great handkerchief to blow his nose and ejected with it a scattering of barley seeds which fell, bounced noisily on the bench and trickled on to the half-bent head of the clerk below him. Mr Henry privately closed his eyes.

'I'm afraid, young lady,' said Mr Brownlow heavily, ignoring what he had done, 'that we have no power to tell the press what to publish or what not to publish.'

'I don't want it in,' she repeated as if it were an order or a threat.

'Do you wish to say anything else about the accused?' asked Mr Osmund impatiently.

'No, nothing,' she said, turning her expression slowly to him. 'It's just that he's an old man. You can see that.'

Sergeant Fearnley moved towards the girl and touched her arm as she descended from the witness-box. She glanced at her grandfather and then looked again at Andrew. Then she sat down.

'Anything known?' asked the chairman, eyebrows going towards the constable.

The policeman stepped back into the witness-box and consulted some spread papers. 'Previous conviction, sir, for stealing thirty-five newspapers from a vendor's stand, fifteen *Star*s, five *Standard*s, and the rest *Evening News*es, sir. Put on probation for three years. Acton magistrates court, sir.'

'That must have been years ago,' pointed out the kindly Mr Brownlow. 'The *Star*'s not been published for ten or twelve years now.'

'Yes, sir,' agreed the constable. 'The conviction was in 1950, sir.'

'Why didn't you say so then?' said Mr Brownlow.

'I was going to, sir, when you spoke.' The policeman looked at the corn merchant steadily and the corn merchant, abashed, picked up one of his previously scattered grains lying on the bench before him, and ate it remorselessly, rolling it in exaggerated manner about his rural cheeks and gums.

After the pause the policeman said with studied firmness,

'There is another conviction – for cruelty, sir.'

He glanced up to see the court stir at that. Andrew was watching the girl again and saw the disbelief and alarm on her pale face.

'Cruelty?' queried Mr Osmund, looking sternly at the old man in the dock and then returning to the constable. 'What cruelty?'

'Apparently, sir, he was fined five shillings at Acton for painting a sparrow yellow, sir, and attempting to sell it as a canary.'

The grim man who always sat sideways like someone in his coffin in the public gallery began to honk with laughter, the first time he had made a sound in court in years. Others were grinning or laughing. Andrew could feel Brenda rolling inside like warm water in a plastic bag and he briefly turned his own face down to the table. When he looked up there was still the pale, laughterless face of the girl.

'Sparrow? Canary?' muttered the chairman.

'Very unkind,' said Mrs Prentice severely.

'Guilty, guilty,' cried the man in the dock.

'It was a long time ago, sir,' said the constable as if sorry it were not more recent. 'Nineteen twenty-one, sir.'

'That's all there is?' inquired the chairman wearily. 'This seems to be getting out of hand.'

'Yes, your honour, that's all,' said the constable. He stepped down.

'Charles White,' sighed Mr Osmund, as though considering every syllable of the name. 'You have admitted this charge and we have heard your previous record. Is there anything else you want to say?'

'Guilty, guilty,' said the old man with dry doggedness.

'I am going to fine you twenty-five pounds.'

There was a moment when the grandfather half-turned and looked at the girl. She nodded and reached for her handbag.

*

Outside the magistrates court, at the top of the warm summer road, was a café called The Bombardier owned by a former regular soldier and painted in camouflage streaks of khaki and green. Big Brenda said she had to return to her office and rolled away down the hill, while Andrew walked idly up the incline towards the café. The work he had done that morning would take an hour to write, and after that he would probably be free to go home to Plummers Park. Sometimes Burton, the editor, gave him evening jobs to do, but not many. He was working at twenty-five per cent of his capacity and he knew it. He was living at the same rate. Two years before he had gone to live for six sexual weeks with a beautiful and crazy girl in three damp rooms overlooking the Thames. Every minute of every day and every night was taken. They had lived, feasted off each other, then finished. They walked away leaving the washing-up of their last meal in the sink. He had gone back to slow compromise with his wife. When he had nothing else to think about, which was quite often, he thought about the girl. If he went to London he pretended he might even see her among the hundreds in the streets. But he never did. She had probably gone to America. Audrey thought about her too but she was hardly ever mentioned.

Bessie White left the magistrates court, pulling her grandfather after her like an old handcart. She nagged him up the road and followed Andrew into The Bombardier Café where he was sitting at one of the tables covered with decorated oilcloth depicting badges of Britain's fighting forces. The bombardier himself, short-haired, thick-armed, festooned with memorable tattooes, stood behind the counter watching the steaming spout of a tea-urn as in other days he had watched what he liked to call the smoking arse of a twenty-five-pounder gun.

Andrew looked up from his table and tea and felt a short startled sensation as the girl came through the door. It was as if she were some kind of threat or vengeance. She was ushering the old man before her now. His face was set with elderly indifference and Andrew saw that his medals had gone. Andrew thought the girl was going to sit opposite him at his place, but she knew where she was going. She and her grandfather sat at the next oilclothed table staring directly at him. He tried to look deep into the revolving tea in his cup but he knew that the young face and the old face were both irrevocably in his direction, so he looked up and grinned foolishly.

'Where's his medals, then?' he asked with uneasy friendliness.

'He had to give them back, didn't he,' said the girl with the London rhetorical question.

'How do you mean?'

'They didn't belong to him,' she replied easily. 'Never done a day's fighting in his life, except with my gran or the neighbours.'

'You . . . you just . . . borrowed them?' asked Andrew carefully. She had steady hazel eyes, and they were watching him with an implicit challenge. 'Just for the duration of the case, as it were?' he added.

'As it were,' she repeated with a little curl of mockery. 'The other one was wearing them, the one who was drunk and having a pee. I gave him a pound to lend them to me. He's got them back now.'

'God,' said Andrew. 'You've got a nerve.'

The tea arrived for her and her grandfather, and she peeped around the thickness of the bombardier's embossed forearms to reply. 'Yes, that's one thing I have got, a nerve.'

'I've never heard anything like it,' said Andrew.

'I suppose you're going to shove *that* in the paper now,' she said. Her hostility rose like a spike. A pink spot appeared on each of her pale cheeks.

'No,' he assured her. 'No, I won't be doing that.' He regarded the strange pair. The girl neat and sharp, the old man staring at him and beyond him, punched with age and indifference. 'Can I come and sit there?' said Andrew, getting up and taking his cup and saucer in his hand. He had taken a pace, but the girl put up the flat of her hand to him, a slim white hand like a trout's belly.

'Why don't you stay where you are,' she suggested, to his discomfort. 'There's plenty of room to talk like this. Anyway, you could scare the old boy and he'll spill his tea. He spills things all the time.'

'All right, if that's what you want,' grumbled Andrew uncomfortably, edging back to his seat. When he looked up, having slopped his tea from thick cup to thick saucer, feeling as he had felt when as a teenager a girl had declined to dance with him, she was smiling.

'Don't take offence,' she said. 'It's not your fault you've got a job like you have. Telling about people.'

'Oh, come on,' he said, roused as he invariably was by any attack on the profession he loathed. 'You'd be the first one to read this sort of case if it wasn't your grandfather involved. You'd have a good laugh and a gossip about it in your street.'

'Do you know where we live?' she asked.

'Morrison Way,' he muttered, as though ashamed he knew. 'I live over that area myself. I live on the hill. Upmeadow.'

She grimaced with puzzlement, then laughed as though he had told a shoddy joke. 'Oh, Christ!' she exclaimed. 'Over the other side. Well, you'll really *know* all about us, then, won't you? Like you know about the Chinese.'

'Listen,' said Andrew, Flat-Roof Man rising to battle within him, 'I've seen a girl in riding gear leading a bloody *horse* out of the front door of one of those council houses. So don't give me all the poor people stuff.'

'Remember *you're* the one who pays my dad's rates,' she mimicked accurately.

'I've got more to do than argue with the likes of you,' he said angrily, getting up. He saw that his zip fly was hanging undone and that she was looking at it. He zipped himself up fiercely and defiantly, but caught a piece of his shirt in the metal teeth and it stuck. He tugged up and down violently but he could not move it. The girl was laughing into her hands, still watching him through slight, open fingers. The old man just continued to stare as though he did not understand.

*

He sat at his desk staring so emphatically at a picture of steel-works on a wall calendar that the ring of the telephone almost lifted him out of his seat.

'Hello,' he said, still blinking with the shock. 'Maiby here.'

'You've got a funny name,' she said. 'Maiby. It sounds like you're not sure what it is.'

39

'I'm *not* sure what it is sometimes,' he said. 'And that's not all I'm not sure about either. What do you want?'

'This is Bessie White here.'

'I know. What do you want?'

'Well, to start with, you got up in such a huff from that caff that you forgot to pay for your tea. I paid for it.'

'Thanks,' he said ungraciously. 'If I'd known I'd have had a cheese roll as well. What do you want?'

'Christ,' she suddenly laughed. 'You didn't half look funny trying to get your flies done up. You got yourself in a right tangle.'

'Flies are things that sit on the wall and rub their feet together,' Andrew told her. 'The thing I was trying to adjust was my *fly*. It's not plural. What do you want?'

'I don't care if it's a fly or a centipede,' she said easily. 'It was still funny. I want to talk to you about keeping my grandad's case out of the paper. You went off too fast . . .'

'No chance,' he said.

'I'm willing to pay,' she said seriously. 'I'll give you a fiver if you'll do it.'

Andrew laughed. 'A fiver! My God, you are flashing your wealth about. First you pay for my tea, then you start dishing out bribes . . .'

'It's all I've got,' she replied simply. 'All I've got now, anyway. I had to pay the old sod's fine, didn't I? And that was my holiday money. If it's going to cost more, then you'll have to wait and trust me to pay you.'

'Listen,' he said more gently. 'There's no way either you or I can keep it out of the paper. I've made it as short as I can but I just can't . . .'

'You've not put it in already!' she cried.

'Well, it's written,' he said uneasily.

'Oh no,' she breathed, her voice hardly carrying over the wire. 'You've got to stop it. Can't you understand, Andrew? I can't let my mum and dad know about it, or the bloody neighbours. If they read it they'll boot him out in the street. Honestly. Can't you see?'

'They don't know, your parents?'

'No. I've kept it from them. I was having a day off sick at home when the police came, and they were both out. So I didn't let on. They'll chuck him out.'

'Listen, Bessie,' he said earnestly. 'Even if I could stop it – and take it from me, I can't – what will happen when it appears in the other paper, the *Chronicle*? My editor will want to know why *we* haven't got it.'

'Jesus wept,' she said bitterly. 'You would think it was a war being declared or a big burglary or something, not an old-age pensioner stealing a live eel.'

'I'll tell you something,' he said defensively. 'In normal circumstances I would have telephoned the story over to the evening papers too. An old man stealing a live eel is a good laugh.' Then he added: 'Unless it happens to be your grandfather.'

He could hear her sense of outrage coming over the phone. 'They would put *that* in the evening papers?' she said incredulously. 'A thing like that? And they'd pay you for doing it?'

'It's a rough world,' he shrugged. 'But anyway I didn't. I don't know why, but I didn't. I'm lazy, put it down to the fact that I'm lazy.'

'*You* could stop it going in the *Chronicle*,' she said, her voice changing craftily. 'That should be easy for you, Andrew. That big fat bird sitting next to you in the court, she was from the *Chronicle*, right?'

'If you mean Miss Perry, yes,' he said firmly.

'Miss Perry, that big fat bird,' she confirmed. 'Well, listen, mate, you won't have any bother with her. She'll keep it out of her paper if you tell her. Give her an extra rub of your leg under the table.'

Andrew's head retreated and stared at the mouthpiece as though he were staring at her. 'Really,' he said eventually. 'Honestly, I don't know what to say to you. I've never come across anyone like you before.'

'And I'm only eighteen,' she mimicked bitterly.

'What's the use?' he sighed. 'Listen, girlie, carefully. There is no chance of keeping this case out of the *Journal*. I will go to the editor, but I hold out no hope at all. Okay?'

'What if I said I would sleep with you?' she said.

That stopped him. He said nothing for a moment. Then he pulled all his strings in. 'You,' he said, 'are just a little older than my daughter.'

'That should make it all the nicer,' she said.

'Look, Bessie, you are a remarkable girl. I'll give you that. But I think you'd better get off the line and forget it. I'll do as I promised – I'll ask the editor, but there's not a hope in hell. I know what he'll say.'

*

'No,' said the editor.

'Okay,' nodded Andrew. 'I promised it would be put to you, that's all. But I told the old man's grand-daughter there was no chance of keeping it out of the paper.'

'You were quite right, as usual,' said Burton. 'There *is* no chance.' He was an abrasive man, and Andrew never argued with him. He was a street-born North Londoner, but now on the suburban hem he liked to give an agricultural effect by wearing ginger tweeds and jodhpurs. He made his face a country red by panting across ragged fields behind his house every morning and by frequently pinching his cheeks in private, which also made his eyes watery. Now he was seated astride a chair as on a horse, his heels digging impatiently into the legs.

'That's all we want to say about that, then, isn't it?' he said.

'Yes,' nodded Andrew. 'That's fine by me. I told her I'd ask, that's all.'

'Well, you asked,' said Burton. 'Now, let's move on to something else. I had a call from a man called Ernest Rollett – said he was a neighbour of yours. He was on about a home for maladjusted kids planned for a spare site on your estate. Said he'd already mentioned it to you.'

'He filled my ear with it this morning,' replied Andrew. 'He's one of these petrified pricks who sees a motorway coming through his precious rhubarb patch every time somebody wearing a black raincoat turns up with a tape measure.'

'He sounded very concerned to me,' said Burton.

'The man wears his hypocrisy like his Sunday suit,' shrugged Andrew.

'He said he was a friend of yours.'

'He's a neighbour,' said Andrew logically. 'He's *got* to be a friend. At Plummers Park you do not quarrel with your neighbours. Hate their guts but don't quarrel. Be nice to them, admire their roses, pat their dog, smile, but don't leer, at their wife. In good old-fashioned suburbia people who didn't like each other never bothered to speak, and in the slums they settled it with their fists, but not in a place like Plummers Park. It's an estate, and you don't do things like that on an estate.'

Burton was regarding him cagily. 'Sounds like something you've got strong feelings about,' he observed. 'Why don't you write a feature about it, or a series. "The Hate Behind the Sandersons' Curtains".' He stopped and smiled with thin satisfaction at Andrew's growing expression.

'God, I couldn't do that,' pleaded Andrew. 'I've got to live there . . .' He glanced up to see that Burton had been baiting him, and felt the shame and the relief mix inside him.

'You could always ask the editor to keep it out of the paper,' said Burton. He got up from astride the chair and turned away from Andrew, taking short stiff strides like a horseman in a stable. 'Listen, anyway,' he said reaching his desk and giving it a pat. 'Look into this other thing, the plan for the maladjusted kids place. See how firm it is at county level and then have a wander around Plummers Park asking people for their reactions. This man Rollett says he's going to call a protest meeting.'

'He will,' said Andrew confidently. 'I'll get on with that this afternoon, shall I?'

'Yes, I should. That's if you've finished all the court cases you want to allow in the paper.'

3

When the telephone sounded, Ena Grant was reading the *Daily Express* fashion page, sitting naked in the growing sun on a G-plan dining-room chair placed strategically just inside the open door of her french windows. The new non-peep fence, which her husband Simon had erected because he liked the idea of her brown all over, protected her on both sides of the narrow garden. The waste land stretched from the infant rose-trees at the bottom of the plot, curving away from her view so that the flat tops of the houses over there were only just in sight, like regular tombstones lying in a hilly cemetery. She could quickly see anyone approaching from that direction.

She let the phone ring fifteen times, counting the tones carefully on her fingers. Then she stood, first placing the newspaper over her front, like a breastplate, and then quickly sliding it around to cover her rear, as she turned and walked into the room. It had sounded three times more before she reached it.

'Hello,' she said calmly. 'Plummers Park 9834.'

It was a deliberate rearrangement of the correct number. If it were Simon he would think that she had merely got the digits in the wrong order. He always credited her with that virtue of the beautiful blonde – dippiness.

'North Thames Gas Board,' answered the voice.

'How are you, North Thames Gas Board?' she asked.

'One day it will be,' said Geoff Turvey. 'And that's the day you're going to make some fitter's life very happy.'

'For all you know,' she said deliberately, 'I may already be making some fitter's life very happy.'

'You'd better not,' he threatened. 'Or I won't pay my gas bill, and I'll tell your husband not to pay his.'

'He doesn't pay it now,' said Ena. 'He thinks if the gas man comes to cut off the supply and I get to the door all smiles and wobbling bosom, the man will stagger away sobbing.'

'Good thinking,' acknowledged Geoff. 'For Simon.'

'I've told you before,' she said without heat. 'Don't be snotty about him. He's got time to improve. At your age you haven't.'

'In my case there's very little room for improvement,' he replied blithely. 'Anyway, stop defending him.'

'Somebody's got to,' she said. 'Did you want anything apart from an argument?'

'How about a nice Monday intercourse?'

'You are too romantic.'

'Listen, it was all I could do to tone it down to "intercourse". This afternoon?'

'All right.'

'I love you.'

'For two hours at a time,' she said.

'Same place. One o'clock.'

'All right,' she said. 'I love you too.'

*

She was waiting in her car in the parking space behind The Jolly Grinder when he arrived, curving his white MGB a trifle flamboyantly on the gravel and coasting it to a standstill six inches from hers, pointing in the opposite direction, so that from their open windows their faces were within whispering distance.

'That was a bit flash,' said Ena. 'It's only an MG not an Alfa.'

'Where I work,' said Geoff smiling easily, 'and where I live also, mark you, missus, the MG is still a symbol of freedom and status, a sweet bird of youth and affluence. Where we lived before, at Northolt, it was the Triumph Spitfire. Tomorrow – maybe the Alfa, in Kensington.'

'If we get nabbed you'll be lucky to afford a bike,' she said practically. 'Cynthia would soak you for every penny.'

'Stop it. You may persuade me to turn right round and head for Hemel Hempstead, where I am supposed to be spying out some building land.' He leaned across and so immediately did she and they kissed briefly. As they came apart their faces stopped six inches from each other and his settled eyes and her young full face met seriously. 'Stay there a minute,' he muttered. 'I'm coming across.'

He jumped from the car and strode around to her far door.

He opened it and almost fell in with her, clasping her and pushing his face into her neck and the spectacular breasts beneath the summer blouse, his palms going to their heavy bottom lobes. She responded at once, pulling his head closer as though they both needed the comfort desperately, her open lips against the shaggy sides of his hair, biting him without using her teeth. He suddenly relaxed and looped his hands around her waist. 'All right?' he said.

'Yes, I'm all right,' she replied softly. 'If you are.'

'Christ, I look forward to this,' he said. 'Do you?'

'Every time,' she said. 'I thought it might wear off, but I think I get worse.'

'Good. So do I.'

'Do you think it's really safe here?' she said, glancing around. 'It's only ten miles away and people do come up here from Plummers Park, you know.'

'Now and again,' he agreed. 'But only in the evenings. Nobody is likely to be around here now.' He kissed her quietly again. 'Sit out in the garden. Go around the corner there, by the mill-wheel. I'll get a drink. What would you like to eat, love?'

'Anything they've got. I'll sit over there.'

She walked across the open space to the garden and sat in the bower created by some flowering shrubs and the solemn wheel which came from the days when the inn was a mill. It felt safe and sunny there. She sat gratefully, happy with the anticipation of the next few hours, but already with the seeds of guilt and sadness that she knew would grow once the evening came.

'What did you do today?' Simon would demand, muffled in the folds of her chest. 'Chasing off all the men?' And she would make up some mundane lie. She was an inexpert liar and she preferred not to face him while she was telling them, so she kept his face pressed to her breasts and uttered them over the nape of his happy neck. And he thought it was the clutch of love.

Geoffrey returned with a bottle of white wine, two glasses and two plates of cold meat and salad. They sat, content for a while in their lives, having a picnic on a day full of the trifling sounds of summer.

They were hidden by the mill-wheel as though it were the side of a great armchair, but there was no one else about anyway. A tortoise-shell cat was trying to catch a butterfly on the pub lawn, but that was all.

'Don't let's go to the motel today, Geoff,' she suggested.

He glanced at her. 'Where do you want to do . . . Where do you want to go then?'

'Oh, I don't know. It seems like such a lovely day to be playing Mr and Mrs Smith in a motel, and it's always so nasty having to pack up and go at five in the afternoon.'

'They're used to it,' he shrugged. 'That's the best thing about motels. At least you pay first, so you don't have the embarrassment of creeping down to the desk and saying you've suddenly got to leave because your Auntie Emma is dying in Darlington.'

'There are times when you sound horribly like the voice of an experienced adulterer,' she said.

'No, not at all,' he began to protest. 'Adultery is an older man's pastime. This is love.'

She waved his voice away. 'I don't want to know, anyway,' she said. 'I'm not exactly innocent, am I? As long as you stay faithful to me.' She wagged a finger at him. The wine and the sun worked quickly on her. 'Nobody else – understand? Except your wife.'

He smiled at her. 'You're a little bugger, really,' he said. 'All right. Where are we going to have it today?'

She waved her glass airily at the fields inert beneath the heavy June sun. She elevated it so that she could look at the rays through the wine. 'Out of doors,' she said finally. 'In the fresh air.'

He stared at her grin. 'In a cornfield, that sort of thing, you mean?'

'Yes, why not?'

'It would be cheaper,' he agreed, smiling.

'Naturally,' she said tartly. 'You can put the money you save towards some plants for your garden or a new tin-opener for the kitchen.'

He glanced at her with sharpness, but then he shrugged and laughed and she returned the laugh. He caught her hand and the wedge of bitterness was blunted. 'All right,' he said firmly. 'To the woods.'

They left her car in a lane near the inn and they took his due north until they reached the downs at Dunstable, great green lumps of mid-England, lying with vacant expressions under a sky hanging with summer heat. It was a place for gliding, and they watched the wide silent wings of the gliders like white hands against the blue.

'Do you think they can see us from those things?' asked Ena as they lay in the ferns and crowded grass. They were stretched easily together, side against side, faces up into the large sky.

'I expect they can,' said Geoff. The smell of her and the humid afternoon was going like smoke through his head. 'But they won't come down to get a closer look because the whole object is to get those contraptions up as high as possible. That's where the whole thrill is.'

'I know something else like that,' she giggled. He glanced at her.

'That was a cheap, nasty little suburban joke,' he reproved gently.

'I'm a cheap, nasty little suburban joker,' she said. Her face became abruptly pinched and sad. 'Oh, Geoff,' she whispered, leaning into his shirt. 'Why is it arranged so it's so difficult? It's all so much trouble.'

He put his face against her thick hair, his nose going right through to her ear. 'All life is trouble,' he said. 'It's death's no trouble.'

She looked up slowly. 'That's very profound coming from you,' she said.

'Thanks very much. It's *Zorba the Greek*,' he told her. 'Went to see the film the other night with Cynth.'

'With Cynth,' she repeated miserably. 'Poor Cynthia, poor Simon. They haven't done any harm, Geoff.'

'Errors. They've made errors. Marrying us,' he said. He took her face in his hands and kissed her deeply. 'And it's a fabulous day, and we're out here alone for a couple of hours. Can't we leave it at that and not ask why?'

'All right,' she nodded. 'I want that too. Do you think any-one will see us here?'

He glanced around. They were in a depression, embraced by ferns on the flank of one of the matronly downland hills. Between their upturned feet, hers shoeless, the flat counties ran to the Midlands, distant trees like puffs of smoke, houses and farms and fields disintegrating in the haze.

He looked then at her resting form, her profile stretched beside him on the dry summer hill, her sweet landscape against distant Bedfordshire. Her cascading fair hair tumbled over the grass, her forehead touched by the sun, the green material of her dress pushed up by her gorgeous breasts, then dipping to her flattened lower body; her bare legs and brown feet were pointed slightly out towards Woburn Abbey and Whipsnade Zoo respectively. He turned on his hip, and she looked at him with hardly a blink, as though she had been warned to watch him carefully, while he undid the buttons down the length of her summer dress. He stroked her flat naked stomach with his right hand and turned the fingers around the honed curve of her waist. They turned inwards and moved close, their faces sweating on each other. Her hands went to his zip and she parted his trousers at the front like a banana before putting her topmost hand in to stroke. Somewhere in the air about them an observant skylark began a song and a snail paused in his green journey along a stem.

'You're a dirty little pig,' Geoffrey whispered, kissing her messily. He wiped his chin and then, using the other side of his hand, wiped hers also. She was wearing a pink brassière with a button between the cups so that when he released it the nylon flapped away like the ears of a flying helmet, leaving her breasts blinking in the sunshine.

He examined, surveyed them for a moment before putting his hands and his lips there. Using both hands he could scarcely circumnavigate one – thumb to thumb and little finger trying to touch little finger. With his tongue against the wrinkles of the right nipple, he glanced with low eyes towards the horizon of the other mound across the valley. It seemed miles away. She had caught him below, but was using her hands easily as though she were washing them and thinking of something else.

The lark was noisy and occupied in the nearby air, but the snail had witnessed enough and was continuing on his slimy journey up the stem. Two hundred yards away four little girls were walking down the hill.

'Don't overdo it, love,' groaned Geoff. He had gritted his teeth, only just remembering to remove them from her nipple in time. She eased her manipulations obediently, took his fingers and coaxed them down to her pelvis. Like someone lowering a flag he lowered her pants. Her eyes were tense on his face. Fifty yards away the four little girls were making daisy-chains.

Geoffrey pulled his trousers back from his backside and hot-faced rolled on top of Ena. They were together in a trice, faces clenched with the anxious work, pushing together, pulling away, and pushing again, the shunting of love, until eventually with only a brief pause to regain breath, they collided hard and joyously, and the lark was gone.

The couple lay together, in the lap of adultery and peace. They were there for minutes, with no more worry or hurry than if Bedfordshire were otherwise uninhabited. Geoffrey could feel the sturdy sun baking his backside and he was about to mention it when the snail, which had been mounting the stem during the normal course of its day, was thrown sharply and accurately and bounced on the springy flesh of his right but-tock. It had been thrown by one of the quartet of little girls, who were now seated intently on the ridge above the secluded depression, hung with interest and daisy-chains.

'What you doing then?' asked the child who had projected the snail.

Geoff felt Ena go to stone. He remained with his face buried beside her like a soldier under fire.

'They're dead,' said the second girl confidently. 'I bet they're dead.'

'Why's the man got his bum showing?' asked the third.

A snort of scorn and realization came from the first. 'They're making a baby. That's what they're doing.' Then with an air of throwaway wisdom. '*I* know.'

The fourth child began to cry.

'What's the matter, Daff?' inquired the second.

'I don't feel very well,' sniffled Daff. 'I saw my mum and

Uncle Ginger making a baby once and my mum said if I ever told, or if I ever saw it again, I'd turn to salt. I don't feel well, Lesley. I think I'm turning to salt.'

'Don't be so soppy,' said the first scornfully. She called down to Geoffrey. 'Mister, we can see you. We know you're not dead.'

The snail, shaking its head in a dazed fashion, was hurrying away in the manner of one who does not want to be further involved. Geoff, hot-faced, looked up and saw the quartet squatting above.

'Go away,' he ordered. 'Go on. Go away.'

'What you doing then?' insisted the first girl. 'Tell us.'

'This lady,' croaked Geoff, 'is very ill and I'm a doctor. Now go away and get an ambulance, will you. Please – it's an emergency.'

'Why you got your bum showing?' inquired the third, unimpressed. 'I never seen a doctor with his bum showing.'

They burst into merry laughter, apart from Daff who was still crying and feeling herself all over for signs of salt. Then they began to chant as children do:

I like sherry, I like rum,
Give me some and I'll show my bum!

'I'll kill these little fuckers,' grated Geoff close to Ena's ear. He looked at her and saw she was white.

'Listen to 'im!' howled the leading girl, outraged. 'Little fuckers! We'll tell the police! We'll tell the parkie!'

'Go on then,' snarled Geoff, still unable to move without completely exposing himself. 'Go on, tell the police.'

'Daff,' ordered the first girl. 'Go and tell the copper or the parkie.'

Daff departed, snivelling, still examining her legs and arms, and pinching her nose. The other three, their crumpled daisy-chains still hanging from their small sweaty hands, sat motionless intently watching the equally motionless couple below.

'Offer them money,' whispered Ena.

Geoff turned a gluey smile round to the children. 'Why don't you go to Whipsnade Zoo?' he persuaded. 'It's very nice there. Bears and lions. I'll give you the money.'

'We bin to the zoo,' said the spokesgirl. 'We don't reckon it.'

'It whiffs,' said the second.

Geoffrey had lost the remnants of his erection and now he lost his temper too. Turning swiftly so that his back swivelled towards the girls he tugged up his trousers and, in his shelter, Ena began buttoning her dress. With a roar he got to his knees and made a rush up the bank. But not before the three witches had taken off, screaming down the hill, their excited terror echoing over the sloping summery ground. The adulterers adjusted their clothing quickly and climbed hurriedly the other way.

4

In the same manner that Hercules, the tramp who wheeled his croaking pram around the boxed roads of the estate, was regarded with distant but proprietorial affection at Plummers Park, so the back wall of the saloon bar in The Case Is Altered public-house was revered because it dated, it was alleged, from medieval times. In a place of such shining newness, populated with shiny new people, age and quaintness were things to be treasured and exhibited.

Even before he entered the bar Andrew heard the guided-tour voice of Barney Rogers, 'That's very old stone, that is,' and knew there were strangers present. The pub was built two years before in a mock nineteen-thirties style, and the mouldering lump of wall, wearing its proud plaque like a dog collar, was, with both business sense and sentiment, incorporated into the building.

'Old stone . . .' The hushed American voice was loaded with respect as Andrew walked in, past the juke-box, the fruit-machine and the pile of plastic sawdust that was regularly spread across the floor to give the place a rural feel underfoot.

It was almost three in the afternoon and apart from Barney behind the bar the only people there were a young American couple, Jean and Harry Solkiss, and Dormouse Dan, a pensioner who slept on a remote stool with a half-pint of cider standing like a patient night-light at his elbow. He was always there from opening to closing time, curled in sleep, his beverage hardly disturbed through the hours, although he occasionally slumped to the floor and had to be replaced on his stool.

The Americans were from Kingman, Arizona, and everywhere they went in this foreign place of England and Plummers Park they held hands.

'Old stone,' breathed Jean Solkiss, putting out lean fingers to touch the mystery.

'Stone *is* old,' shrugged Andrew. 'There's nothing it can do about it. All stone is old.' They turned and saw him and smiled recognition and puzzlement together. He had met them a week earlier when they were moving into their rented house on the estate, having come straight from Arizona to Plummers Park.

'This is sure *old*,' went on Harry like an archaeologist who had recently excavated the remnant himself. 'We just don't *have* old stone like this back home.'

'I would have thought the Grand Canyon had one or two old stones,' observed Andrew. 'Pint please, Barney.'

'The Grand Canyon is *not* a wall, though, is it?' said Barney with a truculent smile. Mounted above his head was the dead face of a fox with the same expression. 'That's a *wall*. There *is* a difference, you know.'

'It's great,' sighed Jean Solkiss. 'Just great.' She was already holding her husband's hand tightly, a habit of several years which had curiously resulted in his becoming left-handed. She smiled at Andrew with her arranged American teeth and frank full eyes. She was a bony girl, with a light brown tan, and a thick cable of black hair down her back. Harry was tall and thin and shy, looking through rimless glasses with what appeared to be a plea for truth and simplicity. He wore a Marks & Spencer sweater and jeans. He was a junior officer at the United States Air Force base at Ruislip.

'How's the defence of our realm going?' asked Andrew

lightly. A brief frown of warning went from wife to husband as though afraid he might have secrets to tell.

'Great,' replied Harry. 'Real great. Never saw a realm defended better.'

'It's the Zeppelins,' sighed Andrew with drama. 'If we can stop the Zeppelins, we can win.'

The young woman did not appear to understand immediately, but when she saw her husband laugh easily she laughed too. Andrew bought them a drink.

'But this wall is sure interesting,' reverted Jean touching the damp plaster with her fingers once more. 'Just imagine, Hairy, this was built when our country was inhabited by savages.'

'There were savages around here when the rest of the pub was built,' observed Andrew. 'A couple of years ago. Some are still in the vicinity.'

'Andrew's always kidding, kids,' said Barney from across the bar. 'He's just trying to scare you. Plummers Park is very, very nice.'

'Very, very nice,' nodded Andrew with exaggeration. 'Very, very, very nice. Heaven in Hertfordshire.' He recited:

Bring your kids, bring your dogs,
We've nice fresh air, and we've got no wogs.

Nobody laughed, and the Americans looked at him unhappily. Eventually Jean said: 'Is the fox head a hunting trophy?'

'In a way,' said Andrew before Barney could reply. 'Found stone dead by some dustbins in Hedgerows one morning. Poisoned by a local woman's cookery.'

Harry characteristically sought peace. 'The inn sure has a strange name,' he said.

Jean glanced at him gratefully. Barney, putting a warning glance Andrew's way, said: 'Well yes, I can tell you about that. It was like this . . .'

Andrew wished Barney could afford some teeth that fitted. They clattered away as he spoke, never seeming synchronized with the movements of his jawbone. It was like a man walking with the sole of his shoe flapping. '. . . an inn in Spain was called Casa Alta, or the House on the Hill,' instructed

Barney. 'During the Peninsular War, in Spain, see, the men of a local regiment rested at this place and when they came back several of them took pubs and called them by the same name – Casa Alta. Over the years it's changed to The Case Is Altered. Now isn't *that* interesting?'

'Gee, I'll say,' breathed Jean Solkiss. She wrung her husband's fingers and he grinned a wincing agreement at Barney.

'My house is called Bennunikin,' announced Andrew. '"That's Navajo Indian for "The Wigwam on the Hill", same thing.'

'Gee, you are so *funny*!' said Jean Solkiss, thinking he had made a joke. Then she sighed seriously: 'Everywhere's so full of history.'

Andrew added for her: 'And the policemen don't have guns and the little kids have such rosy cheeks.'

The couple laughed again uncertainly. 'Sorry,' he said. Then: 'Talking about kids with rosy cheeks, how do you feel about maladjusted children?'

'Terrible,' said Barney before they could answer. 'Terrible.'

Andrew took out his notebook and wrote 'Terrible. Barney Rogers, Publican', at which Barney became frightened, for nothing frightens people so much as writing their names in a notebook.

'It's nothing to worry about,' consoled Andrew. 'I'm merely doing a story for the paper. There's some plan to build a home for maladjusted children on the waste ground up the top of the estate, and I'm getting people's opinions.'

'Could we visit with them?' suggested Jean anxiously. 'Oh boy, we both would love to do something like that, wouldn't we just, Hairy?'

'Sure, sure, when's it going to be?' asked Harry with genuine eagerness, his cowboy eyes bright with decency behind his glasses. Barney was straining across the bar like a man about to say the wrong thing.

Andrew restrained him with a stiffened glance and touched the young couple on the shoulders. 'That's very good of you,' he said. 'They haven't finally decided about the place yet, but I'll let you know.'

'Oh thanks,' said Jean. 'We'd sure like to help.'

'Right,' emphasized Harry. 'Any way we can.'

They said they had to go. Holding hands tightly, as though one or the other had just been reprieved from a death sentence, they went from the bar. Immediately they had turned away, her head, it seemed automatically, fell slightly sideways against his elongated arm and they walked out like that.

'Isn't that nice?' observed Andrew, looking challengingly at the publican.

'Why does she call him Hairy?' grunted Barney, his professional good fellowship gone with the custom. 'He's not got a hair on him. He's like a skinned rabbit.'

'It's just the way she says his name,' said Andrew. 'He's called Harry. But it sounds like Hairy.'

'Sending out boys to do a man's job,' muttered Barney, gathering the glasses. 'Fancy *him* having to let off the bomb.'

'Oh, I don't expect it's actually *him*,' said Andrew in his irritatingly soothing fashion. 'They probably have a much heftier chap to do that. He probably just helps.'

'You're a cynical bugger, you know, Andrew,' muttered Barney. He glanced at the clock, like a hint. But it was five minutes from time.

'Cynical? Not at all,' argued Andrew amiably. 'I've just seen something most uncynical go out of your door. True love, that is, Barney. Before your very eyes. You don't often see that these days.'

'Ah, yes,' said Barney immediately. 'And talking about love and that – did you know we've got a flasher in the district?'

Andrew regarded the unromantic man behind the bar, his beer almost to his lips. 'A flasher?' he inquired into his tankard.

Barney leaned forward with horrified eagerness. 'Yes, Andrew, a bloke flashing his plonker. He's been seen this weekend charging around Fairy Copse with his dickie in his hand. No woman is safe.'

'Most of them around here are dead safe,' observed Andrew. 'Who told you this, Barney?'

'Mrs Sissing. She was in yesterday,' Barney fairly hissed across the bar. 'She saw him on Saturday.'

'Take her a month to get used to her Bert again I should think,' said Andrew. 'And where did this revelation take place?'

'Up at Fairy Copse, like I told you,' continued Barney. 'Long mackintosh, opens it out – and there it is! One morning in the week he was seen by some children. I've warned our June. You ought to warn your girl, too, Andrew. Maybe we ought to get together, some of us, and hunt the bugger down.'

'The police know all about it, I suppose,' said Andrew. 'I'd better go and have a word with them.'

'They know, all right,' confirmed Barney. 'Mrs Sissing was able to give them a full description.'

Andrew said: 'I bet.'

*

He had almost forgotten how bright and hot the day had grown. He walked from the coolness of the pub and the sun seemed to pick him out. Taking off his jacket he sat for five minutes on one of the rusting rustic benches outside, trundling a Skol umbrella across to provide himself with shade. The street was an afternoon desert, the void that inhabits such dormitory places in the day, filling it to the house-tops with emptiness. At the far end some brightly-clothed infants, like little coloured bugs, scraped around on tricycles and in plastic cars. He had often thought about children playing like that, remembering his own lonely games in the grit of summer or the mud of a thousand winters ago.

As he watched them at their remote pretending, microbes in a huge world bounded by unapproachable fields, untouchable roads, and with planned trees and flat roofs holding up a sky of nursery blue, he thought briefly of his solitariness as a child; that inward tightness, a refusal of something to let go or give way; a strong and secret box he knew was still there and still locked. When he was dead perhaps they might open it and find him – crouching.

Bessie White had said, 'What if I said I would sleep with you?' She had come straight out with it, with blunt courage and no bungling, because she was someone who could make up her mind about things. All he had needed to say was 'Yes'. One baby word. If he had said it then *something* would have happened, even if it was only a farce and not a fuck. But no, not him. He had whinnied his way out of it, scrambling to put it aside as though he were above such thoughts and things.

'You are just a little older than my daughter,' he mimicked aloud in the exact prissy way he had said it on the telephone. Christ, why do it? Why sling up frantic defences and feel like hell when a girl of eighteen makes an offer like that? Why? 'That's you all bloody over,' he accused himself aloud. 'You did it once before and then what happened? You ran.' The three miniature motorists and tricyclists, on a long trip, had squeaked and trundled along the hot pavement from the far end of the road and were now level with him and observing his selfish conversation. He looked up and saw them seated in or astride their vehicles, regarding him with that dead-eyed, snotty-nosed, droopy-lipped curiosity that grows on the faces of small children.

'Who are you saying to?' inquired a girl in a plastic Jaguar.

'Saying to?' questioned Andrew, regarding them suddenly and guiltily. 'Oh, I see. Yes. Well, I was talking to myself.'

'Why?' She was determined. One day she would have a real car like that.

'I've got a lot of worries,' he replied. Children always accepted that.

'My daddy's got a lot of worries,' nodded a boy like a half-grown apple, giving his tricycle a scuff around the pavement. 'So's my mum.'

'All daddies and mummies have,' intoned Andrew as though he knew the very answers to life. 'Aren't you a long way down the street from your houses?'

'We're having an adventure,' said the girl triumphantly. 'We're going now. Goodbye.'

She led them off, a confident convoy, the boys revving up with junior splatterings of spit, the girl hanging out a casual female hand as a traffic signal before they crossed the vacant, dusty road. Andrew watched her. Another woman. Christ, and they wanted liberating.

He suddenly remembered, thirty years before, strutting with the sudden confidence of the trickster, picking out special children who, he told them, were to be guests at his birthday party. ('You can come, so can you. But you can't . . .') They had to bring their own cups and saucers and knives and spoons, he had said. At that Gloria Penny, her drawers, as ever, sagging like a sporran, her face scarlet with scorn, scoffed: 'You ain't having a party, Andrew Maiby. You *never* have a party!' Nor was he, of course, nor did he. Ever. The guests, secreting on his instructions the crockery and cutlery from their own homes, sat on his patch of council-house back garden and drank water and ground their teeth on iron-hard ship's biscuits which his father, a merchant seaman, had brought home as emergency rations in case the war was further prolonged. He had wanted to play some games but they left him and all went home early and grumbling.

That was the last adventure for him. He never again risked it. Exactly nine years later, on his sixteenth birthday, Mrs Bigbury, his mother's great white friend, had asked him to call around to her house on his way to the weekly parade of the Air Training Corps. Her husband had died fighting the Germans (even after the war she called them 'the common enemy' as though it were some social slur), and as Andrew had been chopping her firewood and running her errands she said that she was going to give him a birthday present.

He arrived in his itchy air-force blue uniform, with the motto 'Venture Adventure' glistering on his badges, to find that Mrs Bigbury had apparently recently left her bath and was awaiting him in an aura of steam and a long and frilly robe. This garment, although in retrospect a trifle on the grubby side, seemed to him at the time to be the most glamorous wrapping he had ever seen, trailing visions of Maureen O'Hara and other unreachable stars even as it trailed along Mrs Bigbury's kitchen floor. It descended around and about her in shades and folds of pink, containing at the top the considerable bulk of her fine untrammelled breasts. From its folds her fat damp knees kept emerging and withdrawing like red-faced men in hiding, as she walked steaming and beaming towards him. Her heavy blonde hair, with its tidemark of black, was suspended like some Valkyrie's mane. She did not look right in a council house.

'Little Andrew!' she exclaimed, her arms opening as barn doors open. 'Happy birthday! Happy birthday!'

'Thank you, Mrs Big . . .' he had trembled. He remembered even now how the remainder of whatever he had intended became merely 'glubby . . . glubby . . . glub . . . glub . . .', like the globular sounds of a drowning mouth, because she had grasped him and slammed his innocent's face into her mature breasts, and he was suddenly engulfed with her boiled flesh and Woolworth's perfume. She rocked him to and fro with her hefty forearms, banging his frightened cheeks against the fat ramparts of her bosom, his saliva from his smothered sentences running down her red valley.

During this passion she somehow noticed his cap badge and bellowed: 'Venture Adventure! What a lovely motto, Andrew!' The powerful clamps of her arms crashed around him again and he was back in there among the titty and the spit, his hands desperately grasping the soft material of her fluffy robe. But then, curses (even now after all these years, curses and more bloody curses) he began to fight to get away. Somehow he pushed her off, ducking under the booms of her arms, and forced a gulf between them. Her face broke up in a strange way he could not understand. He smoothed his tunic and straightened his cap. Then, in a moment of chivalry, he produced his clean air-force blue handkerchief and, while she stood stiff, he wiped his spittle from her chest. Stepping back like an Air Marshal who had just conferred a medal on the breast of a brave but foolish pilot, he said: 'I must go now, Mrs Bigbury. I shall be late on parade.' And then, like the little cunt he was, *he saluted her*, turned, and fled.

*

His sad and embarrassing memories caused him to sink reflectively into his seat outside the pub. The sun was burning his face and the heat was getting inside his collar and down his shirt. He dozed uncomfortably and inelegantly for a few minutes and was roused by revolving and regular squeaks. He thought as he woke that the infant adventurers were returning. Instead, across his opening vision, progressed an invalid chair bearing an old lady of such regal demeanour that she might have been a queen in a carriage. Her face was set as though in a cast and her silver hair was built up like a Tibetan temple. She was being pushed by Freddie Tyler, the Plummers Park station-master, an amiable, olding man, and was immediately followed by a young slender woman piled high and hung low with boxes and bags.

'Wagons Ho!' called out Andrew sleepily from his seat. He stood up and felt a quick riddle of sweat run down inside his shirt. Old Tyler looked round, his lined face wet with effort. The elderly lady looked round too, more of a glare. The other woman tried to see him over the top of her load like someone trying to surmount a stone wall.

'Want a push?' asked Andrew. 'I expect you do.'

'Not much,' said Mr Tyler. 'She's a bit beefy to push on a day like this.'

'I am *not* beefy!' protested the old lady at this ungracious remark. 'It's all the other stuff I'm carrying.'

She was right. The vehicle was festooned with household things in the manner of a tinker's cart. In the lady's lap were three large, old-fashioned flat-irons. Everyone had stopped now, and Andrew took the top two boxes from the pile borne by the younger woman. 'We're just moving house,' she explained, now fully in view. She was dark and tight-looking, but her smile of thanks softened her face.

'It's easier with a moving van,' observed Andrew.

'You're dead right,' agreed Mr Tyler. He was hanging over the handle of the invalid chair, heaving with exhaustion. 'I never thought one old dear would be such a load, Andrew, straight I didn't.'

'Now you know what Hercules feels like with that pram,' said Andrew, winking at the old lady reassuringly.

'He's not pushing anybody in it, that's for sure,' groaned Mr Tyler. 'I just happened to be going home when this lot arrived.'

Andrew saw the younger woman open her mouth sharply, but he restrained her with a pleading glance, unloaded some of her burden and, giving Mr Tyler a hold-all and a carrier bag to manage, he took the rest in one hand and pushed the old lady's conveyance with the other.

'Needless to say, we *did* have a removals van,' the young woman pointed out as they made better progress. 'But it's always the bits and pieces that get left behind. They take up the time and make the trouble. We had a lot of bother with mother's flat-irons on the train.'

'Where I go, they go,' announced the old woman to the bare pavement ahead of them. 'How else could I iron my Herbert's shirts?'

Her daughter leaned near to Andrew's ear. The boxes she was still carrying nudged against him and he could sense her. 'She's a little bit dippy,' she whispered. 'She still irons my father's shirts every night.'

He nodded. She was so close he thought his forehead had almost touched her hair. 'That stops him catching cold anyway,' he observed.

'It's too late,' she whispered. 'He's been dead twenty-two years.'

'Stop swapping secrets with that man,' snapped her mother from the wheel-chair. 'I can hear you, my girl. Whenever there's something in trousers around, you start your whispering.'

Andrew looked wryly at her daughter, and the neat face grimaced back over the boxes. 'Here it is,' she said then. 'This house.' It was one of the older, phase one Plummers Park houses, now in need of attention after ten Hertfordshire winters.

Old Tyler opened the door, and they helped the elderly woman from the invalid chair into the hall. She stumped away as though eager to explore. Tyler decently went with her. Andrew went into the house and saw furniture and carpets left anywhere, books piled on the floor, and a huge and beautiful mirror, heavy with carved ormolu, standing on the floor against a wall. As soon as they walked in, his dusty shoes and the younger woman's sandals were reflected in its oblong.

'You'll need some help to get that on the wall,' observed Andrew.

'I don't have a man around the house, if that's what you mean,' she answered.

'Well, I wasn't prying,' he replied awkwardly. 'It's just that it looks as though it weighs a ton and the old girl doesn't look all that strong.'

She laughed and said: 'You're odd.' Then decisively: 'Well, look, you might as well spread the good news around, because this is the sort of place, I imagine, where people like to know a bit about you. My name is Joy Rowley. I am a Mrs, but there's no Mr Rowley. That should stop the lace curtains being pulled aside too much in the hope of catching a glimpse of *him* anyway. But now everybody will watch to see if I have other men staying the night.'

'They might well do that,' said Andrew sagely. 'They like to keep an eye on their neighbours around here.'

She nodded that she had expected that, and then she said: 'Now you want to know if we're divorced. Well, we're not. He's deceased, as the lawyers say.'

'Oh, I see. I'm sorry.'

'Save your tears. We were divorced and then on top of that he went and died. He was always one for exaggerating a point.'

'I see,' grinned Andrew. 'Now if anyone asks me I can let them know. The dear old place wouldn't be the same without gossip. I have an idea I've seen you somewhere before. Is that possible?'

'It's even probable,' she nodded. 'I'm a faded actress. Faded before I bloomed really. I do the odd commercial on television. By some joke of nature I, who am childless and husbandless, have the loving-mother image that they need. You'll see me baking cakes, washing the boys' football shirts, putting Harpic down the pan, and all sorts of riveting things like that. The station-master called you Andrew . . .'

'Sorry. It's Andrew Maiby, M-A-I-B-Y. I live at Upmeadow, on the top of the hill. I'm on the local newspaper, God help me.'

'God help *me*,' she corrected. 'Now I've told *all* to the press.'

'Your secret is safe with me,' he smiled. Old Tyler came back to the room. 'She's ironing,' he said in wonderment. 'Soon as she got in she had the stove on and the ironing board up and she starts ironing. I've never seen that before.'

'She does it all the time,' said Joy. 'Dashing away with the smoothing iron.' She looked reassuringly at Tyler. 'It's a sort of hobby with her. She's ironing away her sorrow.' She said it naturally and with a smile at him.

'I see, I see,' replied old Tyler. His tone implied that he didn't know what the district was coming to. 'Yes, well I'm on my way then, Andrew.'

It was almost as if he prudishly insisted that Andrew must go with him and not be left with this woman.

'I'll be with you,' replied Andrew obligingly. 'I'm going up the hill.'

'Well, thanks for your help,' said Joy. 'It's nice to know you've got helpful neighbours.'

'At Plummers Park,' said Andrew at the door, 'we rely on respect, esteem and the helping hand, with the odd bit of treachery thrown in to make it interesting. See you again.'

'Of course,' she smiled. He could see that she had a face that was used to trouble. He glanced up at the house. 'They're pretty good houses,' he said as if to give her confidence. 'As houses go these days. And you can see the sunset from here. If you sit on the roof.'

'I'll watch for it,' she promised.

He ran his eyes over the flat front again. He could not know then that one night he would face death at that very place.

*

The nearest that Plummers Park would ever come to a traditional English corner shop was Gomer John's sub-post office, near the station, on the opposite side of the railway from all the other shops. It stood beside a narrow lane which led to the higher houses, and, at the bottom of this, three iron bollards which, although not old, were of antique form, like the upturned barrels of cannons. They, at the foot of the oddly unplanned lane, and the shop were the meeting place for the children and teenagers of the district. There was nowhere else.

Gomer's father had been Welsh; the sub-postmaster himself was a long-drawn-out young man with hair so fine and fair that in a certain light he looked bald. Andrew bought the early editions of the London evening newspapers which arrived, bringing tips for races already run, by the 3.30 ghost train, the empty afternoon service before the evening rush-hour.

'I wanted to ask you what you thought about the idea for a school for maladjusted children on the estate,' said Andrew.

'I heard,' said Gomer lifting his pale young eyes guiltily, as though a serious accusation had been indicated. He had been twenty years out of Wales, but he still had the accent. 'You understand that it's difficult for me to say anything, being in an *official* capacity, you see, but if you'll be so kind as to come to the back I'll talk to you away from the counter, in my private room and as a private person. You've never been in my room, have you?'

Andrew had not. He walked in now, the curtain opened like the door of some secret place, and found himself in the cabin of a ship's captain: a heavy desk, a sextant, a porthole looking out on a tight sunless yard, books, and walls covered with charts.

'Ahoy,' he said quietly. 'My goodness, Gomer, what a place!'

'You like it, don't you?' inquired Gomer, indicating it was important that he did.

'Yes, of course,' replied Andrew. 'It's extraordinary.' He blinked around again. 'I was just surprised, that's all.'

There was a sharp gleam in the fair man's face. 'I wear this sometimes,' he blurted out. He picked up a cap with a badge anchored on its forepeak and placed it excitedly on his head. He sat at the desk and spread his arms in a strong pose, then looked at Andrew with renewed anxiety. 'You don't think it's silly, do you.' It was a plea not a question.

'Silly? God, no, Gomer,' said Andrew, patting the thin shoulder that would never carry anything but the command of a sub-post office. 'You must let me write a piece for the paper about you.'

Gomer looked at him with sincere alarm. 'Oh, no, Mr Maiby. Nothing like that, please, whatever you do. It's only for my own amusement, see, and I don't want any publicity.' He dropped his tone. 'I always think the Post Office might turn a bit funny about something like this. They're a bit strict because of their special responsibility, see.'

'Right you are,' Andrew assured. 'Not a word then.' It occurred to him that all day he had been dealing with people who did not want to appear in his paper.

With a carefully-stitched smile Gomer removed the captain's hat and, brushing the badge with his slim fingers first, laid it on the desk. 'There's no secret about it,' he said. 'People know it's my hobby, but I'd like to keep it local if I can.'

'Naturally,' said Andrew. 'Tell me, what's it all about?'

'These charts,' said Gomer, moving with a distinct nautical roll to the wall. 'They're anchorages in the South Seas. Polynesia, Micronesia, Melanesia. Small islands and atolls, harbours that only see a trading schooner once a month. And such names, Mr Maiby, such names!' His chalk finger wriggled its way around an inked coastline. 'Look here, on the island of Morfuti. Bourgainville inlet, Green Parrot Creek. There's ten fathoms there.'

'You know how deep the water is?'

'Every current, every tide,' said Gomer. 'I've sailed this room, this sub-post office if you please, into many a distant and tropic anchorage.'

'Who would believe it?' said Andrew, meaning it.

Gomer darted forward. 'I've got all the books,' he said. 'Look, rows of them. And I've read them all.' His weak hands ran along the bindings built along the wall. '*Burleigh's Navigation Guide to the Pacific*, *Trade Winds in the South Seas*, *Jason's Seasonal Weather Charts*, *Two Years Before the Mast*, all of them.' He stared at Andrew as though daring him to laugh, then, almost in a whisper, said: 'I could smuggle you, on the darkest night of the year, 23 October to be precise, on to a lonely beach in Morluka, in the Windrift Islands, without even the natives knowing. Do you believe that?'

'I believe you could,' replied Andrew. 'If I'm ever thinking of doing that I'll let you know.'

'Now you're making fun,' said Gomer, his face collapsing.

'No, no, Gomer, I'm sorry. I think it's a fantastic hobby. I like your porthole.'

Gomer shrugged. 'It only looks out on to the yard – bloody place is full of pop bottles, but as far as I am concerned it looks right out to the horizon of the ocean.' He avoided Andrew's eyes shamefully. 'It's just a pastime,' he apologized again. 'It stops me being lonely. Can you understand that?'

'We're all lonely in some way,' replied Andrew. 'It's the great ailment of the world.'

'Listen, listen to this,' said Gomer, encouraged. 'You're a man of words and letters, even if the sea is not in your blood. I think you'll like this.'

To Andrew's further astonishment the young sub-postmaster turned the switch of an old-fashioned winder gramophone in one corner and the room was at once filled with the sounds of a storm at sea. Gomer stood there, eyes half closed, visibly swaying to it, side to side, his knees bending and flexing to the movements of his imagined vessel. Andrew blinked at him in some alarm, as one might regard a person who has suddenly thrown a fit. But Gomer's eyes opened and he smiled. 'It's a wonderful thing and I don't think it's any sillier than dancing or football or golf. Do you?'

'Not sillier, just rarer,' Andrew admitted.

'I'm one of the few subscibers to *Lloyd's Register of Shipping* in Hertfordshire,' confided Gomer proudly.

'Yes, I can imagine that too.' The storm on the record now stilled and its sounds quietened to the slapping of an easy swell against a hull, the shouting of gulls and the crooning of wind in rigging. Compassion and embarrassment brought a lump to Andrew's throat. He felt himself blushing.

'I thought you would understand,' said the sub-postmaster. 'You're a sensitive man.'

'Will you ever go?' asked Andrew.

Gomer's glance went along his charted wall. 'To these places?' he sighed. 'No, I wouldn't think so. I might even be disappointed if I did. They'd probably be full of tin cans and television sets, and all that. I've never been abroad at all, you know. Not even on holiday. There's my mam upstairs and her leg and her dog, that sodding dog. I *can't* go. It's job enough to get anyone to help in the shop and the sub-post office. I'd planned to go to Ostend one day last year, on one of those day trips, but it was all messed up at the last minute. I don't know which will go first, the dog, my mam's leg or my mam, but whichever it is, it will be too late then. It's too late now, I suppose.'

As a final, defeated gesture, he threw a passport on the desk. 'I've had a passport for ten years, see. Two renewals and filled with visas. Look at these.' He flicked the pages like a picturescope, and Andrew saw that the coloured visas with their stamps and signatures covered each page. 'Impressive, very pretty,' nodded Gomer. 'New Caledonia, Indonesia, Philippines, Thailand. There's nothing to stop you getting the visas even if you never go. It costs a bit, but then all hobbies do, don't they?'

Someone was calling from the shop: 'Gomer, I want *Woman's World* and a packet of Smarties.' He went out. Andrew waited sadly, turning to the porthole and seeing, strangely to his own disappointment, only crates of empty pop bottles. Gomer returned and apologized for taking all his time.

'I hope it's not embarrassed you,' he said.

'Not for a moment,' said Andrew. 'It's nice to know somebody in this place has got a spark of poetry in them.'

Gomer nodded shyly. 'Now, you came about the plan for the school. For the maladjusted is it?'

'That's it. Nothing's fixed yet, but I'm just getting a few quotes for the paper. How do you feel?'

'Well, listen,' said Gomer apologetically. 'I've been thinking, Mr Maiby, perhaps it would be better if I *didn't* say anything. I'm in a public position, as I say, and I'm afraid I'm not a very adventurous person.'

*

Mrs Polly Blossom-Smith – as her name indicated – lived in a better, older, nobler house than the others at Plummers Park. She was a full, handsome woman, a sculptress of some talent and note, rumoured to have an Arabic proverb tattooed at the very top of her right leg.

The house had been one of the estate homes in the days when townspeople stayed in their natural towns and farmland grew unmolested from London to the folds of the Chiltern Hills. Fairy Copse sprouted about it like an Edwardian beard, and its own acre and a half of garden was amok with tangles and weeds, lawns gone gratefully to meadow, and stone urns and statues draped with natural tendrils. The growth this summer had become so thick that even birds familiar with the locality had difficulty in locating the two bird-baths.

There was one clearing, hacked to stubble by some frenzied amateur with a scythe, an area of about ten yards in diameter, and in this hollow on this increasingly hot afternoon sprawled Mrs Polly Blossom-Smith on a sagging canvas bed. Andrew thought how grandly she lay: grand as a piano is grand, handsome, with a fine patina and exaggerated curves. She was in her mid-thirties, but her very stature and presence made her seem more senior than anyone who visited her at 'The Sanctuary'. She had layers of black hair, and thick muscular fingers strengthened through the kneading of tough modelling clay and the chipping of marble. She was wearing a cheap turquoise bikini and her trembling torso was slicked with suntan oil. At the top of her right leg was clearly tattooed an old Arab proverb.

This much Andrew observed after timidly creeping round the dull red walls of the house to the rear garden. He approached the elongated Mrs Polly Blossom-Smith side-on, and was able to see and appreciate the large expanse of her. Her hair, built up in the front, lolled like a funeral drape over the back of her bed, her ample, beautiful face was lifted slightly towards the sun, the nose a little superior, the lips fruity, the neck like one of her own well-sculptured pedestals. Some men, Gomer for one, he reflected, would have been proud of shoulders like that, and the breasts sat atop the body like two separate tureens. The stomach was not without fat but ran away smoothly to the swathe of turquoise around her pubis; the motto was clearly embellished just where the leg of the bikini rounded her thigh; then the legs strode away, slightly arched with a distinct underhang below the thigh and calf but looking fine and shapely and glistening under the sheen of Ambre Solaire. Pound for pound she was as fine a woman as you would see anywhere in Hertfordshire on that summer's afternoon.

Andrew allowed himself a little time to take in the vision (and to remember Mrs Bigbury for a second time that day) before announcing himself with a cough across the indolent buzzing of the garden. She turned her face without hurry, her breasts wobbling fractionally his way a moment later. 'Ah, Mr Maiby – Andrew,' she called. 'How lovely. Come on over.'

She sat up to greet him, and two fleeting riddles of sweat and sun-oil ran down her stomach like bandits heading for the forest. 'It's weeks since I've seen you,' she said. 'Not since that beastly party at the Thingies. That awful woman was sick on the parrot, remember. Excuse my bikini, won't you.'

'Don't worry,' smiled Andrew. 'You look um . . . very neat.'

'Neat! Moses, you newspaper people! Always the *mot juste*.' She laughed extravagantly, like someone pouring water from a bucket.

'Anyway I hope I'm not disturbing you too much,' he said. 'I did ring at the front door, but there was no answer.'

'Staff non-existent at the moment, love. I had old scrawny Annie for a few weeks but she kicked up about having to pose in the nude.' She smiled at him. 'But I'm glad to see you, anyway. For a moment I rather hoped it might be the Phantom Flasher.'

'Oh, you know about the Flasher?'

'Know about him! My sweet, I can't wait to get an eyeful of him. All clothed in a heavy raincoat with just his knob hanging out of a trapdoor in the front of his trousers. Very Magritte. When I heard you cough I thought I might look up and see him holding his testicles.'

'Sorry to disappoint you, Polly.'

'Life's full of 'em, dear. Let me get you a drink. Will you have a gin or something?'

'With lots of tonic, please. It's early.'

'All right.' She moved towards the open french windows of the house, where some flowered curtains were sagging into the garden as though trying to get a breath of air. For a big woman her backside was compact, unsagging, like a professionally wrapped parcel. She went in and he remained in the garden, looking around at nature taken leave of its senses in what had been once a place of geometrical order.

'I take lots of gin and a little tonic,' she bellowed from the shade of the room. 'I think tonic weakens the resolve. Want some ice?'

'Please.'

'You'll have to have a bit off the floor, I've just dropped the sodding lot,' she cried happily. 'It's not too bad though, just a few carpet hairs and a bit of cat fluff on it, that's all.'

'I prefer hairy ice,' he called back.

She appeared almost immediately with the slopping drinks, flinging the jaded curtains royally aside. 'You really are a *very* nice man, you know,' she exclaimed. Then: 'Would you say you're a happy man?'

The frank inquiry took him by surprise. He sipped his drink first. 'Well,' he said slowly. 'It's a lovely day and I'm not ill, nor am I entirely broke, and I've got a family and . . .'

'You sound like somebody counting up how many points they're stuck with at the end of a hand of hundred-and-one rummy,' she laughed. She sat on the canvas bed and placed her square bare feet on the ground like a mother paddling at the seaside. 'I've heard that all men over forty are afraid of death,' she said. 'And especially on lovely summer days like this. Would you say that is true?'

'Auden said it's like the rumble of distant thunder at a picnic,' he replied.

'Of course, *he* would do. That's enough to turn you off picnics for life. Perhaps that's where I've been mistaken about you, Andrew. I always think you look so unhappy, but perhaps it's just the poet in you. You've always looked so thoughtful. When I've seen you at parties and what-have-you.'

'Well at that last thing I *was* feeling a bit unhappy about that poor parrot,' he said. 'You would have thought that the silly bitch could have thrown up somewhere else, wouldn't you? Cleaning it was a hell of a job.'

'Yes, very tiresome,' she agreed. 'Nasty mixture, spew and feathers. But you were the one who did it. Everyone else was too convulsed with their idiotic laughter. It was very kind of you. I'm sure the parrot will always remember it. Have you got much of a tricep, Andrew? Upper arm?'

'Pardon?'

'Sorry, I will dodge about so. Will you let me have a decko at your upper arm muscle, there's a good chap? I'm doing a composite man, you know, modelled from bits and pieces of all the males around here. Flat-Roof Man, the twentieth-century phenomenon. In centuries to come he will be gazed upon and studied by people in museums in the same way as we today ogle at the cave-dwellers.'

'Yes, I'm sure he will, Polly,' he replied.

'Let's have a look then, will you.'

Doubtfully he put down his glass, took off his jacket and rolled his shirt sleeve. He folded the arm, watching the muscle grow as he had watched it with doubt when they had contests at school. Mrs Blossom-Smith looked quickly disappointed. 'No,' she sighed. 'It's not that interesting. As muscles go it's neither one thing nor another.'

'I tend to be like that – generally,' he shrugged. He replaced his coat.

A thrush bounced on the lawn. Polly clasped her hands before her like the folding of a pair of bellows. '*Turdus philomelos!*' she exclaimed. 'An embarrassing name for a nice little bird.' She looked up as though she had been talking to herself. 'Would you like to see the work?' she asked. 'It's nowhere near finished. As you will see, there's all sorts of bits and pieces, his dickie for one, to be stuck on. But he's coming along slowly. Come and take a peep.'

Blithely, like some magnified summer nymph, she led the way across the untidily matted grass towards the house. He felt a strange and unjustified thrill following this expansive, rolling woman into the dimness of the cluttered house. He had been inside before, once to a party where he had laid a jam sandwich (Mrs Blossom-Smith served jam sandwiches at her parties) down on a plate and had picked it up coated with vintage dust. Furniture was piled rather than arranged, paintings sagged on the walls like victims of a firing squad, in one corner was a rolled carpet standing upright as a warning finger. A flight of disturbed bats would not have surprised him.

'It's in my bedroom,' she hooted over her shoulder. 'You won't mind coming into my bedroom, will you, Andrew? Will Audrey mind?'

'I won't tell her,' he forecast confidently.

'Well, you're quite safe,' she replied, heavily charging the stairs. 'I've set my heart on the Phantom Flasher. Here we are, this way.'

The stairs had become a gallery and she led him from the gallery into a bedroom, rudely bare except for a single-size iron bed, its covers screwed and churned, and a life-size clay model of a naked man, minus several essential parts.

The bed and the model were only a foot apart and Mrs Blossom-Smith immediately apologized for this. 'It's just that I get taken with the urge to muck about with him in the middle of the blessed night,' she explained. 'And I can't be bothered to get out of bed. Do you like him?'

Andrew described a tentative sideways movement around the bed until he was facing the clay man. 'Hey Presto! Flat-Roof Man!' announced the sculptress and switched on a spotlight which hit and lit the model squarely.

'Christ,' said Andrew softly. 'It's Geoffrey Turvey!'

'Right first time!' enthused Polly. 'Well, the face and head are Mr Turvey. He has that sort of weekend face which typifies the species. Only on Saturdays and Sundays does it really become apparent with life.'

'It's very good of him,' breathed Andrew admiringly. 'Did he take a lot of persuasion to pose?'

'Trapped him, like the rest,' said Polly with quiet triumph. 'The legs you might find difficult to recognize because, of course, they are normally just a pair of trousers, but they belong to Bertram Reynolds, a trifle knobbly and lacking in flesh as you can perceive. Then the ears belong to Mr Henry Jones and Mr George Jones, respectively, the chest and the abdomen are Mr Shillingford's, and the bum is someone whose secret I have sworn to respect.'

'Geoff Turvey,' ruminated Andrew, gazing at the mute face of his friend. 'The old so-and-so. He didn't tell me.'

'Now you will be able to trouble him with hints,' she smiled. She was looking at him quizzically. 'I'd like to give you a part, Andrew,' she said like a casting director. 'But there's not a lot left. There's the arms and hands, the feet, and the genitals. We've discussed your arms. Your hands are too good and your feet look too big even from here, and I really do want to see if The Flasher can fit with the other bits.'

'Please yourself,' laughed Andrew bemused by her. 'Posterity will have to do without Andrew Maiby.'

'You like him, though, don't you?' Polly asked with genuine anxiety. 'Naturally I don't display him to every Tom, Dick or Harry.'

'Just to Geoff, Bertram and Henry,' said Andrew.

'I do believe you're jealous,' she said, giving him a heavy friendly push. 'Come down and we'll have another drink. You haven't told me why you came to see me anyway.'

'After all this, I'd almost forgotten,' admitted Andrew. He followed her down through the grimy house again and out into the garden sunshine. She poured them each another drink. 'Old Geoffrey looks great, really life-like,' he said reflectively. 'He must have sat for you a long time.'

'Most of the time he was stretched out on the bed,' she said airily. 'He gets very tired. Can't think what he does to get like that. But I thought his head was quite right. It's a mildly *worried* head and it's even a little flat on top. He really looks like Flat-Roof Man.'

'He does too,' nodded Andrew. 'I'd never really thought about his flat head before.'

'I saw it immediately,' she said. 'It was as though nature had designed him for his house. Now, tell me why you came.' She lolled back on the scruffy canvas garden-bed again like Goya's Duchess. Andrew felt very strange. He pulled up a small collapsible seat and squatted on it. He could not somehow imagine himself wanting her sexually. She was too jolly. But when she stopped fluffing and laughing, when her jokes and chatter had been taken into account, there she was, waiting to be taken, like a large lump of marginally over-ripe fruit.

'I'm afraid that the reason I came to see you seems a bit ordinary somehow, after all this,' he said.

'All what?'

'Well, arriving here and seeing that model and drinking gin and bits of carpet fluff. It's all a bit exotic.' He paused, then said bravely: 'Listen, Polly, can I ask you something really personal? Is that really an Arab motto on the top of your leg?'

'My tattoo? You came to see me about my tattoo?'

'No, no. Nothing like that. I'll ask you about the other thing in a minute. It's just a thing for the paper. It's not important.'

She pulled the flesh of her leg tightly round so that she could peruse the blue words. 'Yes,' she said as though satisfied she had deciphered it correctly. 'It's an Arab proverb. Well, the sort of introduction to it. I was at school in Damascus at the time – my father was in the embassy there – and I went off and had this done. I was a bit of a little cow in those days. I got found out before it was finished, so I never got the job done properly. It's supposed to run right round the top of the leg. Like a garter.'

'And what's it say?'

'Well, truthfully, I was a bit disappointed with it. I was very young and full of dreams and ideals and I asked this Syrian tattooist to write something profound about the world and our existence. Well, his idea of something profound and mine were a bit different, so, in a way I suppose, it's just as well he never got around to finishing the sentence.'

'What is it?'

'Oh, it's quite a well-known Arab proverb,' she shrugged. 'It says, something like: Life is like a cucumber – the moment you think you have grasped it in your hands it's up your arse.'

His poker face wrinkled and then exploded with laughter. 'My God, Polly,' he eventually choked. 'There's not too many people like you around.'

She hesitated as though afraid of his laughter, but then she laughed too. 'No,' she agreed enthusiastically. 'I don't suppose there are. I really *am* a cheery great thing, aren't I, Andrew!'

He laughed with her in agreement, but her mirth stopped

abruptly and she asked: 'Andrew, will you tell your wife you've been to see me?'

Andrew, surprised, said: 'Yes, I suppose I will.'

'I thought you might. You mean someone might have seen you arrive here?'

'Yes, that's about it,' he agreed honestly.

'But you wouldn't say about my model or going to my bedroom?'

'No.' He realized she was asking the questions like a social surveyor. He added carefully: 'Not everybody's as . . . as free as you, Polly. Inside most women, especially married women, is a rotten apple. It's called suspicion.'

'Fear, more like it,' she said with understanding. 'With women, especially as you say, married women, it goes with love.'

5

They walked along the towpath, some guilty giggling between them, the barge lying like a tethered hippo three hundred yards up the straight run of bank and water. The sheen of evening had settled on the canal, stilling it so completely that they seemed to be walking into a painted landscape. Even the suspended gnats and water-flies appeared almost stationary in the cooling air.

'It's lovely,' said Audrey, stumbling along the path, catching hold of his arm. He pushed away some dangling blackberry thorns so they could get by. She said, 'Thanks,' and he was surprised to see a blush on her cheeks.

'Birds everywhere,' said Andrew joining in the game. 'Listen. Hundreds of them. And to think that we don't know the note of one from the croak of another.'

'It's very nice,' she said looking around. 'And to think it's here all the time.'

'Amazing how it stirs you,' he acknowledged. 'My God! A couple o' pints o' cider, my girl, and I'd be throwing 'ee into nearest hayrick.'

'You farm lads all be the same,' she said, attempting to mimic too. 'You be only wantin' us maids for one thing.'

'Ye be a stocky wench,' he said roughly, standing away and quizzically regarding her suburban face and her best coat. 'Ye look like ye could carry a coupla churns.'

'I be promised, zur,' she said with a rustic curtsey.

'Who you be promised to, the French onion man?'

He knew he had spoiled it. Her expression changed. 'Oh, shut up, Andrew,' she said. 'We were having a good time then. One of us always has to ruin it.'

'Right,' he acknowledged. 'I'm sorry. Still, we can't play yokels for ever. Even those birds are really screaming to other birds to keep off their property.'

They had walked almost to the barge now. 'Do you think it would work for two people to go away somewhere isolated together and try to get to know the *good* things about each other?' she asked thoughtfully.

'Only if they've never met before. Only strangers might. People who are familiar can't. Once you've tasted blood . . .'

'Stop it,' she said again, pleading now. 'We were happy only a minute ago. Don't let these kids hear us fighting.'

'No, they mustn't,' he agreed. Awkwardly he clambered aboard the barge. He noticed, with slight unease, that the plank of wood that did service as a gangway had been pulled on to the deck. He swivelled it out so that Audrey could walk on it, and then called quickly, before, he thought, she could tell him to hush. Their glances met anxiously as he shouted.

'Anyone aboard?' called out Andrew again.

There was a delayed scraping movement from the stern of the barge and a foggy voice replied. They walked along the deck planks and reached a companionway with worn and uncertain steps going down to a door painted in the curly, vanished hand of the canal people.

'Hang on, please, Mr Maiby,' came the boy's voice from within. 'The door's a bit stuck.'

Andrew was going to hold back, but Audrey's foot went out and gave the door a push to which it responded squeakily. 'Open sesame!' she exclaimed with accentuated brightness. 'That wasn't stuck very much.'

'It's easier from that side,' said the embarrassed boy.

'That's all right, Tim,' said Audrey. She examined him quickly, and Andrew looked at him over her shoulder. He was a hollow-faced kid, the twelve-year-old product of Bertram and Gloria Reynolds, both people with oddly curved features. He had long fair hair, lying lank across his shirt which was open to the waist. Around his neck he wore an old half-crown on a silver chain.

'Why shut it?' asked Audrey. 'It's a lovely evening.'

'I was just starting to paint the inside,' said the boy.

'Sorry,' said Andrew. 'Is it safe for us to come in?'

'Yes, Mr Maiby.'

'I meant . . . I thought there might be paint and lord knows what around.'

'Come on in,' called Lizzie. They could see her now, or half of her, in the dimness at the fore end of the long covered hold of the barge. She was standing in the well of an open trapdoor, her hands above her head fixing something to the dark low roof.

'It's half a woman,' laughed her father, bent almost double in the low space. He squatted down on his haunches. With her hands above her head like that, her new breasts swelling her light sweater, she looked more than half a woman. Her hair was fair and brief and curly. It had been a week since he had been prompted to notice she had been to have it cut.

'Hello, daddy,' she called easily to him. 'Why didn't you say you were coming? We would have piped you aboard.'

'It's a bit dim in here,' said Audrey. She was squatting down now as well. 'It's a wonder you can see to work.'

'Oh, you get used to it,' said Lizzie, remaining in her hole, still intent on the work above her head. 'There's enough light coming through the little window up here, and Tim has only just started on the door, so it's been open until now. We were going to pack in soon anyway.'

'Where's everybody else?' asked Andrew. 'I thought there was a whole gang of you.'

'Billy is down below,' said Lizzie. 'Tim's brother.' She curved slightly and called down. 'Billy! My parents are here on an inspection trip. Give them a bang.'

There were three loud bangs on the floorboards almost beneath their feet. 'He can't come up,' interposed Tim. 'He's plugging the hull and if he leaves it too long the barge starts to sink.'

Audrey looked immediately anxious, but Andrew laughed.

'All right,' he said. 'We'll abandon ship.' He touched his wife's elbow. She glanced at him as though she wanted to stay, but then she followed him on to the outside ladder. 'Why don't you knock off and come and have a drink?' Andrew suggested, poking his head back into the dimness.

'All right, dad,' Lizzie called back. 'You go over to The Jolly Grinder and we'll follow. We won't be a couple of minutes.'

He hesitated, then said: 'As you like, Liz, we'll see you in the garden.'

'Right, daddy.'

Andrew and Audrey balanced along the narrow walk of the deck. They stopped when they came to the dirty little window in the deck housing and Andrew knocked gently with his toe. Their daughter's young face, indistinctly smiling through the grime and cobwebs peered out at them. Audrey waved to her and Andrew blew her a kiss and she laughingly poked out her tongue at them.

'They haven't done very much,' said Audrey when they were on the canal bank again. 'Not considering the time they've spent up here.'

'They've done a bit on the outside,' said Andrew, pointing to the newly painted prow. 'And they're following the old design, which must take a bit of time. All those curly bits. She's all right.'

'You think so? You don't think there's anything going on there?'

79

'Oh, come on, Audrey. We're showing our age, love.'

She shrugged unhappily: 'If you say so.'

'Anyway, I don't think we need worry about the two Reynolds kids. Lizzie's miles ahead of them. God, that Tim's got a face just like his mother. It curves inwards like a bowl. And his old man's got a face that's convex, it swells out. You remember when we saw them dancing at that dinner-dance. Their faces looked as if they could fit into each other. Like one porridge bowl into another.'

Audrey turned and looked back at the barge. 'I still don't reckon they've done a lot. Not to the barge, anyway,' she said.

*

'They're gone,' said Tim Reynolds. 'I can see them walking along the bank.'

'God,' breathed Lizzie, still standing in the wooden hole. 'That was really scary. Fancy them creeping up on us like that.'

She clambered from the well in the deck. She was wearing nothing from the waist down. The boy stared at her. Her sweater finished in wrinkles about her middle and her slim legs and rounded buttocks looked luminous in the dim light of the barge.

'Did our Billy have his look?' inquired Tim earnestly. 'I haven't had my look yet.'

'We can't now,' said Lizzie. 'I'd better go over to the pub.' She bent over the hold, the seam of her backside pointing straight towards the boy. His eyes wide, he moved forward as though to put his hand on her but he hesitated and in that moment she had retrieved her jeans and pants from below the deck and was getting her feet into them. 'Sorry, boys,' she said, 'we'll have to do it another day. They would, just when we'd started.'

Billy's plate face appeared from the hatch. He looked flushed even in the dimness. 'Christ almighty,' he said profoundly. 'Was I bloody scared. I was shivering under there, trying to get my things on. I reckon I've got a spider in my pants. I can feel it.'

'Go on!' the girl exploded with delight. 'You haven't.'

'I reckon I have.'

'Not a spider!'

'There's *something* in there,' said Billy. He pulled his trousers out at the waistband and stared down. 'And it's not my dinga either.'

'Let me put my hand down,' suggested Lizzie excitedly. 'I'll find out what it is.'

Tim, the twelve-year-old, stared with excitement and apprehension as his elder brother nodded dumbly and the girl put her fingers down inside. She and Billy were standing close and Tim was at a spectator's distance. Her jeans and pants had dropped down to her ankles again and her backside was chubby and curved only two feet away. He thought how thin her legs were at the top. His mother's legs were like sides of beef.

'*That's* not a spider,' muttered Billy as the girl, a wicked smile filling her face, explored.

'I can tell that,' she burst out. 'It's more like a lamp-post!'

They all fell into childish laughter at this joke and Lizzie stepped back and said: 'Take it out then, go on, like we said. And I'll show you mine. But, we'll have to get a move on.'

'All right then,' answered Billy carefully. 'But Tim had better keep a look-out at the door.'

'That's just like you, mate,' protested his brother. 'Tim can keep a look-out. Good old Tim. He won't mind. Maybe I want to have a butchers as well.'

'You've seen my thing plenty of times,' replied Billy artfully.

'Get off! I mean hers. I haven't seen hers, have I?'

'Go and keep watch, kid,' ordered Billy.

Lizzie smiled beguilingly at the younger boy. 'Go just for a minute,' she persuaded. 'And then you can come and see as well.'

Head bent venerably because of the lowness of the roof towards the after part of the barge, Tim went off to his post. He pushed the door cautiously open and, half hanging out on to the deck, looked round the corner at the empty towpath. He glanced back. His brother and the girl were kneeling down on the rough boards. He decided to abandon his post right away.

'There's nobody there,' he reported, scampering back

through the splinters and dust. 'Honest. They're gone to the pub.'

Billy had taken his member from his trousers, white and solid, and the girl was bending down in the dimness to examine it.

'Harry Phillpot's got a bigger one than that,' announced Tim maliciously. 'Twice that.' He was staring, though, wondering how his brother could have made it so impressive.

'No he ain't,' said Billy, glaring up. 'Nothing like. I'll give him a bloody contest any day.'

'I want to touch it,' said the girl. 'May I?'

Doubt spread across the boy's face for a moment but then he nodded as though he had weighed up the question. 'Be careful though,' he said.

Lizzie pressed down on the end of the penis with her middle finger, pushing it down like the key of a cash register, then releasing it so that it jumped up.

'It's ever so springy,' she observed. Her voice was thoughtful.

'It goes better than that,' boasted Billy. 'Give it a good press. I put a conker on it once, ask our Tim, and it jumped about three feet.'

Lizzie pressed the contraption again, right down as far as she could, using two fingers now, and let it go so that it flipped up strongly. 'It's like the school diving board,' she said. 'Do you like me doing that?'

'It's not too bad,' said Billy strangely. 'Now let's have a decko at yours.'

'You can see mine if you like,' interpolated Tim, touching the girl's shoulder hopefully.

'She don't want to see yours,' argued Billy disdainfully. 'Once you've seen one in our family you've seen them all. Except his is smaller.'

'I'll have a look if you like,' offered Lizzie. 'I don't mind, really.'

The younger boy unzipped his trousers and out flopped a flaccid little willie. All three stared at it in the dim light.

'What's the matter with it?' asked Lizzie. Billy began to laugh cruelly.

'It would! It sodding would!' bellowed Tim. 'Just my sodding luck.'

'Put it away before it gets cold,' advised Billy. 'Come on, Liz. Let's see like you promised.'

'I'll just look at the door,' said the younger boy. He scuffled away, his eyes near tears, angry and humiliated. He stared out but he could scarcely see down the towpath because of the moisture in his eyes. Billy glanced at Lizzie in the dark. 'He's all upset,' he said knowingly. 'But he's only a little kid.'

'I know. I understand,' said the girl. She stepped out of her jeans and pulled them towards her to make a seat on the ragged floorboards. Demurely she sat, arranging the jeans for comfort, and then opened her slight legs. 'There you are,' she said.

There was a mouselike scamper as Tim came back through the dark. His brother warned him off with a hand. 'Don't rush, sonny,' he said. 'You can have a peep in a minute.' He rolled forward on his knees and peered up the shafts of her legs like a plumber looking for a leak. He shuffled forward, almost on his stomach and she obligingly opened her thighs further. 'I can't see nothin',' he announced eventually. 'It's too dark.'

'I'll get the torch,' said the ever eager Tim. He went to the back of the barge and returned with the hand torch. 'Do you want me to shine it?' he asked. 'I'll shine it if you like.'

'No need,' said his brother with an impatient sigh. 'Give it 'ere. I can manage.'

He switched on the beam so that it shot up the tanned flesh of the girl's legs to the narrow, white bottleneck of her thighs. 'Can you see it now?' inquired Lizzie.

'Er, yes,' Billy muttered doubtfully. 'Yes, I think I've got it. You've got quite a few hairs, haven't you?'

'Of course I have, silly.'

'I didn't think you'd have as many as that. They're getting in the way a bit. That's why I can't see it clear.'

Lizzie shifted on her bottom, drawing her knees up higher. 'Is that better?'

'A bit better.' Billy's voice was like someone in a tunnel now. 'Can I move some of them to one side?'

'No you can't,' said the girl very firmly. 'I'll do it. But you're not to touch me, Billy Reynolds.'

Billy's face emerged from his endeavours between her legs. 'You touched *me*,' he protested. 'I let you.'

'You're a boy. It's different with a girl. You're not to.'

'*I'll* look without touching,' interrupted the hopeful Tim. 'I'll be able to see. I've got good eyes.'

'Shut up,' ordered his brother. 'Wait your turn.'

'That's right,' grumbled the smaller boy. 'You're always bleeding first. *You* have what you want on the telly. *You* get a new bike and *I* have to wait until it's too small for you. Every time it's like that.' He nodded at Lizzie for sympathy and she touched his hand with hers. 'It'll be your turn soon,' she said soothingly. 'It'll still be there.'

'I'm not sure it's there now,' grumbled Billy, still shuffling for a better position.

'Oh, Christ,' muttered the girl. 'If you can't see it now you never will.'

There was no sound from Billy. A prolonged, profound silence. Then he backed out carefully and handed the torch to his brother. 'Go on then,' he said. Then, cautioning, 'It's different to what you think.'

Tim went down between her legs like a mole in a hurry. The girl shifted impatiently. 'Don't be long, Tim,' she called down to him. 'We've got to get going.'

Tim eventually emerged. 'Cor,' he said. 'That's fantastic! That's the first one I've seen.' He saw the expressions of his brother and the girl. 'Close up,' he added.

They dressed hurriedly and, laughing, went out on to the deck of the barge and along the plank to the shore. The sky was in its final shade of day, but the birds still sounded and the water had become thick with diminished light. 'It's half-past nine,' said the girl, looking at her watch. 'Come on, you two. I'll race you to the end of the path! Last one's a silly nit!'

They ran.

*

Even when the day had almost seeped away it was still warm. In the garden of the inn the landlord had hung four lanterns, and moths and other evening creatures came to flutter blissfully against the light.

Geoffrey and Cynthia were already there when Andrew and Audrey arrived. They were sitting in the little arbour formed by the mill-wheel. Geoff was sitting in the place where he had sat earlier that day, and his wife was sitting where Ena Grant had sat. He was drinking beer and she a Martini. She had wanted to go there and he had reluctantly agreed, although he was apprehensive. There were other people distributed around the garden that had been empty in the early afternoon sun; sitting on the bench outside the door of the saloon bar, anonymous kids holding hands and having a shadowy fumble and kiss, young executives, in their evening skins of suede, or carefully stitched jeans, laughing in young executive manner, old people crouched vacantly over a solidified pint of a night-black Guinness, inwardly comparing that dusk perhaps to other dusks long ago.

Under what had once been an apple tree, but was now only a soured trunk, sat a man and his daughter, close together but not conversing, both drinking lemonade.

'We were just saying,' said Cynthia to Audrey, while Andrew went for the drinks, 'they're a funny pair, those two. Always together like man and wife.'

'Who is it?' said Audrey peering through the dusk. 'I can't see properly.'

'The Burville girl and her father,' said Cynthia. 'Sarah.'

'Oh yes. I see. I saw her mother this morning, poor soul. She was sloshed then by the look of it. Trying to pick flowers and she couldn't cope with that. No wonder those two stick together. I suppose they have to rely on each other a lot, having her in that state all the time.'

'The girl's very bright.'

'Yes, clever,' agreed Audrey. 'Mrs Burville does mad things, so they say, and she can be very nasty. Apparently she went round to her husband's office in Ruislip and fisted the commissionaire. Apparently she gets violent as hell. They had to carry her out.'

'Did you hear the dogs kicking up all that row in the street tonight?' said Cynthia. 'They all went for old Herbie Futter as he was going home.'

'They've done that before,' said Audrey. 'It's the smell of the stuff he uses stuffing those animals. It sends the dogs mad in the hot weather.'

'Well,' went on Cynthia, 'they would have had him for tea tonight if Gerry Scattergood hadn't turned his garden hose on them. They were as vicious as anything. There was a horrible big black thing. But he must pong. I wouldn't like to sit next to him in the train.'

Andrew had come back and set the drinks down. 'It's the big black dog from Hedgerows that's out to get Herbie,' he said. 'There's a personal feud there.'

'If they actually set on him, instead of just barking, then he'd have no chance,' said Geoffrey. He had not contributed much to the talk for he was disturbed at being in the garden again. He glanced sideways at Cynthia, her slightly sagging chin over her glass. She was his second wife. Not many people knew that, although Andrew and Audrey did. They had a little girl, Tania, who was five. Now he was spending his afternoons screwing again. He looked at Cynthia's chin again and remembered that's how he got her – afternoon screwing.

'How are they getting on at the barge?' asked Cynthia.

'Oh yes. Just fine,' replied Audrey easily. 'Lizzie will be here in a minute. They were just finishing some painting.'

Cynthia paused over the rim of her Martini. 'Everything proper and above-board?' she inquired.

Audrey felt herself flush and Andrew glanced fractionally at the other woman. 'God, yes,' Andrew said for his wife. 'We only wanted to see what they were doing to the barge.'

'Of course,' smiled Cynthia through the gloom. 'That's what I meant.'

'She's there with the two Reynolds boys,' said Audrey.

'Oh, I see. Well, you've nothing to worry about with those two. God, those kids look so dim they make their parents seem positively bright.'

'We weren't worrying,' insisted Audrey. 'We just wanted to have a look, that's all.'

'Just to show an interest,' confirmed Andrew.

'Andrew went to see Polly Blossom-Smith today, didn't you, Andrew?' said Audrey. She had curious ways of steering a conversation.

'Yes,' said Andrew to the others. 'I've already confessed to my wife. She was in her bikini too, a stirring sight.' He caught a new anxiety in Geoffrey's eye and he gave the briefest shake of his head in reassurance.

'Does she have a tattoo, like they say?' asked Cynthia.

'An Arabic proverb,' confirmed Andrew. 'At the top of her leg.'

'You didn't tell me you'd seen that,' said Audrey.

'The suspicions of women,' sighed Andrew. 'She was in her bikini, I couldn't help seeing it. It's something about life being like . . .' He hesitated. '. . . like a bowl of cherries.'

'Very Arabic,' sniffed Audrey.

'Well something like that,' said Andrew. Her innate suspicion was such, he knew, that she could not have accepted that the true translation was told to him by a woman in a friendly manner. A cucumber up the arse could only be the words of an intimate.

'I also went to see Gomer John,' said Andrew. 'He's busy navigating the sub-post office around the world.'

'It's all done out like a ship's cabin,' said Cynthia. 'His mother told me. She thinks he's mad.'

'Just one of the maladjusted we'll be having at Plummers Park soon,' said Audrey. 'That'll do the property values no end of good.'

'It's only a vague proposal,' sighed Andrew. 'It's just old Ernest getting two legs in one knicker leg again.'

A man emerged through the incandescence of the garden lanterns. It was the landlord of the inn. He looked uncertainly for a moment and then leaned towards Geoffrey and held out his hand.

'Open your hand, sir,' he said as though he were about to perform magic.

All four looked bemusedly at him from their seats. Geoffrey, with an accommodating grin, put out his hand and the man put a fifty-pence piece in his palm.

'What's that for?' asked Geoffrey.

'Lunchtime, sir. You didn't take your change at lunchtime. I recognized you getting out of the white MG.'

'Not me,' said Geoffrey stiffly through the silence of the others. He pushed the coin back towards the man. 'I'll take it if you like – money is money. But it wasn't me.'

The man leaned forward again as though he were peering through smoke. 'Not you?' he said. 'I could have sworn it was . . .' He caught the look, the iron look, and drew back. 'Oh no, sir. Well, now I come to see you I realize it wasn't.' He looked around accusingly. 'These lamps are a bit dim, for a start. Sorry about that.'

Geoffrey laughed easily and held out his hand. 'I'll still have it,' he said. 'I'll keep it if you like.'

'No, sir,' said the landlord taking the coin. 'But I think I'd better wait till the right gentleman comes in. If he don't then it can go in the polio box.'

The man backed away and the three looked at Geoffrey. He laughed again. 'What about that? I could have been fifty pence to the good.'

'You shouldn't be so honest,' said Cynthia choosing her words.

'The best policy, they say,' said Geoffrey. 'Who wants another drink?'

'Here come the children,' said Audrey. 'Could you get some lemonade for them?'

*

'Andrew.'

'Yes.'

'Wasn't that strange at the pub. That man bringing out the fifty pence. Do you think it was really Geoff?'

'No. He said it wasn't. Geoff wasn't there at lunchtime.'

'You don't think so?'

'Audrey love, if he says he wasn't, he wasn't.'

'It just seemed funny, that's all. He seemed so certain.'

'Oh, I don't know. The light was very dim. I didn't realize it was Burville and his daughter sitting across the way from us until someone pointed them out.'

'I suppose you're right. I mean, Cynth's his second wife, isn't she?'

'Look, if Geoff's playing around he's hardly likely to go to the same place twice in one day, is he? He's not that daft.'

'I told Cynth that we were going there. Perhaps he couldn't get out of it.'

'Why don't you forget it, love. It was nothing. Nothing to do with us anyway.'

They lay with just a sheet over them. The night was close. They had left the curtains open and they could watch the stars above Plummers Park, with the roving lights of stacking airliners over Watford waiting their turn to go into London Airport.

'Andrew.'

'Yes?'

'You wouldn't leave me again, would you?'

'No. That's all finished. You know that.'

'But you wouldn't. For anybody. I get afraid, you know. Married women do get afraid.'

'I get afraid too. I'm afraid all the time.'

'It's not too bad together, is it?'

'No. It's fine.'

'Andrew, put your hand around my bum.'

'All right. Is that okay.'

'That's fine. I love you, you know.'

'I do you too. I love you, I mean.'

'Good. Goodnight, love.'

'Goodnight, baby.'

*

'Geoff. Come on to bed.'

'Just coming.'

'Geoff.'

'Yes, love?'

'Wasn't it funny that man thinking you'd been there at lunchtime.'

'A bit embarrassing. Good job he realized.'

'Yes, he *did* realize.'

'It was nice up there, wasn't it?'

'Yes, we ought to go again, Geoff. It's not far.'

'What about the two Reynolds boys, Cynth? Have you ever seen a couple of thicker-looking kids? They have that prehistoric look about them. Polly Blossom-Smith should use them as models.'

'What about Lizzie though? She's a beautiful kid, isn't she?'

'I'll say. She's going to be a stunner.'

'She's well on the way now. Andrew and Audrey are going to have trouble with her.'

'All life's trouble. It's death's no trouble.'

'That's very true.'

'It was in *Zorba the Greek*. Don't you remember?'

'No. I can never remember anything like that. Once I'm out of the cinema it goes.'

'It's not often I do. But that stuck.'

'Perhaps it means something to you.'

'Me? Not me. It's Andrew remembers things like that.'

'Good old Andrew. Do you think they're happy?'

'Andrew and Audrey? Oh, they're all right. The same as all of us.'

'We're all right, aren't we?'

'Us? Of course. You ought to know.'

'I do. Of course we are.'

As she said it he turned round at the side of the bed, away from her, standing naked. And she wondered sleepily why his buttocks were so pink. Almost sunburned.

6

Susie Minnings was an anguished young woman with a boom-ing cloud of red hair like coloured smoke rising from the com-bustion of her extraordinary face. The flying arches of her eye-brows, the banging black eyelashes, the zooming eyes, the thick fiery lipstick and the pink cheeks gave her a perpetual expres-sion of surprised explosion. Tonight she was having a party.

Her clothes were purples and puces, and heavy beads, rarely smaller than walnuts, flew on strings about her neck like a dan-gerous whirligig. She wore beads all the time, even in bed, and her swinging of them, by accident or design, sometimes injured her small children. Her size-eight feet, clad, on this the night of her reunion party, in emerald Aladdin slippers with tingling bells on the toes, were set like the hands of a large clock at ten to two. 'Do you know,' Andrew confided to Geoffrey as they watched her, 'I could never bring myself to have an affair with a woman whose feet stuck out like that.'

'Up! Up! Everybody!' Susie cried scattering her guests from the settee. 'Time to feed the hammies!' Three snot-encrusted children in foul nightwear jogged around her excitedly, each one ducking with almost synchronized reflexes the scything of her beads. In her off-white hands with their mauve finger-nails she clutched a fire shovel loaded with grain which she shovelled down the seam at the back of the settee. 'Listen to the little sods now!' she shouted with delight. 'Can you hear them scam-pering after it?' She smiled around in her smashed fashion. 'All right, you can sit down again,' she invited. 'The hamsters don't mind. If one gets caught in the springs you'll soon know. They let out the most Christlike squeak.'

'How many hamsters are there, Susie?' asked Andrew.

'He-llo, Andrew,' she said kissing him. He wiped his cheek because a kiss from Susie looked like a nasty wound. 'How many? Hamsters? Don't know, dear. Half a dozen at least. They've lived down there for generations. They never come up and I can't say I blame them.'

Her three infants were congregating just out of swinging

range of the beads. Two were sharing a glass of wine. 'Come on!' Susie bawled at them. 'Up in the bath, you lot! Let the nice neighbours see you do have a bath now and again.' She shooed them off. 'Then go to kip. Dry yourselves first.' The children went, and she turned to Andrew and Geoff. 'Last time they went straight from the bath into bed. Didn't bother to dry themselves. They're mad. They're like their bloody father.'

'Where is their bloody father?' asked Geoff. 'Wasn't this a reunion party for you two?' Before she answered, Audrey and Cynthia had appeared from the cloak room and were hovering near their husbands, nodding oddly at Susie, as timid spectators might nod at an exotic zoo animal known to be dangerous.

'Hello, girls,' she replied blithely. She looked at Geoffrey and then quickly at Cynthia again. 'You two haven't gone and got in the club again, have you?' she inquired loudly. She poked Cynthia's stomach. 'Or is that just a good lunch?'

She stopped. Her eyes revolved like a fruit-machine at the aghast couple. Andrew had a quick drink and Audrey covered her mouth. 'Oh shit,' said Susie. 'I've done it again. Sorry, love. Don't take any notice of me.'

'I don't,' said Cynthia bitterly.

'Good for you. Christ, I say the maddest things. I judge everybody by me. A hamburger and a couple of pints and I swell out like I'm having triplets.'

'What about Doug?' asked Andrew quickly. 'Is he around?'

'Oh, that craven bastard. Well, he's buggered off back to his black bint in Wembley and good luck to her. He's been shacking up with her for a month – one of his usual capers – but he came back and that's why I put it around that this was a re-union party. Now he's gone again. It was too late to cancel the reunion so I thought I'd make it a separation party instead. Thank Christ it's only a party. When he came back once we had a celebration kid – that brat Regina.'

'She's the one who breaks the eggs in the supermarket, isn't she?' said Cynthia tartly.

'They all do that,' answered Susie. 'Little swines. Anyway, Bollockchops won't be here tonight, so you're spared him.' She waved extravagantly to them and went off like an armed raider through the crowded room.

'She's damned well impossible,' said Audrey. She glanced sympathetically, but with something funny in her eye too, at Cynthia. 'Poor Cynth. Fancy her saying that.'

'Silly cow,' muttered Cynthia. 'It's just this dress. I'd have spat in her eye and cleared off right there and then, but I didn't want to bring myself down to her level.'

'I'm glad you didn't,' said Geoffrey. 'We might have missed something.'

Cynthia leaned over the side-table by which they were standing and wrote 'Do Not Disturb' in the dust.

*

In a shed in the garden next to the Minnings house, across the fence from the coloured lights hanging from the line-posts and the children's swing, a paunchy acne-splattered youth called Brian Harvey, known as Brain Harvey, was crouched at the controls of his specially-designed baby-listening network. His receiver was connected to twenty houses in the area where children were sleeping, each one with a small microphone in the bedroom. Parents who paid fifty pence per night for the service made periodic visits from the party, and at the pull of a switch Brain could tell them whether or not their offspring slept undisturbed.

Geoffrey was making his second check call of the night and found himself going in the same direction as a young woman who was a stranger. 'I think I'm the only person who's doing this in reverse,' she said as they waited for Brain to make contact with her house. 'I'm a child checking on my mother.'

'That's a new twist,' admitted Geoffrey. 'Does she cry much at night?'

'No. She irons shirts. All the time. It's a sort of fad with her and I thought I would take advantage of this idea to listen in and make sure she was all right.' Brain pulled the switch and the woman leaned forward. 'Ah, yes. She's okay. I can hear her singing.'

'How do you know it's not the radio?' asked Geoff.

'They don't sing "Goodbye, Dolly Grey" much on the radio these days,' she said. 'She sings that all the time.'

'Are you ready for contact Mr Turvey?' inquired Brain. 'Shall I attempt to get through?' He crouched and fiddled with anxious sweat like the eternally pessimistic wireless-operator in jungle war films. He was very serious about his function.

'Roger,' said Geoffrey, and Brain smiled at him appreciatively. The young woman gave an amused twitch of her nose. He thought he recognized her from somewhere. Brain operated the switch and Geoffrey leaned forward to hear the blameless breathing of his child. He smiled fondly, as even adulterous fathers do, and patted Brain on his rubbery shoulder. 'Roger and out,' he said.

He walked with the young woman across the garden, back to the party. 'My name's Geoffrey Turvey,' he said. 'We haven't met.'

'Just moved in,' she said. 'I'm Joy Rowley. You're a friend of Andrew's, aren't you? I saw you talking.'

'Andrew?' echoed Geoffrey, not querying the name but the fact that she knew it. 'Old Andrew. He didn't tell me . . .'

She laughed engagingly. 'Why should he? He helped me to carry some of my belongings to my house the other day. With the station-master. Is that your wife next to Andrew? And that's his wife, I imagine.'

'Yes, sure, come on over,' said Geoffrey.

He led her across and watched for the little arch of suspicion to shoot up on Cynthia's face. It appeared immediately but dropped quickly again when Andrew stepped forward and in a friendly way held the younger woman's hand before introducing her.

'This is Joy Rowley,' he said. 'She's a famous dramatic actress and she's come to live in Plummers Park.'

'He's kidding,' laughed Joy. She was so easy that the other women relaxed. 'I'm the Sarah Siddons of the washing-machine. I do the occasional television commercial, that's all.'

'A celebrity!' exclaimed Audrey, only half-mocking.

'We could do with a few more around here,' said Cynthia

seriously. 'A couple of pop singers and somebody who's on telly regularly and gets in the scandal columns. The property values would go up like mad. You're a start anyway.'

'Thank you,' said Joy politely. 'I try to be as scandalous as possible.'

'Is Mr Rowley here?' asked Audrey.

'If he were he'd be a sensation,' Joy replied. 'He's dead.'

'Oh dear, what have I said? I'm sorry.'

'Don't worry. Don't be silly.'

'I often wonder which is best, or worse, a divorce or a bereavement,' ruminated Cynthia seriously. 'Even a divorce doesn't seem quite so final as the other thing. People have been known to get back together after a divorce.'

'It's difficult after death,' admitted Andrew sagely.

'Well, we were both,' said Joy. 'Divorced – then he died.'

'I bet that made the estate difficult,' said Cynthia, sticking her nose forward. 'Did he have another woman to keep?'

'Cynthia!' laughed Geoffrey not very convincingly.

His wife looked stupidly surprised, first at him and then at the others. 'Oh, I'm sorry. I didn't mean to pry,' she huffed. 'I like to know where people stand, that's all. The problem pages are meat and drink to me, I'm afraid.'

'Have you had a chance to meet many people around here yet?' asked Audrey.

'She means besides me,' said Andrew.

'I didn't at all,' denied Audrey tartly. 'For all you know I might have meant the onion seller.'

'The onion seller?' laughed Joy. 'Who's that?'

'Most fantastic man in Plummers Park, next to Hercules the tramp,' put in Andrew. 'Has the wives round here in tears. I don't know whether it's frustration or the onions.'

'Well, I've got that pleasure to come,' Joy assured them. 'This is the first time I've really been anywhere. I met Susie in the post office. She hit my mother across the head with her beads. She certainly knows how to entertain.'

'She's made an effort this time,' sniffed Cynthia. 'She's even taken the dead moths out of the light bowl in the hall.'

*

Gerry Scattergood, who lived across the road from Andrew and Audrey, was a contraceptive salesman, a young bulky man, fair-haired, waist and paunch overhanging his belt, a large laugh and a quiet sniffy wife called Min who was childless. He sat cross-legged in the centre of a circle of Susie's guests in the manner of a man selling snake medicine. 'The spoggie,' he announced seriously, 'the french letter, the condom, the sheath, the noddy, the bladder, the nosebag, the Friday night blessing and the vicar's friend, whatever you like to call it, is a remarkable contraption that has afforded great benefit to mankind, and womankind incidentally.'

'Prophylactics,' said the tall American voice of Harry Solkiss. He and Jean were holding hands on the fringe of the audience and he spoke without stretching over the heads before him. The English people turned with a collective slow pout, as they do with foreigners.

'The same to you,' said Gerry looking up. His neighbours laughed.

'Yes, sir, that's smart,' agreed the amiable Harry, laughing more than anyone and shaking his head at the unbounded wit of the Englishman. 'Real smart. I meant that *we* call them prophylactics.'

'Yes,' said Gerry carefully. 'Yes, I suppose you would. But it's not something that would catch on over here. I mean, by the time you'd said that mouthful you'd have forgotten what you were supposed to be doing with it.'

'Right!' exclaimed Harry with polite over-enthusiasm amid the laughter. 'I guess you would!'

His wife squeezed his tall, thin hand and laughed her confirmation. 'You sure would, Hairy.'

'Today,' pronounced Gerry Scattergood, with a glance at the Americans which did not invite further interruptions, 'this evening, ladies and gentlemen, spoggy-users all, I trust . . .'

'Not likely!'

'You'd be lucky!'

'What about the pill?'

Gerry stared about him, hurt astonishment cracking up his

face. 'Please, please,' he implored softly. 'Ladies and gentlemen. Do not mention such things. Do not upset the performer. The pill? The pill? A gob-stopper, madam, a sugared bon-bon. *I* speak, sir, of no chemist's concoction, but of a game for two, of titillation and technique, something as engrossing as a toy and as much fun, an art form . . . poetry . . . joy.'

He revolved his wide eyes round the amused faces with challenge. His trousers, from habit, had parted from his shirt at the back and the great melon of flesh was bulging out. 'An art form,' he repeated softly. 'And I demonstrate.'

From his waistcoat pocket he produced with a professional flourish a wriggle of purple rubber which he put to his lips and blew into expertly. It expanded with a squeak like something rudely awakened, and became before everyone's eyes a little plum-coloured dragon with bright eyes and pointed horns.

'The Purple People-eater, our new model,' he announced modestly. Women had their hands across their mouths and regarded him and the rubber dragon with hilarious but fearsome fascination. Gerry let go the end and, with a quick raspberry like a rude comment to the watchers, the dragon disappeared, to be replaced, with the facility of a conjuror, by another rubber creature, its head covered with small horns and ticklers.

'An importation from Honolulu called Invitation to Love. Note the colour – Pacific Twilight.'

'The Japanese Gorilla,' he said immediately, producing another condom from his waistcoat. He glanced about him sternly. 'Not to be used, gentlemen, unless there is a full moon – and only if you love your wife very, very much.' The laughter burst out again, all around.

'And here,' he said, hanging out what appeared to be a small three-fingered rubber glove, 'Is the triple-teat treat.' He glanced about him mischievously. 'For doing it left, right and centre.'

'Note our array of colours,' he continued with a new burst of energy. 'Black Midnight, Passion Puce, Sligo Green – our line for the Republic of Ireland – and this lovely new creation, a tender pink, which we call After The Ball.'

Most of the party guests were crowding about now; the Indian music from the record-player was not altogether inappropriate to Gerry's market-place posture. 'And strength!' he attacked again. 'Such strength, ladies and gentlemen. Not only do you have the enjoyment of trying these products in private, of adding a new dimension to your marriage, a new width to the bed, if you like, but . . . but . . . you have the famous assurance of my company – Joy Through Strength!'

*

'Talking about Joy,' Geoffrey said as they stood watching Gerry Scattergood gather his wares at the conclusion of his act. 'You didn't tell me you knew her.'

Andrew grinned. 'Joy? Well, I have some secrets. Don't we all?'

'What's that mean?'

'Who's been modelling his lovely self for Polly Blossom-Smith, then? Whose magnificent brow is to be immortalized as Flat-Roof Man?'

'Christ, she told you?' Geoffrey's eyes darted around with abrupt alarm not quelled until he saw Cynthia safely at the distant end of the room.

'She didn't just tell me, old friend. She showed me.'

'Ah, she's done you then, as well. You slimy bugger. If you tell on me, I'll tell on you.'

'No chance, son. She's not "done" me, whatever you may mean by that. But she did show me her masterpiece – and there *you* are. Well, bits of you.'

'Has she got the cock on it yet?'

'You thought that might be my contribution?'

'Boasting again.'

'The function of this statue, as far as I understand it,' said Andrew calmly, 'is to depict *typical* Flat-Roof Man. He is far from Superman. In fact from what I saw of it he looks very much like Homo Sapiens Gone Wrong.'

'Cheeky bastard. Just because she didn't use you.'

'Not at all. No bit of him is there because it's the biggest or the best, but because it's typical of our breed. So it's open to argument whether the sexual organ would be big or indifferent from neglect. Some have it, some don't. It's obviously a matter for Polly to ponder.'

'It's a point,' conceded Geoffrey. 'Perhaps she ought to use Gerry Scattergood, as it's in his line, so to speak.'

'I think she's intrigued by the Phantom Flasher,' said Andrew. 'If she can capture him she'll be well pleased. She'd broadcast it everywhere around Plummers Park.'

'God, yes, what about that? Who do you think it is?'

'It's not me,' shrugged Andrew. 'I won't go to a public urinal unless there's nobody else there.'

'It's certainly not me.'

'No, I'm sure of that. Half the women around here would recognize you immediately.'

'I should be so lucky. With Cynthia around I couldn't so much as raise my hat let alone unzip my fly.'

'What about the other night at The Jolly Grinder?' asked Andrew. 'The landlord coming over like that.'

'A mistake,' said Geoffrey, looking at him firmly. 'A case of mistaken identity.'

'Here's Ena,' said Andrew, suddenly looking across Geoffrey's shoulder. 'And Simon close in attendance.'

'As ever,' said Geoffrey turning to see her. 'He never lets her out of clutching distance.'

'Would you?' asked Andrew. 'They don't grow many like that around Plummers Park.' They stood, glasses in hand, admiring her together, as others were.

She wore a pink dress that flowed spectacularly about her. She bent minutely forward to catch something a man was saying and her breasts beamed at them. Her fair hair was piled high. She was genuinely beautiful. She looked too good for the party.

A few yards away their wives were watching. 'Diamond Lil,' sniffed Cynthia.

'That dress,' said Audrey. 'It's not very suitable for here, is it? They say *he* chooses all her clothes.'

'I reckon he pumps her up when she's in them too,' said Cynthia.

'Oh, Cynth!'

'Well, I ask you. You'd think she was going to Buck House instead of 43 Hedgerows.'

'Where's Buck House?' asked Audrey genuinely.

'Oh Audrey, for goodness sake. Buckingham Palace.'

'Oh I see. Well I didn't know. I never go there.' The look she returned to her neighbour said: 'And neither do you.' But the comment remained a look.

Cynthia turned her back to the french windows through which Simon and Ena had entered and where they were now talking with the bead-whirling hostess. 'I can't look,' she said. 'She's like a prize from Hampstead Heath fairground.'

Geoffrey had looked away too and was staring bitterly into his drink. He was tempted to tell Andrew. To say simply: 'I've had her, Andrew. I have her regularly. I've had those breasts in my mouth. I've had those lips and my hands full of that hair, and I've been right inside that lovely flat belly.' Instead he said: 'Have you played much golf lately?'

'Golf?'

'Yes, you know, golf.'

Andrew laughed. 'Sorry. I was looking at her. She certainly is pretty spectacular. I think she's truly beautiful.'

'Our wives don't,' said Geoffrey, nodding across. 'There's blood dripping from my loved-one's fingernails. Look at her. Don't you think women are ugly when they get screwed up with jealousy?'

'Do you want to talk about golf or women?' asked Andrew.

'Women,' agreed Geoffrey reluctantly. 'I don't really know much about golf.'

'But you know about women?'

'Sometimes I think I do. At others I think I know more about golf.'

'You're miserable about something,' said Andrew.

'I was okay,' said Geoffrey, swirling his drink around in his glass. 'Until I looked up and caught that sneer of envy on Cynthia's face. That hatred. Only women have that sort of hate. And only *some* women. I'm married to one of them. That's what has pissed me off so suddenly.'

Andrew shrugged: 'The best you can hope from marriage is a good clean fight,' he said.

'Christ,' Geoffrey said, 'I sometimes think I'll run away, abroad, somewhere tropical, where all the women have nice light-brown titties and pleasing smiles.' He let a thought drop into his glass, then looked up. 'You and Audrey fight, don't you?' he asked as though seeking reassurance.

'All the time. Well, we don't really fight, we skirmish.'

'I retreat,' said Geoffrey. 'I'm always on the retreat or behind my defences. I don't want to fight. This is my second bash at it.'

'I know. I've never asked you about it. What was the first one like?'

'The wife or the marriage? Well, they were the same really. Both excruciating boredom. Every day I used to get on the train to go into London and I'd be sitting there wondering what the hell I was going to do to escape, and every day, on the dot, that bloody great overcrowded cemetery at Kensal Green used to straggle past the window. I tried not to look but I still used to. Miles of it. Sometimes I thought I could hear the sods laughing at me. So one day I met Cynthia and I ran off with her. Just to get away. I thought it was my last chance. I might as well have gone to work by bus and missed seeing the cemetery.'

'That's a hard thing to say.'

'It changes, Andrew. Don't you agree? Before your very eyes, it changes. That bitter woman over there is the one I used to wait for with a banging heart.' He looked at Andrew accusingly, as though anxious that he too should confess. 'You went off with that girl, didn't you? But you came back. Why did you come back?'

'I missed my home,' shrugged Andrew. 'Straight up, I did. I missed the furniture and the new prints we'd bought in Watford. That sort of daft thing.'

'What about the bird?'

'She flew,' said Andrew. 'Off she went and vanished into the world. She'll be all right. She was terrific, sexy and really unusual.'

'And you let her go. You preferred your chairs and your prints.'

'I was afraid. I couldn't handle the situation. I scuttled back in a blind panic – and there was Audrey standing on one of our chairs trying to bang a nail in the wall for one of the prints.'

'Did you ever see her again. The girl?'

'No. I used to walk around looking for her, just playing a sort of ghostly game, looking for her in the streets, in London, imagining I would see her face in a shop window. But I never saw her and after a year or so I stopped looking.'

'Was she a good talker?'

'Yes, she was. She had a marvellous voice too. We used to lie in bed and talk for hours.'

'And you used to tell her how decent and beautiful your wife was. And your lovely little daughter. And all about your neighbours and friends. And about the furniture and the prints.'

'That's it. She was very patient too. And I was the one who cleared out. It's funny, isn't it?'

'What are you going to do now? Settle for it?'

'Of course, settle for it,' said Andrew. 'Audrey has.'

'You could always start digging out a new room beneath your house, like old Shillingford.'

'Ah, I suppose so. But with him it's a hobby. If I did it Audrey would think I was trying to tunnel out. To escape.'

'You would be, wouldn't you?'

Someone took Susie's wandering Indian music off the record-player and replaced it with Sinatra's worn 'Songs for Swinging Lovers' which haunted Plummers Park parties like the ghost of youth. People began to dance, at first an obligatory shuffle with their household partners, but then, as at a silent signal, in the arms of the husband or wife they wanted and who had a fancy for them. It was a game they played at every party: the fresh chest pressed to the fresh breast, the lights dimmed to the jokey laughter of the dancers and to their relief. But, immediately, in the shadows came the clutch in earnest, the suddenly nipping lips and the soughing breath on necks, the touching of bosoms. Hands that daily polished brass door-knockers rubbed recklessly at hardening trouser fronts. Few of the semi-detached people would venture the risks, tribulations and expenses of a real love affair, and this was the next best thing. But like all games it was for a set duration. The following morning it would be remembered but remain untouched, undisturbed, until the next time Sinatra sang songs in some suburban sitting-room.

Andrew and Audrey always backed away from this dancing. Once when they had given a party Lizzie and a young boy from Risingfield had stood watching these married dancers, clutching and kissing, while the record played 'The Second Time Around'. The girl and the boy had gone from the room and Audrey had found them in the kitchen. 'It makes me sick,' Lizzie had said, 'seeing all that. We don't do that at *our* parties. All that pawing from people that age.' Now they stood at the ringside, watching with half-amused embarrassment the increasing fumbling of half-recognized shadows which shuffled and turned and groaned with slow enjoyment and feigned despair. It was as if she and he feared to become involved, like two people who have saved hard for years standing and watching a game of high-stakes roulette.

They danced briefly, and properly, together and they smiled at each other as though in recognition, but that was all, and they were relieved to be interrupted. 'Been up there lately, Andrew? Haven't seen you,' said the voice.

Amidst the sexual fraudulence Gorgeous George was indulging in his own pretence, swinging his eternal, invisible, golf club, slowly back and taking care to follow through. He took up a deliberate stance in front of Andrew and the bemused Audrey, addressing an unseen ball, adjusting his wrists and his feet, then looking up and seeing their expressions.

'Sorry,' he said cheerily. 'Been trying to get it right. Think I'm turning the wrists over at the last moment or something. What do you think, old boy?' He performed an imaginary swing.

'Wrong club,' suggested Andrew, nodding at George's empty hands. 'That's a four iron and you played it more like a nine.'

George grinned beneath his exploded cordite moustache with genuine pleasure at the mild joke. 'You're a funny devil,

Andrew,' he nodded. 'Should get you to speak at the annual dinner.' He turned to Audrey. 'Don't you think he's jolly funny?' he asked.

'A constant hoot,' she agreed dolefully. 'I can't get my house-work done for laughing at him. An absolute tonic.'

'Been trying to line up the putts better, recently,' continued George, actually going through the motions of replacing one imaginary club in a non-existent golf-bag, taking out an unseen putter and putting a phantom ball at his feet. 'All the boys at the club say I'm not lining the thing up right. Playing tomor-row, Andrew?'

'Tomorrow? Tomorrow? No, I don't think so. Is it anything special?'

'Mixed foursomes. Have to play with the girls. Mixed grue-somes, you know. The boys don't really like it, but it's only now and again. It's a different game with the girls, a totally different game.'

'It usually is,' said Andrew. He felt Audrey glance at him quickly.

'Hear about old Fowler?' asked George. 'The head green-keeper. They're giving him the push.'

'Fowler? The push?' Andrew leaned forward, genuinely as-tonished. 'Why, for God's sake? He's been there donkey's years. He must be on retirement anyway.'

'That's just it,' said George with a strange triumph as though at last he had made a remark of some true interest. 'The Com-mittee thought they'd move him along before they had to keep him for the rest of his life. They can get a jolly good rent these days for that cottage of his.'

'That's bloody scandalous!' exploded Andrew. 'I've never heard anything like it.'

George looked taken aback at the outburst. He said: 'Well, it's life, Andrew old chap. Like golf, life is a difficult business.'

He went off suddenly through the crowd, after first replacing the invisible putter in the ghostly golf-bag which he put across his shoulder.

'Rotten swines,' said Andrew. 'If they do that they can stick their miserable golf club up their arse as far as I'm concerned. I'll see that gets in the Sunday papers too.'

Audrey was grinning wryly at him. 'Oh, we're aroused are we? Growling, for God's sake! What *have* those naughty *boys* and *girls* at the golf club done!'

*

Geoffrey Turvey and Ena Grant never danced together or any-where near each other at parties. Not since the party at which they first met. Tonight he was dancing with Susie Minnings's beads wound about his neck like a hawser around a bollard. Susie's children in disgraceful night clothes were charging about the room blowing up Gerry Scattergood's products like coloured balloons. Simon was dancing with his wife, his nose hovering over the scent of her breasts, before leading her in a proprietorial fashion off the floor and towards Andrew and Audrey. It was only in male company that he talked about the extravagance of his wife's personal parts. With other wives around he gained the air of an earnest young man, anxious to discuss serious issues, local, national and terrestrial, and celes-tial, with considered opinions and firm nods of his head.

Ena was towed to the fringe of these discussions and left there, never asked, expected or even allowed to join in. It was as though she were some luxuriously upholstered vehicle te-thered for use once the serious discussions had concluded. If she attempted to make a remark in general company, as distinct from any side-talk among the women, she was given a fond little tug of the wrist or ear-lobe and silenced by Simon's affectionate sentence: 'But I don't think you understand, darling.' It was after one such rebuff in one such deadly conversation months before that Geoffrey had touched her hand and taken her to the floor to dance. Cynthia was in bed with tonsillitis at the time of that party. The first words Ena ever spoke to the man who was to become her lover were: 'There are times when I think I am married to the world's biggest prick.'

Now Simon trawled her through the drinking guests. People were bending this way and that, rolling and staggering too, with the dubious red and white wine that the Minnings provided, plus a bottle of scotch passed secretly around after being burgled from a locked cupboard. Simon only permitted her to drink tomato juice in company, although at home he encouraged her to drink quite extravagantly on some nights. He pulled her in like a tugman pulling in a rope, and immediately engaged Andrew in conversation about the home for maladjusted children. Andrew contributed little but watched the young man, swaying around on a firm base like some sort of talking toy. 'As far as I can see, and I've thought damned carefully about this, Andrew,' he affirmed, 'it's not only a matter of people's comfort up here, and the price of their assets, but their safety too. Maladjusted kids are maladjusted kids no matter what fancy names you would like to call them. Now take this, as an example, and I'd like you to listen damned carefully to this . . .'

Audrey turned slightly to Ena. 'Only a tomato juice?' she inquired, nodding at the young wife's glass.

Ena lifted it past her half-exposed breasts and drank it deeply. She smiled at Audrey. 'I've been looking forward to that all day,' she sighed.

*

Cynthia came from the bathroom and automatically surveyed the room for her husband. The cold nose of a nasty feeling poked into her as she saw him dancing with Joy Rowley. She did not trust actresses. Cynthia crouched and waited for them to move in front of the table-lamp by the far window. She spied carefully and was relieved to see that there was light between their bodies. But they were talking deeply. She was distrustful too of women who could talk deeply. Creeping around the edge of the dancers she sprang out on them like an ambusher. 'Oh, there you are!' she cried, making both jump. Then: 'Oh, Geoff, go and listen for Tania, will you, darling?'

'Sure,' he said, his face only tightening a fraction. 'After this dance, I'll go.'

'No, please go now,' suggested Joy easing herself away from him.

'Perhaps you'll listen for my mother too, will you . . . er . . .'

'Geoffrey,' filled in Cynthia. 'And I'm Cynthia.'

'Of course. I'm sorry, Geoff.' She turned sweetly to Cynthia. 'I've had the listening service hooked up to my house for my mother,' she said. 'She's alone and she's a bit strange, you know.' She smiled fully at the wife. 'A bit potty, I'm afraid. Irons my dead father's shirts all the time. You ought to come round one afternoon for some tea, Cynthia. You'd like my mother.'

The other woman's panicky polite and only half-comprehending smile was interrupted at that moment by the appearance at the french windows of the impressive and fiery form of Mrs Polly Blossom-Smith, a gin bottle in each outstretched hand. She always took her personal gin to parties. Her face was in the light and splattered with excitement. 'Invasion!' she cried dramatically. 'Invasion! Plummers Park is invaded! There's a whole lot of blackies coming up the road!'

That stopped the party in mid-dance, mid-laugh, mid-kiss. Mrs Polly Blossom-Smith was more exotic than Susie Minnings, and larger, and she now filled the doorway, a scarlet robe hanging from her like the evidence of some recent massacre. Then the garden outside was bobbing with black faces. Polly turned and, screaming 'They're here! They're here!', tumbled into the crowded room.

'A demon! It's a demon!' the leading negro retaliated, pointing a long finger at Polly hanging on to the guests like a battered heavyweight on the ropes. 'It's the Bad Red Zombie!' He walked easily into the room, a strong humorous-looking man wearing a good suit and pork-pie hat which he courteously doffed about him. He was followed by further coloured men and women, and eventually, solving the mystery, by Douglas Minnings, Susie's husband, arm around the waist of a bouncing West Indian girl.

'You lousy bastard!' Susie's voice hooted from the back of the crowd. She wriggled her way through for a confrontation with her cheerful husband. 'What do you mean bringing this tribe here like this?' She glared at the West Indian girl, doubling the expression on her already explosive countenance. 'And her! Fancy bringing her!'

'Ah, Dorcas,' said Douglas, as though he had suddenly remembered something. 'This is my wife Susan. Susie, this is Dorcas.'

To everyone's astonishment the two women shook hands almost formally, but immediately Susie spun about and, catching her husband by the lapels of his light jacket, howled: 'Come on, get this lot out of here. We're having our reunion party – or don't you remember?'

'Sure, sure,' soothed Douglas. 'That's why I *had* to get here. I thought I'd bring a few of the gang from Wembley and we could gee it up a bit. Parties here tend to get a bit stodgy. We've brought some rum and soda water and some bits of chicken, and Alfonse over there has got his mouth-organ, and Boney's got his drum. We're going to have a great time.'

'No you are not!' argued Susie. 'You are taking this minstrel show back to Wembley. And now.'

'And who's going to throw us out?' asked Doug.

'My friends here,' said Susie, recklessly swinging her arm about. The faces of the Plummers Park men took on uneasy shades. Their womenfolk looked at them for bravery and reassurance and were, without exception, disappointed.

'Doug! Doug! Doug!' The three Minnings children rushed from the direction of the kitchen like raiding bedouins and embraced their father's legs. He lifted them all at once, like bundles of disreputable rags. 'Look at this, Dorcas! What about these then?'

'Sure, what about them?' replied Dorcas ambiguously.

'Hello, Dorcas!' 'Hello!' 'Hello!' the children enthused. 'Are you sleeping with our daddy?' inquired the eldest.

'Not right now,' answered Dorcas, eyeing Susie.

'We put Mrs Brown's tom cat down the toilet,' exclaimed the middle child.

'And pulled the chain!' added the youngest as though anxious to complete the news. 'We pulled the chain! We pulled the chain!'

'Listen,' demanded Susie, 'are you getting this lot out of this house?'

Douglas touched her soothingly. 'This house, baby,' he

pointed out, 'is my house. Ask the solicitor. And I'd just like some of my friends to join the party, that's all. If you and your friends don't like it I suggest they go out into the garden or piss off home.'

'All right,' breathed Susie. 'Let them stay. But *this* is *my* party. If you want your own party, have it at the other end of the room. We'll push up this end. You have the other half and a gap in the middle.'

'What a great idea,' enthused Doug, kissing his wife on her truculent nose. He walked the width of the room making a corridor with his hands. At the end of this he was confronted by his own children again. 'Give these three machine-guns and they can patrol it like real life,' he suggested.

'No need for that,' replied Susie. 'We'll keep to our bit if you keep to yours. And no banging that bloody bongo thing louder than our record-player.'

Everyone, the Plummer Park whites and the Wembley coloureds, allowed themselves to be recruited into the farce by the husband and wife whose entire existence was built on battle and compromise. They shifted and shuffled, pushing against each other, making space, clutching glasses and loved ones closer, so that in the end there were two distinct ethnic groups at each end of the room, with the vacant corridor between them. Sinatra, the high and unseen priest of Flat-Roof Man's culture, remained incanting the older songs at one extreme, while at the other the West Indians swayed so quietly it was almost a slow tremble to the sound of the drum touched and tapped unprovocatively. But it was an uneasy armistice. The whites had been drinking all the evening and the blacks now began to distribute the rum among themselves. The corridor became narrower as each side tried to gain a few inches of extra room. The atmosphere was becoming hostile when Mrs Harrington, a woman like a frigate bird, who was in the front-line position, stood to spontaneous and courageous attention and began to sing flatly: 'There'll Always Be An England.'

She bleated through the first bars before anyone on either side recognized the song, and then other voices joined in, the West Indians as well, all chorusing the words about country lanes and turning wheels and a million marching feet. The black voices were not only of better quality than the whites but they were louder and expressed the patriotic words with infinitely more feeling. As they bawled at each other, 'Red, White and Blue, what does it mean to you?' the little Minnings children appeared, charmingly bearing trays of small glasses filled with green liquid. 'My God, they've found the crème de menthe,' shouted someone, and hands, black and white, came from all sides to grab the glasses, some to be sipped, but some, in that charged and alcoholic atmosphere, to be brazenly swallowed at a gulp.

Screams and cries and bubbles followed immediately. People staggered for the kitchen, the bathroom and the toilet, or made for the open air, while clouds of bubbles great and small bounced and danced and squirted about the room. 'Don't drink it!' screamed Susie. 'The little bastards! It's Fairy Liquid!'

The washing-up solution had people everywhere clutching their throats and holding their stomachs. The rainbow bubbles, from both sides of the room, burst and flew. In the middle of it all Doug and Susie Minnings clutched each other with helpless laughter, and their children danced with the excitement of life.

*

In her bedroom, with the light of the street-lamp eyeing her over the drawn curtains, Tania Turvey stared through the dimness towards the loudspeaker they had fixed on her wall as part of the listening network. She was hearing strange voices, screams and ribald laughter coming from that direction. It was difficult for her to understand but she was not afraid, for she was a composed and intelligent five-year-old.

Brain had left his post at the switchboard to go for his supper and drunken hands were trying the switches at random. Eventually Tania sat up in her small bed and said loudly: 'Hello Wall, what in God's name do you want now?'

7

Dormouse Dan hung over the bow of the bar in The Case Is Altered. It was Sunday morning and he had been the first customer. His half pint of cider now lay dead and flat in its glass and he was snoring mildly.

'They're going to put a preservation order on that bit of wall, you know,' Barney Rogers said, leaning towards Gomer John from his side of the counter. 'It's very fragile, very fragile indeed. After five hundred years it's got a right to be, of course. What it wants is a sort of iron grille around it. Stop people leaning against it.'

'It's a lovely bit of wall, Barney,' agreed Gomer, after letting his lips barely brush the surface of the beer in his half-pint mug. For a young man he was a notoriously slow drinker. Barney eyed the token sip with disdain and looked towards the door for the vanguard of the Sunday morning people from the newer houses. If he needed to live on the likes of Gomer he would starve. Still he had not long opened the doors and let the Sunday sunshine fly in on to the plastic sawdust, and there was no one else to talk to unless he woke Dormouse Dan, and he had only just dozed off.

'S'pose you've heard about the Flasher?' said Barney.

'Oh yes, at the sub-post office we hear about most things, you know. That's the sort of brain centre around here. Seems a funny occupation to me, running around displaying your private parts to the opposite sex. In the Pacific, of course, in the Fogufu Islands in Melanesia, they have a sort of Flasher's Festival – I suppose you could call it – where the young men, at a certain day in the year, or night time I expect, rush around the various villages showing themselves off in the most indecent way to the women.'

''ave you been there then?' asked Barney suspiciously.

'No, no, I haven't,' admitted the pale sub-postmaster guardedly. 'But I make a study of it.'

'What? Flashing?'

'No, for goodness sake, Barney. The Pacific. The islands and the customs of the people, navigation and all that.'

'Of course he does,' said Andrew, walking in from the sunshine. Geoffrey followed him and made a drinking sign to Barney for their usual pints. Barney looked grateful for their arrival. Andrew put his hand on Gomer's thin Welsh shoulder. 'Round the world in eighty threepenny stamps, isn't it, Gomer?'

'It's only a hobby,' mumbled Gomer. 'It's a private hobby, that's all.'

'Sorry, Gomer,' said Andrew genuinely, seeing he was hurt. 'I wasn't making fun. Here, let Geoffrey buy you a drink.'

'Thank you,' said Gomer, quickly taking the first definite bite out of his beer. 'I'll have a pint, please.' He looked with slight embarrassment at the half-pint mug he had put down. 'I always have a half when I first come in,' he said uncomfortably. 'I like to start off a bit gradual, see.'

Others, nearly all male, came in from the heat of the Plummers Park forenoon until the bar was filled, and there were people sitting all around the terrace. It was the expression of Sunday ordinariness so beloved of the middle-class Englishman, when in his carefully casual clothes he drinks beer with others of his tribe and they can talk as men.

'How it is that all the au pair girls in this area look like the bum of a buffalo? I'll tell you why. Because the women around here pick them to look like that. Anything decent and she's pushed off very smartish. The one we've got has hair on her arms . . .'

'. . . I don't see why we should pay our rates to subsidize those layabouts over the railway. Everybody's got a car over there, council houses or not. The money that's going in some of those houses. Someone saw a damned horse being brought through somebody's front door the other day . . .'

'. . . That new six-cylinder job is just beautiful . . .'

'. . . So this Irishman takes the nun's panties down with a spanner . . .'

'. . . We found if you just went up the coast a bit you hardly found any English people, Majorca or not . . .'

'. . . The one with the big knockers in our Costing Department . . .'

'. . . The Government should stamp on them right away . . .'

'. . . All right, why don't we organize a race for naked au pair girls? A tenner for the winner. Run it at midnight along Hedgerows . . .'

'. . . Nuns don't have panties. Whatever they have it's not panties.'

The men moved very little as they talked, but they performed a very slow revolving dance, a suburban saraband, so that the one whose turn it was to next buy the drinks in that group found himself at the right moment adjacent to the bar. Women came in occasionally from the terrace to have their own glasses replenished or buy crisps for the children. They were greeted and kissed by their husband's friends and then ushered out again so that the conversation could continue. Andrew was listening to the joke about the Irishman and the nun when he saw Bessie White sitting like an apparition on the oak settle near the door. She was regarding him with the same pale, engrossed expression as when she had looked at him in the magistrate's court.

He looked away at once, telling himself that he had not seen her, then admitting that he had, but reasoning that whatever she was doing there it was nothing to him. He returned to listening to the joke. '. . . so the nun said, "I'll recommend you to the Mother Superior" . . .' and looked back at the girl again, as though he were reasonably confident that she would not have vanished. A fat man was blocking his view. He leaned marginally backwards to look round the man's rump. She was still there. Regarding him.

Well, there was nothing to prevent her coming into the place, was there? Maybe she had just taken a walk under the station tunnel because it was a nice day. She could drink there if she liked. They usually kept to their own pub over there, but she could come over and have a drink. There was no law against that. It was just that she wasn't drinking. Just looking at him. He felt he was sweating more than the others.

The girl had not moved. He began to suspect that she was there only as a prelude to something else, and he was right. A big, ham-faced man sauntered into the bar, his frame almost filling the doorway. He wore a dark blue suit with white open collar, with his muscled neck projecting from it like the trunk of a banyan tree. It was easy to see he was from the other side of the railway.

'Ah, you're 'ere,' he said loudly to the girl. 'You might 'ave bleedin' waited for me.' Conversation crumpled all around. Everyone looked towards him but he remained cockily unaware of it. 'Is the geezer 'ere?'

'Yes,' said Bessie. Andrew saw her rise beyond the fat man. 'He's over there.'

'Mind your backs, gents,' advised the man as he worked his way through the drinkers. The weekend executives turned and stared at his wide-suited shoulders as he went past. The men in Andrew's group were at the most distant extremity of the bar and they sensed the intruder was making for them. Geoffrey's pint was fixed halfway to his mouth, Gerry Scattergood, who had been telling the joke, was frozen at the last line, Gorgeous George had just joined them from the golf course, and sitting at the little table across the sacred old wall were Harry and Jean Solkiss holding ritual hands across their two half-pints of cider. Barney was leaning over his bar with that incredulous reactionary glare of his kind witnessing the arrival of a four-ale bar type in the lounge of his pub.

The man got to Andrew's group. 'Who's Mr Maiby?' he said to Geoffrey.

'It's him,' swallowed Geoffrey, nudging his beer gratefully towards the paled Andrew. All eyes now turned to Andrew.

'Ah,' said the man, on the half-turn. 'It's you.'

'It's me,' admitted Andrew.

The visitor glanced about him with working-class haughtiness. 'I've got a bit of business with you,' he said. His voice had dropped but was so hard and grating that it was heard easily throughout the now almost silent bar. 'But not in 'ere. Would you care to step outside?'

It said much of Andrew's friends and neighbours that they fell back to a man, making an avenue through which he walked with the man behind him. The man had said, 'After you,' and waved a great horny paw. Andrew walked like someone riddled with guilt at the moment of arrest.

The tracking eyes went to Bessie, who from her prim seat had risen and now followed the two men out to the terrace. Once they had gone the voices and the eyebrows went up.

On the warm terrace the trio emerging from the door provoked less attention. The wives and children were out there, a concoction of gossip and gin, cries and crisps, sitting at the iron tables beneath the Skol umbrellas and on the imitation rustic benches. Andrew looked behind him, uncertain which way to turn, as though the other man were pushing him forward on the end of a shotgun.

'This'll do,' said the man. They stopped under the board which said 'Gentlemen'. Bessie walked to them, and the three faced inwards towards each other.

'I'm Bessie's dad,' said the man.

'Bert,' added Bessie glancing at her father as though he had forgotten his lines. 'Bert White.'

'Hello, Bert,' said Andrew uncomfortably. 'What's the trouble?'

'There's no trouble, mate,' said Bert. He appeared appalled at the suggestion. 'I just wanted to give you this.' He pushed out a hand clenched downwards in the manner of a schoolboy giving a toad to a nervous girl. Andrew automatically, but tentatively, put out his hand and found two ten-pound notes pressed into it.

'Twenty quid,' said Bert. Bessie nodded her fair hair as though encouraging Andrew to take it.

Andrew stared at the notes. 'What's this for?' he said.

Bert's matey, iron hand touched his shoulder. 'For keeping the old boy's name out of the papers,' he answered. 'It's to sort of pay you off. I found out about the court an' all. There's not much they can keep from me in our 'ouse. Anyway, there it is.' He glanced up truculently. 'Is that enough?'

'Yes, yes,' Andrew assured him. 'But I don't want this. I didn't even . . .'

'Yes you do,' insisted Bert as though he recognized a direct lie when he heard it. 'Everybody wants money. If it ain't enough, say so, mate, and I'll put another fiver to it.'

'No,' argued Andrew feebly. 'It's not that. You see I didn't . . .'

'Tell it to Bessie,' said Bert shortly. 'She's got to buy you a drink out of her own money. I've told her that, Mr Maiby, and she's got to do it.' He glanced at the pub and the garland of faces at the door. 'I can't come in,' he said with no regret. 'I got a darts match at our boozer and I got to get to that.' He turned, slapped his hand powerfully on Andrew's shoulder, smiled a jagged smile and then, with a curiously sweet ''Bye, 'bye', crunched about and strode away.

Andrew glared at the composed and smiling Bessie. 'What the hell was all that about?' he insisted.

'Christ, Andrew,' she giggled. 'You ought to have seen your face. He's a big bloke, isn't he?'

Andrew looked down at the twenty pounds held in his hands like some ill omen passed to him. He thrust them towards Bessie. 'You take this back,' he said. 'I don't want it.'

She half glanced to the right of his shoulder. 'All your friends are looking,' she said. 'I wouldn't make any more bother if I was you.'

Andrew looked too. The faces, Geoffrey, Gerry and the others, were grinning now. Ill-temperedly he thrust the notes into his pocket. 'How do you think that damned-well looked?' he said to Bessie. 'You being there and that big, hulking so-and-so dragging me out of the pub? I've got to live around here you know. They'll be thinking all sorts of things.'

'And your wife will find out,' she said smugly.

'Find out? It wouldn't surprise me to see her belting around that corner any minute. And none of this is my doing. I didn't keep your grandad's name out of the bloody paper. I didn't even notice the story wasn't in.'

'Well, it wasn't,' said Bessie simply. 'And it wasn't in the other one neither.'

'It was nothing to do with me,' said Andrew angrily. 'So get that straight for a start.'

'You're getting all upset,' soothed Bessie. 'Let's go in and I'll buy you that drink.'

'You keep out of there,' growled Andrew. 'That's my pub, that is. I have to drink in there.'

'In that case I reckon you *ought* to take me in. At least you can tell them the truth, or something anyway. Just so's it don't look like you've got me pregnant or something and my old man came up to sort it out. I mean, it did look a bit funny.'

Andrew groaned and wiped his damp forehead. She was still smiling. 'Listen,' – he leaned towards her nastily – 'they *saw*. They *saw* your old man give me money. I'll show them. Nobody, not even your lot, goes around giving money to men who have seduced their daughters.'

'Our lot? What's that mean, our lot?'

He was immediately embarrassed. 'Well, your family.'

'You didn't mean that,' she said. 'You meant "our lot" from the other side of the railway, didn't you?'

'I didn't mean that at all. But, I ask you, what a way ...'

'I'll come in and buy you that drink,' she said briskly. 'Or you can go and buy it and I'll stand out here if you think I'll spread some sort of disease in your rotten pub. But I'm going to buy it for you because my old man told me to. Otherwise he'll belt me.'

'He'll belt you?'

'That's right. They still hit the kids over there, see.'

Andrew sighed. 'All right. Come on in and we'll have a drink.' He looked at the notes again. 'I can't take this, though. I mean, I didn't ...'

'Put it in the poor-box then,' suggested the girl. 'If you've got one on this side.'

'Come on,' he said glaring at her.

'All right,' she replied blithely now. 'I'll behave. I won't let you down, Andrew. Honest.'

They took two paces towards the door. All the heads were

immediately pulled in. Bessie was slightly behind him. He stopped and turned. 'I thought you guaranteed that your father would never know about the old man being in court. That didn't last long, did it?'

'Sometimes things go wrong,' she shrugged. 'Even with me. You know I told you that I'd given the medals back to the other bloke. Well, I didn't actually do it myself. I told grandad to do it. I thought he had, but the thieving old bugger kept them. Nicked them. The other bloke came around the house to get them back and all the story came out. My dad went mad.'

'A regular old magpie your grandfather, isn't he?' said Andrew bitterly. 'Cocktail sticks, wasn't it? And live eels . . .'

'*A* live eel,' she corrected. 'There was only one. Don't make it worse than it is.'

'All right, *one* live eel. Now some poor old soldier's medals. He certainly collects things.'

'He's not going to be collecting his pension for a few weeks,' said Bessie. 'Not all of it, anyway.'

'This twenty pounds is coming out of his pension, is it?'

'Too bloody right it is. Two quid a week. He's lucky my dad let him off so lightly. Even then he cried, the old sod. He's always crying. But he won't get out of it. The only way he's going to get out of paying is to croak.'

'Give it back to him,' said Andrew, feeling for the notes which he had put in his pocket.

'You're joking,' she said, genuinely shocked. 'It'd be more than my life's worth. Do what you like with it, but don't expect me to take it.'

Andrew thrust it away. 'You people,' he sighed in his annoyed way.

'Us people,' she said, looking at him.

'I'm sorry,' he said. 'Let's go and have that drink. My reputation is already smashed beyond hope; standing here talking to you won't make any difference, I suppose. Bruiser enters pub, accosts respectable man. Young girl weeps in the background. It's a melodrama.'

She laughed in her bright way. 'You ought to write that in your paper,' she said.

'And that's another thing. *I* didn't keep that out. And I certainly didn't stop it getting in the opposition either. I don't know how it happened.'

'Go on,' she teased. 'I thought you'd been around giving a bit of comfort to that fat bird on the other paper.'

'Well I haven't,' he said. 'And I wouldn't. Even I have my standards, you know.'

'Oh, you admit that you do 'ave a look around then. I thought you were all married and that.'

'I *am* all married and that,' replied Andrew. 'And I need a drink. This is all getting too much for me.'

They walked into the lounge bar, and through the dimness and the contrast from the sun outside they could see the smiles standing out on indistinct faces. 'Cheshire cats,' muttered Andrew, as they went through the smirking men. His own group had retreated to the distant end of the bar and were waiting for them. Andrew purposely stopped short and turned the girl towards Barney's bar. 'What would you like, miss?' he asked with his back to his friends.

'No,' insisted Bessie. 'I got to buy you one.' She did it purposely, he knew, in her squeakiest Cockney. Andrew grimaced. 'Just a pint of bitter, please,' he said carefully.

'You don't want no egg-flip nor nuffink?' she inquired.

'A pint, please.'

'Pinta bi'er, please, mate,' smiled Bessie at Barney. 'An' drop o' port an' lemon for me.'

Andrew leaned close to her. 'Will you please, *please*, pack up this Eliza-sodding-Doolittle stuff,' he grated. 'What are you trying to do to me? And *I'll* pay for the drinks. You can pay me back outside if you feel you must.' Even as he admonished her he was aware of her sweet, fresh, open smell that belied the slum accent. Barney, with a knowing smile, handed the drinks over the bar. Andrew was about to pay for them with one of the ten-pound notes when he realized what it was. Unthinking, he pushed them towards the girl and said: 'You'd better have these.' He felt the landlord's eyes glow, turned, swallowed in anger and confusion, and thrust the notes back into his own pocket.

The drinks in his hands, he turned her towards the watching smirks of his own friends. 'This is er . . . a young friend of mine, Miss White,' he began.

'Bessie White,' she completed with a wide, bright smile.

'Bessie,' Andrew continued, 'this is Geoff and Gerry and George. And those two over there are the nice people around here, Harry and Jean Solkiss. They're Americans.'

Everyone nodded at the fair girl, and Harry and Jean, looping their held hands over the table, stood and joined the group. No one seemed to know what to say to her but she did not appear at all uncomfortable. She stirred her foot among the sawdust on the floor.

'What's this stuff for?' she asked.

'Well, it's to sort of give the place a traditional air,' said Andrew. 'I suppose.'

'What? Sticking sawdust on the floor!' she said. 'That's a joke.'

She gave the sawdust a stout kick sending a little spray of it over Gorgeous George's suede boots. He backed off, but continued to stare at her as though she were from some outer world. 'In our pub,' she continued, 'they've got those nice modern lino-tiles. It's easy to mop the beer up afterwards, I s'pose. It's a very good pub, really. Juke-box and a couple of fruit-machines and there's usually a singsong or a bit of a knees-up. Do you have singsongs here?'

'Not generally,' said Geoffrey. He was regarding her with quiet disbelief. 'Nor knees-ups. I've tried it once or twice but nobody will join in.'

'Oh, in our pub the trouble is stopping them when it's chucking out time,' smiled Bessie. 'They're a boozy lot.'

'Where is this pub of yours, love?' asked Gerry. He was firm and more confident than the others as if, through his varied trading journeys, he had come to know her type and learned her native tongue.

'Bull and Bush,' she answered. 'Cross the line.'

'The line?' It was George leaning forward now. They were like missionaries questioning a little captured savage.

'The railway,' explained Andrew. 'Over the railway.'

'I live over there, Attlee Park,' said Bessie, pointing over Barney's head.

'Ah,' they said, looking at her even more closely. 'Ah, do you now,' Geoffrey continued for them all. 'Whereabouts?'

'Morrison Way,' she replied. 'Know it?'

'No,' Geoffrey disclaimed hurriedly. 'No, I don't actually.' The others all shook their heads. Harry and Jean had failed to detect any difference in the girl's accent or demeanour from that of any other English person they had met. To them the exchange seemed to be some sort of stark and absorbing ritualistic play.

'It's the street that goes up from the cake-shop,' said Bessie as though that would fix it, and it apparently did for they all nodded.

'How do you know our Andrew?' asked Geoffrey lightly. The two men each sent a fraction of a glance towards the other.

Bessie put her hand on Andrew's sleeve and recited in the manner of a line from a film: 'It's a long story. You tell them, Andrew.' Andrew sensed his mouth and throat contract. He felt sure that Audrey was going to stalk into the bar at any second. He changed hands with his glass so that her fingers slipped away from his arm.

'Well,' he said. 'It was a bit complicated, really . . .'

'Take your time,' advised Geoffrey enjoying it, watching him profoundly.

'I will, I will,' muttered Andrew. 'It was Miss White's . . . Bessie's grandfather, you see. He was in a little trouble . . .'

'With the narks,' added Bessie.

'Er . . . yes. Well, he was unfortunate. You see he was in court and I was there for the paper. Yes, he was in court . . .' He tailed off lamely.

'Heroin pushing,' nodded Bessie.

The others fell visibly away before Andrew laughed in a strange abandoned way and said: 'No, No. Nothing like that.' He grimaced at Bessie. 'You and your inimitable humour,' he said. He returned to the others. 'No, the old chap was in court.

No fault of his own really, just bad luck in fact. One of these technical offences . . .'

'Well, what?' asked Gerry after some moments of vacuum.

'No lights on his bike,' said Andrew desperately.

'And aiding and abetting prostitution,' added Bessie.

'No!' Andrew howled it so loud that all the pub's customers turned to look. He stifled his voice. 'No. She's only fooling. No lights on his bike and . . . er . . . yes, um stealing by finding. Yes, that was it. He found the bike at the side of the road and thought somebody had abandoned it so he rode it home.'

'So it wasn't *his* bike?' pursued Gerry.

'No.'

'But they charged him with having no lights on it?'

'Oh, for God's sake! Listen, I was there. I can't remember it all. Anyway he was fined twenty pounds, but he didn't have the money so my paper, the editor, decided to pay the fine for him. It was a touching sort of story, as you can see.'

The group nodded sagely. 'Very touching,' said George.

'And that's about it. Bessie's father got to hear what had happened and he's brought the money back to be repaid to the paper. He's a proud man, her father.' He took a triumphant drink of his pint and regarded them challengingly.

'He's a big bloke too,' said Geoffrey.

'Very touching I must say,' added Gerry Scattergood.

'I said it was,' replied Andrew.

'You English,' sighed Jean Solkiss. 'You're so . . . so . . . noble in such little ways. Aren't they just, Hairy.'

'They surely are,' agreed Harry. 'I guess *noble* is the right word.'

'It's the big things we're not noble about,' said Andrew. He was relieved now the explanation was over. It sounded so convincing that he would hardly have minded if Audrey had put in an appearance.

'Pity your old man couldn't 'ang around for a drink,' said Gerry, slipping easily into the patois. 'He looks an interesting bloke.'

'He does demolitions,' said Bessie. 'Knocks down buildings and that.'

'He looks as though he could do it with his fist,' nodded Geoffrey giving Andrew another glance. 'I wouldn't like to get in a rough-house with him.'

'He can be ever so nasty,' agreed the girl. 'Once he knocked my Uncle Tom right through our reeded-glass kitchen door. Not a scratch on him, he went through so fast. He had to go off today because he had a darts match. Anyway he wouldn't drink in here. He said this wasn't no pub, it was a pansies' parlour.'

This information had such a stunning effect on the group that nobody said anything for more than a minute. Bessie seemed serenely ignorant of the chasm she had cut. She smiled privately into her drink. Eventually George rumbled: 'We don't think it's too bad. Bit of atmosphere here, anyway. Do you like the fox's head over the bar? That was actually caught on this estate.'

Bessie lifted her small nose and smiled at the fixed grin of the fox. 'Hello, Bruin,' she said. Andrew closed his eyes quietly.

'That wall,' continued George portentously, pointing at the relic, 'is said to date from the Middle Ages. It's part of the old inn that stood here then. Mind how you touch, it's very fragile.'

The girl had leaned forward to put her fingers on the wall and as she did so Andrew saw how slim and finely arched her body was, the backside tight in red trousers, twin small bumps, and the hooped front of her summer blouse sagging as she leaned so that for a moment he could see the first gentle white risings of her breasts. Bessie dug her fingers into the powdery stonework. George's eyebrows rose apprehensively. But she withdrew before he could say anything.

'When we lived in Kilburn,' she sniffed, 'before we moved out here, all the bloody walls of our house had damp like that. You could stick your finger through into next-door, just about. They used to say it was only the wallpaper keeping them up. Nobody wanted to show *them* off, I can tell you.'

She smiled around at the group, a pure, lovely smile, as though she were some princess talking to a group of commoners. 'I've got to be on my way,' she said. 'Blimey, my mum goes berserk if we're not there on the dot for Sunday dinner. Thanks kindly for the drink.'

'I must go too,' said Andrew. That quick movement from Geoffrey's eyes again. 'I'll walk you down to the . . . tunnel.'

'Right you are,' she laughed. 'I know my way from there. I'm in my own country, like.' She blew a quick series of kisses all around and made for the door with the reddened Andrew following. As they went he sensed the eyes and the curving mouths all around. The conversation dropped like a breeze at sea. He was relieved that at least the terrace was less occupied now.

He and the girl walked silently in the widespread sun. She was on the outside but he let it stay like that. 'Funny how different it is over here,' she said. 'Especially when it's really only a few yards. One day I'd like to live somewhere a bit posh. I'd like to live somewhere where . . .' she paused thoughtfully, '. . . where people don't plant their old Christmas trees in their gardens and expect them to sprout.'

'A graphic ambition,' he said. For some reason he now felt calm and unworried. He did not want to say anything about the things she had said in the pub. It did not matter.

They reached the entrance to the tunnel. 'Do you want me to walk through with you?' he said.

'No, dafty,' she laughed. 'There's no need to fall over yourself for me. I've been coming through this tunnel ever since I was eight and nothing's ever happened to me yet, worse luck.'

'I'll walk through anyway,' he said. They started forward together, a few inches dividing them, and went into the cool gloom of the tiled arches. 'I honestly had nothing to do with stopping that story getting into the paper,' said Andrew, his voice booming strangely around them. Some council house boys were playing on small bicycles at the distant end, black against the vivid sunlight of the exit arch. Together they shouted 'Bollocks' and the word bounded and bounced the length of the tube. The boys cawed like crows and turned their cycles away. The girl did not seem to have noticed them or heard their shout.

'Pay the money into some kids' charity or something then,' she said. She was walking very straight, very upright, almost marching through the tunnel. At the far end they paused and she said openly: 'When it's a fine day I take my sandwiches into the churchyard in Watford and eat them there. Why don't you come there as well?'

He looked at her. She was turned towards him now, the fresh face upturned, the fair hair drifting a trifle in the small breeze that always lived in the tunnel. Christ, he thought, this is *it*. This is where you run as you ran from Mrs Bigbury when you were young. Now it's the ages reversed. Go on, *run*.

'All right,' he heard himself saying, his voice making a minute echo against the tiles. 'Perhaps I'll come on Tuesday.'

She nodded seriously. 'Right you are. See you then, Andrew. 'Bye.'

He watched her walk up the slipway and stood there until she gradually went from his view as though she had descended a ramp on the far side. On impulse he went to the top of the slipway and saw her talking to the two boys who had shouted 'Bollocks' from their bicycles. He could see all three were laughing. The council estate seemed barren to him even in the sunlight. Great sheets of Saturday night's newspapers were lying like corpses in the road. He retreated and made his way back to his own familiar territory.

'Christ, what have I done?' he whispered to himself as he went towards his flat-roofed house on the hill. A grin forced itself on to his face and stayed there.

8

The girl from Cowacre walked tightly along Upmeadow to Risingfield on her Monday morning way to the station. Mr Brewster, Mr Reynolds, Mr Burville, Mr George and Mr Henry Jones, Mr Shillingford and poor old Mr Henty followed at their appointed paces. Andrew stood on his spot and drank his coffee like a casual general reviewing a familiar parade. Gladstone circled his legs like a hairy pipe. 'Action-Dog,' said Andrew, 'I am watching my world go by.'

Herbie Futter smothered his wife with kisses before taking the daily risk of parting. Cynthia Turvey folded Tania's vest and shorts for the school sports. Simon Grant, eagerly opening a parcel from the postman, found the anniversary body-stocking for Ena had arrived a week early. His eyes shone. Gorgeous George was practising pitching and putting on his lawn but his thoughts were elsewhere. Ernest Rollett was beginning a week's holiday during which he intended to properly organize the protest against the school for maladjusted children. The youngest and grubbiest of the Minnings family had caught her head in the springs of the settee while trying to view the hamsters. An ambulance and the Watford fire brigade had arrived.

Joy Rowley was setting out to do a television commercial, taking her mother with her. They let her mother do ironing in the wardrobe department. Gomer John, trembling, opened an envelope in his sub-post office and saw the words: 'So You Have Applied To Join The Royal Navy'. Mrs Burville was pouring her first drink of the day and measuring herself against her wartime ATS uniform hidden in a cupboard. Big Brenda, her knitting-bag slung like a papoose over her shoulder, trundled to the magistrates court where she would press her weekly thigh against Andrew. Mr Brownlow, the oat-growing magistrate, was preparing for the same court with a bad conscience. Mrs Polly Blossom-Smith was telephoning the police station:

'Hello, hello. Ah, there you are. I thought I'd never get you. Mrs Polly Blossom-Smith here.'

'Oh, yes. Hello, Mrs Blossom-Smith. I'm sorry we didn't answer. We're very busy.'

'Lots of crime?'

'Crime? Oh no. It's just it's Monday. It's the start of the week.'

'A fantastic deduction, officer. Is the station sergeant or somebody of rank there?'

'He's ever so busy, Mrs Blossom-Smith. But I'll tell him. He'll come for you, I expect.'

'Tell him I've been raped and mutilated.'

'Yes. All right. I'll pass the message.'

She waited. 'Station Sergeant here,' said an eventual voice.

'Did your constable give you my message?' asked Mrs Blossom-Smith.

'Yes.'

'He told you I'd been raped and mutilated?'

'Yes. Do you wish to make a complaint?'

'Oh, sergeant, you are terribly funny.'

'Thank you. What was your call about, Mrs Blossom-Smith? We're up to our ears here. There's three lollipop men haven't turned up for work and the panda car has broken down.'

'It sounds like toytown,' said Mrs Blossom-Smith brightly. 'No, sergeant, I was merely ringing about the . . . this man who is dashing about exposing himself.'

'Ah! Have you seen him?'

'No. Not yet.'

'Oh, I see. You're just worried.'

'Anxious more than worried.'

'Yes, well living with all those woods around you I expect it's a nasty feeling. He's been seen twice this weekend. Once at the back of the golf course and on Sunday evening, late, down at Sheep-Dip where he stopped a young girl, exposed himself, and then asked the way to the Catholic church. The girl, with great presence of mind I must say, gave him the required directions without even looking at the exposed part of his body. Fortunately she was a Catholic and knew the location of the church. It's in Watford so the directions were quite complicated.'

'It's a marvellous thing, religion,' sighed Mrs Blossom-

Smith. 'So you think he might be around today?'

'We don't know. He appears mostly at night or at weekends, so he must have a job to go to.'

'He's just a part-time flasher, you mean?'

'Er, yes. It would seem so. If there's an outbreak of occurrences during the day we'll know he's on his annual holiday – and then we've got him! We check on every man in the district who's on holiday.'

'Ingenious, sergeant.'

'We're paid to be, Mrs Blossom-Smith. But don't worry. I don't suppose he'll bother you.'

'How kind you are.'

'Well, I like to be reassuring. But don't count on it. You'll know him if you see him. Medium height, raincoat, furtive look.'

'Any other distinguishing features?'

'Oh, well. Only the obvious one. He exposes himself.'

'Easily recognizable, what?'

'Oh, you'll know him if you see him. And don't worry. We're nearly always here, and when we've got the panda mended we'll come and have a snoop around Fairy Copse.'

'I'm sure the fairy cops will be pleased to see you. Goodbye, sergeant.'

'Goodbye, Mrs Blossom-Smith. *Who* will?'

But she had gone.

*

Monday was the day of destiny, decided the Reverend Malcolm Boon; the day when he would cross the tracks and attempt something which until then had eluded him and his predecessors in the parish of St James the Less, Plummers Park. He would go, from his vicarage safe among the council houses, and journey into the land of Flat-Roof Man, and there try, at least, to establish some contact for Christ.

The mission seemed to him to be fully accommodated within those terms. The people about him he knew and understood. The girls were always white brides in his church, he baptized their children (sometimes spectacularly soon after the wedding) giving them the names of Cheyenne, Darren, Scott, Desiree,

Crystal, Melody, Ossie, or whatever was the fashion or the footballer of the moment. Generally they did not bring their dead to the church but took them straight to the cemetery chapel, for which he was grateful. Funerals were even untidier than weddings. The local teenagers had cheerfully excommunicated him. They inhabited the coffee and hamburger places of Watford, caring nothing for eternity. For them, he had reflected glumly, the world was less likely to end with a bang than with a Wimpy.

Some of the older people actually attended church on other occasions too, and the Sunday School was what he, a gentle man, liked to describe as robust. One volunteer teacher had a lawsuit outstanding against the parents of one of the pupils, and two others had left not only his church but Christianity in general because of what they suffered at the hands of little children who had come unto them.

But those people beyond the railway line were of another country. There was no church over there and not even a list of souls who would be glad to see one established. He prayed long and hard late on the Sunday night while his wife kept shushing him because she was watching an Edward G. Robinson film on television, and on Monday he set out on his mission.

He set out dressed, not inappropriately, in a khaki bush-jacket and camouflage green shorts, his clerical collar and bib poking coyly from the open shirt neck, with blue woollen socks and open-toed sandals. He abandoned the idea of taking a scout stave with him as being a trifle too theatrical. It was not very far.

Timidly he left his departure until the bulk of the morning march to the station, through the tunnel, would be finished. He was not one to meet the heathen head-on. By ten o'clock, however, they were all departed and, after a quick prayer in his own church for blessing on his project, he set out in the Monday sunshine.

He went through the tiled coolness of the tunnel and emerged into the emptiness of the Plummers Park estate. He knew only one person there by name, Mrs Polly Blossom-Smith with whom he had judged a children's art contest in Watford the previous year. She had not, it was true, struck him as a likely disciple but she was a kind if somewhat awry woman who might be able to give him names and addresses. In such a manner, he told himself comfortingly, did Christ begin his church. Contacts.

Sheep-Dip, the road that led from the station, was vacant except for an anguished man trying to re-inflate the flattened tyres of an elderly open sports car. He looked up at the vicar's approach, his face running with a confluence of tears and perspiration. He appeared to come to an immediate decision, as though the Reverend Boon had been sent especially.

'I wish *you'd* have a word with her,' he implored. 'Anything.'

'Who? What?'

'In there,' shuddered the man, pointing at the house.

'What about?'

'This. This sort of thing,' he sobbed, nodding at the car as though it were some injured human. 'Letting down the tyres, now. Or she throws things, muck, anything, at me, or she scratches the paintwork – look at that there – or pulls wires and things out. She'll ruin it one day.'

'I'm terribly sorry,' said the Reverend Boon inadequately. 'Terribly, terribly sorry.'

'You are a minister, aren't you?' inquired the man. 'I mean, you're not dressed up for something?'

'No. No. I'm a clergyman.'

'Go and see her then, will you? It might appeal to her better nature if she saw your collar. She's superstitious like that.'

'Well, er, no,' declined Mr Boon. 'I have to be getting along.' Disappointment crumpled the man's face. 'I'm visiting the sick,' lied the vicar desperately.

'Well, you could start right in there,' said the man, nodding again vigorously at the house.

'No, I must be off.' He nodded helplessly at the defunct tyres. 'I hope you get them up.'

He walked briskly off, the weight of guilt and defeat banging around in his stomach like the clapper of a cold ball. He decided to avoid the climbing pavements of Risingfield and Upmeadow and to continue to the boundary of the estate with the main road, where a screen of trees had been left, a slim plantation that bulged eventually into the wider expanse known as the Fairy Copse.

He liked it in there: the enclosed grass and the cosseted wild flowers, the trees, slender as organ pipes, the sun flicking through the leaves, the birds hidden and singing. He saw a squirrel and raised a hand to it. It would have been nice, he thought, to have been St Francis or Robin Hood, or someone else who inhabited a forest.

Mrs Polly Blossom-Smith, he knew, lived in the Victorian house called 'The Sanctuary' edging the copse. He felt a little shy at approaching her property through the trees, but he intended to call from the fringe to see if he could attract her attention. This was not necessary, however, for Mrs Blossom-Smith leapt out upon him as he approached the edge of the woodland with such enthusiastic ferocity that he was severely shaken.

'Mr Boon!' she exclaimed. 'Not you!'

'Yes, yes,' the vicar assured her. 'It's me.'

Her enthusiasm deflated quickly, he was sad to see, and she shook her head. 'No, not you. I'm dreadfully sorry. I thought it was someone else.'

'Oh, you were expecting someone.'

'Well, more anticipating them, shall we say. Never mind. What a lovely day again! Will you come and have some coffee?'

'Thank you. I would love that. I came over because I need your help.'

Polly led the way across the wild lawn. She was disappointed it was only the vicar, but she hid it. She was wearing a large yellow outfit of trousers and blouse, with a hat shaped like a grand buttercup shading her face down to the end of her nose. She looked at the clergyman sideways from its deeper shadow. 'How can I help, vicar?'

'Well, truthfully, you are the only person on this side of the railway line that I know at all. Since all Plummers Park estate is officially my parish I feel I ought to do something about . . . well . . .'

'Colonizing it,' suggested Polly sympathetically.

'Claiming it, I suppose,' nodded Mr Boon. 'I am neglecting

my duty if I do not. I need to know some people over here who would form the basis of a church, who would serve on committees and say the occasional prayer. Do you think that would be too much to ask?'

'I don't know,' sighed Polly sincerely. 'I'm afraid if you gave these people the choice of the Kingdom of Heaven and a fortnight in Benidorm they'd be down the bank getting their pesetas like a shot.'

'I was afraid it would be like that,' said the vicar gloomily. 'It's going to be very difficult.'

He sat in the garden while she went for the coffee. He liked it there in the hushed sunshine with the enclosing green and the flowers and the squirrel he could still see floating in the trees. St Francis had certainly been very fortunate. How would he have fared with Plummers Park?

It was very warm. He undid the back button of his clerical collar and let it sag around his thin neck like a ring about a prize on a hoopla stall. He would do it up later when he went into the streets again, for nothing looked sloppier than a vicar with a drooping collar.

'Yes, vicar, it's a great task that faces you,' boomed Polly cheerfully as she returned with the coffee. 'I'm afraid there aren't many paid-up Christians around here. Still, when Jesus started I suppose he felt very much the same.'

The Reverend Boon pondered this for a moment. He sipped his coffee tentatively. 'How do you feel about it, Mrs Blossom-Smith?' he asked. 'You would be the sort of pillar of strength the church would need over here.'

She smiled extravagantly from beneath the huge buttercup hat. 'I'm very touched that you should ask,' she assured him. 'But I have to confess to being an agnostic, I suppose.'

'How do you mean – "I suppose"?' he inquired with hope.

'Well,' she hesitated. 'I'm not really a *practising* agnostic. I think, quite honestly, that the best thing I can do is to give you the names of a few people who might be of some help to you.'

'It's as though we were trying to start up some entirely new religion, isn't it?' said Mr Boon sadly. 'Not something that's been going on for two thousand years. It's my fault, I suppose. But I've never been able to think of a way to make contact with the people over here. It's not as though they die or get married. They're married when they get here and they're not ready for death yet. The generations haven't had time to move up. Are there many babies, Mrs Blossom-Smith?'

'Oh yes, quite a few latish ones I think,' she said. 'But most of the wives are reaching their thirties, so they're past the first rush on babies. And when they get here they're all for having a dishwasher and going out to nice places to dinner, so the late addition frequently never arrives in Plummers Park. It's a bit like the London evening papers.'

'What is?'

'You know, how they come in by train and sometimes they never arrive at all. Late editions or late additions, it's all the same.'

He looked at her a little glassily over the small curve of his coffee cup. 'Yes, yes, I see,' he wobbled.

'The first wave of Plummers Park kids is not quite old enough to start begetting yet, although by the look and demeanour of some of them it won't be too long. Whether the trade will come your way, I don't know. They seem to like to get away from here for such things as christenings and weddings. They go back to the places they came from originally. I don't know why. I suppose they think things are more *established* there.'

'Like the Church of England,' sighed Mr Boon.

'Everything,' said Polly consolingly. 'This is such an unreal sort of place. It's manufactured and it's slow to grow. It's just been dumped here in the middle of all these fields and chewing cows. People come here for big sitting-rooms and bright kitchens and something called Blo-hole heating. But it'll take years to puff the breath of life into this baby, vicar. And the people don't expect it. They know it's prefabricated. That's why they go elsewhere for their traditions.'

'What about the people on my . . . the other side?' he asked. 'They have the breath of life. They've been dumped here, as you put it, too.'

'Ah, those are evacuated cockneys,' she said. 'They're different. They'll always *live* as long as there's enough of them to keep each other warm. They live on each other just as they always did when they were in London. They know, by instinct, how to keep the fire burning. Their doors are always open, neighbours in and out, fights and all-pals-together. All that sort of thing. The people over here don't barge into each other's houses to borrow a squeeze of the bluebag or half a pound of margarine. Even if they live next door they talk on the telephone. They're a new breed, you see, and even *they're* not sure what they're like.'

'My goodness, you seem to know them very well,' said the vicar, professional admiration lighting his sombre face.

'Oh, I've had a good look at them,' she laughed. 'They all think I'm potty, of course. I've got a funny name and I live in this draughty old house and I do clay modelling and sculpting and that sort of suspicious activity.' She looked at him uncertainly. 'Actually, vicar, I've made a special study of Flat-Roof Man, as I call him, and I'm modelling him at this moment. Would you like to see him?'

'Yes, I really would,' said the Reverend Boon sincerely. 'It might help me to recognize him, as it were. I'd also be very grateful for those names and addresses, Mrs Blossom-Smith.'

'Of course. Let me tell you now. I don't know these people's religious convictions, you understand. It's not something that's very widely discussed here. If you asked me their feelings about the rates or the preference in motor-cars I might be able to help. But they're the *sort* of people who could be useful, if you know what I mean.'

'I understand very well,' said the Reverend Boon. He produced a pencil, which he wet with a businesslike flick across his tongue.

She watched the small action with amused curiosity; he looked up and saw her expression and realized immediately why she smiled. 'Wetting the pencil,' he acknowledged with a sigh. 'Yes, that must come from working on the other side. Over here, I suppose, only meter readers and plumbers do that sort of thing. It sort of gives me away, do you think?'

'Over here,' said Polly kindly, 'the felt pen is the thing right now. Licking the end of the pencil might *just* put them off a shade.'

'It would betray me,' he agreed sadly. He smiled at her: 'This is something like training as an agent to drop into Occupied France during the war. It's exciting in that way too, I suppose.'

'If you knew all about the latest Alfa Romeo or you could claim to have met one of the Beatles it might help to gain sympathy, to identify with them,' she said helpfully.

'The Beatles? But surely, aren't they old hat now? The teenagers over the other side laugh when you mention the Beatles. I've tried it.'

She nodded. 'Exactly. That's the difference. Over here they're busy beatifying them. They are spoken of in the very same breath as Mozart.'

'Ah,' he said. 'Now we may be on to something. In a modest way I'm considered to be something of an expert on chamber music. I even wrote a small tract on Vivaldi. Would that be a let-in, or wouldn't it?'

'Vivaldi might be taken for the ice-cream man. Stick to Mozart,' she advised. 'And then only in relation to the Beatles.'

'I see. I shall have to tread warily, won't I?'

'You may be all right,' she said, regarding him carefully. Then she added: 'As a sort of curiosity.'

He looked down the front of himself from the witless grin of his sagging clerical collar through his crumpled khaki bush-shirt and olive-green shorts to the woollen socks and sandals projecting from the ends of his white straight legs. 'A curiosity?' he said.

'Yes, and a good thing it would be for you. The people here, well, they like to grasp on to *something*. They're all seeking something because they're so new to it all. It sounds very patronizing I know, vicar, and I don't mean to be, but that would be your major chance. They might *take* to you because you are part of something *old*, something *established*. There's a piece of wall in the pub which is said to be medieval, although I have my doubts. Believe me, St Albans cathedral is not more sacred. *That* could be your way in.'

'Could I have the names, please?' asked the clergyman.

'Oh, now I've upset you,' said Polly, truly concerned. She reached out and patted him on his bib. 'I didn't mean to. I'm so sorry.'

'No, not at all, Mrs Blossom-Smith,' he replied. 'It's just that the whole operation looks more complicated than even I had believed.' He paused and spread his pale hands. 'As you say, they're a new breed of people. They're not like my people over the line, they're not like settled suburbanites, they're not like people who live in old places like St Albans. They're something completely new and different. I suppose I should pray about it.' He glanced at her. 'Later, of course.'

'Let me tell you the names,' she said hurriedly as though he might fall on his knees immediately. 'First there's a man called Ernest Rollett. His name suits him. He undoubtedly is a rather earnest man. Always canvassing for this or protesting about that. I can't vouch for his Christianity, but I feel sure if you offered him some sort of official position, as church secretary on this side or something of that nature, he might well be your chap.'

Wetting his pencil again, looking up guiltily, and then pressing the lead with unseemly hardness into his notebook, the Reverend Boon took note of the name.

'Simon Grant,' added Polly. 'He's another. Always talking very seriously at parties and what-have-you about local issues. Very opinionated, but he's young and he has an attractive wife. She would get the children to Sunday School, especially the lads. He lives just down the road from Mr Rollett at Risingfield, although you'll have to ask because I don't know the exact numbers. Then there's Gomer John at the sub-post office. He's a bit wet, I always think, but he's Welsh and they're often religious, aren't they?'

The vicar wrote industriously. 'Yes, I've seen the chap in the sub-post office. He asked me once about how one became a missionary in Polynesia, but I didn't know. He's certainly a possible. Anyone else?'

Polly hesitated. 'Well, there is,' she said. 'It's a long shot though. His name is Andrew Maiby. He's a reporter on the newspaper in Watford and he lives at Upmeadow. I don't know why I'm suggesting him. It's just he seems to be a thoughtful person, and I think he's kind. I believe he would like to be a good man. He's certainly looking for somewhere to go.'

'You mean he's moving from here?'

Polly nearly said: 'No, stupid fool!' Instead she said: 'No, I mean spiritually. He's a bit lost, I think.'

'I will make you fishers of men,' quoted Mr Boon writing down Andrew's name.

When he had finished his jotting, Polly said: 'Would you really like to see my sculpture? It might give you some notion of recognizing your quarry, so to speak.'

'Yes, yes, I would love that. That's very kind.'

'It's upstairs,' she said, leading the way. 'In my bedroom, I'm afraid. Still, I suppose you are used to going into strange bedrooms.' Decently she added: 'Visiting the sick and suchlike.'

'Oh yes, indeed,' agreed the Reverend Boon, trying to remember the last time anyone asked him into a bedroom. He hurried after her, sniffing familiarly at the churchy dust hanging in the gloomed air of the house. She banged up the stairs ahead of him shouting, 'I sometimes work from bed, you see. Whenever I get inspiration.'

'Oh yes,' he called after her. 'I do the same.'

She stopped and turned around: 'You work from bed?'

'Oh no! When I get the inspiration.'

'Ooooops! Sorry. Right, here we are.'

The curtains were open wide and the first thing the vicar saw was the spread and sunlit view of almost the whole of the Plummers Park landscape. He went to the window and looked on it. 'And the devil took him up into a high mountain and showed to him all the Kingdoms of the Earth,' he mused aloud.

'Thank you, vicar.'

'Oh dear, my dear Mrs Blossom-Smith. We seem to get at cross purposes all the time! I was merely quoting. I didn't mean that you were the . . . er . . . devil.'

But he saw she was laughing. 'I'm afraid the view isn't all the Kingdoms of the Earth either,' she said. 'Just Plummers Park estate.' She sighed and fitting her big hands into her substantial hips she viewed it with him. 'It's like a tented city, isn't it?' she observed. 'Wake up tomorrow and they might have all crept away in the night.'

'That would solve the problem for me,' said Mr Boon wistfully. 'Now please let me see your sculpture.'

She was standing beside her untidy bed and with a little flourish, one of the few *small* movements of which she was capable, she flicked away a drape from her model. 'Presenting Flat-Roof Man,' she announced.

The vicar was both impressed and nonplussed by what he saw. The work was strong and individual. 'Very fine,' he nodded. 'Really very fine. You are most talented, Mrs Blossom-Smith.'

She swallowed the compliment easily. 'I'm not bad, I suppose,' she beamed. 'The different parts of the anatomy were taken from different models. All residents here on this estate.'

'Real men?' he exclaimed. 'And they came up here and . . . and . . . sat for you?'

'Loved it,' she confided. 'It's curiosity value, you see. This is what I meant. The face and the head are from a chap who lives at Upmeadow, and the trunk and the arms and legs are spread out all over the place. It's like a dismemberment in reverse.'

'Indeed, indeed,' said the vicar sagely.

'You notice that he is incomplete, vicar.'

The Reverend Boon found himself backing away from her.

'Yes,' he said, 'I had observed that.'

She gave a fat giggle. 'Don't worry, I'm not asking for volunteers. I have someone in mind. The difficulty is – capturing him.'

'Of course,' agreed the vicar as though he understood fully. 'Flat-Roof Man would look very odd left like that.'

'I suppose I could exhibit him as he is and suggest that Flat-

Roof Man is sexless,' she said. 'But it would not be true. There's even an individual form of sexuality about here. It's not the Saturday-night grunt and groan of your other parishioners, vicar. Nor is it the prim jiggery-pokery of ordinary suburbia. Here, vicar, it looks so . . . so bland, look out of the window and see.'

He turned and they both walked to the window. 'Bland,' she repeated. 'But it seethes with unsatisfied demands and emotions. If this place ran amok, vicar, the Borgias would look like tea-party people.'

He looked at her, worried, and saw she was serious. 'It looks innocent enough,' he said. The raft roofs floated down and up and down again over the crammed landscape, trees and telegraph poles and street lights projecting between them like the arms of drowning people. All was sun and silence. 'All those people,' he whispered wistfully. 'Hundreds of souls. Waiting, just waiting for something.'

'I'd get out there before someone like the Hare Krishna rabble do,' she advised. 'If people don't believe in something they'll have anything.'

Hercules the tramp, hunched like the perpetual handle over his dogged perambulator, progressed along Cowacre below them. The air was so quiet they could hear the rhythmic squeak of the pram's wheels.

'Hercules,' nodded Polly in introduction. 'The conscience of Plummers Park you could call him. He pushes that pram around here day in and day out and the people give him things. He's their charity, their let-out. But only him. He's the *local* tramp. Another one would be ignored or hounded out.'

'I woulder if he's a Christian?' mused the Reverend Boon. 'He would be most valuable.'

'If cleanliness is next to Godliness, I doubt it. Anyway, he used to be a car dealer. But he's been *adopted* around here. If you could be adopted like that . . .'

'I see, I see,' sighed the vicar. 'To be accepted. That's what it needs.'

'We have another itinerant,' said Polly. 'A French onion seller, the most gorgeous man. Eyes, hair, biceps, the most magnificent thorax you ever did see. He's Mephistopheles, I think. Yes, Mephistopheles, with his dangling onions and his bicycle. You can almost imagine the man wearing wicked horns. The women are mesmerized and terrified by him.'

'In other words he's a moral danger?'

'No. In a strange way I think not. It's the Plummers Park thing again. I can't see any housewife around here bringing herself to have an affair with a man who habitually uses a bike.'

9

Miss Dora Jankin, a short, rude woman, was headmistress of Plummers Park Primary School, which many of the young of the estate attended. Later, if they did not attain a grammar school scholarship, they were often farmed out to surrounding private schools, thus circumnavigating the necessity for them to attend the local secondary modern school with the children from the council houses.

It was school sports day and all about her children ran knock-kneed with eggs balanced on the ends of spoons, fell heavily over ropes they were intended to leap, and scampered races urged on by the screams of competitive and near-hysterical mothers. She viewed it all with distaste. Mothers and children, in that order, were the reasons why Miss Jankin had never married and had a family. Children in baggy shorts snivelled and hung around her as she made a tour of the picnic panic of the sports field. Her school, behind her shoulder, was one of those which might easily have been assembled from a kit. She was not in the best of tempers and she would be greatly glad when the holidays arrived so she could give full attention to the miniature dachshunds she bred so devotedly. They were much more rewarding than children.

She snorted like a compact dragon when she saw the Reverend Boon approaching across the sports field, smiling like a lost imbecile, patting infant heads indiscriminately. He walked un-heedingly into the three-legged race just at the moment it had started and wondered why his blessings and benedictions aroused such fury in both children and parents.

He looked up from his reckless route at the second steamy snort from the advancing headmistress. 'Ho, ho!' shouted Miss Jankin. 'All things bright and beautiful! Look what the sun's brought out!'

He dithered across to her, knowing that of all the oddments on the field his shorts were the baggiest and his legs the whitest. 'Good afternoon, Miss Jankin,' he said. 'What a lovely day.'

She snorted aside the greeting. 'If you did at Kempton Park what you've just done to our three-legged race you'd be warned off the damned course,' she told him.

'Oh dear, what was that? What did I do?'

'Messed up the start doing your blessings bit,' said the head-mistress. 'That's a very dangerous race to interrupt too. Pride can be hurt, bets lost, and little legs broken.'

'That's terrible,' agreed the Reverend Boon, his hand going to his mouth. 'I must go back and apologize.'

'Don't do that,' she warned. 'They've just got their limbs sorted out. They're starting. The mothers might ravage you.'

The clergyman considered her miserably. He had not had a good day. He was sweating and he wished now that he had acknowledged the cowardice of his convictions and worn an open-necked shirt instead of his collar and bib. He had undone the back button and it was damp and sagging now. Nor had his visits been greatly successful. Mr Ernest Rollett, whom he had found at home, had agreed to become an officer of his church as soon as they built the church right behind his house instead of the school for maladjusteds. Neither Simon Grant nor Andrew Maiby had been at home and Gomer John had said that he intended to join the navy if his mam would let him.

But he gazed around the field with attempted ecclesiastical benignity. 'What a lovely day for it, headmistress,' he observed.

'For what? This rubbish?' She glared at him as though he were mad. 'As far as I am concerned it's one day nearer the holidays when I can get out of this howling biscuit-tin they call a school and look after my dogs. What are you doing over on this side anyway? I'm surprised you haven't got a native guide with you.'

'Yes, yes, Miss Jankin, I fear you are right,' admitted Mr Boon dolefully. 'That is the reason I'm here. I have failed so thoroughly with these new people. I thought if I came over and made some contacts, it might encourage people to come to church.'

'You'll be lucky,' she leered brutally. 'The blinding kids only come to school because it's the law. The parents are so damned indulgent they'd let them squat in front of a television set all day if they could. It would save the mothers having to get up early. Some of them want a fleet of buses to tour the district to bring the brats here and take them back in the afternoons, thus relieving the parents of further responsibility.'

'That's not true of all the people, surely?'

'It's true of enough of them,' she replied. 'And then because little Johnny can't read like the kid next-door who's three years older, and brilliant, they come up and threaten me with their fists.'

'Oh dear, oh dear, headmistress, you sound so bitter. Surely middle-class children like this ...'

'Middle-class my backside! I've worked in the East End and it was easy-street to this. At least you knew where you were with the slum kids. They were rough but you accepted it and there were ways of handling them. These kids are so sneaky. I caught a nine-year-old boy urinating in the bloody staff teapot the other day.'

'How revolting!'

'It didn't make the Typhoo taste any better, believe me.'

'You tasted ... you still used the pot?'

'I made the little sod wash it out but I wouldn't be surprised if he wee-weed in it again afterwards. Elevenses tasted dreadful and Miss Thornby had stomach pains in the afternoon.'

'Oh dear.'

'Vicar, for Christ's sake, stop saying "Oh dear".'

'Really, Miss Jankin.'

'Yes, really. I'm sorry, vicar, but I can't deal in your ephemerals. It's all happening right here, around my blasted feet. Go about your missionary work, with pleasure, but I have to go and organize the sack race. The way I feel I might put the bags over the little swines' heads.'

She strode away and the vicar, further defeated, went dejectedly out into the field, smiling this way and that, trying to engage wary mothers in conversations which he hoped would, by some touch from God, turn in the direction of local religious life. But no help arrived and when he blatantly opened the subject himself he found the women evasive. They could not promise anything regarding anything, particularly church, before consulting their husbands on their return from work. Others made excuses. The church was too far, Sunday school would entail their children walking through dangerous streets on the other side of the railway. There were other difficulties. 'If church was any other day but Sunday it wouldn't be so bad,' a young mother sighed.

The vicar wandered disconsolately to where a man was selling ice-cream at the school gate. The vendor was cheerful but blunt. 'What you want then, mate?' he inquired.

Mr Boon thought a Strawberry Trinity sounded appropriate and ordered one. Because of the heat it ran very quickly and he had splashed some on his bib before he caught up with the drippings. Two older girls in the summer uniform dresses of the local grammar school watched him working his tongue around the confection while they waited for their own ice-creams. He smiled with embarrassment and, having contained the pink flow, nodded acknowledgement. 'You're from St John's,' he said.

'Yes, sir,' replied the shorter of the two, who smiled at him brazenly. 'We're helping with the junior sports.'

'Ah, good,' smiled the vicar. He knew that a pimple of pink ice-cream was suddenly sitting like a joke on the point of his nose. He could feel its coldness. He squinted and confirmed it. The girls had seen it too, of course, and were restraining a giggle. He wiped the ice-cream away. 'It's very nice to see older children assisting the young,' he continued.

'We got the day off to do it,' replied the taller girl. She had a dark and serious face and she regarded the vicar's forlorn appearance with real interest. 'You're the Reverend Boon, aren't you. From the church.'

'Yes,' acknowledged the vicar, pleased that he had been recognized. 'I shall be at your prize-giving, with the bishop, at the end of this term. Now, who are you?'

'I'm Lizzie Maiby,' said the shorter girl.

'And I'm Sarah Burville.'

'Ah, yes, now I've heard of you,' said the Reverend Boon. 'Do you have some prizes to come this term?'

'Yes, I believe so.'

'She's won everything,' said Lizzie without envy. 'Haven't you Sarah? She's won so many things she'll have a job to carry them home.'

'Ah, yes, yes,' said the vicar trying to remember. 'I'm sure your headmistress told me something about you last year. She hopes you will go to university. But your mother's ill, isn't she? Your head did say something about her. Is she better?'

A scarlet blush rushed across Sarah's face. Lizzie stared at her. She trembled in the sunshine. 'Yes, thank you,' she said eventually. 'She's much better.'

*

Simon Grant was home early from work. The afternoon children were only just returning from school and the sports field when he walked from the station. His jacket and his tie were off almost as he entered the house.

'Have you tried it on yet?' he asked Ena eagerly.

'No,' she hesitated. 'No I didn't.'

'Well, why not, darling?' She had been sunbathing. Now she was wearing a short light dress. He caught her brown forearms and pulled her to his shirt. He unzipped his trousers and let them fall ridiculously about his ankles as he embraced her.

'You don't hang around do you?' she said. 'You've only been in the house twenty seconds. Don't you want a drink or a cup of tea or something?'

'Let's have the something,' he smirked boyishly. 'All the way home I've been sweating in the train and thinking about you in that body-stocking. I thought you would have tried it on. Why didn't you?'

'I thought it was for our anniversary,' she said.

'It's here! Don't let's wait, baby. Come on, let's go up now.'

'All right,' she agreed with a sad patience he failed to notice. 'Let me give the kitten a drink. He needs a drop.'

'So do I,' said Simon coarsely. He picked up his trousers from the floor and went upstairs. 'Don't forget to bring the right pussy up,' he called down to her. 'And the parcel.'

Ena closed her eyes momentarily, miserably. Still, it was a change for him to pick up his own trousers. She poured the kitten's milk into the saucer and looked out to the garden and the sun-blue sky over the houses. She wondered where Geoff was. She felt very lonely in this house with her husband. Reluctantly she picked up the unwrapped parcel and touched the nylon garment inside with distaste. Then she walked up the stairs.

Simon was lying in the middle of their king-size bed, still wearing his shirt with his penis standing up from beneath it like an admonition. The curtains were closed and the room was humid. The sun seemed to be pushing against the blue curtain fabric, trying to force its way in. From outside came the 4.30 sounds of the Plummers Park children going squeakily home to tea.

'See how I feel,' said Simon nodding down from the pillow to his projection. He was so insensitive he did not even notice how his insensitivity injured her.

Ena nodded: 'I noticed.'

'You don't seem very enthusiastic, darl. Is anything wrong?'

'No, nothing. I've just been a bit tired today, that's all. I thought we were going to leave it until our anniversary. It will be a bit hot wearing that thing.'

'Oh come on, sweetie,' pleaded Simon. 'Don't let me down now. Give me your hand.'

She stretched her fingers towards him smiling wanly through the muted light of the room. He caught them and twirled them about his erection. 'They're cool,' he said. 'Your fingers.'

'Anything would be cool against that,' she said. 'It's burning.'

'Like a poker,' he agreed. 'How can you expect me to wait?'

He pulled her forward while she still grasped him and guided her lips to his. He felt the large breasts, under the short light girlish dress, roll freely forward. He took his mouth from hers and while she still arched above him undid the top pair of buttons of the dress and with both hands pulled out the big right breast from the thin brassière that held it, like a man lifting a puppy from the litter. He laid his tongue against the supple nipple. She released him and his member nuzzled its way under the short skirt of her dress and between her glossy legs. Simon put the breast away and lay back on the pillow, his wife's lovely face and falling fair hair a few inches from his eyes. 'I'd love to have you now, darl,' he said. 'But I'm going to control myself. Will you put the thing on? I want to see how you look in it. I wouldn't mind having a drink.'

'A drink? I thought you said you didn't want one.'

'Well, I sort of fancy just lying back here like a sultan sipping something cool and watching you walk about in the body-stocking.'

'All right,' she sighed. 'I'll get you something. Do you want me to put that garment on in here?'

'No! For goodness sake don't do that,' he said anxiously. 'You'll spoil the effect. Put it on in the other room and put your negligee thing over it. The pink fluffy one that I like. Then you can sort of take it off.'

'In other words, a striptease.'

'Aw, you don't mind, do you?'

'No. No, I don't mind. I'll get you a beer.'

'*Not* a beer! I can't watch my wife cavort while I'm drinking a measly beer. Have we got a lime juice? That's a bit more exotic.'

'We've got some tinned shandy,' she said. 'Will that do?'

'If I didn't know, I'd swear you were trying to mess this up.'

'I'm not. I'll go and get it and put the body-stocking on for you.'

She went and he lay luxuriating in the private, dimmed warmth of the room and the anticipation of what was to come. He looked down at his penis with proprietorial satisfaction and rolled his body one way and another so that the member dipped and rose like the mast of a small boat in a choppy sea. He thought of his wife's fine untiring body, and smiled. He was a happy man. There were not many wives around Plummers Park who would look anything in a body-stocking.

He tried to imagine what it would be like. The advertisement in the Sunday paper had indicated it was the last word in glamorous garments, with an erotic aperture for each breast and what the wording described as enticing divided legs.

She came back into the bedroom then, lovely in the pink robe he liked so much, her hair arranged, a glass in her hands, her legs black-nyloned. He took the glass from her. 'No shoes?' he said. 'Why don't you put those very high heels on.'

'Will you want me to do high kicks so you can see the grating they've left between the legs.'

'Oh, don't be so mean, Ena darling.'

'Well,' she said more softly, 'it *is* a bit of a creation, Simon. I was embarrassed to put it on. Do we *need* this sort of thing . . .'

'You promised,' he pointed out. She was standing at the bottom of the bed now and he had to keep peering around his own upstand to see her properly.

'All right,' she sighed. 'Do you want me to reveal all now – in a flash?'

'No wait,' said Simon, half sitting up, his drink balanced in one hand. 'Do it properly, lover. With a bit of show.'

She smiled at him for the first time. 'You really are a boy, you know, Simon. You enjoy it so much, don't you? All this.'

'Of course I do. Better than having some sort of formal sex every Sunday afternoon like half the people around here. My God, you know we've seen them wearily drawing the curtains. Right after the Big Match on television. It's fun like we do it. Don't you think it is?'

'Yes,' she said, still smiling a trifle pityingly at him. 'Right, are you ready for this?'

'I'm ready,' he sighed, lying back again. 'On with the show.'

She went along with his wishes now, swaying theatrically and turning her head and then pushing the negligee away from her shoulders, inch by inch until it slipped and dropped away from her. Simon stared at her. Her splendid body – always a surprise and a thrill for him – was entirely cased in the tight black nylon except for the two gaping holes at the front from each of which her breasts thrust spectacularly, the flesh rounded, the tips rosy. She smiled at him. 'How do I look?' she inquired.

'Good God! How do you look?' gasped Simon. *'How do you look?'*

'Coo-ee. Cooooooooooooeeeeee. Cooo . . . Coooooooeeeee.'

The sound came from outside the house and then immediately from within. Someone was yodelling up at the window and then poking their head into the hall.

'Oh, Christ, what's that?' demanded Simon.

'Wait, wait, I'll see,' she whispered.

'Not like that! He'll see.'

'I know, I know.' She caught hold of her dress from the adjoining room and stepped quickly into it.

'Coooeeee. Who's at home?' came the voice from below.

'Fuck,' swore Simon. 'Bloody fuck.'

'Quiet! It's a clergyman,' said Ena, peering down through the curtains. 'You must have left the front door open. He's looking in.'

'Nosy bastard,' complained Simon. 'What are we going to do?'

'You stay here,' said Ena. 'I'll go down.'

'Keep him outside the door, then,' said Simon. 'Once those buggers get in you can never get shot of them.'

She went from the room as the third 'Coooooooooeeeeee' hooted through the house. Simon lay fuming, his manhood collapsed, his fists clenched with frustration.

Swear words hissed from him like short escapes of gas. He could hear the voices from below, the professional hushed bray of the clergyman and the agreeing sounds of Ena. Eventually he heard her coming upstairs. There was a suggestion of amusement on her face as she entered the room. 'You'll have to come down for a minute, Simon,' she said. 'He knows you're in.'

'What in Christ's name does he want?' demanded Simon in a whisper, unconscious of the aptness.

'I think he wants you to become a leader of the church,'

replied Ena. 'You'd better get your trousers on.'

Simon was such that, sexually interrupted though he had been, the thought of some recognition from the church, or any other well-known body, quelled his bad temper. He sat on the side of the bed and a sudden vision of himself in the raiment of an archbishop came to him. Standing like a golden bird before thousands. Quickly he put his lolling organ into his trousers, slipped on his shoes and socks and followed his wife downstairs.

The Reverend Boon, dangling apology, was sitting in one of their Stag armchairs. His shorts hung from his legs like abject flags, his sun-flushed face was choking from his clerical collar which he had buttoned again in the interests of propriety. He greeted Simon with a damp church hand.

'I sincerely hope I am not intruding at an inconvenient time,' said the vicar.

'Not at all,' Simon assured him with a beam.

'When you get in from the city it must be very nice just to put your feet up for a few minutes.'

Ena, who had retreated to the kitchen to get the vicar a lemonade, heard the remark and muttered privately: 'Don't give him ideas about his feet.'

She returned to find her husband and the Reverend Boon in profound and friendly conversation. 'Certainly if I can be of any assistance, as a lay preacher perhaps . . .' Simon was saying.

Ena smiled grimly to herself again. 'What does a lay preacher do, Simon?' she inquired innocently.

'Now, now, darling,' he said putting up his barrier hand. 'If you start getting involved we'll be here for hours. The vicar wants some help in establishing a church over here, that's all.'

'That's all,' repeated the vicar doubtfully. He got in before Simon could speak again. 'What we need is a group of people as a foundation, a rock, a beginning. I think that a young couple such as you could be a great help and influence in Plummers Park.'

'I'm sure we would be delighted,' said Simon blandly. 'Ena is good at organizing teas and suchlike, aren't you, baby?'

She nodded, not so much puzzled as amazed by him. The rampant sultan had been turned with a few ecclesiastical words into a missionary. The vicar, finishing his lemonade, rose politely.

'I won't intrude on you any further,' he said. 'I must get back for my confirmation class anyway. If I'm not there they all escape and go home. I'm afraid enthusiasm is not a strong point at St James the Less.'

'Good name for a church,' said Simon in a businesslike way. 'It's got a sound about it. Did you pick it yourself?'

'No, no,' answered the vicar cautiously. 'That's a matter for the higher authorities. I must be off. Goodbye, Mrs Grant, Mr Grant. God be with you. I shall contact you quite soon.'

They saw him to the front gate and then returned to the house. 'You can't be serious,' said Ena.

'About the church? Of course I'm serious.'

'But you . . . me . . . ?'

'Listen, think of the contacts you make that way. Once you're in you get invited to this, that and the other thing. Dinners, garden parties and the like. You'll have to cover up your boobs, but we could get a lot of kudos like that. Meeting Lord this and Lady that and the odd bishop here and there. It's like in business, you have to *know* people.'

Five minutes later they were on the bed again. 'Now for St Simon the Most,' he boasted. She lay and closed her eyes and felt him enter her. She wanted to tell him she was pregnant but even when they had finished she could not bring herself to do it. She knew how it would upset him. And he was having such a good time.

*

Andrew left the office with studied casualness and walked along the main street. He decided he would stroll by the churchyard, not through it, just to see if she had meant what she said. It was a cooler day with a short furly wind mixing with the sunshine.

The old graves in the churchyard had been grassed over, and girls and men from the offices and shops now lay there sun-bathing above the former inhabitants lying in similar positions in the darkness beneath.

Three times he sauntered deliberately by the wise, worn steps of the entrance but he could not see her. Then, glum with doubt, he turned in through the gate and went slowly along the old path, crazed with the tombstone slabs of two centuries before. Bessie was sitting on a wooden bench talking with a young man in jeans with his shirt open to his navel. Andrew almost walked by but she rose easily and said to the youth, 'I've got to be off now.' She walked alongside Andrew over the old stones.

'Do you think these people who were buried underneath the stones would mind us treading on them like this?' she asked without a greeting, as though they had been conversing for hours.

'They're not really in a position to mind, are they?' Andrew pointed out.

'No. It's a shame really, I think. Having people walking all over your name.' She smiled at him. 'I wondered if you'd come,' she said.

'Oh, I was going through anyway,' he said absently. 'I thought I'd keep a look-out for you.'

'You walked past the gate three times,' she grinned. 'I spotted you. Have you got any sandwiches or anything? I've eaten mine.'

'Er . . . no . . . I don't generally bring sandwiches. I have something in the pub as a rule. That's where I was going. Why don't you come and watch me eat my pork pie? I'll buy you a drink.'

She had stopped and was looking at a memorial tablet on the church wall. 'Have you ever read that, Andrew?' she asked. 'I often look at it.'

'Never read gravestones,' he advised. 'It's fatal. Whatever advice they give, it's too late. A forlorn afterthought. What last-gasp goodies has this one got?'

He leaned forward and read aloud: 'The wonder of the world, the beauty and the power, the shape of things, their colours, lights and shades; these I saw. Look Ye also while life lasts.'

'It's really nice,' said Bessie sadly. 'I think it's ever so nice.'

'It has an icy ring about it when you get a bit older,' answered Andrew.

'You talk as though you're eighty,' she said. 'From the minute I first met you, mate, I could see you were getting the miseries about your age.'

He glanced at her sharply. She was watching him in her half-laughing manner, her face clean with youth, the town sun on her gentle hair. She looked lithe and carefree. Her hand came out to him encouragingly. He felt a groan of joy growing within him.

'Who was that chap?' he asked.

'What chap?'

'The one you were talking to on the bench.'

'I don't know. I was just chatting to him.'

'You kids talk to anybody today, don't you? When I was your age you wouldn't start a conversation with someone like that unless you had *intentions*.'

'What's that mean? Intentions?'

'Well, unless you thought there was something *in it*. It took a lot of guts when I was young to just sit down and talk to someone of the opposite sex and in your own age group. You swallowed several times and then . . .'

'I know – she dropped her lace handkerchief and you picked it up!'

'Go on, have a good laugh. If you want to know the truth, when I was eighteen I *carried* a lace handkerchief around with me – so that if I saw a girl I fancied I used to drop it and pretend I thought it was hers. I'd belt after her and ask her if she'd dropped it.'

'Blimey,' she said admiringly. 'That's not bad. I bet you pulled a few like that.'

'Pulled a few? My God, the richness of the language these days. You make it sound as though it's something to do with teeth.'

'All right, you *had* them then. Is that better?'

'Not much,' grunted Andrew. 'And I didn't *have* them anyway. It wasn't like it is now, or what I'm told it's like now. In those days if you got a kiss on the third date you went home walking three feet above the ground.'

'That's nice,' she approved. 'It's a pity you couldn't talk to people though. Me, I'll talk to anybody.'

'I've noticed. Are you sure you didn't *talk* to anybody at my newspaper? I've tried to find out who stopped that court report going in, but nobody seems to know.'

'Grandad was just lucky,' she shrugged. 'Not that it made much difference: my dad found out dead easy anyway. But at least the neighbours didn't know.'

'Well, *something* happened. You don't get the same thing omitted from both papers by coincidence. I could believe you'd seduced my editor, but the other editor is an old woman.'

She laughed. 'I'm not particular,' she said.

'But you're rude,' he replied. He almost said 'crude' and he changed it at the last syllable.

They had reached the far end of the churchyard now, where the traditional yew tree shaded out over a paved area with tables outside the public-house. She drank half a pint of beer with him and watched him eat his pork pie, refusing to have anything more to eat.

'How do you reckon you get to be a saint?' she said.

He looked up from his pie, not so surprised at her now, to see she was studying the gold lettering on the church notice-board.

'You're too late,' he observed. 'I wouldn't bother if I were you.'

'No, but I mean Saint Adrian, like it says up there. Who was he when he was home?'

'Mostly away,' said Andrew. 'His real name was Nicholas Breakspear and he came from around this area. Probably the council estate.'

'Don't be funny. I'm trying to learn. Did they call the crematorium after him?' she said.

'Yes, they did,' he said encouraged. 'But the name is all around here. He was Adrian, the Fourth or Fifth, I can't remember, the only Englishman ever to become Pope. He had a white palfrey and the Emperor Frederick of Germany kissed his foot in the stirrup.'

'Is that a horse?'

'A palfrey? Yes. Frederick led the horse while Adrian rode it.'

'He must have been a good bloke. I wouldn't mind being a pope if I could have a white 'orse and be led around by an emperor who kissed my feet. I'd reckon that.'

'You've got no chance,' he said.

'Listen,' she added thoughtfully. 'I was thinking about you at work yesterday and I thought it seems a bit funny really – like you being so clever and yet you're only working on a tinpot local rag. Why don't you work for the *Daily Mirror* or one of them?'

'Thanks,' sighed Andrew. 'You sound just like my wife.'

'Your wife's bound to ask you. Can't say I blame her.'

'To start with I don't think I'm clever. I know a few things which I've read in books – all about Nicholas Breakspear for instance because he was a local chap – but whatever I know or I can do is counterbalanced by the fact that I'm bone lazy. I do the easiest thing, the minimum effort for the most amount of pay I can get. Does that answer the question?'

She nodded. 'I'd worked that out already,' she said. 'And I bet you're like that with everything, not just your job.'

'Well, I don't keep a lace handkerchief to drop if I see somebody I fancy. Not now.'

'You ought to read that thing on the tomb again, Andrew,' she advised. 'About looking while you're alive.'

'Oh, I look. Don't get the wrong idea. I'm *looking* all the time.'

'It's just you don't move your arse to *do* anything?'

'A fair assessment.'

'I've got to get back to the shop,' she said rising suddenly. 'It's my half-day tomorrow. Do you want to meet up and go somewhere?'

'Go somewhere?'

'Yes. Just go somewhere. I don't know. Do you want to, or not?'

'Yes,' he said. He hesitated then added, 'Here about the same time?'

'All right,' she nodded. 'I'll be here. I'll try not to talk to anybody.' She bent and picked a daisy at the gate to the churchyard. 'You know why they call this a daisy?' she asked.

'No, I don't.'

'Thank Christ for that. Well, it's because it used to be called the day's-eye. People said it looked at the day from the very minute it opened in the morning. They learned me that at school, anyway.'

*

The next day was suddenly drooping with cloud after two weeks of hot weather. The wind increased about the town and there was a trace of rain at noon. Andrew went to the church-yard and saw her sitting alone in the deserted place, a large carrier-bag on the seat beside her.

'New clothes?' he said.

'No. Some old ones,' she said cheerfully. 'They're for you.'

'Me? Why?'

'Well, I thought, Andrew, you might like to come around to my house for a cup of tea, and since we've got so many nosey bleeding neighbours I thought you wouldn't mind putting these things on.'

'A cup of tea?' he said.

She looked at him steadily. 'Yes, that's what I thought. Nobody else will be in except grandad and he's stuck to the television all the time.'

'What are these things?' He stared at the bag.

She said doubtfully, 'It's a sort of gas-meter reader's out-fit. You know, a cap and a long mackintosh and that. It's a good job the weather's gone off. You'd have looked a scream wearing that heavy mac if it was still hot.'

Andrew touched her arm. It felt very slender under her light coat. 'Here, now, just a minute, Bessie. Isn't all this a bit elaborate?'

'Do you want to come or don't you? To my house?'

'Yes.'

'Have you got a car?'

'No, well yes, but my wife uses it. I don't drive.'

'You don't drive? How do you manage for your work then? Do you run to the scoops?'

'No. We have an office car with a driver. I use that sometimes. We don't have to hurry so much when it's a weekly paper.'

'Christ,' she said studying him. 'I reckon you get worse.'

'I'm sorry, but I don't have a car.'

'I thought everybody had a car.'

'Well, I haven't.'

'Right you are. We'll have to go on the train,' she decided. 'I'll go first. You catch the next train after me and come down the road in this gas-meter man's outfit and come to the front door.'

'Look, couldn't I just be the insurance man, or something?'

'No. If you're in ordinary gear they'll still want to know who you are. It will get around to my dad in no time.'

'I'm getting to like this less all the time.'

'Do you, or don't you?'

'Yes, all right. I've said so. But why don't we go to a hotel . . . and . . . have some tea.'

She looked aghast. 'Hotel?' she whispered as though it were unmentionable. 'If you think I'm going to start creeping into hotels with you, mate, you're mistaken,' she said hotly. 'I'm going now. I'll go home and if you're not at the door in half an hour then I'll wash my hair and forget about it.'

Bessie went. He watched her, the decisive legs, the straight hair dropping over the slim back. She turned towards the station at the churchyard gate and did not look back. Andrew sat down dejectedly with the carrier-bag. He looked with misgivings inside. Folded, the raincoat weighed like a stored tent. The cap was greasy. There was a record book with a wooden back and a pencil. He was amazed and disgusted with himself, but there was an unfamiliar excitement too and he knew he was going to wear it.

*

He knocked at the door and she must have been standing directly behind it because she opened it right away and almost tugged him in. He could hear the old man's ratcheted voice calling: 'Who is it, Bessie? Who is it?'

'Nothing, grandad,' she called after leaving a pause. 'Wrong house.'

She put her finger to her mouth and, eyes laughing at the sight of him in his disguise, she beckoned him quietly from the hall through the small living-room, within a couple of feet of the old man's back. Her grandfather was watching a programme in Spanish on a huge colour television set. It was a crammed room, with narrow channels between the furniture and across one a bamboo and walnut bar, with bottles in clips like ammunition, and bull-fight posters on the wall. He went from the door, through the room and out of another door without the old man knowing a thing. The stairs were linoleumed and he climbed them tentatively until at last he was in her bedroom and the door closed behind them.

'Oh, Andrew,' she whispered, enthralled. 'You look fabulous. I'm crazy about men in uniform.'

'God,' he breathed. 'I never thought I'd ever get involved in anything *quite* like this.'

'You're *not* involved yet,' she said, smiling quietly at him. He returned the smile and she helped him from the great tarpaulin raincoat.

'Where, in God's name, did you get this stuff?' he asked.

'My Uncle Brett,' she said. 'But he don't use it now because he's in the nick. He kept the money from gas meters. It's been hanging in the hall ever since he went.'

'It's a wonder the Gas Board didn't want it back,' said Andrew.

'Well,' she said cautiously. 'He never actually worked for them. That's why he got done. He just made out he did and emptied the meters. The cops brought the mackintosh and the cap and the book back after he'd gone. Don't ask me why. Maybe they're hoping to nab him again as soon as he gets out.'

'There's never a dull moment with you, is there?' He was regarding her carefully. She had a white sweater curving modestly over her bust and a pair of flared red velvet trousers tight around her thighs.

'You say nice things,' she said. She sat on the bed. It was a small room with space enough only for the single bed, a dressing table and a wardrobe. On the wall was a childish painting of a Dutch windmill. The curtains were pulled across the window.

'All right,' he said. 'Where's the tea then?'

'There ain't no tea. It was a trick to get you here.'

He leaned quickly down to her then and they kissed, tenderly, her quiet lips against his grown mouth, their hands friendly on each other's forearms. He bent at the knees and crouched beside her. 'I honestly don't know how all this has happened,' he said. 'But it's doing something for me.'

'I know,' she acknowledged softly. 'It's doin' the same for me. Ever since the time I saw you in the courtroom I wanted this. I don't get much fun living here.'

'There's such a difference between us, ages and everything.'

'That's why I wanted to have you,' she said firmly. 'It's the *difference*. One thing I don't want and that's to talk. I'm going to take my things off. Close your eyes. I'm shy.'

'Now you're *certain*?' he said, touching her face.

'Christ,' she sighed. 'I told you, didn't I? I'm *sure*. If you're not then you'd better get out before I start undressing.'

He kissed her again. She cut it short. 'Close your eyes now,' she said. 'Go on.'

He sat on the edge of the childish bed. 'Can I talk?' he asked.

'You usually do,' she said. 'Don't start on anything too long though. I won't be a tick.'

'You're amazing,' he said sincerely. 'I've never known anyone like you. Honestly, Bessie, I don't know what to do about you.'

'Would you like to adopt me?' she giggled. She paused. 'Now, take a decko.'

He opened his eyes and saw her standing at the foot of the bed, slender, white, naked, smiling at him, her breasts small, their nipples like pink flowers, her stomach long and curved inward and then out to the pubic hill with its brief copse of fair hair. 'There's not much of me,' she apologized.

Andrew found he was trembling. He stood and put his hands out to touch her. She smiled uncertainly, then said brazenly, 'Get your trousers off,' but then, in a moment, fell against him and he engulfed her in his embrace. He felt her, skin and lively flesh, against his chest, her legs slotted between his, her face and hair crushed into his neck. 'Come on Andrew,' she nagged breathlessly in her cockney voice, 'let's see you. Be fair.'

Quickly he undressed. He looked at her and saw a strange blush coming to her face. Eventually they were naked and facing each other. He pulled her to him again and felt his penis spring and lodge easily between her thighs. He was gentle with her, the points of her breasts barely touching his lower chest, her stomach resting against his loins.

'You're sure?' he whispered.

'I'll give you my knee in your crutch if you ask me that again,' she answered. 'I'm *sure*. I'm *sure* I want it. I'm *sure* we're going to have it. I'm *sure* the old boy won't come up the stairs. Anything else you'd like to check.'

'It looks a small bed,' he said mischievously.

She seemed oddly hurt. 'It is, but we don't all live in posh houses. It had to fit the room, didn't it?'

'I didn't mean it like that. I wondered if it would hold us, that's all.'

'It's all there is. I'm scared to use my mum and dad's bed.'

'So am I,' agreed Andrew. He eased her back and she lay, at that moment half afraid it seemed, thin and pale, a half-stopped smile on her lips, anxiety in her eyes. He eased her legs apart and leaned forward and kissed her on her clump of hair.

'No,' she said immediately. 'I don't want any of that. I want it properly.'

They had it properly. There were few preliminaries. He merely leaned towards her and sank deep into her, seeing the expression of relief and gladness flow across her face as he did so. Still arched away from her with most of his weight on his forearms he dropped his head forward so that his face fell into her hair and her neck. They lay savouring the suspended luxury of it for a while and then he began to move. She was very undemonstrative through it all. As though she were intent on committing it to memory. When they lay together after their climax, she said: 'It took forty-three before you fired. Well, forty-three and the last one which you could reckon to be a half, I suppose.'

'Fired? Oh, you counted?'

'Yes, I nearly always do.'

'I see. Was I up to standard?'

'Lovely,' she said, kissing his face. 'I had a fabulous come.'

'Good.' He eased himself away from her. Then without looking directly at her he said: 'Have you done this a lot then.'

'A fair amount,' she answered readily. 'Have you?'

'I'm married,' he said.

'Excuses, excuses,' she giggled. 'Answer the question. Have you?'

'Well, yes. On and off, I suppose.'

'I bet you've never had anyone as young as me. Eighteen.'

'No. I haven't.'

'I've never had anybody as old as you either,' she said, cocking her head as though trying to remember. She glanced at him and smirked at his expression. 'Worse luck,' she assured. She leaned towards him on her elbow, her small breasts dropping to the left only slightly like the eyes of his dog when it looked to one side. 'When you're old, well older, does it make you very tired having sex?'

'Tiredish,' he said.

'It makes me feel I could run up to the sky,' she said. 'Honest.'

'I don't think I've got much time to drop off, and neither have you for running up to the sky,' he observed. 'I don't think I ought to hang around too long.'

'You're *not* going yet,' she said stubbornly. 'What do you think this is, a bit behind the bike shed?'

'But what if anyone comes back, your parents?'

'They won't. They're both on overtime tonight. They're going to Spain next week and they're grabbing all the money they can. They won't be back yet.'

He was about to mention the old man sitting downstairs when a disembodied voice groaned up through the landing: 'Bessie, Bessie.'

'What d'you want?' she called back unruffled. She put her face only a little closer to Andrew's and said: 'He'll never get up here, don't worry. He did once and the silly old sod fell arse over tip all the way down. So he won't now.' She turned her mouth away from him again and shouted: 'Grandad, what's the matter?'

'I want some fags, Bessie,' came the painful voice. It sounded as though it were coming from a deeply-welled spiral staircase instead of a few feet from the bedroom door. 'I want some fags. I ain't got no scratch.'

'He's got scratch all right,' she muttered, crawling on all fours from the bed. 'He's always bleeding scratching.' Andrew watched her from the bed. She went like a wraith across the linoleumed floor to where her handbag was sitting on the dressing table. She took some money from her purse and went lightly to the door. "Ere y'are,' she called, and tossed the coins down the stairs. Shutting the door quietly and firmly she returned to the bed.

'Bessie!' complained the voice again. 'Bessie! It's another three. I ain't got nuffink.'

'Christ,' she swore. She slipped across the bed again and looked in her purse. 'I haven't got three,' she said to Andrew. 'He'll never bring back the change from ten. Have you got any?'

'Have a look in my gas-man's coat,' he advised. 'I put my small change in the pocket when I changed into it.' She laughed, mischievously and silently at him and felt in the wide, rough pocket, producing some brown coins. She examined them. 'Blimey,' she said. 'There's one of the old pennies in here. That's not yours, is it?'

'No,' he answered. 'I cashed all my old ones in.' His head was on her pillow which was embroidered with a bluebird, and he watched her with a subdued amazement. She went to the door, stepping like a fawn. "Ere?' she bellowed down the stairs. "Ere's the other three. Now bugger off. I'm washing my hair.'

She flung the coins and Andrew heard them bounce on the linoleum and then the old man's grunts as he sought to retrieve them. She waited by the door and after a minute or so opened it a fraction and looked down through the aperture. Satisfied that her grandfather had gone she turned with her wan smile and regarded him. 'You asleep?' she inquired softly.

'No,' he said. 'I was watching you.'

'Do I look all right without no clothes?'

'Beautiful,' he replied.

'That's gone to sleep even if you're not,' she said, coming on to the small bed on all fours, her little breasts hanging below her like an animal's. She put her finger under his penis and lifted it. 'Poor Tired Tim,' she said. 'Let me give him a kiss.'

She put her lips softly to the implement's head and laughed at the reaction under her nose. 'That woke him up, didn't it just?' she said.

He thought she might do something further, but she did not and he was willing to lie and watch her do what she wished. She lay flat on him, her thin form hardly brushing his flesh, then began to crawl upwards, an inch at a time until their faces were together. 'Let's have a bit of a lie like this,' she suggested. He nodded against her cheek and put his hands protectively over the small humps of the backside. 'Put him in,' she said. 'But don't do nothing yet. Let's have a chat.'

She felt under her as she was speaking and catching his member in her right fingers guided it like a short hose to her place. Then she backed up, moved on to it, and they lay there hooked in the dim afternoon light of the small room.

'Now don't do anything silly,' she warned. 'Just have a natter.'

'What do you want to talk about?'

'Anything.' She came to a decision. 'Where did you get changed into the gas-man's stuff?'

'That wasn't easy,' he grunted. 'God, if anybody had told me yesterday I'd be walking up Morrison Way in a thick mac and a peaked cap I'd have said they were mad.'

'Wasn't it worth it?'

'Every frightened step,' he smiled. 'I've still got to get out of here yet.'

'Blimey I hadn't thought about that. What you going to do, Andrew?'

'I'll go out like I came in,' he said like an old campaigner. 'And I'll take the stuff off in a phone-box just up from the station. I put it on in there and it doesn't take a moment. You'll have to follow me and pick it up from the phone-box.'

'Right. That's good. I reckon you're really enjoying this.'

'Well, you're winning me round,' he smiled.

'What else shall we talk about?'

He thought, then suggested. 'Where are your parents going on holiday?'

She gave a brief laugh. 'Parents?' she said. 'It's funny but over here we never call them parents. They're mums and dads. It's when you get over your side they're called parents.'

'I see. Your mum and dad, then.'

'They're going to Spain. They always go to Lloret. They like it there because there's pubs and things. They always go to the same hotel and they come back ever so brown and they win the frog races and the tango championship.'

'I see. It's well worth their while going then,' he said eventually. 'To win the frog races and the tango championship.'

She examined his expression anxiously. 'You're not taking the piss, are you?' she inquired.

'No, of course I'm not.'

'Well, you'd better not. They practise all the winter for their holidays. They have strings stretched out along the passage and they jerk these cardboard frogs on them. Every time you jerk the string it sort of jolts them along, and when they're at Lloret they have races in the hotel and they always win it, easy. They win quids like that. And they really like the tango. Love it, they do. They practise it downstairs, in and out of the furniture.' She moved her head violently one way, then the other, as tango dancers do, but she was very serious about it – poised over his body, her head just lifted, her nipples nibbling his chest.

'They must be pretty good then, eh?' he said. 'And yet, somehow, your dad doesn't look the tangoing sort, does he?'

'Oh, they're fabulous,' she sighed. 'I wish I could do it. My mum's ever so small too. She's only a squinchy five foot and you've seen how big he is. He whisks her around all over the place.'

'He'll whisk me around all over the place if he catches me here,' said Andrew.

'He would too,' she replied as though she would approve,

'my dad. They won't be back yet, though, so stop bothering.'
She looked at him sagely. 'Do you want to start doing it again
now?' she inquired.

'We could try it.'

'I reckon we could. You lie still and let me do the moving.
I want to start and stop and keep on starting and stopping until
we can't stand it any more.'

She began to move, very slightly, on him and then rolled
easily from one side to the other, before jerking hard at his loins
with sharp predatory jabs. He felt her bottom going like a small
powerful piston. Then she stopped and looked down at him,
smiling brightly. 'Is it nice?' she asked.

He sighed. 'If I'd known it was going to be like this, Bess, I'd
have joined the Gas Board years ago.'

10

By evening the heavy clouds had queued away to the east and
the remainder of the day's sun lingered across the uncaring
cattle in the back fields, mellowed the Plummers Park houses,
and touched the trees with selective grace. Some people were in
their small-portioned gardens, and children were playing on
the waste land and by the sub-post office, but the place was still
largely empty. The cars had been nosed into garages and under
carports, the homing trains had emptied and now the English-
men were in their boxed castles again, most of them not to
emerge until morning.

'Where did you go this afternoon?' asked Audrey. 'I rang the
office and they said you'd gone out but they didn't know where.'

He was quickly grateful she had added the second sentence.
It gave him time to think. 'Oh, *they* wouldn't,' he said with
more ease than he felt. 'They never know a damned thing. I
went up to have a chat with old Fowler, the greenkeeper at the
golf club.' It was a risk, but he did not think she would check.

He had been to see the man the day before.

'The one you were so upset about? Are they going to give him the boot?'

Andrew shook his head. He picked up the evening paper so that he did not have to look at her. 'They think they are, but they're not.'

'Why not?'

'Because he's been there longer than anyone else – and he's clever. He's got a trump card. He knows something – I don't know what it is but he does. He's not worried. He's not as simple as they think.'

'He sounds like the man with the key to the lavatory,' she observed.

'I think he is. Or the key of Life. Maybe both. Maybe they're the same thing.'

'Where else did you go?'

Now he was tempted to face her but he resisted it. God, the intuition of the married woman. He knew if he did not panic, then it would be all right. She didn't know anything but she felt something.

'I had a sniff around after the infamous Plummers Park Flasher,' he said. He walked to the window so he would not have to look directly at her for a few moments more. He told his heart to be quiet and made sure his voice was normal and regulated. 'I had a natter with them at the police station but they're not exactly Scotland Yard calibre across there. They're more worried because they're a couple of lollipop men short at the moment.'

'Do you think it's someone who lives around here?' she asked. He knew then that he was safe, like a man who has trodden the last stepping-stone. She had rejected her intuition, her suspicion, and was ready to push along with the conversation.

'It's got to be,' he said. 'The way he keeps popping up and vanishing so quickly, he's got to live in this area.'

'It's nasty, though,' she grimaced. 'It's not nice for the kids.'

'I expect most of the girls around here would have a laugh at it,' Andrew said. 'I can't see them being very frightened. He must look ridiculous.'

'Lizzie would,' she interrupted brusquely. 'She'd be scared.'

He caught her expression. Her face was a little flushed, half angry. Lizzie always had her tea immediately she came in from school, before doing her homework and then usually going out again. Her parents always ate their evening meal together at the kitchen table, half watching the portable television in between any conversation. Tonight it was on but the sound was switched to below a mumble. 'Lizzie's not been going up to the barge lately, has she?' asked Andrew.

'Not so much,' said Audrey. 'She went up there tonight, though, with Sarah Burville and that fair-haired boy from Sheep-Dip.'

'Sarah Burville, well that's an improvement.'

'I'll say. They were helping at the little school sports yesterday. They seem to be pretty pally. She's a nice kid. It's a crying shame about her mother. I feel sorry for her father too. Fancy coming home to that every night. Anyway, Lizzie and Sarah have gone up there with the boy, what's his name, Whiting, Keith or Ken I think it is. The Reynolds kids seem to be out of it now.'

'Just as well. The rate they were working it wouldn't have been ready before the Flood.'

She smiled. 'I'm not sorry either about the Reynolds boys. She would never have got into any trouble with them, but God help us . . .'

The sentence was truncated by an abrupt howling of dogs outside the window. 'Herbie,' said Andrew, getting up from the table. 'It sounds like the whole pack tonight.'

They went to the window to look out. 'God, Andrew, they've got him!' cried Audrey. 'Rollett's Alsatian's there!'

As she called, Herbie Futter was pulled down by the savage attack of a dozen dogs. The Alsatian, which was normally fenced in Ernest Rollett's garden, and the big black dog from Hedgerows were on top of him. They had caught his coat and he stumbled, and in a moment all the animals were at him and on him barking and biting and rolling him over. Andrew ran for the door calling, 'Get Gerry, over the road.' He took a broom from the cupboard in the hall and ran down the garden path and along the road to where Herbie Futter was almost buried by the savage pile.

Andrew ran at them with the broom held like a lance. He caught the Alsatian in the ribs as he arrived and lifted another animal with his foot, sending it howling. But the pack instinct in them was fully roused and they snarled and bit at him as he tried to get to the old man crouched beneath the pile bleeding hands over head, like a rugby player in the middle of a dangerous scrimmage. Andrew was panting and fearful. He was making no impression on them. Shouting, he swung the broom and then jabbed them, kicking out and trying to grab at the bristling hair with his hands, but they would not back off. The black dog tore his shirt sleeve down and he felt blood running on his forearm. He waded into them then, dropping the broom and flinging them angrily aside, trying to get to Herbie. A small dog went for his face. He kicked the Alsatian again. He was very frightened now. Sweat and blood were in his eyes. He felt the teeth of one against his ear and he punched another on the end of the nose as though he were fighting another man. Then Gerry Scattergood arrived with a hosepipe, picked up at the run from his front garden, charging and squirting the heavy stream of water as he advanced. The dogs, howling still, backed away as Gerry soaked them. With his free hand he was hurling clods of earth and Andrew, relieved now, joined him in the bombardment. Eventually they had all gone, standing barking at the junction with Risingfield, as though regrouping for another attack.

'Bastards,' breathed Gerry. 'Mad bastards.'

Gently he and Andrew picked up Herbie. The old man's face was paper-white and smeared with blood; he was half breathing, half sobbing, his clothes wet from Gerry's hose; he was trembling so much his bones seemed to rattle. Andrew said: 'Take him over to my place, Gerry.'

'I'll carry him,' said Gerry. He lifted the old man up and bore him easily up the path to Andrew's house. 'I'd take him in my place,' he added, 'but my missus is out. So's his wife, I think. I saw her go by about six.'

'Take him in then,' said Andrew. 'We ought to get him look-ed at in hospital. He's no youngster.'

'No, no, no,' Herbie Futter protested feebly, rocking his head. 'My wife will do it. She will do it.'

They took him inside Andrew's house and gave him some brandy. When he had taken a drink, Andrew, who realized he was shaking too, took a swig of the bottle. Cynthia and Geoffrey had come across, and Cynthia bathed Herbie's head while Audrey did the same with the bites and scratches on his face and hands and neck. His trousers and coat were torn. Andrew sat down, pale-faced, with a towel around the gash in his fore-arm. Audrey saw him and pulled the torn shirt back and saw the wound. She kissed him quietly on the cheek and bathed the blood away.

'I think you'll both need a bit of stitching up,' said Geoffrey. 'Gerry's getting the ambulance I think.'

Herbie stared at them, black eyes set in ashen face. 'Fucken dogs,' he groaned. 'I sorry, ladies. Beg pardon. But I kill those fucken bludda dogs.' He lay back heaving. Audrey gave him another sip of brandy and then handed the bottle to Andrew.

They all watched Herbie anxiously. His eyes were closed as he lay back frailly in the chair. The cuts on his forehead and cheek still ran blood. Eventually he looked at his neighbours and gave them a crooked smile. 'You know,' he said slowly. 'In the First War, in Germany, my fadder he had a suit made of the stuff they call shoddy. Yes, shoddy. My two brothers, his sons you understand, killed at the front, and he was walking in Hamburg in his shoddy suit and it rained, you see, and the suit fell to bits on him.' He gave a little shaky laugh. 'Like a funny man. First a sleeve, then a leg from the trousers. It all fell to bits in the rain. And his sons were dead. He sat in the gutter and he cried, my fadder. So what's a little thing like this, hey?'

Audrey suddenly began to cry and so did Cynthia. To An-drew's intense relief he heard the ambulance siren and in a mo-ment the vehicle stopped outside. Gerry came in with the two ambulance men.

'Savaged by dogs,' wondered one as they persuaded Herbie

to lie on their stretcher. One of them looked at Andrew's arm and nodded for him to go also to the ambulance. Andrew felt rather foolish walking through the small assembly of neighbours and excited children who had gathered on the pavement. He could hear children shrieking excitedly down the street. 'Savaged by dogs,' repeated the ambulance man as he and his companion carried Herbie into the vehicle. 'I don't know what the country's coming to.'

*

Jean and Harry Solkiss, thin as pipes in jeans and Western shirts, their customary fingers intertwined, sauntered along Sheep-Dip going towards Risingfield and the meeting which Ernest Rollett had called to discuss the establishment of the school for maladjusted children. Their normal peace was not with them, both were aware of this. Only Harry knew why.

Joy Rowley came from her house and they heard her call back: 'Don't iron too late, mother. He won't need all those shirts this week. 'Bye, 'bye.'

She saw them and smiled. 'Going to the meeting?' she guessed. 'It seems such a nice evening, it's a pity to occupy it gassing.'

'Gassing?'

'Talking,' she said. 'Chin-wagging. But it's got to be done sometime I suppose.'

'Gassing,' said Jean studiously, taking out a dwarf notebook. She wrote the word. 'I guess it's spelt like it sounds?' she asked. 'G-a-s-s-i-n-g?'

'That's right. You're compiling an English oddity dictionary, are you?'

'Right. It's real interesting. Yesterday I found out that twig was not just something on a tree. It means to realize something.'

'You twigged it,' said Joy.

'And chin-wag, I've just *got* to have that beauty.' She wrote it down.

Harry laughed. 'I've been thinking maybe I'd tell her some of the crazy words from the base, but she said she didn't go in for that sort of classification.'

'I think air force words ought to be kept in the air force, like at twenty thousand feet,' Jean answered. 'It's the typical English I'm rooting out.'

Joy Rowley said thoughtfully: 'I hope you don't think *this*, this around here, is typically English. It's a strange thing to all of us, all these big windows and flat roofs and carports and lost-looking people, all just dumped here in the middle of the fields. We're strangers here ourselves. Nowhere else in this country would a self-respecting street allow itself to be called Sheep-Dip, for instance.'

'Yeah, I guess we've worked that out,' agreed Harry. 'It's a little like being on a US base in a foreign country. You're kinda lost. And so are all the other guys.'

'*You* don't seem to belong here,' Jean said to the other woman as though she had just realized. 'It's not the sort of locality . . .'

'To find a wicked actress living without a man,' Joy finished.

'Oh, please, don't get me wrong.'

'Not at all,' said Joy. 'I know you didn't mean that. But I'm an oddity here, even more than most. I hear about it. In a place like this, rooted wives and restless men, I'm as good as a scarlet woman.'

'Oh, please, I really didn't mean that at all!' exclaimed Jean.

'No, Jean didn't mean that,' confirmed Harry. 'She just meant that we imagined an actress would live in some area like Chelsea. Like she said, you don't seem to belong here.'

'Sure,' agreed Jean anxiously. 'That's what I meant.'

'I'm sorry,' smiled Joy. 'Jumping to conclusions, that's me. I'm probably a bit touchy about it at the moment. I came out to this district purposely because I thought there might be some sort of magic about open green fields. English people actually believe that, you know. Like a fool I believed the builders' advertisements.'

'And now you regret it?'

'No, not altogether. I don't suppose I will ever find what I want unless it's on top of a mountain where no one's ever been.' She grinned. 'And then I'd never get my mother up there. Not with her ironing-board and everything.'

'We feel real settled here,' sighed Jean. She glanced at her husband to note the enthusiasm of his nod. It was screwing her up because she knew he was keeping something from her that day. 'We try to keep open minds about everything and to listen and find out what makes a place like this operate – go.'

Joy nodded seriously. 'In that case,' she said. 'When you've drawn some conclusions perhaps you'd let the people around here know. They don't know now. This evening, I fancy, we are to enjoy the spectacle of some fine old English middle-class hypocrisy. Smuggery at its best.'

'Smuggery?' asked Jean, reaching for her notebook.

'An invention of mine, I'm afraid. You're welcome to it if you think it's apt. It means mugging with a smile. They'll say all the right things and then turn the whole thing upside down so that they'll die rather than have a load of maladjusted children on their doorsteps.'

The young Americans stopped walking and looked shocked. 'Oh, no,' Jean said slowly. 'We were going along to see if we could help to get it *established*.'

'You Americans are such nice people,' said Joy. 'Watch for the British tiger.'

'That's sure come as a shock,' ruminated Harry. 'It's a good thing you warned us.'

'Just do some of your watching and listening this evening,' advised Joy. 'It will be an interesting lesson.'

'I wondered why people kinda clammed up when we seemed so enthusiastic about helping,' sighed Jean. 'I guess we should have watched and listened more carefully.' She shook her ponytail thoughtfully. 'On the other hand that nice guy, Andrew, the newspaperman – he didn't seem to be against it, or against us for accepting it like we did.'

'Ah, Andrew,' said Joy. 'I don't know him very well. He seems to want to do the right things but he can't get the steam-up to do them. He flaps his hands at the universe. He's like Don Quixote without a lance or a horse.'

'But he tries,' said Jean.

'He *thinks* about trying,' amended Joy. 'And then sometimes he does try. On Monday he tried to fight off some dogs who were attacking some old boy and he got bitten, so I heard today.

Generally speaking I don't think he has a lot of luck.'

'That's terrible,' said Harry. 'Poor guy. Is he okay?'

'I believe so. He'll be there tonight I expect. Maybe he could rally the forces of humanity and carry the day for the maladjusteds.'

'*You* support the idea?' asked Jean cautiously.

'Yes,' nodded Joy. 'But they'll say it doesn't affect me because I don't have any kids, because I live some distance away from the site, and because I've got a maladjusted mother anyway. In the same way they would say that you were only supporting it because you thought it was the progressive, smart thing to do. And anyway, by the time it's built you will be safe back in America.'

'Jeeze, I never thought I'd hear anyone use the phrase "safe back in America",' grinned Harry.

They had reached the point where Sheep-Dip made an angle and its last section turned towards the tarmac hill of Risingfield. The man with the old open sports car was sprawled on his back in the road, half under the carcass of his vehicle, trying to untangle a fist of barbed wire wound around the front wheel.

His mauve face shuddered from beneath it as they passed. He glowered at them as they nodded, but said nothing and again inched under the running board.

'That was barbed wire,' whispered Harry as they went on. 'Did you see that? Nobody gets barbed wire around a wheel by accident. Not wound around and around like that. That guy's been sabotaged.'

'His wife,' said Joy confidently. 'So I gather. She hates him and she hates his car, although I'm not certain in which order. It's one of those incompatible situations. She's violent and he's peaceful. He'd be better off going to live in sin with the car.'

'Wow, that's really terrible.'

'Revenge,' said Joy thoughtfully, 'echoes through these parts like the sound of somebody chopping trees in a wood. A man, so I heard, burned all his household furniture in the garden, and a woman drilled holes in her husband's bath.'

'That's real sneaky,' agreed Jean.

They turned and walked up the gradual slope of Risingfield,

the American wife in her jeans and pony-tail and with the sharp face looking like a small girl alongside the measured maturity of the Englishwoman. Harry, stooping with the everyday embarrassment of every exceptionally tall man, strode oddly beside them, trying to shorten and adjust his wide strides to their short steps. Risingfield was empty apart from a man hosing down his Austin, and two small children sitting on a low wall, surrounded by the excessive roses of someone's front garden.

'It's so peaceful,' enthused Jean. 'Don't you feel it, Hairy?'

'Empty,' corrected Joy. 'People vanish in these parts. Just disappear. There's a legend that their riches turn to rags after eight in the evening, British Summer Time. But there should be a few at Ernest Rollett's place.'

'Does he have a big house?' asked Harry.

'Same as everybody else,' replied Joy. 'But it won't be in the house. Not the meeting. You can bet it will be in the garden. People will go because they like to have a nose around in their neighbour's places, just to see what they've got, but from what I hear Mrs Rollett will turf them out, if you'll excuse the pun, on the lawn. She'll make the excuse that they thought there would be too many people for the house and as it was a nice evening they thought it would be pleasant in the garden. Then she doesn't have to do too much clearing up afterwards.'

'You seem to have gotten to know this location real quick,' observed Harry.

'Instinct,' said Joy. 'Pure instinct.'

They reached the high fence of the Rollett house and heard the talk of people on the other side, the muffled talk of people at a failed picnic. The American couple glanced acknowledgement at their companion. The high gate was ajar and they walked through to find a vapid group of about thirty sitting self-consciously on small school-like benches sipping the most wan orange squash poured into their glasses from a long enamel sanitary jug.

'Wow, drinks!' enthused Joy secretly to Jean.

Jean smiled, unsure how the remark was meant. 'I'm sure thirsty,' she said politely, and her husband nodded from the top of his stoop. 'Me too, honey.'

The Englishwoman gazed, rapt, into the pale potion plopped into her glass, as though trying to detect a trace of orange in it. 'Is it a fly?' inquired Mrs Rollett, who was dispensing the liquid from the jug like a relief worker at a disaster.

'No, no,' replied Joy. 'No, it's perfectly clear, thank you, Mrs Rollett.' Mrs Rollett went along the ranks of her neighbours seated on their forms, jerking her jug in the manner of someone ministering to the poor and wounded. 'Cheers,' said Joy to Jean and Harry Solkiss.

'Cheers,' they replied, their response stranded between politeness and embarrassment.

'They're bound to have a collection after this,' said Joy. 'To defray expenses, as they say, and to start the fighting fund to stop the maladjusteds in their tracks. Nothing brings out the Dunkirk spirit in the British so much as a threat to their property values.'

Andrew and Audrey came through the gate followed by Geoffrey and Cynthia. Andrew, his arm bandaged to the elbow, smiled at Joy and the Solkiss couple, surveyed the people, the straight forms and the orange squash, and said: 'Blimey, it's Sunday school!'

'How's your arm?' asked Joy. She was already aware of Audrey and Cynthia watching her like the twin muzzles of a shotgun.

'It's like a bit of embroidery,' answered Andrew with a grin. 'Mr Rollett's dog has an artistic bite.'

'It was *his* dog, was it?'

'The starved monster that normally inhabits this garden,' said Andrew evenly. 'But which has been removed to some refuge tonight in case I get my boot up its jacksie.'

'Good evening, Andrew, Audrey, Geoffrey, Cynthia,' intoned Ernest Rollett as he moved to the front of the crouched assembly. 'Arm all right, Andrew?' And then: 'Good evening, everyone.'

The talking stumbled at his opening voice, to an eventual silence spoiled only by Andrew taking a long sucking drink from his glass of insipid orangeade. Ernest looked at him with annoyance as the faces turned towards the sound. 'My God,' said Andrew with loud cheerfulness. 'I *needed* that drink.'

'Perhaps,' pouted Ernest, 'we can get the meeting started.' He looked about him truculently, challenging any disagreements, and was almost immediately interrupted by the arrival of the Reverend Boon, who charged through the high gate like some guilty cleric in a French farce. Faced with thirty strange and instantaneously half-hostile expressions, he smiled through his sweat and mouthed the silent 'Good evenings' while making short stabbing bows from the waist in all directions. He accepted a glass for his orangeade. Mrs Rollett had measured well. The great narrow jug was lifted until it was all but upside down and the final drip of the pale refreshment had riddled into his glass. 'In the nick of time, Mr Boon!' chuffed Mrs Rollett. 'In the nick of time!'

Her husband was beginning the proceedings. 'Ladies and gentlemen, friends,' he began, 'this meeting has been called tonight to discuss the proposed establishment, in the very midst of our homes, of an institution for the maladjusted. The plan is that the open land at the rear of this house, and abutting many of your houses, should be used for the erection of this place. Need I say that such a happening would have a disastrous effect upon this community, upon our daily lives, on the value of our property ...'

'They've called it off.'

It was Andrew's casual remark. It stopped Ernest a few sentences short of his appeal to launch a fighting fund. Everyone turned and looked at him.

'What's that?' asked Ernest brusquely.

'They've abandoned the idea,' repeated Andrew. With some difficulty he took a piece of paper from his inside pocket with his uninjured hand. 'I only heard tonight. I rang my contact at County Hall and told him about this meeting and he said that the plan has been dropped.'

Ernest's mouth had sagged. 'Why ... why didn't you say?' he demanded.

'I've just said,' pointed out Andrew. 'I wanted to hear a bit of your speech, that's all, Ernest. But you're wasting your breath, old lad. The county council committee decided this afternoon that the environment at Plummers Park would not be suitable for the establishment of the home for maladjusted children.'

Somebody began to clap, and Ernest, determined to lead something anyway, applauded with loud exaggeration and urged the others to join in. The sound of the hands was strange over the evening void.

As the applause diminished, Andrew held up a hand. 'I had not quite finished,' he said, glancing at the paper. 'The committee felt that the environment here would not be conducive to the well-being of these children under their care.'

He turned to go out through the gate not bothering whether Audrey or anyone else was following. At the fence he turned and called back. 'Thanks for the drink, Ernest.' Some fool, even then, began to clap.

*

The Reverend Boon walked towards the railway, and the tunnel that led to the council estate, still deeply puzzled by this curious land and these outlandish people. It was dark now. He had spent the last two hours playing chess with Andrew Maiby and tasting the first scotch whisky of his life.

The drink had left him a little light in the head and he hummed a snatch of 'All People That On Earth Do Dwell' to a strong rock beat as he went down Sheep-Dip.

There were few lights in the windows now and apparently nobody about. Then, ahead of him, through the night, four large, white, trotting, naked girls appeared, giggling and wobbling as they ran. He pressed himself back against a hedge in horror and astonishment. They bounded by, pounding, pounds of undressed flesh, great feet smacking on the road. He was witnessing the Plummers Park Nude Au Pair Girls Derby, heavily backed and with twenty pounds to the winner.

The clergyman pulled his jacket about him and fled for the tunnel which led to the country he knew and understood.

11

Bessie climbed the stile with the awkwardness of a non-rider trying to mount a difficult horse. 'Listen,' she said sulkily. 'I didn't want a bleeding walk in the country. I've seen all this stuff before.'

'The canal?' said Andrew helping her down. She descended gracelessly, as though she had four legs. 'You've been along here before then?'

'No, but I've seen it all on the box, haven't I? It's the same. Water and grass and insects buzzing around. At least with the telly you don't get bitten by the things. Andy, I'm not this sort of girl . . .'

'Call me Andy again and I'll give you a nudge into the canal.'

'Sorry, I meant Andrew. But for Christ's sake, Andrew, tell me where we're going. We're wasting a lovely afternoon messing about out here in the country.'

'See that barge just up there. We're going on that.'

'That? You must be joking, mate. You're not getting me on that?'

'Why not, for God's sake?'

'Crummy old thing, that looks. It might take us straight to the bottom.'

'I'll go straight to your bottom in a moment.'

She flushed and then laughed as though released from her anxieties. 'Oh, all right. Anything for a giggle. Is there a bed on it?'

'No. But we'll manage. We might get the odd splinter but we'll pull them out for each other.'

'Shut up! You give me cold shivers.'

'What can I do?' pursued Andrew. 'You won't go to any hotel and I can't do all that carry-on with the gas-man's outfit. Not again. I couldn't think of anywhere else apart from this, except the mortuary, and I thought you might grumble about that.'

'Too bloody right I would,' she grimaced. 'How did you know about this barge thing? How do you know it's not all locked up?'

'A relative of mine has an interest in it,' he replied carefully. He put his arm around her waist, thin and curved sharply inwards beneath her summer dress, her hip-bone projecting like a horn. She pushed herself closer to him and he dropped his fingers so that they slipped into the hip-bone's groove, and then he pushed them further down so he could feel the bun of hair beneath her summer dress and knickers. The towpath was cross-banded with sunshine and the obese shadows of the edging trees. As they walked the shade and the sun moved across them like a slow, moving belt.

'Have you had a lot of affairs, Andrew?' she asked casually.

'No.'

'But you have *had* affairs?'

'You are witnessing the final threshings of a randy old fish,' he muttered.

'Never mind the fairy tales. Have you?'

'I lived with another woman for a while a couple of years ago,' he said. 'Just for a few weeks.'

'Who left? You or her?'

'I left. Not that there was anything wrong with her. We were really absolutely right for each other.'

'Why go back then?'

'Because of my wife, I suppose, and my child. All the reasons people do go back.'

'They're mad. I always think they're mad, going back just because they think it's the right thing to do,' she said. 'I wouldn't go back unless I *wanted* to go. It's no use doing it and then being sorry is it? You screw up everybody then. You've got to do what you want to do. In the end it's best for everybody, all round.'

Andrew nodded and watched the path ahead. 'To yourself be true,' he muttered.

'Well, if you put it like that, yes.'

'Shakespeare put it like that.'

'Well, he was talking sense. He probably had some bother

himself. Everybody has bother at some time. But if you meet somebody and they feel just right, then I reckon you ought to stay with them, you see what I mean.' She paused and then said with almost comic misery: 'We don't feel right together, do we?'

He stopped and turned her shining face to him and kissed her gently. They were alone except for a water-rat beginning to swim across the canal. 'We don't even *look* right,' smiled Andrew.

'There's a rat!' she screamed stamping her feet like a baby. 'Oh God, look at it, Andrew! Yuk! It's all sloppy and wet!'

'So would you be if you lived in there,' pointed out Andrew calmly.

She said 'yuk' again, but subdued now. They watched the animal stroking determinedly and, reaching the other bank, scramble out and disappear into the summer undergrowth.

'He knows where he's going anyway,' said Bessie, the stiffness leaving her frame once the animal had vanished. They walked a few more paces. They were almost at the barge now. 'It's funny,' she mused, 'but my mum and dad are ever so happy. All around we've got neighbours who fight. The people next-door, they throw bloody great heavy metal things at each other – at three o'clock in the morning. You can hear them screaming, effing and blinding, and you can hear the things bashing against the wall. I've never worked out how they get their hands on things like that in the middle of the night. Buckets, all sorts of stuff. I mean, you don't have buckets in the bedroom do you? My dad reckons they take their ammunition upstairs with them every night and then when they have a set-to they bring it out from under the bed and start chucking it.' She laughed. 'He's really funny, my dad. And my mum's nice. And they're happy.' Her voice dropped. 'I'm the only one who's not right in our house.'

Andrew pressed her to him again. They had reached the crude gangplank to the barge. He said. 'You're sure you want to go on.'

'You're always asking me whether I'm *sure* of this or I'm *sure* of that,' she complained. 'I ain't sure of anything. But I'll do it anyway. Did you mean "go on" with you or "go on" this ship?'

'Both,' he laughed. He helped her up the wobbling plank and held her nervous hand as they inched their way along the narrow wooden walk, the wall of the low deck housing pushing against the backs of their legs. Andrew stooped and peered through the odd window at the end, where he and Audrey had seen Lizzie. It had been cleaned and cleared of cobwebs and he could see rolls of sunlight hanging on the walls.

'The door should be open, I hope,' he said as they reached the painted companionway.

'Cor, this is pretty, init?' said Bessie, touching the serpentine decoration on and about the door. 'I go for colours like that. Greens and reds and yellows all flyin' about.'

He almost said: 'So did the barge people.' But he stopped himself and said: 'They're the sort of traditional colours and patterns of the people who used to work and live on the barges in the old days. They even painted their kettles and watering-cans like that.'

'Ever so nice,' she repeated. 'Nice and cheerful.'

'They were cheerful people,' said Andrew. The door was unlocked. He turned the handle stiffly. It opened and they peered into the half-light of the long, dry, low cabin.

'Blimey,' she said, poking her head forward to look further inside. 'Cheerful? I reckon they didn't 'ave much choice. There's no room to scrap in here.'

She shuffled in timidly with Andrew just behind her. He saw that the children had cleaned the inside thoroughly, Sarah Burville's hand he thought, and there were some beer crates, probably purloined from The Jolly Grinder, arranged like chairs in a conversational circle and topped by cushions. An oil lamp hung from the middle beam and there was a second on the floor; in one corner was an indistinct bundle.

'Where're we going to 'ave it?' asked Bessie bluntly.

Andrew, bent like a pilgrim because of the lowness of the roof, shrugged. 'I thought we might manage something,' he confessed. 'But it looks a bit bare, doesn't it? Let's see what this is.' He went to the pile in the corner and found it was a small inflatable rubber dinghy, clean, flat and folded and with a single nylon sail rolled under it.

'It's a dinghy,' he said. 'We could put that down.'

She grinned like an urchin. 'By the time you've blown that up, mate,' she observed, 'you won't have any puff left for nothing else.'

'There's a foot-pump,' he said triumphantly, turning the folded rubber over. 'We'll use that.'

'I hope I don't get seasick, that's all,' she said. 'I generally 'ate boats.' Then, as though the matter was now settled to her satisfaction, she undid the buttons of her dress and pulled it away from her shoulders. It was held about her waist by a belt and it hung down while, without fuss, she unhooked her bra, ran her hands over her nipples and gave herself a furious scratch under the armpit.

Andrew's eyes remained on her. He dropped the foot-pump and, still arched beneath the ceiling, moved towards the girl. She laughed at his stance. 'You look like a hunch-back,' she said.

'I feel like Quasimodo,' he admitted.

'Well I still reckon you look like a hunchback,' she said. 'Or a big ape. You could really be quite scary.'

He stopped because there was a trace of alarm in her face, as though she had suddenly realized, because of the ape posture, that she hardly knew anything about him. He bent forward, not touching her with his hands, and kissed her cleanly, giving her confidence. 'Let me pump this thing up,' he suggested. 'When we're lying down it will be more comfortable.'

'Your trousers are getting all dusty,' she pointed out. 'Why don't you take them off.' She was still naked only to the waist, her dress hanging over from its middle band. As though to get it done quickly before he made any reply, she walked forward, unzipped his fly and tugged his trousers down his legs. Then she knelt and put her narrow arms about his legs, pushed her face and rolled her hair into his groin. 'You've got thick legs,' she muttered with her mouth brushing the end of his agitated penis imprisoned in his underpants. She now reached up and pulled these down so that they joined his trousers in a ruffled pool about his ankles.

'Let me get these off, love,' he said softly. 'Then I'll get this contraption pumped up. It doesn't take a minute.'

The acknowledgement in the final sentence that he had undertaken the operation before, the feel of the pump pedal under his bare feet, once he had got rid of his shoes and socks, brought back to him abruptly the last time he had pumped a rubber dinghy – on the beach at Weymouth when Lizzie was four years old and he and Audrey were content together.

He brushed the image away, annoyed with himself for having conjured it up at all, and pumped steadily with his foot. Bessie, her hands on her narrow naked middle, grinned at him. 'You don't half look funny,' she said. 'Doing that in your shirt tails.'

'It feels a bit strange, Bess,' he said.

'Do I look funny?' she asked, suddenly anxious.

'No. You look . . . sweet. Yes, sweet.'

He had half inflated the dinghy, so that it breathed flabbily. He picked up the nylon sail and threw it across the upturned rubber floor of the boat. 'Your couch, my lady,' he announced.

'That's ever so clever,' she acknowledged. 'Are you sure you haven't done this here before with some other bird?'

'It's not experience,' he said. 'It's ingenuity. If we were on a desert island, Bess, I would surprise you with the things I can do.'

'*You'd* be more surprised at me,' she promised.

'Come on, love,' he said softly.

An unusual intensity came into her face, as though she had been hiding something, ashamed of it, and was now about to relieve herself of that burden. She moved forward half stumbling on to the sagging rubber with its covering sail, knees first, then hands and knees, the dress still like some voluminous skirt about her lower half. Then she eased herself over and lay there smiling up at him in the dry dimness of that enclosed place.

Andrew undid his shirt, threw it off and went down on his knees at the side of her makeshift bed. She put a fond hand on his penis, stroking it as though it were some pet. He reached forward and kissed her nipples, briefly first and then taking each breast and enclosing as much of it as he could accommodate in his mouth. While he was occupied at that end of her she put her hands to her waist and pushed and wriggled her way out of the rest of her clothes. His head still lay across her chest; he moved his extended palm down the straight course of her body, feeling her ribs corrugated beneath the cool layer of skin, feeling the abrupt little hill of flesh that was her stomach and then, with his hand travelling like a train over a smooth country, he pushed his fingers down in the culvert between her barely opened thighs. He rubbed her furrow gently for a while, never taking his head from her breasts, and felt her body's response on his finger-tips.

'You don't arf get me worked up, mate,' she breathed.

'Let me lie beside you,' Andrew muttered, easing himself on to the rubber boat. There was room for them both since it was a dinghy normally meant to carry five persons in a calm sea. He felt his large man's body touched by the slightness of her form, the light sweet smell of her filling his head. His arms encircled her to him as though they sought mutual protection. He felt her flesh at points all along his body. They settled into each other.

'Why do you call me Bess, Andrew?' she asked drowsily.

'You ask questions at the most inconvenient times,' he replied. 'Do I call you Bess?'

'All the time. Always Bess. Is it because it sounds better, well posher, than Bessie?'

'No,' he said, considering the point guiltily. 'Nothing like that. I just like Bess, that's all.'

'I'm silly,' she said. 'There was I thinking it was for the other reason. Like you don't like me calling you Andy instead of Andrew.'

He eased himself a fraction from her. There was already a little sheen of sweat between their bodies and it parted like a cobweb as they came away from each other. 'Have we come here to argue over names?' he said. 'Or would anything do?'

Bessie regarded him sorrowfully. 'I'm sorry,' she said. 'I'm doing my best to bugger it up. I always try to spoil things, even the things I want most. Come back, right up close, Andrew.'

As he moved back to her he felt his compassion stir. 'You're as lost as I am, aren't you, Bessie?' he said.

'Call me Bess,' she whispered.

'I thought you didn't like it.'

'I didn't say that. I was only asking you *why* you did it, that's all. I like to hear it coming from you. Do it again.'

'All right, Bess.' He smiled so close to her cheek that she felt his mouth parting. 'Do you want to call me Andy then?'

'No,' she whispered. 'Let's keep it a bit posh. I'd like it to be like that.' Her voice assumed an attempted refinement. 'Do you wish to have intercourse now, sir?'

'If that's what we're calling it today, yes,' he smiled. He eased himself above her, making sure his weight did not press on to her, and then lowered himself into the recess of her legs. They loved immediately and easily, and they paused and she whispered: 'Can I come on the top deck now, skipper?'

'Aye, aye,' he said. Without taking himself from within her he turned his body carefully below and eased her weightless form up with his arms and a shove or two of his thighs until they had revolved and she was suspended above him. They smiled, congratulating each other on their accomplishment and then she dropped her cheek on his jawbone and said: 'Andrew, can I ask you something?'

'You usually do at this juncture,' he observed, looking up patiently. 'What is it now?'

'Do you like Christmas?'

'Christmas! What a time to ask.'

'Well, I thought I would.'

'Er . . . well, no I don't actually. Now you ask. In fact I would exchange Christmas, New Year, and Pancake Tuesday for just one afternoon of a summer's day. Particularly this afternoon.'

'You're lovely, you are, Andrew.'

'You're not bad yourself.'

'I wasn't really going to ask you about Christmas.'

'I thought you weren't.'

'No, I was going to ask you something else. But I got scared.'

'What is it?'

'We know each other very well, don't we, *really*?'

'Yes, I'd say that,' he agreed patiently. 'Better than some people know each other all their lives.'

'Will you do something, then? One thing?'

'All right. What do you want me to do?'

'Smack my arse.'

'What!' He half jerked up from the horizontal in his amazement, but she pushed him flat again with surprising force.

'Sorry, I mean my bottom.'

'Christ. You are the limit.'

'Well, will you? Quite hard,' she continued hurriedly. 'I've wanted to ask someone before, but if you ask some boy your own age he's bound to think you're kinky or something.'

'Yes,' agreed Andrew, still startled. 'He might too.'

'Go on,' she encouraged. 'Do it then. You've got a big hand.'

'Oh, Bess, what am I going to do with you?' he moaned.

'Smack my arse, I hope.'

'I can't.'

'Go on. Please, I want you to.'

He sighed. 'All right. But I'm not doing it hard.'

'Quite hard,' she insisted quietly.

His hands went around her buttocks from each side, each warm globe just over a handful for him. He held them and rolled them gently, feeling them wobble and brush against each other. Then he withdrew his hands and felt, to his anxiety, her body stiffen with anticipation. He drew his right palm back but it was as though another hidden hand was holding him and he kept it there, a foot from her expectant buttock.

'Come on, then,' she said cheerfully. 'What you hanging around for?'

'I *can't*,' he croaked. 'Honestly, Bess, I simply can't.'

He felt her inner muscles giggle. 'You can do it,' she encouraged wickedly. 'Just force yourself.'

He brought his hand down with a weak flap like the tired movement of a bird's wing and said: '*There*, was that what you wanted?'

'Is *that* all there is?' she inquired.

She eased her face up from his body pushing her hands out for leverage and stared at his confused expression. She was pink-cheeked but confident as ever. 'Are you a man or a wet flannel?' she asked. 'If you're a man do it proper.'

She relaxed against him again and lay there waiting. He gritted his teeth as though it was he who was to get the blow. Then he pulled his right hand back and brought it down smartly on her backside. She gave a truncated squeak and began moving against him. 'Do it again love. A few more.'

He did, bringing his hand up and down against the small portion three times and then again on the other side. It opened a great door in him and he felt his whole sexual gases vibrating and heaving as she plunged more savagely against him with each smack. They climaxed together very quickly and they lay there drained and sweating. He screwed his eyes together and felt his hands caressing the area he had just chastised. Bess began to laugh happily against his neck. She stopped and kissed his jugular vein and said: 'You know, I really enjoyed that.'

'You make it sound like a steak and kidney pie,' he observed wearily from beneath her. His arms went around her strongly then, around her back, and he crushed her to his wet chest with a great feeling of love and regard, kissing her face, and her hair and her eyes.

'Get off,' she protested bashfully. 'You'll muck up me eyes.' He stopped and studied her with an expression short of belief. She returned his look seriously: 'You're ashamed of me, I bet,' she said.

He kissed up at her with tenderness. 'No, Bess,' he said. 'I feel a bit ashamed of myself for doing it, that's all.'

'But I *wanted* it,' she replied, looking down. 'Don't you go and blame yourself. It had to be someone like you. Somebody older.'

'Kraft-Ebbing would understand, I suppose.'

'Don't you go tell *anybody*,' she said alarmed. 'You did it, don't forget. It takes two.'

He laughed. 'I wouldn't tell.'

She looked at him with pleading. 'You liked it as well, didn't you, Andrew? A bit?'

He nodded fondly. 'Of course I did, Bess,' he assured her. 'I don't like the idea of hurting you, that's all.'

'It's not hurting,' she insisted. 'It's like having an icy cold shower. It's a sort of thrill. That's what my parents, my mum and dad, get from the tango. A thrill.'

She eased herself away from him entirely and he looked down the stretched length of her body, the colour of planed soft wood, arched above him as though she were doing press-ups, and admired it again in its slimness, in the unblemished flesh, the cheekiness of the breasts, and the indomitable smile that crowned it. She rolled from him and knelt on the floor. 'Is my bum red?' she asked. She had turned it in his direction and now she shuffled backwards so that he could view it more conveniently. The insides of the backs of her legs were wet, glistening. He touched her with both hands.

'You're a bit pink,' he said. 'But if you don't go around showing people it ought to be all right soon.'

She turned about, still on her hands and knees and bent towards him, kissing his stomach and his groin and then moving her lips lower. 'Sleepy head,' she said.

'I want a cup of tea,' announced Andrew, sitting up.

'Oh, blimey,' she said. '*You*, Andrew! With muffins and strawberry jam, I s'pose!'

'That wouldn't be a bad idea,' he confirmed. 'I'm all for doing things to excess. Get your clothes on.'

She began collecting her garments while he let the air escape from the dinghy, helping it out by pressing his foot on the walls, and began to fold it. Then she found the piece of paper by the beer crate where she had left her shoes.

'Looks like somebody's been here before us,' she said studying the paper with amusement. 'Kids too. Little buggers.' She handed it to Andrew. It was a crude crayon drawing of a naked girl facing a naked boy whose penis bridged the gap between them ambitiously. In the middle was another girl, face on, big-breasted, watching them. Above the first girl was the name 'Lizzie', above the boy 'Ken', and the girl in the middle was labelled 'Sarah'.

Andrew felt a sickness surge in his stomach and his hand trembled as he crushed the paper. Bessie was not watching him. It was nothing to her and she had turned to retrieve her skirt.

He crushed the drawing so hard he felt his nails digging into his palm.

'Fancy kids getting in here and doing that,' said Bessie blithely. She was pulling her dress up her body, wriggling into the waist. 'Still, I s'pose everybody's got to start somewhere.'

He almost shouted at her, but he restrained the impulse and turned away from her so that she would not see his face. She was quickly dressed and, telling him cheerfully to hurry, she hopped out of the companionway and climbed like a child herself on to the roof of the barge. He could hear her running about above his head. Miserably, slowly, he put his clothes on, and then taking a match from the box at the side of the oil lamp on the floor he lit the piece of paper, and then the lamp. He carried it to the trapdoor at the far end of the long cabin, the same well in which his daughter had been standing up to her waist on the evening he had gone there with Audrey. Below was a pile of sacking and a scattering of paint tins. He suspended the lamp over the hole for a moment and then deliberately opened his fingers and let it drop. It broke and the flame burst out. He watched it a moment then shut the trapdoor on it and walked out.

The girl was already ashore on the towpath. 'Tea and muffins,' she called to him as he walked along the deck.

She had not noticed his face and now he attempted to compose it. 'Tea and muffins,' he agreed.

'Cor, Andrew, we're doing all the exciting things today!' she laughed.

They walked along the flower-decked towpath without looking back. Had they done so they would have seen a sliver of smoke seeping out of the timbers of the barge.

12

Plummers Park Golf Club always had a splendid view of the evening. Its clubhouse was far from sumptuous, more like a large bungalow with pieces added without thought to each end, but it spread itself with the grinning comfort of a satisfied man in an armchair on the highest plateau in southern Hertfordshire with views as far as the Chiltern Hills in the north-west and London to the south. Had this been Red Indian country it would have been the natural place to observe smoke signals from Hampstead Heath.

It crouched benignly overlooking fairways dropping away all around, like the pleats of a voluminous skirt. In the dulcet light of the final two hours of the summer's day the greens looked rich, emerald shading to olive; the distributed trees, ash and elm and birch on the course itself, and doyen oaks all around, were draped with late sunshine, and even the difficult bunkers smiled a sandy smile.

Groups of members were out on the course, as slow, distant and indistinct as the crunching sheep in the farm fields beyond. They were observed from the terrace by other members drinking and playing a serious but juvenile game of trying to recognize the identities of players on the remote greens. As pairs and quartets of players completed their contests at the eighteenth hole beneath the clubhouse, they were addressed with the gentle and meaningless buffoonery that is part of an imaginary world.

'Humbled again, Percy!'

'She's killer, that Clementine!'

'You took so long to play that putt I thought you were dead, old boy.'

The players, the majority into middle age but some elderly and some young, walked ritualistically, all smiling, up the path to the terrace and with pleasant weariness joined the drinkers, talkers and watchers there. They were joined by Group Captain Fernie Withers, the secretary, a man with the fierce expression only attained with a florid face and a wall-eye, both of which he had. He ruled the club and the course like a little king, and with a rough charm that is the acquisition of his breed.

'Damned beautiful out there tonight, isn't it, Cartley?' he inquired of one of the returning players, an older man in unsuitable multicolours. The member grinned respectfully and agreed it was, damned beautiful. Since the club was far from exclusive and its members mostly drawn from the minor professional people living in the Ruislip latitude, the secretary treated almost everyone with a sort of jocular aloofness, which they accepted as a part of his former rank of Group Captain.

Bertram Mason, the captain of the club, nicknamed Mauler, was under-sized, bald and mean-eyed. He strode with all the self-importance of a small man in authority on to the terrace, wearing the hues of a varied hors-d'oeuvre, clasping to his little chest a full pint of beer in a tankard that almost obliterated his Shetland pullover.

'We'd better have a word with Fowler this evening, don't you think? Better get it over with,' he said to Withers.

The Group Captain regarded him doubtfully. 'Yes, I suppose we should. You definitely want me to be there, do you?'

'Of course,' replied Mason in his hot small voice. 'Dammit, you're secretary of the club. We'll do it together. We can't let sensitivities stand in the way, you know. He's past it now, he's as good as useless on the course, and we could use that cottage of his. We'll have a good whip-round for him, don't worry.'

'All right,' said the secretary. 'He's working on the third tee. I'll get somebody to fetch him over.'

At that moment the Plummers Park police panda car made as dramatic an entry to the club car-park as it is possible for a panda car to make. It rolled in quickly like a large blue and white ball, sent up a modest hail of asphalt as it came to a skidding halt, and sat panting as two members of the constabulary jumped out.

'Hello, hello,' said Group Captain Withers. 'What's the excitement?'

'Sorry to interrupt you, sir, but it's the Flasher,' said the sergeant in the lead. He glanced with quick alarm at the ladies turned towards him in their terrace seats, and amended it. 'The exposer, sir. We think he's on the golf course.'

'Good God, that indecent chap?' exploded Group Captain Withers. 'On the course. And some of our girls are out there.'

'We'll get him, don't you worry,' vowed the sergeant. 'Before he can do much harm.' He turned to his companion constable. 'Right,' he ordered. 'Fan out.'

The lone PC blinked at this difficult instruction but set off, nevertheless, at a good professional jog, down the first fairway. Before the sergeant could embark in the other direction, Mason slammed his pint of beer down on the rustic table and said: 'We'll assist you. We've got to catch this beast.'

'Indeed!' howled Group Captain Withers, a sudden blood-lust lighting his retired face. 'Come on, chaps. Ladies – inside the clubhouse and stay there until it's safe.'

The men, most of whom had just walked five miles round the course in the sun, began getting hesitantly to their feet. Within a minute Withers and the minute Mauler Mason were leading the posse, each brandishing a golf club and a courageous expression, on a wide encircling movement to drive the Flasher into the waiting net of justice.

*

The Flasher stood trembling behind a holly bush at the back of the thirteenth green. By the very nature of his vice he disliked holly, blackberry or any form of bramble, but this provided his only chance of concealment.

He was dressed in a long fawn mackintosh beneath which he wore only the legs of a pair of trousers. These covered his shins but terminated above the knee, where they were held by elastic. He wore plimsolls and no underwear. Over his face he had pulled the recognized disguise of a nylon stocking which gave his features the look of plasticine, and on his head was a light-coloured canvas hat which he thought he would replace when winter came with a warm cap. He was trembling because he was afraid, as he always was, not only of those who hunted him but of his own compulsion. He had tried most things, gardening, learning German, taking cold baths, reading good books, and in the end, miserable and excited, he always crept back to the old mac and the topless trousers.

The four ladies now approaching the thirteenth green were at once his prey and his predators. He knew that the moment he had accomplished what he had to do he would be on the run like a hare. He had only rarely worked the golf course before for many reasons, one of which was that it was too open. After uncovering he needed quick cover.

Four was also a good number at one exposure. It provided a proportionately greater thrill than the single victim, but was not so many as to turn the quick deft act into a performance for the mass. He judged their ages to be about right too, three of them young women and the fourth mildly round with middle-age. To display it in front of old women was, he felt, unnecessary generosity.

The quartet dithered a little short of the green and one lady had to pitch her ball out of a bunker, but eventually there were four balls on the green. In a moment, the Flasher thought with a quiver, there would be a couple more.

One of the younger women was hunched over her ball, preparing to putt it three feet to the hole, and the other two were intent on her actions, so that it was only the older of the quartet who observed him walk casually from behind the holly tree and open the front of his mackintosh to reveal all his private hangings. With true golf grit and tradition she did not scream, or indeed utter a sound, until her opponent's putt was safely made. Only after the ball had plopped into the hole did her frenzied cry break through the murmurs of approval for the accurate play.

They turned with her pointed finger and saw him standing. He pulled the curtains of his mackintosh wide again and let his appendage look at them and they look at it. Four screams, frightened or baffled at first, then strengthening to sheer fury, issued from the peaceful green. He was an experienced flasher and he knew that this was the time to leave. He bowed politely to the ladies, gave them another quick glimpse, and then in an almost leisurely fashion, trotted away.

Behind him he heard the urgent, ambiguous cry: 'Was it a

member?' Then the summons: 'After him!' which made him increase his pace through the beard of woods. Then he realized he was in trouble. There was a police car on the road behind the course, which was his escape route, and he saw a line of bright men fanned out to cut his retreat the other way. Suddenly frightened he turned and ran through the gorse and undergrowth in the opposite direction, causing untold discomfort to his naked regions. Letting out little squeaks of pain he had covered two hundred yards across this punishing terrain when he saw the unmistakable blue blob of the law ahead. The policeman did not see him, so spinning about he doubled back and then made off at yet another angle. Plunging and sprawling through ever more agonizing undergrowth he suddenly found himself confronted by a police sergeant and the golf club secretary. In panic he turned again as they saw him and ran back towards the other policeman. Sweat was sticking the nylon stocking to his face and his tears of fear were soaking it also. He quivered as he ran, abject terror now making him unheeding when the brambles caught him. The one thing he must not be: exposed.

There was no doubt they were closing in on him. He could hear the men golfers and the unnaturally excited women calling to each other in the thicket. One policeman was blowing his whistle. He decided to make a brave break through the open golf course itself. Fearfully he worked his way along the fringe of the undergrowth and then at the edge of the twelfth fairway essayed his run. His audacity paid off and he was able to make about a hundred yards or more across the open grass before anyone spotted him. Then they were after him in a howling pack. The older ones were tiring, but two younger but fortunately overweight golfers were running with masculine fierceness after him, and one of the young women from the quartet, who must have been something of an athlete, was speeding like a gazelle on an almost parallel course to his. He must not let *her* catch him. That would be ignominy indeed.

His big advantage was his almost total lack of clothing beneath the mackintosh, and the plimsolls on his feet. The golfers without exception were in heavy studded golfing shoes. He went like a ragged hare over the course, his pursuers baying through the quiet evening. He knew that they were enjoying it now. He distinctly heard someone shout 'Tantivy!'

At the incline on the long arm of the course leading up to Fairy Copse his breath began to sag. He turned and saw they were nearer. On the road to his left he observed the pale blue top of the panda car bouncing like an Easter egg beyond the hedge. Sobbing with fear and gulping for breath he stumbled into the thick copse, paused with panicky uncertainty, then turned right, hoping to reach the open sheep fields beyond. But he heard running voices as he reached the fringe of the wood and he knew his escape that way was impossible. The panda car, he reasoned quickly, would be on the road to his left. There was no way to go but straight ahead. The half-idea had been in his mind for some time, now there was nothing else for it. The rumours had reached him. He ran, fell, picked himself up, and then ran again until he reached the rear of the house of Mrs Polly Blossom-Smith. Above the arch leading from the copse to the dusky garden were the vivid words 'The Sanctuary'. The Flasher went in.

*

'For God's sake, sergeant, why didn't you bring tracker dogs?'

The policeman regarded the Group Captain with morose patience: 'We've only got one, sir, Rexie, and he's on leave.'

'On leave! Don't tell me the bloody dogs have leave.'

'They've got to, sir. Regulations. We'd be done by the RSPCA otherwise. The only dog we've got at the station is a stray Pomeranian, and he's not trained for this type of work, sir.'

'There's no need to be facetious, sergeant,' interjected Mauler Mason. 'We are aware that a Pomeranian would not have been suitable. The fact is the swine got away. Four of our women violated . . .'

'Violated, sir?'

'Yes violated, sergeant! Visually violated. It will be rape next.'

'I doubt it, Mr Mason,' intoned the policeman. 'The man

who flashes is very rarely the man who actually *does*. They're a different kettle of fish altogether.'

Group Captain Withers glowered at him: 'We don't have time for amateur psychology now, sergeant. We've got to *do* something about this chap. The girls will be too frightened to go out on the course until he is caught.'

'Human frailty is a difficult thing, sir,' said the sergeant shaking his head. 'I often think that if it was only the other way around – females indecently exposing themselves to males – skirt-lifters instead of shirt-lifters if you see my point, sir – there would be a lot less complaints.'

The secretary and the club captain looked at each other with exploding astonishment. 'Christ almighty, sergeant,' protested Mason. 'Don't sit there philosophizing. What are you going to do? Maybe you had better call in the Yard.'

The sergeant scratched his head industriously. 'We can't do that, I'm afraid, Mr Mason. Anything less than a murder and they get upset and fidgety. He must have given us the slip before he got to the house. Mrs Blossom-Smith had not seen him. I've asked my constable to check on your groundsman, sir.'

'Fowler? For heaven's sake, it wasn't Fowler. He's too old to run like that.'

'I didn't assume it *was* him, sir. It's just he might have some ideas.'

'Well, you'd better ask him soon because he's not going to be here long,' said Mason maliciously.

'Oh, sir?'

'He's retiring,' said Group Captain Withers waving the matter away.

'I see. Well, I suppose he would be. He's getting on. Been up here years, hasn't he? Before all the houses were put up or all these people lived around here. I've always thought he was here first and they built everything else around him. Grand old chap.'

He did not seem to be looking at either of the other men, so the embarrassment and annoyance that flew about their faces missed him. He got up slowly in the unique manner of disappointed policemen everywhere and shook hands with quiet finality first with Mauler Mason and then the Group Captain, as though he could not reasonably expect anything further from the investigation. 'If Chummy returns, sir, then you know . . .'

'Chummy? Who's Chummy?' asked Mason blindly.

The sergeant appeared surprised. 'Chummy? The criminal, the suspect. It's a police word, sir. We call them all Chummy.'

Withers humphed. 'Well, sergeant, if this particular Chummy does return, what chances have we of catching him next time?'

A shrug enveloped the sergeant's body like a wrinkled glove. 'I can't give guarantees. Not for anything. We're watching all the time, but we have our problems too. We've had three lollipop men away and we've had to put constables at the school crossings. And the car keeps playing up.'

'Somehow it all seems a long way from the police series we see on television,' commented Mason.

'It is, sir,' agreed the sergeant sadly. 'It is. If you cared to drop into the station one day you would perceive that a policeman's lot is the pursuit of the trivial. Lost property, lost children, men flashing themselves. Even the houses around here don't attract burglars. They're not established enough. We would welcome a nice murder, sir, just to break the monotony. Our Black Museum, at the moment, has only got the relics of suicides. That's the nearest we get to violent death. No killer to hunt. The victim and the killer are one. It's a story without an end, so you can't tie it up nice and neat.' He turned with a professional weariness to each man and shook his hand again; then, straightening his cap at the door as though he expected someone important to be outside, he went. A moment later they heard him trying to start the panda car.

'What a miserable so-and-so for a policeman,' said Mason.

'The rot's set in right through the country,' agreed Withers. 'They don't seem as enthusiastic as they did before the War.'

Mason glanced at the window. 'Here's Fowler,' he said. 'Will you tell him, or shall I?'

'We'll do it together,' answered Withers unsatisfactorily. 'Don't worry.'

'I'm not worried,' returned Mason sourly. 'I've got more to do than worry about an old man.'

Fowler knocked and came into the office at the secretary's call. He had obviously been home and washed his thin red face and combed the outcrops of hair about his ears. He was a little man, brown and red, but with a wise jauntiness about him like a small old tree.

'Ah, Fowler,' boomed Mason, who was even shorter than the greenkeeper. 'Ah, Fowler, Fowler, Fowler . . .' He paused as though he had forgotten the next line. Then he said: 'Sit down, old chap.'

There was a smile arranged on Fowler's face, as though he were puzzled by the invitation but rather hoped it would turn out for the best.

'Fowler,' began Group Captain Withers when it seemed that nobody else was going to speak. 'Just how long have you been with Plummers Park Golf Club?'

'Many years, Captain,' said Fowler enigmatically. 'Years, years.'

'Yes, well we thought it would be about that. You don't seem to have even signed any sort of formal agreement, any contract, with the club when you came here, terms of employment and suchlike. We can't find anything in the records.'

Fowler lifted his contented eyes. 'No, there wasn't one, Captain. It was a gentleman's agreement.' He turned and smiled at both with confidence and pride as he said the final two words.

'We've been talking about your retirement,' said Mason bluntly. 'You're well over sixty now, aren't you?'

'Well over, sir. Seventy-four.'

'Good gracious! You look jolly well on it,' said Withers.

'It's the nice atmosphere around here, sir. That's what's done it.'

'Yes,' put in Mason, sharply again. 'Now – retirement.'

'I'd like to retire, Mr Mason,' said Fowler quickly, but moving his head slowly to follow the words like a ventriloquist's dummy. 'I've thought about it, I can tell you. I know how these old bones feel early on a frosty morning. But I feel it would be letting you down, sirs. Letting the club down ...'

The two listeners adopted looks of pretence, surprise and pleasure as he spoke and were both ready to interrupt, but there was something dogged about Fowler's delivery, something that advised them he was not going to be interrupted. '... You see, Mr Mason, Captain Withers, I worried a lot about this. I knew I ought to retire because I've worked since I was twelve and a body needs a rest. But I'm worried about the drains.'

An unsurprising silence greeted this remark. Then Withers ventured: 'Drains, Fowler? What drains?'

'The drains of the course, Group Captain. The lot. All the system, all over the course. I'm the only one what knows where they all are. Every inch of them. And I know them by instinct, as you might say. Nobody else knows them. A little bit here and a little bit there, maybe. But I knows every pipe, every cock, every bend. I'm afraid if I went you'd have the course flooded in no time. One storm and that would be that. I couldn't have that on my conscience, now could I?'

Withers turned to see the suburban anger was bursting to get out of Mason's tight mouth. 'Oh come on, Fowler,' said the little man, controlling it. 'Surely there are plans of the drainage system.'

'Disappeared before the War, sir. Vanished. Never found. That's what's been worrying me. I'd draw a plan for you, sir, and then I could retire happy and contented, but I'm no hand at drawing and I wouldn't get it right. It's all done by instinct, now. Like playing the violin, I suppose. By touch, if you understand me.'

The two men understood him. He shook his head, for his sorrow seemed to have deepened. 'The only thing I can offer, sir, is to try and teach somebody younger the lay-out.' Their faces brightened but fell again when he added: 'A little bit at a time.'

'How long would that take?' asked Withers.

'Years, sir. I only hope I'm spared to pass on all the knowledge.'

'We hope so too, Fowler,' said the Group Captain, glancing sideways at the thoroughly depressed Mason. 'Don't we, Mr Mason?'

'Yes, oh yes,' nodded the club captain bitterly. 'Of course.'

If they thought Fowler had finished, he had not. 'But, as I say, Mister Secretary, I do feel the cold in the mornings once the year goes on. I thought the club might be kind enough to let me sort of half retire. I could be in what they call an advisory capacity, don't they? I could start a bit later and finish a bit earlier, if you see what I mean.'

They gave no reply, but he did not need one. He rose. 'And one more thing,' he smiled. The two officials backed involuntarily away from what might come next. Fowler said: 'That bloke what was being chased across the course tonight.'

'Yes, Fowler. What about him?' said Withers.

'I think he was a club member, sir. I didn't say as much to the policeman, but I think he was.'

'Good heavens! Whatever makes you say that?' exclaimed Mason.

'He jumped right over the new bunker on the twelfth, sir. And you just can't see that bunker when you're going towards it, from the back, like. It just looks like a hump of grass and there's a whole lot of little humps just there. But he *knew*, sir. He knew it was there, all right. He went over it like the favourite at Beechers Brook. And another thing. Even though everybody was on his trail he ran *round* the tenth and the thirteenth greens. It would have been a sight quicker to run across them. But his golfer's feelings, like his instincts was too strong. He ran round the putting surface and so did everybody else chasing him, except the police sergeant, who has got big boots I must say. That green will need watering and rolling tomorrow. But that gentleman, whoever he was and whatever he had been up to, was a sportsman, sir. I'll say that for him.'

*

'Geoff.'

'Yes, darling?'

'Can you take your leg off mine for a minute? I've got cramp.'

'You're getting old. Do you want me to rub it for you?'

'Yes, would you?' said Ena.

He reached below the motel sheet and smiled into her eyes as he played his hands into the tightened muscle of the leg until it was soft again.

'All right now?' he asked.

'Yes, thanks. That's much better. It felt very nice.'

'It felt all right for me too.'

They were naked and face to face in the impersonal bed. The curtains cut out the afternoon light and she had the sheet pulled almost over her head like a veil. Her face and her shoulders and the mounds of her breasts looked luminous.

'Here we are again,' she smiled sadly. 'These motel bills must cost you a fortune.'

'We have had to postpone the new fitted carpet for the lounge,' Geoff grinned. 'Perhaps we could have wall-to-wall motel bills instead.'

'Poor Cynthia,' she said.

'Oh, don't start "poor Cynthia-ing" again,' he pleaded. 'Nor "poor Simonizing". We're here to enjoy ourselves.'

'But *why* do we do it?' she insisted softly. 'Why do we creep away and have sex and then go back with a big innocent smile?'

'Why? Christ, trust a woman. Because we like it. I like it, and you like it, and our lives would be empty without it. That's why.'

'Your emptiness and my emptiness,' she said thoughtfully. 'I suppose if you pour two lots of emptiness into a pool you still get an empty pool.'

'There are times when going to bed with you is like going to bed with *Old Moore's Almanac*,' he grumbled.

'I'm sorry, Geoff. It's just that I feel I would like to do other things with you – for you – for a change. You may laugh at this, but I'd like to go to the cinema together or bake a cake for you. Do you understand?'

'We are *not* spending our illicit afternoon making cakes,' he said firmly. 'Or at the pictures.'

Ena smiled and pushed her face and the top of her body to him. His went down to the full barrel of her breasts. She scratched his head. 'It's silly, I know. But this always seems so temporary. There's no conclusion with it.'

'There's a salesman I know,' sighed Geoff, 'an old boy, been in interior design for years, and he's fond of saying: "Geoff, my boy, never forget the four Ws – wine, wool, wood and women. There's nothing that tastes or feels like any of them." What he doesn't say is that the first three don't argue.'

'I'm not arguing,' she argued. 'I'm worried, that's all. I'm worried about you and me, you and Cynthia, me and Simon. What's to become of us?'

He kissed her anxiously. 'Do you remember that party the night we met? The leaf-sweeping party at the Reynolds.'

She giggled reluctantly. 'A leaf-sweeping party,' she mused. 'Have you ever heard anything like it? And you made me laugh when you said most of the women had ridden in on their own brooms.'

'A leaf-sweeping party,' repeated Geoff. 'Good old Plummers Park. We didn't worry too much about conclusions then, did we?'

'That wasn't the time to worry about them. We needed each other so badly.'

'Don't we still?'

'Yes, of course. I was really at a low when I saw you for the first time. I knew before we had spoken two sentences that we would be doing this. It's funny how all the things you say to each other then, clever or idiotic, all point down between your legs.' She sighed, 'I never told you then but it was my birthday three days before, and do you know what Simon had given me?'

'At a quick guess – an album of photographs of himself.'

She smiled tiredly. 'Not quite. He had set up a treasure trail. All over Watford and Stanmore and down to Northwood and Ruislip. You know, clues in little notes. It started from home and I had to follow up each clue on to the next one. They were in shops and pubs and even a book in the library. I thought it was very romantic and it took me two days and goodness knows how much in bus fares. And the prize was at the end of it in an electrical shop in Watford. It was an electro-vibro massager.'

Geoff whistled noisily under the bedclothes. 'What every woman wants for her birthday,' he said.

'He said it was to keep me in trim, as he put it, but the first night he wanted me to use it on him.' Suddenly to Geoffrey's astonishment she erupted into tears, sobbing and thrusting her head hard against his chest, her breasts banging against him as she sobbed. 'Oh, Geoff,' she cried hopelessly, 'I'm pregnant and he wants to move to Wimbledon.'

Geoffrey felt his breath tighten. He said nothing for a few moments, then eased her away and looked down into her rainy face. 'That could be a funny line in some plays,' he said. 'You're pregnant and you're moving to Wimbledon?'

Snivelling she nodded her head. 'It does sound a bit comic, doesn't it?' she wept. 'But it doesn't seem like that to me.'

'It could be *my* baby,' he said.

'It could be. I got all careless with my pills, silly fool that I am. Those little bastards, they wriggle inside you so sneakily.'

'The human sperm does not know the meaning of sportsmanship,' said Geoffrey glumly. 'What are you going to do?'

'Move to Wimbledon and have a baby, I suppose,' she sniffed. 'Simon's been offered a promotion but it would mean moving down there. Unless you do something I'll have to go.'

'Unless *I* do something?'

She hesitated, then looked at him directly. They moved away fractionally from each other because when they stared so closely it made them go cross-eyed. 'Unless you and I put this on an honest basis and go off together. You leave Cynthia and I'll leave Simon and we'll go somewhere else and live together. Anywhere, New Zealand if you like.'

'New Zealand?' he whispered. 'This is getting serious.'

'It *is* serious,' she replied. 'I've told you how serious. Unless I get out *now* there's going to be *no* getting out.'

'Wimbledon and motherhood,' murmured Geoffrey. 'A nasty combination.'

'You're so sodding flippant about it.'

'I'm trying to be,' he said. 'It gives me time to think. God knows I adore you. I look forward to these times we have together like mad. I even thought we might be able to sneak a holiday together later on. But . . . Christ, Ena, you *know* I've made one mistake. I've quit one marriage, how can I do it again?'

'You've made *two* mistakes,' she pointed out. 'Otherwise we wouldn't be lying naked in this room. What you're afraid of now is correcting the second mistake. A third marriage is not a disgrace. The disgrace is being unhappy in the second but still hanging on.'

'I'm afraid,' he said.

'I know,' she agreed softly. 'So am I. Bloody afraid. Can you imagine what it would do to Simon?'

'I could make a rough guess,' he agreed miserably. He pulled her warm body to him. 'I'm stunned,' he said. 'I can't think.'

'Do you want to make love now?' she asked. 'I'd like to. It may be the last time.'

He nodded and without another word they closed to each other in the dark beneath the sheet. Afterwards they lay in silence until eventually she said: 'I'd have an abortion if you were worried about the baby.' She began to cry again and turning to him said: 'Oh, Geoff, I love you so. It's not fair, is it? Nothing's arranged properly in this life.'

No, he thought, it isn't.

13

Thursday 18 July was an important and dramatic day for two members of the Plummers Park community: it was the day Sarah Burville had her prizes and the day Herbie Futter had his heart attack.

The prize-giving happened first. The summer-ginghamed

girls of the Grammar School scraped chairs and giggled in rows, watching carefully the sunshine boxed in the big windows of the school hall, as though they feared it was about to vanish forever. In two days they would be released for the holidays. Parents and other visitors were accommodated in the rearmost ranks. The governors, staff and select visitors were ranged in a wide morose arc across the stage like a large and losing football team. The Bishop was there, wrapped in thought and gaiters, and so too was the Reverend Boon, banished to the extreme wing and, to his discomfiture, placed next to Miss Jankin, the headmistress of the Plummers Park Primary School.

'Ah,' whispered the vicar as though it were some rude secret. 'I see from the programme, Miss Jankin, that we are to have some songs from the Elfin Choir of the Plummers Park Primary School.'

'They're hideous,' sniffed Miss Jankin at once. 'Unreservedly hideous.'

'Oh dear. I would have thought you'd have been rather proud of them.'

'Mister Boon, I have told you on a previous occasion how I feel about my school. Almost every activity, apart from home-time and the blessed breaking-up for the holidays, fills me with dismay and not infrequently disgust.'

'But you're so uncharitable,' he complained.

'Before you speak of charity, vicar, wait until you've heard the Plummers Park Elfin Choir. There ought to be a registered charity for schoolteachers who have to suffer like this. Miss Simister – known, not undeservedly, as Miss Sinister in the school – who conducts them is not only excessively furtive, she's deaf as well.'

'But I understand they have gained a certain amount of popularity in this district,' argued the vicar unhappily.

'Notoriety,' Miss Jankin grimly amended. 'They had them up at the old folks home to complete the misery of the inmates last Christmas. The matron at the general hospital wisely curtailed their concert there to prevent the further spread of gloom and despondency.'

'Surely you exaggerate.'

'Just wait. You've never heard such a lot of tuneless little swines. Not that they're completely without entertainment value. Jason Farley, a child who far from hunting for a golden fleece will be fleeced himself regularly throughout life, sometimes provides a diverting moment.'

'Oh good. What does he do?'

'Wets himself,' said the headmistress uncompromisingly.

'Miss Jankin!'

'Straight up. He doesn't always do it, but he mostly does. He's what you could call an unknown quantity. He's left his indelible stain on half the platforms and stages in Hertfordshire.'

The Reverend Boon rolled his eyes miserably. Miss Jankin said with her nasty eagerness: 'Here they come now. I think Miss Simister has encouraged Jason to pee during the songs rather than between them so that it's a bit less obvious. You can't actually *hear* him doing it anyway.'

'I'm glad, I'm glad,' nodded the vicar haplessly. Then: 'I must say they look very sweet.'

Miss Jankin snorted, but her neighbour joined enthusiastically in the applause for the fifteen small children who now clopped on to the stage. The motherhood barely latent in the girls in the audience burst out and there were sighs and fond eyes as the Elfin Choir, dressed in green crêpe-paper costumes with pointed hats framing their infant expressions, formed a half-circle.

Mrs Mappin, the headmistress of the Grammar School, a steady-looking woman in a pinstriped suit, strode out to the front of the platform on resounding shoes and announced: 'My Lord Bishop, Councillors, Governors, Ladies and Gentlemen, girls. To start off our annual prize-giving this year we have the Elfin Choir from Plummers Park Primary School, and I think you will agree, very pretty little boys and girls they look.' There was applause for this compliment, and the choir stood moon-faced, simpering, holding hands apprehensively and badly wanting to remember the first song.

Mrs Mappin continued: 'With their choir-mistress Miss Simister at the piano they will sing three or four songs for us.

Miss Simister has asked me to explain that unfortunately she has suffered an unfortunate accident to two of her fingers which are I see encased in sticking plaster.'

The dairymaid Miss Simister held up the two fingers, bound so excessively in plaster that they resembled toffee-apples, to the assembly in a sort of indomitable victory-sign. Miss Jankin sighed. 'Silly bitch left them on the keyboard and little Bertie Ringling slammed the lid down on them.' Mr Boon, defeated now, nodded.

Mrs Mappin continued: 'So I am sure you will understand that the piano accompaniment might not be all that it usually is. We have offered to provided an accompanist, but Miss Simister and her Elfin Choir are such a team that they feel they would rather persevere even under these difficulties.'

There was further applause at this news. As it died and the children stiffened themselves for the attack on the first song, Miss Jankin whispered: 'I hope you're ready for this, vicar.'

The performance started badly even by the low standards of the Elfin Choir. Miss Simister's two toffee-apple fingers hit the notes like the hammers of a xylophone player, each blow causing her to jump with pain, and each jump lifted her a few inches from her stool in the manner of a rider mounted on a difficult pony. The children, never over-confident, stumbled over the first few bars of 'Sumer is icumen in', started again, muffed it again, re-started, and eventually trampled through it in great confusion and haste.

The applause was more sympathetic than polite.

'That was written by a monk, you know, in the thirteenth century,' whispered Mr Boon informatively.

'May he return and haunt them,' grunted Miss Jankin.

There followed the choir's decimated version of 'Linden Lea', during which Miss Simister chose to continually remind the audience of her disability by holding up her two plastered fingers at them whenever she could, a sort of 'look, one-handed' sign, causing the girls in the audience to blush and snigger. Then appropriately in the next song, 'The Rain It Raineth Every Day', the risky Jason Farley wet himself spectacularly, a spreading emerald patch appearing on the front of his paper elfin trousers, ever widening, until the paper itself sagged and parted and eventually rolled and fell about the small boy's knees, leaving him staring down in disbelief. The occurrence fortunately came at the end of the song and the near hysterical applause covered both the mishap and the reaction to it.

The small choir was led off the stage, and their mistress did a further innocent V-sign as she was about to disappear into the wings. Miss Jankin dried her eyes on the vicar's shoulder. 'My God, that was their best ever, vicar. I've never seen it all happen at once before. The way that silly cow kept lifting her fingers!' The heaving headmistress attempted to illustrate her point by thrusting her own two middle fingers up until the Reverend Boon almost forcibly restrained her.

He had never been so angry. He feared the Bishop might have caught a glimpse of those uplifted fingers and would think that their owner was something to do with him. 'I really don't know, Miss Jankin,' he gritted, his head low, 'why you ever became a schoolteacher at all. It does *not* appear to be your vocation.'

She was un-angry, unruffled. She laid a comradely hand on his shoulder. 'You don't seem to be much cop as a vicar, not to me,' she said. 'I bet you only went into the Church in a fit of devilment.'

The Reverend Boon's indignant retort was snuffed by the rising once again of Mrs Mappin. She straightened the skirt of her pinstripe and banged her boot on the stage for silence among the girls.

'I am sure that we would all like to thank Miss Simister and the Elfin Choir for er . . . performing here this afternoon,' she said doggedly. 'And to let them know that we appreciate the various difficulties under which they were working.' She came to an almost military attention on the stage and then opened one leg like the prop of an old-fashioned blackboard, thumping her foot down noisily.

She then introduced the Bishop, who gave a condensed lecture on Life, his voice flapping big and slow around the hall like the circular flight of a large tired bird. The Bishop ended with a joke he imagined he had heard when he had tuned in by mistake to a disc-jockey programme one morning. It was meaningless to him but he thought it sounded as though it might be funny because the disc jockey laughed a lot. So he repeated it as well as he could remember, but at the end he knew he had been under some misapprehension, for the entire young audience remained gazing at him with bored respect with not an inch of a smile at the corner of any mouth. He blinked with disappointment, thought about repeating the final line in case nobody had heard, gave it up, treated them to a quick blessing and sat down.

Mrs Mappin stood again and said how marvellous it was to have a bishop who understood young people and their world. She went on to summarize the school year and, finally, announced: 'We have had this year a pupil who has been more than merely outstanding. Never in my experience as a teacher and as a head have I come across a girl with such a unique academic ability – and, I might say, a very modest and pleasant nature to go with it. Everyone will know that I am talking of Sarah Burville.'

There was huge applause at the name, and shouts from the girls in all the rows. Sarah sat crimson-faced among her classmates while they clapped.

'I would hesitate to say that Sarah has "hogged" all the prizes, for hogging is very far from her nature. I think she is as popular with her classmates as she is with the staff. A rare combination, if I may say so. She has not had any undue educational advantages, just an outstanding ability and a modesty which makes her work as hard as anyone in this school. I think it is indicative of her attitude to school and life in general that although she has never claimed to be more than proficient on the sports field, she represented the school at both tennis and swimming this year and was a member of the team which won the county relay at the swimming gala last month.'

She paused and looked across the heads of the six hundred girls. 'I know I am embarrassing Sarah. I can see it from here.' The girls laughed and looked round. 'To save her the further embarrassment of having to troop up to this platform half a dozen times to collect her prizes I propose to read out the list and, if Sarah can carry them all at once, she can come and get them all at once – or in a couple of journeys anyway.'

Laughter came readily from the hall. The guests on the platform nodded and beamed. Andrew arrived at the school at that moment. He had been delayed in the office and had telephoned Audrey to say he would join her at the prize-giving.

He had walked into the front lobby of the school when a car pulled up raggedly outside, and behind him, through the main door, staggered Mrs Burville, sodden drunk and wearing her wartime ATS uniform from which she burst and bloated at every button. He saw her as she clattered against the door and hung on to it with one faltering hand while covering her face with the other. Andrew stared uncomprehendingly. The khaki tunic was bulging and the buttons, bright with Brasso, strained. Her skirt was so tight it forced her middle-aged knees together so that she could hardly hobble, and her peaked cap was smashed on her head like some comic headgear. Andrew moved towards her, his hands going out ineffectually in case she should fall.

'Don't you touch me, you smug bugger!' she shouted. Her hand came away from her face and he saw that it was almost purple, the bitter red eyes sunk so deep it was as though they were looking from behind a lurid carnival mask.

'Mrs Burville, Mrs Burville,' he pleaded helplessly.

'They didn't tell me!' she cried. 'They're fucking well ashamed of me. I had to read it in the paper. My own girl, my Sarah, and even she didn't tell me. God help me, I'll show them who's her mother! It's me! I'm her mother . . .'

Andrew attempted to catch hold of her. But with surprising swiftness she had taken a large silver sports cup from its display-shelf in the lobby and held it above her head like a weapon. 'Let me go by or I'll smash this on your bloody head,' she swore. 'You can't understand. Get out of my way!'

He still made the attempt. Instead of striking him with the cup she flung it furiously. He ducked but it bounced on his shoulder and smashed through the glass door of a display cabinet. That was the first those inside heard.

She went through the gap he had left like a rugby three-quarter, head down. She burst through the double swing-doors of the school assembly hall just as her daughter stood on the stage, books in her arms and about to receive another from the headmistress. Mrs Mappin was saying: 'And yet another First Prize – this for English Literature . . .'

'Sarah! Sarah!' Mrs Burville screeched from the back of the hall. Everybody looked. Mrs Burville was hanging there by one of the brass handles, legs askew all over the polished floor, the ridiculous ATS shoes toes up, skirt torn halfway down her hip, tunic like a lumpy bag, hat fallen backwards, held by a pin, hair wet over red drunken face.

'My Sarah!' she squealed again. 'You di'n tell me. I *wanted* to come! I *wanted* to come!'

'Oh, God,' said the girl, ashen-faced on the platform. 'Oh no, God.'

'Your mother,' said the headmistress quietly.

'Yes, my mother,' said the girl, speaking as though to emptiness. 'She's ill.' The prizes began toppling from her hands on to the platform. She looked through icy tears to see the nightmare woman advancing knock-kneed, arms flailing, down the polished centre aisle, crying like a ghost. Nobody in the hall moved.

Sarah, calmly now putting the rest of the books at her feet, walked down the steps from the stage and advanced towards the sliding woman. They faced each other for a moment, like the two women they were, tears and anger and pity on the girl's face; blank guilt, panic, on the countenance of her mother. 'Come on, mum,' said Sarah. 'It's all over. I'll take you home.'

She put her young arm round the heaving shoulders and turned her mother around to face the door. Turning back momentarily to the platform where the headmistress and the others remained like a frieze, she called: 'She's not at all well.'

They stumbled together to the door. The abject Andrew was there, head down, to open it for them and they went out towards the playground sunshine.

No one in the hall moved. Some of the girls and some of the mothers were crying. Mrs Mappin hesitated, then moved to the front of the stage. 'As an emergency measure,' she announced trying to keep her voice straight, 'I am going to ask for another song from the Elfin Choir.'

'Christ, Jesus,' muttered Miss Jankin into her hands. 'Haven't we had enough suffering for one afternoon?'

*

Harry Solkiss and Gerry Scattergood, the tall, thin, loping man and the broad, striding man, adapting their different paces, walked from The Case Is Altered. It was seven o'clock. Most of the men were home by now and Plummers Park had its familiar air of evening hollowness.

'Don't often see you having a drink without your wife,' said Gerry. 'Can't ever remember seeing one of you without the other, come to think of it.'

'You're correct,' agreed the American dolefully. 'Jeanie and I are real close. In fact I was having that drink to kick up my courage. I have to break something to her.'

Gerry nodded incuriously. 'Telling women things can be very difficult,' he said philosophically. 'There's a lot they don't want to know.'

'Sure. This is going to be tough. Hell, it is. Every day I bus to the base and every night I come home and it's cosy, and up till now that's been fine with me. But they've offered me a job flying around, going to Paris and Rome and places like that, maybe four or five times a month.'

'That sounds great,' nodded Gerry. 'But you don't think she's going to be very sweet on it?'

'I know she won't. We've seen each other every day since we married and I've never slept away from my own bed and my own wife. It's going to come hard.'

'And she'll be thinking that you're having a great time with the birds in Paris while she's worrying at home.'

The boyish American grimaced. 'Not me,' he said seriously. 'I wouldn't do *anything* like that. But she'll sure worry in case I do.'

'Women do worry,' nodded Gerry understandingly. 'And a lot of them in Plummers Park have good reason. Don't believe in it, myself, all this playing around. I suppose selling contraceptives as I do, you get to the basics, if you know what I mean, behind all the romantic mush. In the end it boils down to the same bits meeting the same bits. It don't matter if they're film stars or poor people or a couple of railway trucks, they all couple up in more or less the same way.'

'Is there a deal of it in this neighbourhood? Playing around, I mean.'

'A fair amount. They're all at the stage when they're looking around to see what they might have missed first time.'

'You mean wife-swopping?'

Gerry considered it but shook his head. 'I doubt it. Not your direct *blatant* swop. They have a nibble here and a nibble there but nothing is *organized*, if you see what I mean. Come to think of it that's the one thing they haven't been able to organize around here. Some of the husbands wouldn't mind another man's wife in their bed, but it would upset them to see her cooking the breakfast. See what I mean?'

'I get it. We have these problems at home too, in Arizona,' said Harry anxious, as ever, to politely spread the guilt. 'Some of the girls there get wed at fifteen and by the time they're twenty they're rooting around like little pigs.'

'Maybe that's better,' said Gerry, considering it. 'If you get married at fifteen then at least you're still young enough for another start at twenty. Here, when they start itching, it's generally getting too late to scratch. I'm very settled, myself, like I say; my job keeps my feet on the ground and off the bed. Mind, I *have* buggered about. In the past. When I first got married I was a real tearaway. But I was selling baked beans then. I had a different philosophy, a different outlook on life. One night I went out on the razzle and I woke up next morning stark bollock naked with this terrible ugly bird, also stripped, in the back seat of my car. I couldn't remember anything about the night before, not even her. We were parked right outside a bloody railway station too and there were hundreds of people going to work and gaping in at us through the window. That just about cured me, I can tell you.'

'I imagine,' said Harry, who had begun to stare with dis-belief at the tale. He shook his head. 'And to think, back home people really believe that all the British do is to sit weaving in the fog.'

Halfway up Risingfield they heard the violent howling of the dogs. 'Jesus,' said Gerry, hurrying his pace. 'That sounds bad. It's old Futter being ambushed again.'

He began to run, and the long lean Harry ran easily beside him. 'That's the old guy who always gets the dogs at him?' he asked.

'He's a taxidermist and they go for the smell.' Gerry did not take long to pant and he was puffing heavily by the time they reached the privet hedge corner of Risingfield and Upmeadow. The dogs – a dozen of them were in the road – were still baying and barking, but were backing away from the swinging brooms of Mrs Futter and Audrey Maiby. Gerry's wife Min was running up the road, unravelling the garden hose like an auxiliary fireman as she ran. Andrew Maiby was kneeling over the rumpled figure of Herbie Futter.

'Blimey, they've got him this time,' said Gerry running forward. He and Harry went in among the dogs with boots and shouts and the pack eventually retreated to the far side of the road. People were coming from their houses and looking from their windows. The old taxidermist looked as though he had been assassinated, lying mouth open to the clear blue evening sky. Mrs Futter knelt on the opposite side to Andrew and began to sway and weep. Andrew looked up and saw Gerry. 'He's out cold,' he said urgently. 'I can't get any response.'

Harry Solkiss kneeled down. 'I know a few things,' he said. 'But I guess what he needs is a doctor.'

'He's been called,' said Andrew. 'But he's got to come from Watford. Why the hell we haven't got a doctor here, I don't know.'

Harry began massaging the old man's heart. Someone brought out a bright aluminium sun-bed and they eased him on to the ironically vivid canvas and carried him to his house, with Harry massaging on one side and Mrs Futter howling on the other.

They took the sagging old man to his house. Nobody in the

neighbourhood had ever been inside that house, and now as they carried the improvised stretcher over the threshold their sense of amazement all but overtook their concern for Herbie. For within the uncompromising square Plummers Park walls was a small, ornate palace, a place of rich carpets, chairs with curly backs and cabriole legs.

'On the table,' said Harry ogling around. Then he caught Andrew's glance and turned and saw the exquisite ovalled wood and fine shining surface of the Regency table, with a gigantic candelabra hanging above it, the two pieces taking up almost the entire space of the modest modern room.

'Maybe not,' amended Gerry.

'On the table,' cried Mrs Futter. 'He likes that table.'

They put him on the rare wood, his quaint button-boots sticking out like the hands of a clock, his old-fashioned trousers spread pathetically, his shirt open to the scraggy neck, and Harry sweating as he continued to try and bring some life to the heart.

'Where's that sodding doctor?' cursed Andrew impotently. 'You'd think it was miles.'

'It *is* miles,' said Gerry. 'You ought to get your paper on to that one. We're like a flaming outpost of Empire here.'

As though he had been waiting for the right moment Herbie opened his eyes. He stared around at the anxious faces of his neighbours and reached out his uncertain hand for his trembling wife. 'Bludda fucken dogs,' he said to Andrew. He closed his eyes again. Audrey said, 'He'll be all right,' and took Mrs Futter hunched across the road.

Andrew, Gerry and Harry stood awkwardly around the prostrate old Jew. 'I'll get a mirror,' said Gerry, 'to see if he's breathing.'

He went to the bathroom and returned with a small round mirror. He held it in front of the old man's mouth but no breath showed. At that moment the doctor came in. 'Watch he doesn't wake up and see himself,' he observed casually. 'He looks terrible.' He bent and examined the old man. 'He's gone,' he said. 'Dead.'

'What do we do now?' Andrew asked the doctor. It suddenly

came to him that very few of them had known any dealings with death. Plummers Park had not reached the age when people died within their houses.

'Well, you can't leave him on that table for a start,' said the doctor. 'Not a Regency table. It's like Blenheim Palace in here, isn't it?'

Andrew was about to make some angry rejoinder when he caught the doctor's eyes and saw that he *did* know something about death. Instead he said: 'He'd better go to his bedroom, I suppose.'

'That's more usual than leaving him on the dining-room table,' said the doctor. 'Somebody will look after his wife, won't they?'

'My wife will,' said Andrew. 'She's taken her across to my place.'

'In the bedroom then,' said the doctor. 'You take the other end. He's only a little one.'

Herbie was like a fragile shell. They carried him easily up the stairs and pushed open the first door. 'That's not it,' said the doctor. 'That's a spare room.' He hesitated at the door and said: 'Good God, there's a stuffed dog in there.'

They put Herbie in the next room, and with some brief embarrassment arranged him on the bed as though they were making him comfortable.

'There,' said the doctor as if he were satisfied with some good task. 'He'll be all right there.' He stood back and regarded the dead Herbie. 'Just to think,' he muttered almost to himself, 'whatever we do in this life, we all end up on our backs, staring into space.'

Andrew immediately thought of Bessie. He nodded with brief bitterness and they left the room. He stopped at the first door they had opened and, glancing at the doctor's back retreating down the stairs, pushed it quietly. It opened. There in the middle of the floor was the big black dog from Hedgerows, dead, stuffed and stitched, standing quite elegantly, feet apart, head raised, vacancy shining from its brown glass eyes. Herbie Futter's revenge! Andrew's shock was more than he had felt about Herbie's death. His face paled. He closed the door and went down after the doctor. At the front door, red from his bike, was the Reverend Boon.

'I heard,' he said breathlessly. 'I heard from Mrs Blossom-Smith on the phone. Someone's had a heart attack. Can I be of some help?'

'He's dead,' said Andrew simply. He took hold of the clergyman's arm. 'He's not only dead, but he's Jewish. Or was. Is someone still Jewish when they're dead? I suppose they are.'

'Oh dear,' said the vicar. 'What a shame. What a great shame.'

He shrugged, mounted his bicycle, and free-wheeled disconsolately down the hill. Andrew watched him go. 'You're another one who doesn't have any luck,' he said aloud.

14

There were rooks in the churchyard and cars in the street. Bessie sat eating her egg sandwiches, and Andrew, after carefully surveying the lunch-time people on the grass, sat beside her. They talked, and he ate one of her sandwiches. He was worried about her. He said, suddenly: 'Do you have any plans?'

'You know I'm working this afternoon,' she answered in her shopgirl way: 'I can't just buzz off when I like. Not like you. I wonder how you manage it, really. Don't they ever ask you where you're going or what you're up to?'

'I tell them I'm making inquiries,' he said blandly. 'General calls and inquiries. That's how I put it on my expenses.'

'Christ, you get expenses for it as well!'

'I *have* to charge expenses, otherwise they'd think I wasn't doing anything, wouldn't they? Anyway, I didn't mean this afternoon, I meant generally. You know, in the future.'

'I never look to it much,' she said. She bit crudely into an egg sandwich and left a tail of crust hanging out of her mouth which was gradually munched inside. The next sentence came through a mouthful of bread. 'I get up in the morning and I go to bed at night. Sometimes I see you and sometimes I don't.'

'That's not much of a life for a young woman,' he said.

She examined him suspiciously. 'What're you trying to get at, Andrew?' she said. 'You want me to "make something of my life" do you? Sounds just like my teacher at school. Make something of your life, plan your life, construct your life, she used to say. You'd think it was a bleeding skyscraper. I just let it happen.'

Andrew sighed. She had given him a bit of her sandwich, tearing it off and handing it to him without saying anything. He shared his portion with some path sparrows. 'I get worried about you, that's all,' he said. 'I feel, well, in a way I feel responsible for you.'

'I'm not up the spout if that's what you're getting at,' she said bluntly. 'That's why I couldn't go to bed with you last week. I'm on the pill, in good nick, and everything's working.'

'Not that,' he said. 'Just generally. I ought to be ashamed of myself really, having an affair with someone your age. Taking advantage.'

'Cradle snatching,' she grinned.

'That's right. We used to call it that too.'

'When you lived in *your* council house?' she said mockingly.

'That's correct,' he said hardening. 'When I lived in *my* council house. I told you before you're not the only one who's had the privilege, you know.'

'But I've got the privilege *now*,' she smiled, annoying him. 'I like to see you wriggle.'

'Thanks, I thought you might.'

'Don't let's fight,' she said. 'I've got to be back in ten minutes.' She became quiet, sitting there with one egg sandwich left in its wrapping on her lap. She looked at it, curled up her nose and said: 'Do you want the last one, Andrew?'

'No thanks, Bess,' he said.

She looked straight ahead across the churchyard over the heads of the people on the summer town grass. 'You don't have to worry about me, Andrew,' she said. 'I'm having a good time. And you don't have to worry about us, neither. When the bus stops, I'll know where to get off.'

'I didn't mean anything like that,' he protested.

She bent, touched his shoulder, and said gently: 'I've got to push off. I'll be late back. Is Wednesday all right?'

He looked at her, studied her face. 'I'm very lucky, you know,' he said.

'I know you are,' she replied simply. 'Is it all right?'

'Yes, I'm fixing something.'

*

Andrew waited until everybody but Burton, the editor, and the office cleaner had gone home. He could see Burton roving behind the frosted panes of his room and the cleaner rummaging among the untidy papers at the far end of the editorial room. He picked up the telephone: 'Will you get me County Hall at Hertford please,' he asked the operator. 'Mr Culler.'

She called him back. 'Mr Culler on the line.'

'Thanks. Hello, Dick, Andrew Maiby.'

'Andrew! Nice to hear you. What secrets can I tell you?'

'No secrets, this time, Dick. Thanks for the thing about the school for maladjusted kids, by the way. I was able to give them the news – and the reason about the environment – just as they were starting a collection for protest expenses.'

'Ha! A most opportune moment, I'd say.'

'It was. You ought to have seen the looks on their faces. The trouble was that when I told them that the environment was not considered to be right for the children, some of them thought it was a compliment to *them*!'

'God, you must live among a fine bunch.'

'No, I wouldn't blame them, not altogether,' said Andrew. 'I'm one of them, I suppose. There's no villains. But they've got something, a house and a few possessions, and they get afraid they'll lose them, that's all. I know how they feel.'

He could almost hear the other man nodding. 'Maybe you're right,' he replied. 'We all get like it. I can't sleep at nights because somebody leaves a bicycle in the hall downstairs. It annoys me. I gnash my teeth and tell myself it lowers the standard of the place.'

'That's what I wanted to ask you about. Not the bike, your flat.'

'What about it?'

'When I come up to the county council meeting on Wednesday, do you think I could borrow it for an hour or so.'

He heard the breathing silence at the other end. Then, eventually: 'You old devil. What are you up to? Have you met up with that marvellous girl again?'

'No. It's not her.'

'You old devil,' Culler said again. He did not sound enthusiastic. 'But I take it I'm right in a general sort of way?'

'Yes,' said Andrew uneasily. 'I could say I wanted to borrow the flat to read the council minutes, but you wouldn't believe me. Yes, you're right in a general sort of way.'

'I wish I could operate like you operate,' said Culler without admiration in his voice.

'You *are* single,' Andrew pointed out. 'Adultery is the *prerogative* of the married man.'

'And married woman.'

'Yes, and her. Them.'

There was another pause. Andrew could tell he did not like doing it. Then he said: 'Yes, you can have the flat, Andrew. I'll be in the council chamber with my boss, so I'll pass the key to you beforehand. Without knowing any more about it than I do now, I'd say it was a better way of passing the afternoon than listening to some of the fatuous duffers who'll be doing their usual spouting at the council.'

'Thanks. I'll leave it tidy. There's no point in my being in the council chamber all the time, anyway, as you know. I'm only interested in the stuff that affects my local area, and that's right at the end of the meeting by the look of the agenda. I'll get one of the other press boys to give me a ring when it looks like coming up.'

'Such cunning. You've got it all planned.'

'Yes, it sounds like that, doesn't it? Dick, you don't mind, do you?'

'No. It's all right.'

'You don't sound very enthusiastic.'

'Well, it's not me that's having it, is it? I shall think of you when I'm pressed up against some fat borough planning officer on Wednesday.'

'I'm sorry. It's all right then?'

'Yes, Andrew. I said so.'

'Good. Thanks very much.'

'You're welcome. Have a good time.'

*

'Blimey,' said Bessie. 'We do get some changes of scenery, don't we. I'm never looking up at the same ceiling twice.'

'Don't grumble,' said Andrew. 'You refuse to go to a hotel.'

'No, I told you. There's something nasty about going to hotels. It's immoral.'

Andrew groaned. 'Sometimes I lose track of your arguments, Bess. We've got to have somewhere. It was just our bad luck that barge catching fire and sinking like that.'

'We must have been hot stuff,' she laughed. She was undressing casually, her eyes drifting around the room. 'Who is this bloke anyway, the one what has this place?'

Andrew was sitting on the edge of the bed watching for the moment when she took away her brassière and those pretty nipples blinked in the light. He had not undressed. He said: 'He's an old friend. He works for the county council.'

'Does he know what we are going to do here?'

'Well, he knew I didn't want to lie down because of a headache, but he didn't ask too many questions.'

'But what about your work? You're supposed to be at this meeting.'

'You're always going on about my work,' said Andrew. 'You worry about it more than I do.'

'Well, I worry about *you*,' she said simply. 'I worry about your job in case you should get into trouble, not doing it. Screwing me instead.'

Andrew sighed. 'Bess, it's all arranged, so don't worry. I will not miss a county council scoop. They'll be gassing for a couple of hours before they reach anything that concerns me. I've fixed for one of the other reporters to give me a ring from the press room when the time comes.'

'You've got it all nice and planned,' she said. 'All for me.'

'All for me too,' he said. She was nude now and she lay back with ease and familiarity on the double bed. But there was a remoteness about her too, as if she were only posing. She spread her feet apart but her knees moved towards each other to form a steeple and she closed her eyes as though she were sunbathing. Andrew, remote too, like a voyeur, in his clothes, sat on the side of the bed and eventually put his hand on the upturned bowl of her stomach, then moved it down and rubbed his fingers gently into her hump of hair and against the angles and flats of her bent legs. She opened her eyes. 'What's the bloke like,' she said, 'what lives here?'

'He's a nice chap. About twenty-eight and he's not married. He works in the development department.'

'Building houses and things,' she said.

'Yes, sort of.'

'He had some nice records in the other room, on the player,' she mused. 'What's those cups for on top of the wardrobe? For sex?'

'For squash, I imagine,' said Andrew. 'He plays squash.'

'So do we,' she said, looking at him quickly to see if he approved of her joke. 'Are you doing it with your shirt on today?'

He stood and began to undress. She watched him, her hands going behind her head and her small breasts flattening out with the movement. 'Do you reckon he's had lots of women on this bed?' she asked suddenly.

'Possibly. I don't know. He's a bit of a quiet, thoughtful type.'

'That didn't stop you,' she pointed out easily. She looked around again. 'It's funny somebody from the council living here and having pop records and things, cups and all that, because when you get letters from them they don't seem human, do they?'

'Well, he is,' said Andrew naked now, easing himself on to the bed, crouching beside her. 'And so am I.'

'I can see that,' she said. As though with a sudden idea she opened her mouth and put it low to him, hanging on madly, cradling him beneath, moving him in and out like a piston. She was a girl full of impulses. Andrew's head dropped forward with the acute sensations she gave him so that his forehead rested against the fine skin of her back. They bent, curved into each other, fitting together like the figures in a Japanese ivory carving. He felt as though she was drawing his whole being away through a straw. His teeth gritted and he said tensely: 'Stop it, Bess, no more now.'

Not for the first time he thought what a remarkable girl she was. She pulled away from him, laughed up at him wet-lipped and wicked, and then eased herself back on the bed. 'If we packed up early,' she said in her joking, matter-of-fact way, 'we could go out and do some sightseeing. I wouldn't mind having a look around Hertford. I don't see many old towns. Do you think people in hundreds of years, like, will walk around where we live and think how interesting it is?'

'I can't see the houses on my side staying up that long,' said Andrew.

'Ours will,' she said with confident pride. 'They'll be up. They're not fancy like yours, and they have to be strong because council house people fight and have lots of kids.'

'That sounds like a contradiction in terms, but I'm not sure.'

'What's that?'

'Well, people fighting but having lots of kids.'

'Oh, I get you. Well they do. They fight and they still have kids. Kids is not always to do with love, you know.'

'No, I think you're right.'

'I am, generally.'

'I think you're right there too.'

'Come on top,' she suggested.

'Will you want to be tanned today?'

'Ah, I thought you liked that. We'll have a bit of that later on. I hope these walls aren't too thin.'

'I don't expect they are.'

He embraced and kissed her and they rolled with ease to each other, her knees nudging his thighs, hips and groins locked, the points of her breasts rubbing his ribs, her face against his neck, his lips on her hair. They moved smoothly into and against each other and then, when they paused and lay for a while, she said: 'Did you notice something just now?'

'What should I have noticed?'

'When I said about the walls. I said "I hope they aren't thin" instead of *ain't*, or turning the words arse about face, like I usually do with you, so I don't need to say it at all.'

'You make me feel like Professor Higgins,' he said. He was still buried in her and had leaned forward against her again after their brief conversation, ready to recommence, when the telephone rang. Andrew cursed. 'It can't be,' he said. 'Not yet.'

'Pick it up,' she said. 'I can't stand it ringing.'

Andrew did. It was Audrey.

'Audrey!' he cried. Then croaked: 'Audrey.'

'Yes. *Andrew*, whatever's the matter?'

His eyes were bulging, his flesh was trembling, his erection had withered at breathtaking speed like a released balloon. Several croaks creaked from his throat. Bessie watched him with horror. He thought she was going to say something so he put his shaking hand across her mouth, very hard, until she wriggled from beneath it and retreated across the bed, silent and staring.

'N : . . noth . . . nothing's the matter, love. Nothing.'

'Where are you?'

'A flat,' he said aghast still. 'A friend's flat. I didn't feel too good so he let me come up here. Dick Culler. You don't know him.'

'You're ill? What's wrong?'

'Oh, I don't know.' He was steeling himself now, trying to force his voice into its proper groove, trying to think. 'I almost fainted at the council meeting. Something I had to eat, I expect.'

'Good God! You! You've never fainted in your life. And nobody said anything when I rang County Hall.'

'Oh. Oh, you rang there?'

'Yes, of course. Andrew what *is* the matter? You sound very strange. Very odd.'

'No, I'm all right, thanks, Audrey,' he said weakly. 'But I felt pretty bad and I went off to sleep and the phone woke me. You know how the phone scares you sometimes.'

He heard Bessie whisper behind him: 'And you can say that again.' He made frantic signals to her to keep quiet.

'What did you say?' asked Audrey. 'What was that?'

'Oh, wait a minute,' said Andrew feigning anger. 'I can't get my thoughts together. It was a surprise hearing you, that's all.' He feared suddenly that Bessie would remark on that too, but she didn't. She lay on her back, revolving her thumbs, a look of disgust and sadness on her face.

'Listen, Andrew Maiby,' said Audrey brusquely. 'Don't you get ratty with me. I rang the press room and somebody said you'd be at that number, so I rang. I don't understand why you sound so funny.'

'I told you, Audrey. I feel ill. I feel terrible.'

'Have you called a doctor?'

'No. No I haven't. If I rest for a bit I'll be all right and I'll make my way home. Why did you ring anyway, love? Anything urgent?'

'Fairly urgent,' she said. He could still hear the suspicion hissing around at the other end. 'I wouldn't have tried to get hold of you otherwise, would I? You'd think I was checking up on you.'

'Yes, of course. What was it?'

'About your birthday.'

'My birthday?' His incredulous voice sounded miles away from him. The phone was slippery in his hand. He glanced back at Bessie and saw she was lying like a corpse on the bed.

'Yes,' said Audrey, annoyance spiking the words. 'You have a birthday, don't you? And it's next week. You are thirty-seven, or don't you remember?'

'Of course I remember. Don't turn nasty on me. I'm not feeling up to it.'

'All right.' Her voice calmed, but he knew she was making an effort. 'It's just that I wanted to make sure we were definitely having the dinner party on Thursday – that's the actual day. Geoff and Cynthia have to know this afternoon because they've got to make some other arrangements right away. Do you want me to ask anyone in particular besides?'

'Anybody,' he replied still weakly. 'Gerry and Min. How about them?'

'You don't sound as if you care very much,' she retorted.

'Christ, I told you. I don't feel well, love.'

'All right. I won't ring again. You can get back to bed, or wherever you were.'

She rang off abruptly and he replaced the phone and lay sickly back on the bed. 'I don't feel well, love,' mimicked Bessie with disgust from alongside him. 'Oh dear, I do feel ill, oh dear, oh dear. Yuk, yuk, yuk.'

'What did you expect me to say?' he demanded. 'That I was here having it away with you?'

'Bloody 'ell,' she laughed sarcastically. 'I've never seen anybody so bleedin' scared. You looked like you'd seen your grandad's ghost.'

'I *was* scared,' he confessed miserably. 'I was so scared I still feel sick. Fancy picking up the phone and hearing her. She's never done that before.'

'She *knows* something,' said Bessie in a disinterested voice. 'She doesn't ring up with your birthday plans when you're supposed to be working and you're screwing instead. She's got the sniff on you, mate.'

'You're always so poetic,' he muttered.

'Well, whatever I am,' she turned and shouted at him, '*I'm not pathetic like you*! If you could have seen yourself writhing and crawling. If you'd turned around and told her to fuck off she'd have gone like a shot – *and* she'd have believed you. I know how a woman thinks.'

'I am not in the habit of telling my wife to fuck off!' he snarled.

'Ho, ho, listen to us. We don't use nasty common language like that on *our* side of the railway. Not to our lovely wives.'

He hit her suddenly and hard across the face. She jumped up from the bed, white-cheeked, with the red mark of his hand bright on the skin. He recoiled. 'Oh, Bess, I'm sorry! I'm sorry, darling.'

'Bessie to you,' she said evenly. 'If anyone else had done that, Andrew Maiby, I'd have torn their bleeding eyes out. But I wouldn't like you to go home to your mummy all scratched now, would I?' She moved towards her clothes and began to dress quietly.

'Don't go, Bess, please don't,' he pleaded.

'You don't like wasting the room,' she jeered. 'Well, mister, I don't like being knocked about. Not even by somebody better-class than me.' She paused, standing in her pants with her bra in her hand. 'I might as well tell you something right now,' she continued bitterly. '*I* stopped that bit about my grandad in court getting into the papers. *I* went across and cheered up that silly old bugger who's a magistrate – the one who's got all the bloody cornflakes in his pocket.'

'You? Mr Brownlow. You went to see him?'

'That's right. He seemed a decent sort so I went to see him and let him put his arm around me and pat my arse a few times and he promised to see if he could get it kept out of both papers. He said he used to be mayor and he could pull some strings. And he did.'

'Jesus Christ, you're amazing.'

'I thought you were a bit different too,' she said sadly. 'I fancied you from the first minute because you looked different and dependable and nice. I'm trying not to cry. I didn't want to take you away from your wife. I just wanted to have you to myself a bit now and again. I thought that would be something decent anyway. Now you've hit me. Any fool can hit me.' She put her face in her hands and sat on the bedside chair, still naked to the waist, bent forward into her palms. When she looked up she was red about the eyes but there were no tears.

'Come back, Bess. Come back to bed. I'm sorry. I wouldn't do that again.'

'You're not going to get the bloody chance,' she said bluntly. 'This is the last time we're doing this.'

'But, for God's sake . . .'

'I'm getting married,' she said airily.

'Married! You're not! You're lying!'

'No I'm not lying,' she said. 'I'm telling the truth.'

'But . . . no! Who to!'

'Bloke in our road. Kenny Broad. We've been sort of half engaged for a long time and he keeps on at me to get married, so I thought the other day that I would. I told him last night.'

'Oh, darling, for God's sake you can't! If you don't love him . . .'

'Who told you that?' she said smartly. 'I didn't say I didn't love him.'

'But, what about . . .? How *can* you love somebody when . . .?'

'You love your wife, don't you? Go on, deny it. You kept calling her love, darling. You won't ever leave her. Well, this bloke might not wait around forever. And he's all right. Not all the good people come from your side of the lines, you know.'

Slowly she had been getting dressed. He watched the breasts disappear into the bra as though they were toys being packed away for the last time. He dropped his head in his hands. 'I can't believe it,' he groaned. 'I just can't believe it.'

'It's got to happen sometime,' she said almost blithely. She had put her dress back on and was looking through her handbag for a comb. 'I wanted you for something and you wanted me. We've had each other and that's that. We knew it couldn't go on forever.'

'But that telephone call convinced you, did it?'

'Yes, that was the knock. There's no time like the present. I'm going now. I'll get a train about four o'clock, I expect. 'Bye, Andrew.'

She walked briskly from the room leaving him sitting on the side of the bed like a stunned boxer on a stool. He heard the outer door of the flat shut. He did not go after her. He knew that the longer he sat there the better it would be. The phone rang again and he jumped almost to the ceiling. But it was only the reporter from the Hertford paper. 'Your stuff's coming on shortly,' he said. 'Did you get the call that came for you?'

'Yes, I got it all right.'

'Good,' said the man innocently. 'It was lucky I could tell her the number.'

'Yes, it was. Thanks. I'm just coming across.'

He dressed slowly. He looked at his haunted face in the mirror. His thoughts were not of Bessie. Only how he could compose himself in front of Audrey when he walked in that night.

15

Two magpies patrolled the garden in a constabulary way, numerous other Plummers Park birds sat around in hawthorn, privet and miniature peach tree, singing the songs that kept others from trespassing on their territory or their mates.

'You've been having sex with somebody else in this area.'

'What in the name of God are you talking about?'

'I've had my suspicions for a long time, you crafty bastard.'

'Oh have you? Well, your nasty little suspicions are wrong. *You* ought to know how to detect bloody adultery – after all, that's how I got you!'

The voices of Cynthia and Geoffrey Turvey clattered untidily out of the french windows on to the summer-morning lawn. Adding their complaints, the magpies flew off at the first-flung accusation, the other birds backed away. Neighbours on both sides stopped in their tasks and listened eagerly.

'Adultery's too good a word for you!' Cynthia sneered. 'You're like a greedy little boy: you can't leave something extra alone, can you? What are you trying to prove – at your age?'

'Listen,' said Geoffrey. 'I'm going. I'm going to work. I don't want to discuss this any more.' His voice had dropped to a low threat, a disappointment to the neighbours. They had no such problem with Cynthia.

'You don't want to discuss it any more!' she screamed. 'I should think you bloody wouldn't either!' She bent closer to him with a strangely confiding attitude, as he was arranging some papers for his brief-case. 'Listen, *chum*, you forget that's how *I* got *you* as well. And I know your tricks, because I was on the other side of the fence last time. Never admit anything – that's what you used to say. Lie until your teeth drop out. If you're cornered get out of the house as quick as you can. Christ, I can hear you saying it. So, you're getting out. Go on, clear off to work – so that you can think of something clever to say when you get back, so that you can warn her to cover her tracks. Well, you've got the wrong girl here. I *know*!'

The front door slammed to coincide with the final word. She heard him start the car and she watched from the window as he backed it from the carport. He turned it sharply and drove down the hill. Suddenly she felt very solitary. She turned dejectedly back into the lounge and looked around her at the possessions they had accumulated since they had come together and married. Tania had gone to infants' school, the house was hollow and quiet except for the calls of the birds drifting in from the garden and a muted and crackly disc jockey on the portable radio in the kitchen. Anger and hurt were now joined by a bitter sadness inside her. She decided to go and see the other woman right away. Two minutes later she was on her way to the house of Polly Blossom-Smith.

*

She was undecided as to her approach. A direct attack? Some reconnoitring conversation? A skirmish? Her anger drove her towards 'The Sanctuary' like a small but powerful motor. She seethed and closed her eyes for yards at a time as she strode, once almost trampling over a small child, one of the aimless morning tricyclists under school age, who emerged from a front gate into her blind and fuming path.

'Sorry, little boy!' exclaimed the stumbling Cynthia, trying to blow some cheerfulness into a glassy smile.

'I'm Roddy,' said the child, apparently hoping to prolong the conversation because he was lonely. 'I'm going to hospickle to have my winkie seen to.'

'I know somebody who could go with you,' thought Cynthia. She patted the child on his sparse hair and continued. He pursued her, hopefully, apparently bursting with further private information, until she outdistanced him and he returned to his solitary wheelings along the dusty pavement, beneath the laburnum and the baby beech trees. He had been warned by his mother that the seed pods of the laburnum would poison him and he wondered whether it would be worth trying. He might get some attention that way.

At the main gate of 'The Sanctuary' Cynthia hesistated, but a small booster explosion of wrath within her propelled her forward quickly and she strode up the path and banged on the hideously grinning gargoyle knocker. She poked her tongue fiercely at its metallic amusement and then steeled herself as she heard the catch being rattled within.

She had determined to keep a civilized front before launching into her accusations, but her tactics were immediately baulked by the appearance at the door not of Mrs Polly Blossom-Smith but of a thin scraggy old woman wearing a girl's bikini. She had a void expression and a feather duster which she continued to flick unambitiously around her as though seeking to do some token work.

'I'm the daily,' she said. 'Mrs Blossom-Smith's not in. She'll be back soon. Do you want to wait?'

Cynthia had hardly recovered from the first sight of the woman. She must have been seventy and her hips stuck up each side of her like the pommels of a saddle. The bikini which sagged like a hammock between her loins and drooped emptily across her chest was bright pink satin. She looked like a bone tied up with ribbon.

'I'll wait,' decided Cynthia.

'Come on in then,' muttered the grey woman. 'You'll 'ave to excuse my swimming suit but that was 'er ladyship's idea. She's doing some sort of statue and she studies me as I walks about doing the 'oovering and suchlike. She reckons it 'elps her get the bone structure right. Well, she can see every one of mine.'

Cynthia nodded understandingly, then craftily said: 'She uses live people for models all the time, doesn't she?'

'I'll say she does. You want to see the bloke up in the bedroom. Balls and all, 'e is.'

A cold hand touched Cynthia's stomach. 'In the bedroom?' she inquired.

'That's where she's got 'im,' nodded the old lady. 'I ain't never seen nuffing like it and I ain't led a sheltered life I can tell you.'

'I'd like to see that,' said Cynthia, She reached for a handkerchief from her purse and dropped it, a pound note floating down at the same time. The old woman, who seemed to know exactly what to do, picked up the handkerchief and the money and returned only the former. She tucked the note into her bikini pants with all the adroitness of a stripper at a stag party.

'The missus told me to feed the birds,' she sniffed. 'So I'll go and get on with it. Make yourself comfy.' She glanced around the moribund house. 'If you can,' she added. She stuttered down the passage like the victim of some famine, turned at the end and nodded helpfully towards the upper landing. 'Door right in front of your nose,' she said.

She vanished to the garden and the birds, and Cynthia stood, momentarily afraid, at the foot of the stairs. Then her bitterness began knocking again, so with a determined breath she mounted the Victorian stairs two at a time and without hesitation threw open the door.

The model of Flat-Roof Man was standing like a braggart beside Mrs Blossom-Smith's bed: Geoffrey Turvey smiling out at the window on to Plummers Park. Her breath shuddered and she crept towards it as though she needed to catch it unawares. She stopped three feet in front of it, feeling as though something had suddenly hollowed out her inside. Geoffrey, her husband, standing naked in clay, grinning confidently into her face. Her gasp went audibly around the room. She stood back, as though she feared it, and put her hands protectively across her blouse. It was Geoffrey right enough, just as she had heard, the face she had loved enough to throw away a marriage. It seemed to nod its grin at her: 'I told you so.' Her eyes went inevitably down to the loins and the detailed appendage hanging there.

Abruptly the model was flooded with white light and Mrs Blossom-Smith's voice said: 'Do you think it's a good likeness?'

The whole gigantic effrontery of the thing suddenly exploded before Cynthia's baffled eyes. The eyes narrowed and then went wild. 'You great cow!' she screamed across the room. Polly's expression collapsed. Cynthia turned back towards her clay husband and with a vicious grab she tore away the modelled penis and flung it like a flying sausage at Polly whose face filled with a scream for her creation. 'It's not his!' she protested. 'It's not his!' She caught the clay roll with both hands close to her stomach. Frantically, her artistic reflexes overcoming her wrath she began to try and remould the member from memory.

'Stop! Stop!' she pleaded. Cynthia was amazed that the big woman had not rushed her, but merely hung by the door begging for the life of her creation. A frontal assault might have been more effective from Polly's point of view, for Cynthia, encouraged by the disinclination to attack, turned upon Flat-Roof Man again and with an echoing cry of vengeance drew back her housewife's fist and smashed it into the grinning face of the immortalized Geoffrey. The nose bent comically and the eyes almost closed with the blow. She laughed without restraint, as though this were some sort of recommended and enjoyable therapy. She hit him with a left then, flattened the cheek and withdrew with the right ear dangling pitifully. Then Polly came across the floor at her like an unbraked railway train. Cynthia tore the head from the clay shoulders and threw it at the sculptress as she rushed. It caught her square on and caused her to stagger sideways. With an abandoned whoop Cynthia leapt the bed, ran around its foot and out of the bedroom door. She half fell down the stairs. She reached the sunshine and continued to run. The bedroom window was flung open behind her and Polly's howl followed her through the unoccupied morning air: 'Vandal woman! Vandal! Philistine!'

Cynthia did not mind. A great exultation gripped her heart; freedom seemed to fly around her. As she ran she laughed, her feet skipping above the pavements of Plummers Park. The small tricyclist with whom she had conversed on her downward journey watched her coming with lonely interest. He began to pedal towards her hopeful of some more brief companionship. 'The doctor won't hurt my winkie!' he called in advance. 'Mummy says it won't hurt.'

*

Geoffrey sat with triumphant if surprised composure on his satin settee. Cynthia had poured him a concerned vodka and tonic and he manoeuvred the ice about in the foot of the glass with enjoyment of the moment. Mrs Polly Blossom-Smith had just left. Cynthia was huddled, very chastened, on the chair opposite.

'You should have told me, Geoff,' she complained. 'If you'd

told me I am sure I would have understood. I'm not that jealous.'

'It was going to be a surprise,' he said easily, making his hurt sound convincing. 'When it was unveiled, there I would be – for posterity.'

'And it truthfully wasn't your thingy?' she pleaded, looking coyly from the rim of her glass.

'Couldn't *you* tell that, of all people?' he smirked.

'Well, I didn't look that close. When I could see it was your face, just like I'd been told it would be. Mrs Reynolds told me. That old gossip. You might have wanted to keep it a surprise, but it was all round the estate. And I had the feeling, which I know was wrong now, that you were having an affair.' She began to sniff plaintively. He thought the time had come to put his arm about her. He called her over to the settee and she went obediently and sat beside him wiping her eyes. 'When I thought about it, you know, about the man at The Jolly Grinder saying you'd been up there that day, and one night – this might seem really silly – when you were undressing I noticed all your bum was red, almost as if the sun had been on it. I thought nothing of it at the time, but when all this suspicion started growing in my mind it suddenly came back to me. I thought you'd been out in a field with somebody.'

If she had watched her husband's face she would have seen the pleased look quickly replaced by a sick expression. He skilfully managed to dismantle this by the time she faced him. By then he had replaced it with a measure of incredulity. 'You thought I was in a *field*?' he repeated, as though he could not believe his ears. 'A *field*? Me? With Polly Blossom-Smith? Christ, Cynthia, you want to go and get somebody to examine your head!'

'I know, I know,' she acknowledged miserably. 'But I'd got myself into such a state I'd believe anything. It sort of festered inside me.'

He composed a hurt sigh and released it. 'How could you do it beats me. I thought she was very decent about it.'

'Yes, yes, she was,' admitted Cynthia. 'I felt such a fool.'

'There were bits of men from all over Plummers Park in that model,' said Geoffrey. 'You must have seen it wasn't all me.'

'Whose was the thingy, I wonder?' ruminated Cynthia.

'The Flasher,' answered Geoffrey dramatically.

Cynthia's astonished face came up to meet his eyes. 'The Flasher? That man . . . who . . . You mean the indecent exposurer?'

'That was the story,' said Geoffrey smugly. 'She wanted that bit reserved for him. Somehow she must have got him. All I can tell you is it wasn't me.'

'How amazing,' acknowledged Cynthia. 'But, then, she's an extraordinary woman. And she was very nice about it really, wasn't she? Sitting down here and not getting mad. I really took to her. I wonder what happened to *Mister* Polly Blossom-Smith? Nobody's ever asked that, I bet. She seems so, well, *complete* without a man, doesn't she? She's a very clever woman and not only in her work either. I was glad when she said she wasn't very happy about the model anyway and she had thought about starting again with just the inspiration floating about in her mind. It must be marvellous to be able to do that, Geoff. Marvellous. Perhaps I'll go to pottery classes again in September. I used to be quite good.'

*

Apart from Dormouse Dan and Barney Rogers the publican, the bar of The Case Is Altered was empty when Andrew walked in. Barney pulled the pint he ordered then walked through to the back of the bar, to his private quarters where Andrew knew, by the steaming smells, his early evening meal was cooking.

Andrew sat and opened the evening paper. After a moment he sensed someone looking at him and glanced up to see Bessie White's father in the doorway. Apprehension fluttered inside him.

'Well, well, it's Mr Maiby,' said the man.

'Hello . . . Mr White, isn't it? Nice to see you. Have a good holiday?'

'Who said I'd been on my 'olidays?'

'Oh, well, nobody. But you look nice and brown. Will you have a drink?'

'No, I drink in my own pub, thanks.'

'Did you want to see me?' Andrew's smile was hung with trepidation. 'I put that money in the paper's polio fund, incidentally. I couldn't keep it.'

'Very good of you that was. Yes, very decent. I came to see you about our Bessie. She's been cryin' at nights and I never 'eard her cry before, not since she was a nipper. You've been seeing a bit of her, 'aven't you?'

'Seeing her?' Andrew felt his inside solidifying. The man's attitude was menacing but matter-of-fact. Andrew shrugged: 'Well, I do see her some lunchtimes when she has her sandwiches in the churchyard.'

'You're a married man,' said Mr White. 'She's a young girl. You upset her, mister, and you'll be in the fucking churchyard for more than your sandwiches.'

Andrew rose guiltily and looked over his shoulder in fear that Barney might be back at the bar. The other man saw his glance and knew what it meant. 'Don't worry, mate,' he said. 'Nobody's heard. It won't get back to your missus.'

'Now, look here,' said Andrew with as much whispered outrage as he could summon. 'What do you want?'

'Our Bessie's getting married on Saturday to a kid in our road. So I've come to tell you to keep to your own side of the railway line, mate. If you get busy with her again I'll knock all the piss out of you. And there's a lot to knock out.'

He reached out and gave Andrew a short push. Then, as though deciding all at once to do it, he reached forward, caught Andrew by the lapels and threw him violently the length of the bar.

Andrew careered backwards through the empty chairs and tables, crashing them to each side. Dormouse Dan awoke and looked at the scene with gradually focusing eyes. Andrew had fallen near the medieval wall, and picked himself up wondering whether he would be wiser to stay down. White strode through the chairs after him and caught hold of him easily in immensely powerful grips and flung him back again. All the breath went from him in a great wheeze. A darkness banged through his brain and he could hear Barney's voice shouting: 'The wall! The wall! Be careful – that's an old wall!'

Mr White stared at Barney for a moment, then turned on the wall and with four mighty blows with the sole of his boot he smashed a great hole through the old powdery stone and plaster. Barney howled his horror and tentatively reached for the telephone.

'Put that thing down, guv'nor,' said Mr White with menace, 'or I'll make a *bigger* hole in you.'

Barney prudently replaced the receiver. 'But it's five hundred years old,' he whispered piteously. 'Five hundred.'

Mr White turned to the debris again. Some of it had fallen across the prostrate Andrew. The man from the council houses gave it three or four more kicks sending the rotten materials tumbling again. Then he picked up a piece of plaster and examined it, smelled it, crumbled it in his fingers, and eventually tossed it away.

'Listen, mate,' he said to the speechless Barney. 'I'm an ignorant bloke, but I know about walls. I'm knocking them down all fucking day. I'm in demolition, see. That wall is no more than a hundred years old. You can smell the plaster and tell that, dead easy.'

'What . . . what about the damage?' stammered Barney.

'Sorry,' said Mr White. 'I got carried away. There's a lot of things I don't like over this side and that wall was one of them. It's about as bleeding straight as most of the people. But don't worry about the damage, old friend. I'll come over with my mate on Saturday morning and we'll have it all built up nice for you in no time. All right?'

'No. No, don't bother,' hurried Barney. 'I'll get it done.'

'Please yourself, squire. But no talking to the coppers about it, either,' warned the other man. 'One word and you might find this boozer a bit more crowded on Saturday than you likes it to be. And then you might find *all* the fucking walls knocked down. Got that too?'

'I have,' nodded Barney, thoroughly frightened by the threat. 'Nothing will be said. Are you going now?'

'Yes, I'll be on my way.' He turned easily to Andrew who was retching among the debris. ''Night then, Mr Maiby. I'll think about you on Saturday. 'Bye, 'bye.'

16

He was considering his reflection in the blade of a table knife, the rubbery, spread face, the blobbed nose, the eyes drawn out orientally. A good likeness, he thought. He gave it a cursory polish and set it on the dining table beside the cork place-mat with the picture of Old London Bridge.

'Andrew,' Audrey called through the hatch from the kitchen. 'You *do* want this dinner party, don't you?'

'Want it? Yes, of course. That's a funny question at this stage.'

'You don't seem over pleased. Is there anyone else you would have liked to come? Your girlfriend, perhaps?'

He dug a kings pattern fork into the palm of his hand with exasperation. 'If you keep on about this mythical girlfriend,' he called back controlling his tone, 'I shall go out and obtain one. I'll get some little scrubber from the council estate and bring her.'

The moment he said it, he felt ashamed, not because of Audrey but because of Bessie. He blinked away a momentary picture of her.

'Good idea,' she echoed from the kitchen. 'She might bring a little fresh light into our lives.' He nodded miserably. 'You don't seem to be looking forward to this very much,' Audrey went on. 'After all it is for you. It's your birthday.'

'Age is nothing to applaud,' he answered carefully. 'Even the most stupid people get it. As for me, I can see forty squatting on the dark horizon like a large malicious moon.'

The telephone rang. He answered it. 'Audrey,' he called. 'It's from Cynthia. She wants to speak to you.' As Audrey came wiping her hands from the kitchen, he added: 'She sounds bothered.'

He returned to laying the places at the table. Audrey put the receiver of the phone down on the hall table and walked through to him. 'Geoff's parents have turned up. Nobody expected them. Cynthia says they're horrific and she and Geoff don't mind staying away tonight. But I said bring them over. Is that all right?'

'Yes, of course,' said Andrew. 'Maybe they'll bring a little fresh light into our lives.'

She poked her tongue out at him. 'Not these two, if Cynth's anything to go by,' she said. She returned to the phone. 'Andrew says you've got to bring them. He wants somebody fresh to impress. Yes, he means it. See you at eight.'

She returned to Andrew. 'That's going to be great,' she sighed. 'He's sixty-nine and she's sixty-two. She keeps showing people photographs of Geoff's ex-wife who she thought was lovely. They're from Lancashire, you know. He used to be a miner.'

She paused and looked down at Gladstone slothfully patrolling the table legs. 'Is it possible that Action-Dog could be shut up somewhere this evening?' she requested. 'You know he gets under the dining table and makes those sickening smells.'

'How can we shut him up anywhere?' answered Andrew. 'He'll howl the damn' place down. They'll think we've got the Hound of the Baskervilles locked up.'

She sighed. 'If you ever do decide to leave again,' she said, 'will you take that bloody dog with you?'

'I wouldn't be without him,' he replied.

*

'Listen, pal,' confided Geoffrey almost as soon as his parents had been ushered into the lounge. 'Let me warn you. These two are dynamite. She's been sitting in the garden all the afternoon waving her hankie to the airliners stacking over Watford. She's convinced that the passengers hang out of the windows and wave back. And given encouragement he'll give you the history of the northern coalfields.'

'I haven't got any beer,' said Andrew.

'Beer? Don't worry about that. They order like they drink in the Savoy every lunchtime. I don't know where they get it. He'll tell you about Tufton Main pit disaster while sipping an extra-dry Martini.'

Andrew cautiously served the drinks. Mrs Turvey, bright red from her afternoon's plane-waving, her corrugated hair banging as though it were on springs, said she would like a Cinzano Bianco with a twist of lemon, soda and three ice cubes, an order which Andrew received with gradually ascending eyebrows. Mr Turvey, already settled back in the armchair, his short legs jutting from his brown suit in the forlorn ambition of touching the ground, had a vodka and bitter lemon with two ice cubes.

'Ah,' the old man sighed, a strange crackling coming from his chest as he moved in the chair, 'it's like paradise down 'ere, lad. Seems a shame that folks 'ave to die when there's places like this.'

'Alf's right,' agreed his wife. 'All these houses with these contemporary flat roofs, fields right next-door, and two cars in every alleyway, and people with lovely contemporary homes like this, and divorces. It's like America. Like you see on the television.'

The chimes rang, and Gerry, bursting from a pair of scarlet trousers, and Min Scattergood arrived. Gerry coaxed Andrew aside just within the door and whispered. 'I just want to pop into the dining-room a minute. A birthday surprise for you.'

Andrew smiled, and put his hand on the suet shoulder. 'Not a lifetime's supply, I hope?'

'No chance,' said Gerry. 'You'll see soon. You can't come in. It's got to be secret.'

Andrew grinned gratefully and waved an invitation at the dining-room door. He returned to the lounge. Geoff's father was saying to his son: 'Mind, we don't like the idea of flat roofs in the north, do we, Annie? It don't seem right some'ow. God meant roofs to be pointed.'

'Like on Noah's Ark,' confirmed his wife. 'They tried to 'ave these contemporary flat roofs up our way but the folks didn't take to them. They had to build pointed roofs on top, didn't they, Alf?'

They were obviously accustomed to confirming each other's statements and Alf nodded and said: 'Aye, they did that.'

The old man put his lips to the edge of his glass and sucked loudly. The ice crowded to the rim. Andrew wondered how low a chair would have to be cut before his feet touched the ground. He could imagine him in a coalmine. More crackling came from the man's chest.

'Were you in the pits all your life?' asked Andrew.

'Aye, same seam for twenty-eight years.'

'I bet you were glad to be out of that.'

'No, fair do's. There's nowt wrong with workin' in the pit. It were a bit damp . . .'

'Water up to your knees,' muttered his wife.

'Damp,' said her husband firmly. 'But it were nowt to grumble about. There's no germs down pits, you know, lad. And no women either.'

'Well there was *something* down there,' said Cynthia. 'Listen to your chest.'

'Aye, I've got a bit of a crackle,' he agreed.

'He used to wear a hearing-aid,' said Geoff. 'He wasn't a bit deaf but he used to pretend the crackle came from the battery.'

'Ah, I was vain then, lad,' said his father. 'Now I don't care what folk think.'

'That's one of the compensations of age,' smiled Andrew. 'I'm beginning to feel like that.'

'He's thirty-seven today,' retorted Audrey. 'He talks as if everything's over.'

'Many 'appy returns,' offered the elder Mrs Turvey.

'An' many of 'um, lad,' said the husband, raising his glass. He adroitly continued the upward movement to give Andrew the glass to be refilled. Andrew took it with a grin.

'Geoff left his Mary on her birthday, didn't you, Geoff?' Mrs Turvey said as though she had just remembered. 'When you went off with Cynthia.'

*

'Andrew came home with a black eye the other night,' said Audrey conversationally.

They were around the table. Beneath it lay the elongated Gladstone, a tube seething with captive gases. Andrew watched Audrey making regular sniffs but the hound had contained itself so far.

'You had a fight in the pub or something, didn't you?' asked

Gerry Scattergood. 'Some bloke was smashing down the old wall and you tried to stop him.'

Andrew raised his eyebrows, not displeased at the rumoured explanation. 'Some character from the council estate,' he shrugged. 'A big one too, unfortunately. Suffers from what I call agro-phobia – love of agro. Just looking for trouble. A nasty bit of work. Came in and started kicking the old bit of wall about and I told him to be careful. The next thing I knew he's knocked me down *and* the wall.'

'What I simply could not understand,' said Audrey, 'is why it had to be you.'

'Like the mountain,' said Andrew simply. 'Because I was there. It was either me or Dormouse Dan, and he was kipping. All I can say is I'm glad he didn't use his boot on me like he used it on that wall.'

Geoff laughed: 'They're now saying it's not old at all. After all the fuss old Barney used to make about it being medieval.'

'Early Fred Astaire's more accurate, I think,' said Andrew, and Audrey said: 'It's amazing how things never seem what they are at Plummers Park. Nothing.'

Geoffrey's father had been silent at the table. He had made a pleased examination of everything in the room, nodding and smiling at prints, ornaments and the furniture as though in considered approval. Now he turned to his wife and said: 'They 'ave some right funny candles down 'ere, don't they, lass?'

'Aye,' she replied without emphasis. 'I was wondering about them meself.'

The attention of everyone went to the two single candles in their stainless steel sticks.

'Dear God,' said Cynthia eventually when she was certain. 'Do you see what I see?'

'But ... but I only bought the usual candles,' gasped Audrey.

Andrew began to laugh. He dropped his face into his hands and looked out between his fingers at the two objects. They had been burning for several minutes now, but the wax had melted to a peculiar design so that now exposed on the table were two phallic symbols, upright, domed, leaving no doubt as to what they were supposed to represent. 'Gerry,' laughed Andrew accusingly. 'Your birthday surprise?'

'Gerry!' exclaimed Min. 'You didn't . . . ? You *did*, you rotten pig! Fancy doing that!'

Gerry began to laugh, but only he and Andrew seemed to be doing so. Geoffrey was grinning sheepishly, Cynthia and Audrey were staring with awe and fascination at the objects running with hot wax, while the old couple nodded in unison as though this was just another facet of the decadent southern life they had been shown.

Gerry now looked confused and said: 'Sorry, but I saw them when I was getting an order at this sex shop in Paddington and I thought they were a great laugh. You should have seen all your faces!'

He looked around again as though to comfirm his first impression but, Andrew apart, the expressions remained cool, glum or puzzled. 'Oh, come on,' he said uncertainly. 'It was only a bit of a joke. Wasn't it, Andrew?'

'Of course,' shrugged Andrew. 'I thought it was funny anyway.'

'A *bit* of a joke, is what it was,' said Min tartly. 'I wish you wouldn't bring your work home, Gerald Scattergood.'

'Now wait a minute . . .' began Gerry, becoming angry.

'Wait nothing,' soothed Andrew, making a calming motion with his hands. 'Don't let's fall out about the candles.'

'I'll move them,' said Min determinedly. 'Where are the proper candles, Audrey dear?'

'I hid them,' muttered Gerry unhappily. 'They're in that cupboard over there. I'm sorry, Audrey.'

It was Audrey who went to the cupboard and retrieved the normal candles. She stood at the side of the table, one in each hand, waiting for someone to blow out the phallic candles and take them from their holders. There was a funny awkwardness, and then Gerry, grunting with annoyance, blew them out and took the offending objects from their sconces.

'If it's not a rude question, what shall I do with them?' he inquired.

Andrew laughed at his discomfiture, standing sorrowfaced at

the table, a big white penis in each hand. 'Listen,' he said reasonably. 'I think it's funny and it's *my* bloody birthday party – so there. Here, Gerry. I'll take them. I'll put them in the kitchen.'

Audrey glanced at him quickly. 'Don't leave them where Lizzie will see them,' she said. 'She'll be in soon.'

'Give them to Polly Blossom-Smith,' suggested Cynthia airily. 'She's always looking for models.' She smiled with craft and sweetness at her husband.

Geoffrey's father, who after carefully tasting Andrew's red wine was drinking it thirstily, suddenly said: 'If no bugger wants them I'll 'ave 'em. It'll be a laugh at Christmas, won't it, lass?'

'I'll wrap them for you,' promised Andrew. 'Now will everybody have some more wine and let's get on with my birthday party.'

The old man took another long swig of the wine and said philosophically, 'It's damned 'ard to make a woman laugh, yer know. The only time we ever did see eye to eye with women is when we're layin' inside 'em.'

'Go on,' said his wife good-humouredly. 'We've 'ad some good times.'

'Aye,' he agreed. 'We didn't have much but we 'ad some good times.'

'We never seemed to want much,' she said.

'No, tha' right, lass. And you could always leave your door unlocked. We never locked our door.'

'No,' confirmed his wife. 'Nobody stole from you in those days.' She looked at her son and then at Cynthia. 'Whatever you 'ad was yourn.'

An atmosphere of frosty inebriation settled around the table. Andrew leaned back and regarded his guests and their wives. 'She was a lovely kid, that Mary,' said old Mrs Turvey. 'I could never fathom it. I've got some snaps 'ere.' She fumbled in her handbag and passed around a photograph of a young woman in a garden. She even showed them to Cynthia, who had seen them before.

Then, as though on cue, from below the long table seeped an

insidious smell, drifting up around the edges until the guests were looking around suspiciously at their neighbours. 'There's a bit of a niff,' said Geoffrey's father.

'Andrew,' said Audrey grittily, 'get Gladstone out from under the table. He's letting off again.'

Andrew got his head under the table with difficulty. There between the trousers and the shoes and stockings of his guests was the basset facing him, its face riven with sorrow and apology.

'You've done it again, Action-Dog,' he said, patting the dog on its patent-leather nose. 'You've got to go. Come on out.'

The animal moaned an apology, but Andrew dragged him out like a half-filled sack. 'I'm sorry, friends,' he said. 'I'll just eject him.'

'By Christ,' said Geoffrey's father with some admiration. 'I swear I've never niffed anything like that since they opened the old coal seam at Preston Main Number Five.'

Andrew dragged the dog to the door and pushed him out into the garden. It was a warm night with the stars mounted above Plummers Park and a bored moon just rising over the railway line. He was glad to be away from the table. He allowed himself one flying look across the flat roofs of the estate to where he knew, a mile away, Bessie would be trying on her wedding dress before her bedroom mirror.

*

Andrew, packed with wine, sat back and dimly and grimly perceived Audrey sitting opposite him. The others had gone now, early because it had not been the most successful of evenings. The lights of Plummers Park were going out in little spasms, leaving the night to the local stars.

They had gone out on to the terrace for it was still warm. Drunk as he was he knew he had to keep his voice down out there. They were sitting in deckchairs facing each other like old people in armchairs each side of a fire, their years of marriage tying them, their sprouting hostility screaming for them to get away.

Audrey said sadly: 'Do you remember, when this house was

just foundations, coming up here and sitting on piles of bricks, trying to think how it would be?'

'I remember, I remember. The day this house was born,' he recited drunkenly.

'And yet we're so unhappy half the time,' she said.

'Who isn't?' asked Andrew. 'The only people who weren't fighting tonight were the old couple, and they're not match-fit. You have to be fit for marital combat like you have to be fit for football. Anybody around here knows that.'

'*Some* people are happy,' she persisted pleadingly.

'All right,' he challenged. 'Let's count them. The only pair I know are the Yanks, Jean and old Hairy.'

'She's had the onion man in,' sniffed Audrey.

'Get off!'

'So I was told. Her husband's flying off all over the place and she had the onion man in. His bike was outside twenty minutes, they say.'

'The whole world's crumbling,' groaned Andrew. 'I'm pissed off with it anyway. Personally I don't understand why it was arranged that men have to have anything to do with women.'

'I'll second that,' she said. She looked hard at him: 'You're frightened because it's your birthday.'

'I begrudge every damned one, Aud,' he admitted. 'I begrudge every Christmas and every New Year and especially every birthday. Soon the hair starts to come out and then the teeth rattle loose and clatter on to the floor. It's a wonder that, as the final insult, God didn't arrange for a man's chopper to fall off as well.'

She stood up. 'I'm going to bed,' she sighed firmly. 'I can't listen to any more of your great thoughts. I'm tired.'

'I'm going for a walk,' he said.

'A walk? Now?'

'Yes, now. I'll trot old Gladstone for an inspection around Plummers Park by night. I'll be like a watchman making his tour. Perhaps I'll peep through a few windows.'

'Why don't you come to bed. You've had a hell of a lot to drink.'

'I'm going for a walk,' he insisted.

She leapt up from her chair in a burst of anger. 'Oh, get stuffed!' she snarled at him. 'Go for your walk. Go and see what you can pick up.'

'You never know your luck,' he retorted viciously. She strode through the french windows slamming the metal door behind her and drawing the curtains emphatically. At the moment before the drapes finally came together he caught a swift view of his lined and coloured books and the prints on the wall. Then he was left standing on the terrace like an actor on a stage. He called the dog, and, hunched and doleful both, they set off down the slope of Upmeadow.

*

It was only just past midnight. The late train rattled its lights along the Metropolitan line, the trees fidgeted in their sleep, a dog howled like a coyote in the Hertfordshire night. At the bottom of Risingfield he saw the small, old, open sports car standing by the pavement, and just short of it the defeated figure of its persecuted owner. He was sitting with his feet in the gutter, his left hand patting the wheel of the car as though he were comforting a sick animal.

Andrew felt very drunk, his walk was haphazard, and he needed to shuffle every thought and each word. He stopped short of the man. 'Camping out?' he said.

'Locked out,' said the neighbour pathetically. 'I can break in easy enough, but I'd just as soon stay out here. There's nobody in there anyway. She's gone off, the lady wife. Gone off with her amour, her lover, you understand.'

'I've heard of such things,' nodded Andrew sympathetically. 'Well, you've still got the car.'

The man nodded. He was not looking at Andrew. 'Yes,' he said hoarsely. 'The car I've still got. Just she's gone.'

He stood up and walked with no further word into the darkened enclosure of his front garden. A moment later a pane of glass broke, the door opened and quietly shut again.

Andrew walked about the vehicle twice and Gladstone urinated against both front wheels. Andrew shambled on, not knowing where he was going, only knowing that now, as he shambled and ambled, he was only howling distance from Bessie's window. He felt tempted to climb the railway embankment and to shout 'Bessie! Bessie!' from his side to hers, but he knew it was too late.

Gomer John was standing by the pillar-box just outside his sub-post office, an instrument held in his hands and up to the sky.

'Hello, Gomer,' said Andrew. 'Waiting for the eclipse?'

The thin young Welshman jumped nervously. 'Oh Mr Maiby! That was a scare. Didn't expect anybody to be about as late as this.'

'What are you doing?'

'Taking a fix on the stars,' answered Gomer, returning professionally to the instrument. 'With my sextant, see.'

'Making sure the old sub-post office is not off course, eh?'

The young man brought the instrument down. 'I don't blame you laughing, Mr Maiby. My mam thinks I'm mad. But it's a passion, see, and even in Plummers Park people have passions.'

'Here more than anywhere,' agreed Andrew soberly. 'I wasn't making fun, Gomer. Do you think I could have a go? Could you show me how to do it? Let me look at the stars. I've had my feet in the gutter too long.'

'You really want to?'

'Yes, of course. I've never tried to fix the stars before. Nor anything else come to think of it.'

'Well, well, who'd have thought you'd be interested?' said Gomer warmly. 'I'd like to show you. It's all a matter of angles, see. The word sextant means to measure in one-sixths.'

'It's nice to hear it used that way,' nodded Andrew.

Gomer showed him how to look through the telescope eyepiece of the instrument, but only a moment after he had begun to squint through the aperture the young man caught his arm. 'Mr Maiby,' he said, 'I don't think I'm mistaken, but does that look like a house on fire over there?'

*

There was a terrible idiocy about that night which was never to leave him. Even when he had hours and days to relive it in the hospital he was never able to think of it as more than a drunk's dream, long and stretched out in places, yawning yards of it, and then quickened to the pace of Mickey Mouse voices in the smoke and the bruised glow of the fire. And, on top of that, there was Gomer.

It was Joy Rowley's house. As they ran he counted the staggered walls and realized it was hers. There was a deep glow in the upstairs windows like the light thrown by a red table-lamp. From one of the big swivel windows, swung open, black smoke uncoiled like a long pipe reaching into the street.

'Gomer, I'll go!' shouted Andrew to the younger man who was running ahead of him. 'You get on the phone.'

Gomer pulled up. 'All right, Mr Maiby,' he panted. 'Are you sure?'

'For God's sake hurry!'

There was a phone-box outside Gomer's own sub-post office. He ran and opened the door but called after Andrew again: 'I haven't got any change.'

Andrew stopped, fooled. Then he bellowed back: 'It's free, you bloody idiot!'

He ran on. For some reason it had never occurred to him that there would not be a crowd at a fire. He had always associated crowds with fires. But there was only him. The houses on either side slept undisturbed. There was hardly a light in the street. For once nobody was watching.

The upstairs floor of the building was burning like a torch, but the downstairs rooms were strangely quiet and untouched. He looked into the sitting-room. It was still and dark with the shapes of the furniture hardly distinguishable. He began to ring on the doorbell, almost politely. Something inside stopped him shouting fire. On the garden path Gladstone, hunched like an oriental bridge, was straining over a turd.

Then at the closed upstairs window he saw Joy Rowley. He waved both hands to her. She was wearing blue pyjamas and he felt surprised that she should wear pyjamas. He had always concluded she was a nightdress girl. It seemed as though his voice had left him for he wanted to start shouting, but some-

248

how no words were coming out. She stood like a ghost in the window, then bent to the catch and opened it. It swung out. They stood like some odd Romeo and Juliet, facing each other. 'I can't reach the stairs, Andrew,' she said almost conversationally. 'My mother's at the back of the house somewhere. I can't get to her.'

'The fire brigade is coming,' said Andrew hopefully. 'You'd better get out of there, Joy. Do you think you could jump? I'll try and catch you.'

'I've got the door closed,' she answered calmly. 'But the wall started burning when I opened this window.' He could see the glow behind her increasing.

'Jump,' he urged her. 'Listen, climb over the window ledge and drop feet first. It's not that far. I'll catch you.'

'What about my mother? She must have left the iron on. I've only just let her use the electric iron.'

'I'll see if I can get her. But you come on out now.'

She turned her back on him and cocked one leg over the window ledge, then the other, supporting herself by her elbows. She looked very slim and small in her pyjamas. He had the odd thought that it was like a child escaping from a school dormitory. 'As you drop,' he called, 'shove yourself away from the wall with your arms and feet. You won't hit anything on the way down then.'

'Andrew,' she suddenly called in a stifled voice, 'I must get my mother.'

'Come down!' he shouted, almost screamed. 'I'll see to her. I told you. Come on – now!'

She jumped backwards and he caught her. He gave at the knees but her dropping weight astonished him, knocking him over on to the front lawn. They sprawled there like some knockabout acrobats, and Gladstone, sensing some fun, loped around them, his clownish face rough with excitement.

Andrew had a passing sensation of her body, a waist as slim as Bessie's, the slim kicking legs in the blue pyjamas. He was sprawled beneath her, for the fall had left them breathless, but she remained calm.

'I'll see if I can get to your mother,' he said, helping her to her feet. 'You go and bang on some doors. Do they all take bloody sleeping pills around here?'

'You'd better have this,' she said. 'It's the front-door key. I remembered to pick it up.'

'Good, that's fine,' he said. 'Go on now. Go next-door. Gomer John is calling the fire people.'

He felt somewhat foolish opening the door of a burning house in such a conventional way. He turned the key and pushed the door open before him. Smoke was loitering in the hall and a heat came out from the enclosed space but there was no fire. First he took his jacket off and then realizing it was a fire not somebody drowning he put it back on again. He wished he was not drunk. He poked his head in the sitting-room, then went through the hall into the kitchen at the rear.

A wide path of moonlight was coming innocently through the big window, illuminating the tiled floor, the dish-washer, the packet of Persil on the draining board, the two pairs of tights hanging to dry. In the moonbeams smoke wandered un-hurriedly as though having a good look around before consuming the place.

He had a notion to switch the lights on, but he desisted since he had no idea what effect that might have. Instead he took a tea-towel and put it under the cold tap for a moment. Hardly a cupful of water soaked into it, but the inadequacy did not occur to him at the time. He put it around his mouth like a bandit's mask and, after a moment at the bottom of the stairs, ran up into the fire.

It was the most terrible and terrifying thing. In a second he was engulfed by hot red air. No flames, but a monstrous glow that burned his clothes and his hair. The shock was so great when he realized what he had done that he cried out and the tea-towel fell from his face and he felt the red-hot air rush into his mouth and against his face. Black smoke was thick as fur about him with the crimson glow at its centre. He knew his coat and his hair were on fire. His face was stinging, his lungs full of oily smoke.

'Mrs Rowley!' he shouted once, as though he was crying for

her to rescue him. 'Leave the ironing, Mrs Rowley.' Then he had to get out. He knew it was that or death. His bare skin was blistering all across his chest. He wondered where the front of his shirt had gone. He couldn't see. His mouth was full of smoke like oil. Heat was searing up his legs. His shoes were on fire. He stumbled forward in the blackness and his hand miraculously touched the top pedestal of the stairs.

He launched himself into the blackness and tipped and rolled screaming down the stairs. There were a collection of people at the bottom and he plunged through them, tumbling among the faces so they parted and let him roll through. He could hear Gomer's voice shouting, 'I'll go, I'll go.' In terror and pain and panic he picked himself up and ran like a burning ghost out into the indifference of Plummers Park night.

Some of the people began running after him now, pursuing him, and he ran madly at the head of the grotesque chase. His body was in rags, he could feel his skin sagging like chewing gum. He wept as he ran. From behind he could hear the shouts of his neighbours and the baying of Gladstone who was running joyfully with them. There was no sense or object to his flight. He went madly along Risingfield, through gates and gardens and finally rolled and rolled in the dew of Gorgeous George's front lawn. Even in his state he knew where he was lying because of the golf holes cut into the grass. He threshed about in the dew and then sat up, cross-legged, his skin hanging, his hair gone, his clothes charred shreds, like a leper begging in some eastern street. There was a strong smell of hamburger.

'Oh Bessie!' he howled loudly. 'Oh Audrey, Bessie, Audrey! Oh, what the fuck have I done now!'

*

Audrey sat down patiently but awkwardly, as people do in hospitals, that deep trench between the visitor and the sick, the uncomfortable chair, the watching the clock for the time to go, the sensation of an interview.

'When do they say you can read?' she asked.

'Next week, they promised. They're going to have another look at my eyes to make sure they're really all right and then the sister says I can read the papers and have a squint at a book.' He held up the panda-like hands, covered in bandages. 'They put a strap around one paw with a thing like a knitting needle attached to it. You turn over the pages with that. It's marvellous what you can do without fingers.'

'Thank God you're not without them for good,' said Audrey. 'They told me today they've only got one more lot of skin grafts to do.'

'Yes, a couple more bits of jig-saw and I'm a complete picture. And all new skin like a baby.'

'You were very lucky.'

'I know.'

They waited uncomfortably.

'What's happening?' he said eventually.

'At Plummers Park? Nothing much. Let's think. Oh yes, you know Mr Shillingford was digging out another room.'

'Yes. Has he finished?'

'Struck an underground stream,' said Audrey with satisfaction. 'It poured through the lounge. They had to have the fire brigade.'

'We're keeping them busy at Plummers Park,' said Andrew.

They both waited again.

'Are you all right?' said Andrew eventually.

'Fine, thanks. Yes, fine. So is Lizzie. She's got a new boy-friend. That nice Cowley boy. And . . . oh my goodness, yes! . . . that golfing chap, the one you call Gorgeous George. He was in court yesterday. It was in the paper. Indecent exposure. Long raincoat . . . everything.'

Andrew's start made his skin hurt. 'Oh no,' he muttered. 'George. The Phantom Flasher. Poor George.'

'Arrested by a woman police constable too,' added Audrey with female satisfaction. 'Cost him a hundred pound fine.'

'And drummed out of the golf club,' sighed Andrew. 'Poor George.'

'You keep saying "poor George",' she said, and at once they were aware that, even in the hospital, they were sliding towards one of their arguments. Audrey sniffed: 'After all it's not a very nice thing to do.'

'Flashing was just his hobby,' said Andrew patiently. 'Golf was his life.'

They fell to silence, both unwilling to fight. Then she asked lamely: 'What do you do all day?'

'Checking up on me again,' he grinned ruefully. 'I'm safe in here. My only female indulgence I have is listening to Woman's Hour.'

The yawning gap opened between them again, she on the small wooden chair, he swathed in the bed. It was as though they had never known each other, never been close, had nothing, no common experience about which to converse. She dropped a glance to her watch.

'Only five minutes gone,' he said.

'Don't. I didn't look for that.'

'If you're ever in hospital I promise I won't visit you,' he said. 'We sit here like two bad actors trying to remember our lines.'

'I know,' she said miserably. 'It's funny how we run out of conversation so quickly. Don't you want me to come?'

He reached out with a quick sympathetic paw. 'Yes, of course. I'm only saying it to hurt you. As usual. God knows why I do it. The hours go slowly enough in here. Five weeks and another three, four or five, to go.'

'You seem to be much more cheerful when other people come. They say you're always making jokes,' she said. 'Would you like Joy Rowley to come and see you again? I think she wants to.'

He caught the old warp of suspicion in her eye, the hurt inquiry. 'Why do you say it like that?' he asked. 'If she'd like to come I'd like to see her.'

'She says she wants to explain about her mother. When she came last time you were too ill for her to tell you. But I told her you knew what had happened.'

'What, about the old girl being in the house down the road all the time?'

'Yes, I saw those people yesterday. They felt terrible about the whole thing. They said they weren't sure who she was when she knocked on their door at midnight. God knows why she went there. She seemed quite batty. She had gone to tell them that the house was on fire because she'd left her iron on, but when she got talking to them she forgot all about it. She said she was having such a good time chatting with them it went right out of her head.'

'Why didn't she tell Joy?'

'You can't get any sense out of her. She says she went up the road to tell the people there because she was afraid her daughter wouldn't understand.'

'Silly old cow,' he said bitterly. 'Gomer died for nothing.'

'There was no need for you to have been in there at all,' she said. 'It was a terrible mess-up all round.'

'Poor Gomer,' said Andrew. 'Getting lost in there. And he wanted to be a navigator. Whatever will I say to his mother?'

'She's potty as well,' said Audrey. 'She's apparently furious because she found out after the fire that he'd been planning to go in the navy for ten years. She's more upset about that than the fact that he's dead.' She sniffed sadly. 'The vicar, what's his name, Boon, was a bit put out because Gomer turned out to be a Methodist. Apparently he was very annoyed.'

'Robbed him of a hero's funeral, eh?' grinned Andrew. 'First old Futter, then Gomer. I'm Church of England and I didn't die.'

'Shows even a vicar can't have everything he wants,' she replied, not looking at him. 'But Gomer's mother was the worst. She was really angry about the navy.'

'Strange logic,' he agreed.

'None of it's very logical,' she replied bitterly. 'I nearly lost my husband an hour after his thirty-seventh birthday. Or had one crippled and disfigured for the rest of his life.'

He felt ashamed. 'I should have thought about you first,' he nodded. 'And Lizzie. God only knows what made me go in there. Stupidity, bravado? I don't know.'

'Suicide,' she said flatly. 'You were in the mood for it that night.'

He said nothing to that. Instead he said: 'The ward sister was saying that she thinks you have behaved remarkably.'

'Me? What did I do?'

'You stayed with me,' he replied simply. He felt a lump in his throat stretching his sore skin painfully. 'She says it's far from unknown for a wife to come and see her beloved burned to a frazzle and to piss off forever the same day.'

'That's more reasonable than it sounds,' she nodded. 'I wouldn't do it because I love you.'

She said it just as simply but he felt the tears suddenly begin to rise in his face. She spared him by getting up and going to the window. It had been raining all day. He had spent hours watching drips of rain working to bend a rose thorn just outside the pane.

The silence between them sagged like a rope bridge across a chasm. He could think of nothing but to splutter with his sore mouth, 'I love you too. You know that.'

'You always say "You know that" when you say you love me. As though we were having an argument,' she said, still not turning about.

'Sorry. I'll remember not to say it.'

She remained at the window studying the rain intently. 'There's some wicked buggers at Plummers Park, you know,' she said suddenly. 'The story has gone around that you were inside the house with Joy Rowley when the fire happened. I don't believe that's true, but that's what's going around.'

He felt himself go dry. 'That's a bloody terrible thing to say,' he whispered. 'A terrible thing. Especially with Gomer dying like that. Audrey . . . you don't believe that do you? Have you asked Joy?'

'She came and told me it wasn't true,' said Audrey. 'When she explained about her mother.'

'You don't believe it, do you?'

'No, I don't. It's just the sort of story that gets around.'

She turned casually. 'Geoffrey and Cynthia are talking about moving,' she said. 'Just talking about it. They had a look at a house down at Southfields last Sunday. He says he would like to go down there.'

'Southfields? That's Wimbledon way, isn't it?'

'Yes. He says he'd like to go south of the river.'

'Half the neighbourhood are moving south of the river,' he said. 'Simon and Ena went down there. It must be the attraction of Victoriana after Plummers Park.'

'Somebody's moved into Simon and Ena's house,' she said, just remembering. 'From across on the council estate. She's a blonde girl. I think they've just got married. It shows that as soon as they can afford it they hop across the railway line as quick as they can. As long as they don't have washing hung everywhere it will be all right, I suppose.'

He stared at her through his sore eyes, but they were so red she did not notice the difference. She said she had to go. She kissed him on the new skin on his cheek. For weeks she had been unable to bring herself to do more than peck her lips near him.

She walked to the window, a neat dark woman nearing middle age. She sighed at the rain. 'I suppose the summer's gone now,' she said. 'I don't suppose we'll see another one like that.'